# YAHTZEE CROSHAW

**DARK HORSE BOOKS®**
Milwaukie

Cover Design by David Nestelle
Cover Illlustration by Matt Cavotta
Book Design by Krystal Hennes

Special Thanks to J. Harrison Barber, Jemiah Jefferson, Chris Koeppel, Jonathan Quesenberry, John Schork, and Robert Simpson.

Published by Dark Horse Books
A Division of Dark Horse Comics, Inc.
10956 SE Main St., Milwaukie, OR 97222
darkhorse.com

Library of Congress Cataloging-in-Publication Data

Croshaw, Yahtzee.
 Mogworld / Yahtzee Croshaw. -- 1st Dark Horse Books ed.
   p. cm.
 ISBN 978-1-59582-529-2 (pbk.)
1. Internet games--Fiction. 2. Fantasy games--Fiction. I. Title.
 PR9619.4.C735M64 2010
 823'.92--dc22
                            2010010939


ISBN: 978-1-59582-529-2
First Dark Horse Books Edition: August 2010

Printed at Offset Paperback Mfrs., Inc., Dallas, PA, USA
10 9 8 7 6 5 4 3 2 1

*To Blizzard Entertainment, for the three months
of my life I will never get back.*

# PART ONE

# PROLOGUE

QUEEEEEEK QUEEEEEEK QUEEEEEEK QUEEEEEEK
QUEEEEEEK

A dream about my father chasing me through the fields with a pig sticker took an even more nightmarish turn when he started emitting a rhythmic high-pitched screech. Then I swam dizzily into full wakefulness to find an alarm sprite floating through the dormitory.

It had to be an emergency. They didn't deploy alarm sprites lightly—it takes two fairly high-level mages to shut the damn things up. And I'd spent enough time at St. Gordon's Magical College to know that any emergency involving magic is something you want to get away from as fast as you can.

After a minute of confused bustle in which dressing gowns were thrown on and several sets of slippers thudded their way downstairs, I and the rest of the second-years followed the squealing ball of light into the entrance quad. The ear-molesting noise was immediately joined by the screams of several other alarm sprites as the rest of the student body filed out into the pre-dawn gloom.

That's when I knew that something was really wrong. An alarm in itself wasn't that unusual, especially not in the second-year dorm. After spending the entire first year learning theory and taking the mandatory psychological tests, students tended to be overly enthusiastic with their first firebolts. But a full evacuation of the entire student body (57) and faculty (four) wasn't usually necessary.

"Jim!" called Mr. Everwind, my tutor. Sweat was dripping from the brim of his pointy hat. "Line up the second years at the back."

We were too rattled to do anything but obey, taking up position behind the third years. All of the students had been arranged by year into a rather haphazard rectangle that didn't seem to have anything to do with the usual drill procedure.

Suddenly, the sun began to rise, spilling orange dawn over the rolling green hills of the surrounding plains. I noticed that the horizon was a lot more textured than I remembered, and more bristling with siege weaponry.

An army was advancing towards the school. Just as I had done on my first day, I deeply resented the fact that St. Gordon's Magical College was not, in fact, a castle.

"All right, chaps, settle down," said the headmaster, resplendent in his star-patterned cardigan as he strode back and forth in front of the student body. "Let me assure you all that there is absolutely no reason to panic." The rising tension was not eased in the slightest. "It's probably just some misunderstanding—stop chewing, Haverson—but a Stragonoffian army appears to be attacking the college. Now, don't worry. You are only here as a precaution. We have enlisted a former graduate, Ponyleaf the Enchanter, and his adventuring party, to aid us. And I want you to show them the same respect you'd show to me, understand? I said spit that out, boy."

Ponyleaf was tall and thin, with a curly beard and the kind of rugged tan and fidgety nervousness that comes from a career adventuring through the gnoll-and-goblin-haunted wilderness. He stepped forward, separating himself from a bored-looking Loledian dwarf and a poorly dressed Anarecsian warrioress who looked chilly in every sense of the word.

"Good morning," he said with a cough, turning his staff over in his hands.

A furious ongoing roar was slowly edging into earshot, punctuated by the clash of swords against shields. "Good morning, Mr. Ponyleaf," droned the bewildered student body dutifully.

"Now, what we're dealing with here is a loose alliance of student fighters from the warrior schools just over the border in Stragonoff. Obviously not much of a match for veteran adventurers like us. They're here because the king of Stragonoff has put out a quest to recover the Stone of Solomus that was left with this college by its founders hundreds of years ago. Now, obviously we will never surrender the stone to such bully-boy tactics, but I would ask that I and my fellows be allowed to look after the stone for its protection, and so that we can wave it at the enemy for purposes of psychological warfare."

"We don't have the stone," said the headmaster, as Ponyleaf met his gaze hopefully.

"You what?"

"We've only been open six years. There's no such thing as the Stone of Solomus. The king's mad. Last year he made his son marry a koi pond."

An awkward silence passed. Or at least, it would have been a silence were it not for the increasingly loud warcry and wet thudding of booted feet upon the dewy morning grass, not to mention the subtle clinking of light armor as the two other members of Ponyleaf's adventuring party attempted to shuffle towards the back gate unnoticed.

"Can I be perfectly frank?" said Ponyleaf eventually. "We're kind of only doing this because we were hoping you'd let us have the stone as a reward."

"Well, that's obviously not going to happen."

"No, no . . . I see that." He looked behind him and did a double take that was just a little bit too obvious. "Sorry, it seems my colleagues have wandered off somewhere. I'm just going to . . . see where they went. And . . . come . . . right back." Then he left, quickly.

The frontmost rank of armored fratboys was now over the last hill and had broken into a run. The ground was quivering in almost perfect synchronization with my stomach.

"Right then," said the headmaster, tight-lipped, eyes fixed on the fence over which Ponyleaf had just vaulted. "I know most of you didn't really expect to be practicing this level of combat magic this early in your career. But I think I can say that if I were an invading army I'd certainly be given pause for concern by such a formidable rank of enchanters as—God damn it, Haverson, I told you once before about—" The vibrating rear half of an arrow suddenly appeared in his temple. He concluded his sentence with a few spit bubbles before falling over.

A large chunk of our defense force took this as the invitation to run away. But I didn't. Furious tears were forming in my eyes. I'd spent my last vegetable tray on tuition fees. Home was at least five turnips' worth of journey away and, more to the point, the last place I wanted to go. St. Gordon's might not have been the most prestigious magic college in the world, and its graduates generally couldn't entertain any ambitions beyond running a pest control business, but it was all I had.

The creaky wooden gates were pulverized into splinters under a whirling cloud of iron boots and training warhammers. I extended a hand and began to incant. "Arcanus. Inferus. T—"

I don't actually remember if I was able to get a firebolt off. I have a vague memory of seeing orange light splatter harmlessly against a spiked breastplate, but that might just have been sparks from all the metal rubbing against metal. Then there was a sound rather like a bag of wet laundry being hurled across a gravel driveway, and that was the first time I died.

Everything seems a whole lot more peaceful when you're dead. Even watching your own pelvis being kicked around the quad by guffawing adolescent berserkers has something transcendental about it when you're looking down on it from about six feet up and ascending. Maybe it was the way everything was tinted a strange bluish-gray, and seemed to be glowing with an eldritch light.

As I continued to drift upwards, the world began to fade. The majestic sight of the warrior hordes breaking all of St. Gordon's front windows blurred, and not just from distance. At the point of death, all sound had suddenly crashed into silence, as if I'd thrust my head into ice-cold water, but now the quiet was somehow deepening. What I had previously accepted to be complete silence was a cacophony compared to what I wasn't hearing now.

The land of the living was still there, barely. It had been reduced to a collection of dim shadows that were almost invisible against the cosmic brilliance of the beyond. What I remember most vividly of all is the light. Bright as anything, and my ghostly eyes were open wide, but it didn't dazzle me. It wasn't just a light at the end of a tunnel, unless the tunnel was also made of light. It was everywhere, all around me, and I was part of it. I was watching the light, and at the same time, I was the light watching me.

I think I was still ascending, but it was becoming harder and harder to tell. The world was turning below me, reduced to little more than a faint smear against the light. I saw the college, the surrounding county, and the lands of Stragonoff toiling under the heel of demented monarchs. I saw the kingdom of Borrigarde, where I had been born, along with all its neighboring territories, their ancient borders and writhing battlegrounds now made meaningless. I saw the entire continent of Garethy, a thousand rural hues of brownish-green and greenish-brown spreading from ocean to ocean like rotting seaweed on a calm beach. I saw the entire planet, from the jungles of Anarecsia to the urban sprawl of Lolede City. I saw the glittering sphere hanging in the blackest darkness, and somewhere at the back of my mind, I realized that "Flat World" Frobisher owed me twenty quid.

I could see it all, but I was still ascending. The world of my birth shrank from a planet to a moon, to a beach ball, to a pea, to a grain of sand, to . . . gone.

Now there was nothing but the light, and a new sound was drifting through the stillness. A beautiful voice was calling me, singing songs of beckoning, and as the delicate tones passed my ears I felt a giddy and instinctive state of rapturous love. For just a few more songs I would have done anything for that voice. I would have—well, I wouldn't have died for it, obviously, I was ahead of the game there.

The light took form around me, breaking off bits of itself like clay and reshaping them into—what else could they have been?—angels. Their blank, featureless faces were strangely beautiful, shining with a golden inner light. They took my spectral arms, holding them ever so gently, and aided my ascent. Their every touch, every movement, every sound they breathed into my ears, all communicated the same thing: love, undying and all-powerful. I had passed on from life, from the world of struggles and hardship and big fat women with annoying laughs, and entered a glorious new existence of utter peace, and joy, and love.

And then some git brought me back to life.

# ONE

It began as a soft pulling sensation, and grew violently in strength. The light went away fast. The world was speeding back towards me, a gigantic custard pie hurled by a universe determined to make me the butt of some cruel, cruel joke. I scrabbled for purchase with my astral fingers, desperately clawing for something to cling to, anything that would mean I wouldn't have to go back down there. . .

But no. The universe refused to see things my way, and my spirit returned to my body like a punch in the gut.

I sat bolt upright, or at least tried to; my forehead discovered something hard and wooden overhead, and my skull fell back down with an audible crack. A handful of dust in my lungs interrupted my attempts to swear and I spent a few instructive moments in a wretched coughing fit, clutching at my head. I noticed that most of my hair was missing, and as my hands travelled down, that my face was thin and sunken.

Okay, I thought. I'm not going to panic. I'm going to take a deep breath—okay, I'm not going to take a deep breath, but I'm going to count to ten, and take stock, and I'm going to stay calm.

"I died," I recalled, mouthing the words airlessly. "Oh well. Could happen to anyone. Everyone, even. And now I've come back to life. So I can't exactly complain, can I? I'm in a coffin. That's where they put dead people. It makes sense. Ho hum. There's no air in here. La de dah. Who needs air? Not me, anymore, apparently. My body seems to have been wasting away for many years. Well I never."

A loud rumbling from deep within the bowels of the earth shut me up. The ground shook violently. I could feel the spiders in my lungs clinging to alveoli for dear life.

"And there's an earthquake going on. Fiddle de RAARGH LET ME OUT LET ME OUT—"

The nails were old and gave way almost instantly, but then there was something heavy on top of the coffin, pinning down the lid. I strained until both wood and limb were creaking like talkative garden gates, until finally I felt weight shifting, my lid flew off and I was catapulted bolt upright.

Light drilled uncomfortably into my long-unused retinas. Normal, boring torchlight, not the glorious holy light of recent memory. I knuckled away a succession of fat pink after-images and coughed up something that looked very much like a cobweb.

I was in a crypt. That made sense—I was dead, after all. The walls were lined with alcoves containing battered coffins like my own, mostly smashed open. The torches on the walls were freshly lit, and the thick piles of dust on the floor were disturbed by very recent track marks.

There came a clattering to my immediate right. I glanced over just in time to see the coffin that had been on top of mine burst open and a skeleton tumble out. "Khak!" it went. "Khakkhakh khakh!" Then it fell apart.

I was attempting to crawl along the ground away from it when another quake shook the crypt. A large portion of plaster and stone disassociated itself from the rest of the ceiling by an inch or two, and reddish dust rained down. "What the hell is going on?!" was what I tried to say, but my lungs were still dusty and it came out more like "Whrrf kkkrghhaff?!"

It did the trick, though. A grayish head peered around the corner of a nearby tunnel. It was a corpse, his complexion pale and scarred, one glassy eye dangling down a waxy cheek. His body had clearly been dead for quite a long time, but the message apparently hadn't reached his brain.

"Oh, hello," he said, his voice reverberating as if his throat was full of gravel. "Do you have any idea what's going on?"

"No!" I had coughed out the last of the dust, but my voice was just as rough and raspy as his. "No I do not know what's going on! I was dead! I kind of expected things to stop going on!"

"It's just a bunch of us just woke up in here and no-one seems to know why." He offered a hand and helped pull me to my feet. "You got off pretty lightly."

"Got off lightly?!"

"All four limbs. Both eyes. Shame about your nose. But you should see the state of some of the others."

I was fingering a rather ghastly triangular hole in the middle of my face when the room shook once again, in the way a human would say "Ahem." With a noise like the enthusiastic mating of giant stone golems, the far wall buckled inwards and part of the floor gave way. The skeleton, still trying to stand up, fell from sight with a terrified "khakk," followed by the remains of my coffin and presumably my nose.

"We'd best get out of here," said my new friend. I nodded, took a step, and fell flat on my face. It would have probably been quite traumatic for a person with a nose, but fortunately I was ahead of the game there.

"Sorry," he said, helping me up again. "You're a bit wobbly. Expecting to wake up fresh and ready to go after being dead for a while would be a bit optimistic."

"Well, yes. Expecting to wake up at *all* would have been a bit optimistic."

"Hey, don't take it out on me. I'm trying to help."

Specifically, he was trying to help me run away from whatever was causing all the rumbling, and from the increasingly collapsing floor. Old and long-unused signals from my brain were having trouble making the long climb down my spinal column to my limbs. I stumbled through the underground chambers on my colleague's shoulder, sensation returning to my feet and joints by tiny increments. The thought was sinking in with greater and greater certainty and considerably greater discomfort: I was dead. I was alive and dead at the same time. I was un-dead. My current biological status was aggravatingly inconsistent.

I had seen zombies before. There had been a necromancer's tower in the village near my family farm and you'd sometimes see an undead slave lurching through the marketplace. On shopping days me and a few other kids used to flick bits of bread at them so that hungry seagulls would chase them around. And then later, at college, Mr. Everwind was in the habit of raising undead teaching assistants, and a popular hazing ritual was to steal the Undead Command Stone from the staff room and use it to make them pole dance on the school flagpole. I remembered how amusing it had been at the time to watch them move around as if their joints were held together with elastic bands. Now I just wanted to know how they had made it look so easy.

Getting to grips with myself would have to wait, because now the floor was rumbling continuously. We staggered through another archway moments before it cracked and into a wide nexus of passageways at the bottom of a steep flight of stairs. Moonlight shone invitingly down towards us, but in our current state, the steps might as well have been the north face of Mount Murdercruel. Several of my fellow undeads were milling around waiting for someone to take charge.

"Found another one," said my helper, jiggling me.

"Ohh," said a balding woman with no arms. "Look at this fancy dan with his four functioning limbs."

"And his skin hardly flaking off," said a man with no face on his skull.

"Aaa ih ee oo uh aaa," said someone else with no lower jaw.

"I bet he could still maintain an erection," grumbled a decrepit old corpse who probably had issues.

"Uh uh aaaa!"

Between us there were about six complete bodies, spread out over around ten individuals. There was more exposed bone and sinew on view than in a dumpster behind an abattoir, and everyone was wearing expensive funeral attire that had become faded and torn by the passage of time. The whole effect was rather like the aftermath of an explosion at a high-class dinner party.

For the first time I took a moment to examine myself properly. I was wearing what had probably once been a basic mage's robe, creamy brown linen stitched into a pattern that the nearest convenient tailor to the funeral home had probably thought was mystic and artsy. Time, however, had not been kind to it. Both elbows were worn right through. Threads all over the garment had come unstitched, and now dangled shamefacedly from all over my body. The tailoring had been utterly spoiled by whatever thoughtless person had cut a huge slit in the back, from neck to arse.

A particularly loud clash of falling ceiling echoed through the subterranean halls, and the floor was starting to shake again. I and the assembled undead collectively realized that we were still far from safety. A section of nearby wall slid into the abyss that was all that remained of my tomb, and a huge cloud of dust billowed out.

Now half-blind and fighting off a powerful desire to lie down and go back to sleep I tottered over to the stairs, fell forward and began wildly flinging my elbows and knees upwards in an impromptu attempt at climbing.

"Look, he can even climb stairs!" said the man with no face, struggling to follow.

"God, life's wasted on the young, isn't it?!" said the woman with no arms.

The fellow with no lower jaw was probably planning to add something, but then the ground cracked open beneath his feet and he was swallowed by the earth with a tongue-flapping wail of fright.

It's amazing how imminent peril can aid recovery from rigor mortis. I was making decent speed, and was already halfway to fresh air. At this rate I'd be perfectly fine as long as I was never called upon to do anything complicated, like shake someone's hand or sit in a chair. The rumbling was turning into a roar, the stairs were starting to shift beneath my hands and feet, and small bits of rock were raining down upon us constantly. A much larger bit of rock decided to join in the fun and thundered down the steps, but it flew over me and collided wetly with someone I hadn't had time to care about.

Being the most functional horrors present, I and the chap who'd found me were the first to reach the top. My arms and legs continued spinning through thin air for a few moments before I collapsed onto dead grass. A handful of the others were able to escape before the crypt entrance uttered a final impatient cough and caved in.

"Wait a second, I know this place," said the man with no face, who had been the third to emerge. "This is the graveyard near Whitbury Farmstead. In Goodsoil County."

I knew of Goodsoil County, but I had never been there in life, because of the rumors that circulated about the native farmers and what they got up to with domestic animals and unsuspecting travelers. It had not, as far as I could remember, been fingered as a dark and sinister place that oozed an atmosphere of tangible evil from every square foot of ground, but that was the sort of thing that could easily be overlooked if you were concentrating on keeping your private places away from backward rural folk.

The crypt had been the centerpiece of a vast graveyard that rolled away in all directions, a stark navy of gray stone slabs sailing upon an ocean of dead grass. It was hilly country, surrounded by a black pine forest from which emanated the growl of predators and the abruptly cut off squeals of their prey.

Once again, the ground began rumbling underneath me. *Oh, for crying out loud*, I thought. Was a single moment to myself too much to ask? I jumped back just as the dying grass split asunder and a zombie hand burst forth, flesh hanging from it like puff pastry from an aging apple turnover. It clawed the air for a moment, and an involuntary yelp of terror escaped from my lips. After that, though, it seemed to be having trouble, so my new colleagues and I helped pull it out, closely followed by the owner.

"Thanks," he said, re-attaching his arm. "Why am I alive?"

The same question was occurring to the graveyard's entire population, who were popping up like extremely fast-growing, foul-smelling daisies. That was what had caused the cave-ins, I realized: the graves were so packed together that the simultaneous stirring of their residents had caused massive trauma to the local geology. Of course, the huge green crystals probably weren't helping, either.

They were sitting on makeshift towers made from metal girders, thin and flimsy-looking but tall enough to loom over the treetops, and which were erected at regular intervals around the graveyard's perimeter. Mounted on the top of each tower was an irregular lump of green crystal—probably magical stone, judging by the way it glowed and the arcs of chartreuse lightning crackling around. As we watched, some unspoken signal caused the crystals to become connected for a brief second by a huge circle of green magical energy, which detached and drifted off into the sky like a smoke ring.

"This is necromantic magic," I thought aloud.

"Well, DUH," said someone.

"I mean, it has to be, but I've never seen anything like it. I didn't think it was done with crystals. I thought it was all blood sacrifice and that kind of thing."

I tapped my chin thoughtfully, felt exposed bone in my fingertips, and resumed taking stock of my current condition. My hands were skin and bone—in some places, just bone— and my flesh was discolored to a sickly grayish-green. None of my fingernails were less than an inch long. My toenails were poking out the front of my flimsy cloth boots. Miserably I unbuttoned the front of the robe and ran a clawed hand across my chest and belly. A deep scar ran diagonally across my torso, held together with rusty metal staples. At least my nerves had warmed up to the point that now I merely felt as if all four of my limbs had fallen asleep at the same time.

"Do you want to . . . take a look around?" asked the zombie who'd found me. Now that the earthquake had stopped, everyone in the graveyard was milling around uncertainly.

"No," I said, folding my arms with a series of unpleasant cracking noises. "I'm not moving until someone or something comes along and explains what the hell's going on. And only if it's a good explanation with lots of apologies."

Suddenly there was a thunderclap of magical energies colliding and a vertical sheet of flame burst forth along the ground several feet away, walling off access. More firewalls started igniting, forming a zigzag that seemed to be bearing down on us.

*That'll have to do*, I thought. Somehow I'd leapt to my feet, and I found myself forced to run again. More flaming barriers were bursting up all over the cemetery, and the undead masses were soon high-speed shuffling away from them and towards the graveyard entrance, where a crowd was frantically shoving against a pair of massive iron gates. A few attempted to scatter in different directions and were turned away by pointed bursts of flame. The word "shepherding" came to mind.

"What's going on?!" I said, repeating myself somewhat.

"It is a sign for the righteous," said someone next to me, who was gazing at a point above and to the left of him. "We have been resurrected for the Day of Judgment."

Too late I noticed his suspiciously cassock-like robe and collar. Mages, even student ones, don't get along with priests. Priests are all about using magic to heal wounds, and mages are all about using magic to create the wounds in the first place. Still, religion was probably the best place to start looking for an explanation, since there was a definite apocalyptic taste to current events. "Day of Judgment?"

He looked down at me in that way priests do, with what remained of his lips smashed tightly together and his eyes staring like I'd just widdled on his daughter. "The LORD has returned the righteous to life in time for the Rapture."

I looked around for my cryptmates, but they had been absorbed by the crowd, and once they reach a certain stage of decomposition, all corpses start to look alike. "Er," I said, glancing toward the spooky and unhelpful forest. "Does Almighty God say anything about the itinerary for Judgment Day? I mean, are we supposed to meet him somewhere?"

Almost all the resurrected were now gathered around the entrance gates. A couple of forward-thinking undead were rattling the padlock with numb fingers, but they jumped back in terror when a colossal explosion rang out. As one, the crystals disintegrated, filling the air with tiny shards of twinkling green glass. A fork of lightning split the night sky, a boom like the crashing of worlds. The wind picked up, fluttering our rotting rags insanely about our bodies. Something was obviously trying to get our attention.

"This is it," said the priest. "I am returning to my father!" He kicked me in the leg. "Stand not so close to me, demon, and stain not my soul!"

"Ow."

A laugh screamed out over the graveyard, a hearty and insane laugh, about as far removed from polite after dinner laughter as you can get. This was the kind of insane laughter even the truly insane have to practice for years to get right.

There, standing on top of the gate with legs wide, one fist pointed skyways and one clinging to a nearby pillar for stability, was a cackling silhouette. A bolt of lightning set alight a circle of fuel, obviously prepared beforehand, and a fire quickly rose around his perch.

"Rise, my hordes of darkness!" he shrieked, then he did that laugh thing again. With the firelight, I could now make out his features. He was very tall and very thin, with the body and skin tone of one who has placed far too many pieces of his soul in far too many evil magic artifacts. He had tried to disguise his skinny build with a thickly padded black cloak and a pair of spiked shoulder pads the size of watermelons. Framing his sunken face was an ornate obsidian helmet carved somewhat predictably into the shape of an angry fanged skull. In addition to all that, he was addressing a bunch of dead guys, so he might as well have been wearing a sash with "NECROMANCER" writ big.

"Rise!" he repeated, throwing up his hands. "Rise, and join the ranks of my unholy horde!"

He seemed to notice for the first time that we weren't exactly rushing to his side, but were mainly watching him as a zoo patron would watch a crazy monkey, curious but ready to move at the first sign of poo-flinging. There was a minute of awkward silence before someone near the back with their head held under their arm said, "Who's this twat?"

"Are you God?" asked someone else.

The necromancer clearly wasn't prepared for either of those questions, but to his credit he recovered quickly. "Perhaps I am!" he said, flashing a winning smile. "Your ruler, certainly! And soon the ruler of the world!" He stretched out the word "world" until a roll of thunder served up the exclamation mark. "March, my undead minions! We ride to my fortress of darkness!"

Glances were exchanged between the undead minions in question, most of them directed towards the agnostic speaker of the previous question, who was apparently being groomed as company spokesman. He was a turquoise fellow with missing ears and piles of gravedirt on his shoulders. "Do we have to?"

This time, the necromancer's improvisational skills abandoned him. His arms dropped to his sides, and when he replied, the booming insane qualities were missing from his voice. "Well . . . yes, I mean . . . you're my undead minions. I raised you from the grave. You have to do everything I say." Doubt was clearly nagging at him. He extended his hands again, holding his gnarled ebony staff horizontally. "I command thee to march!"

"Your commands are the futile bleating of the damned, bedfellow of the Serpent," growled the priest.

"March!" A spark of panic materialized in the necromancer's eyes as if it had finally dawned on him that he had just placed himself right in the middle of a cranky, unstoppable army of unwilling zombies and identified himself as the source of their misfortune. "March! Walk . . . jump up and down . . .

do a little dance . . . er . . . " The staff wobbled nervously in his grip. "You've got free will, haven't you."

"Sort of," said the spokesman.

"They've got free will!" called the necromancer, to a trio of men in full suits of spikey black armor who had been tending to a quartet of horses some distance away. "How the hell have they got free will?!"

"I dunno what to tell yer, Lord Dreadgrave," said one of the soldiers, his voice echoing nicely in his senselessly huge helmet. "It's your ritual."

Dreadgrave smacked himself in the face with a full open palm. "It's my ritual. It's meh reh teh meh. It's meh meh meh meh. I came in here for a horde. What the hell am I supposed to do with a bunch of smelly . . . independents?"

"Why don't you just ask us to join your horde?" said the haughty lady with no arms. "Like polite, decent people do."

"Would you really? If I asked? Gartharas, would you put this fire out, please, I think it's coming straight for my shoes—"

"Maybe," said our spokesman, as the armored men began stamping on the dwindling ring of flame. "I mean, we've never really been in any undead hordes before, so we might be interested in the opportunity to try new things."

"And it's not like we've got much else to do with our time now that we're piles of rotting meat and bones that no-one besides the utterly depraved would ever want to sleep with," said the decrepit old corpse (whom I still felt had issues).

Dreadgrave tapped his staff against his palm pensively. "Do you want to join my horde?"

The undead closest to the spokesman, and the ones who had appointed themselves senior members of the undead community, went into a huddled conference. For a few minutes, all eyes were on a muttering scrumdown of assorted abominations. Someone put forward a motion, someone else seconded it, and the meeting was adjourned. "What does it pay?" asked the spokesman, after a cough.

"Pay?" said Dreadgrave distastefully. "Why should it pay anything?"

A collective moan descended on the crowd, and some of them started drifting away, losing interest in the whole stupid affair.

"But . . . wait, wait, wait, don't go, don't go, don't go," said the necromancer, flapping his arms to avoid losing his audience. "What I meant was . . . why do you want to get paid? What could you possibly want the money for?" No-arms opened her mouth to reply, but no answer was forthcoming. Dreadgrave continued. "You don't need food. You don't need water. You don't need to sleep, so you don't need shelter, so you don't need rent money. You can't get tired so you don't need to pay for carriages and things. What else is there?"

"Prostitutes?" tried Gartharas, leaning amicably on a tombstone.

"Well, like he said, they'd need to be blind or open-minded to a completely shameful degree. I just don't think any of you could have any possible need for a regular wage."

"Just because we don't need it doesn't mean we couldn't find a use for it," said our spokesman. "We could donate it to charity. Arrange trust funds for our surviving loved ones. Take up antique collecting. Go to the opera."

"They wouldn't let you in at the opera—"

"Well, that was just an example, wasn't it? We could go to a pantomime or some low-budget musical production or something. The point is, you can't expect to hire an army without incentive; if everyone could do, that the whole economy would collapse."

People were starting to drift off again, as they do when words like "economy" enter the conversation, so Dreadgrave was spurred to interrupt. "Okay, listen, listen. What would you say to . . . a profit sharing scheme?"

The drifting stopped. The crowd cocked a collective ear.

"Join my horde, and every time we fall upon a town or village, you get to keep everything you loot, minus a small percentage—no! Wait! Come back! No deductions, no deductions! Maybe a small deduc—okay, none at all! All yours! And free room and board at my doom fortress."

There was a lot of conferring going on among the shambling dead. I waited to see their decision; I'd been in enough angry mobs in my time to know that the smart money was always with the majority.

"And every month, I'll take you all to see a low-budget musical production."

A lot of heads were nodding approvingly now. The spokesman counted a show of hands, then relayed the result. "Done."

"Then march, my undead horde!" screamed Dreadgrave, holding his arms aloft and getting back into the swing of things. "We ride to my fortress of darkness!"

# TWO

Dreadgrave's request that we march to his doom fortress could only be obeyed creatively at best, since every zombie had to master his own interpretation of walking. We were learning fast, though; I and the other guys fortunate enough to have both legs had almost totally shaken off rigor mortis by the end of the first night, and even the guys with no limbs at all had worked up a decent pace using only their teeth or their buttocks. In the spirit of marching, Dreadgrave's horde lurched, goose-stepped, crawled, shuffled, and chewed its way through Goodsoil County.

That was what the guy earlier had called the place, and what was written on the older road signs, but the countryside had seen a lot of changes while we'd all been out of touch. The newer signs seemed to believe they were in a place called "Greydoom Valley," which seemed a lot more appropriate. The day was overcast and grim, while the night was just plain cold and dark. It was like a black cloud had descended to ground level and refused to move on, squatting in place like a big fat toad.

The peasants we passed on our way to the doom fortress didn't seem to think there was anything good about the soil, either. They came out of their tiny hovels to line the roads and gaze at us from under their heavy brows with slack-jawed wonder. They had the skinny builds and pale skin that come from a diet with too much reliance on potatoes and cabbages. All in all, standard local color with low to middling potential for pitchfork-and-flaming-torch-wielding mob-forming.

I did have a pleasant conversation with one of the shrewder ones, who was going down the ranks trying to sell sticky buns. It was from him that I learned that my homeland of Borrigarde had been invaded and conquered by the neighboring kingdom of Pillock forty years ago. I wasn't that bothered: I had never been patriotic. Whenever the King's carriage had rattled through my home village during his monthly "parades" through the land, I had usually joined the other kids to run behind him throwing old peaches.

But it did mean that I could estimate how long I had been dead. At the time of my sudden and tragic death I was fairly certain that the fragile peace between Borrigarde and Pillock was about due for another collapse. There was a lot of very old, very stagnant bad blood between the royal families. Apparently, in their youth, the two kings had been roommates at Rolledgoat University and there were several outstanding issues regarding eating each others' food and bringing girls around late at night. Anyway, at the time I had died, I had given it ten years at most before another big war. Therefore I must have been dead for roughly fifty years before Dreadgrave came along and proved my eternal slumber to be nothing of the sort.

After four days' march we came to the top of one last hill, and Dreadgrave's distinctive voice echoed throughout the plains. "Behold!" he yelled. We laboriously climbed the rise and beheld.

We were looking down into a wide valley, and while I had thought the rest of the surrounding country was gloomy, this place made it seem like Happy Smiling Bunny Rabbit Junction. Except for the oily foliage around a small decorative swamp the color of ancient lettuce, there wasn't a scrap of vegetation. The very earth of the valley slopes was gray and cracked, all life drained. A snaking river of unhealthy greenish-brown water bisected the landscape, and a gigantic black cloud hung in the sky, spiralling and swirling madly above the only man-made building in the valley, which squatted over the river like an incontinent titan.

Dreadgrave's doom fortress looked exactly like doom fortresses are supposed to look: a big gnashing skull from the front, and a great sprawling insect from above. Veins of obsidian ran across shiny black marble. Black pipes and black chimneys placed randomly around the black roof and walls emitted occasional bursts of decorative black flame. The tallest tower (black), which I took an immediate interest in, was a magnificent hundred-foot affair studded with black stone gargoyles of the kind of terrifying hideousness that has to be specially imported from countries with higher suicide rates.

"Ooooooh," went the undead horde.

"Pretty snazzy," I said aloud to no-one in particular, as we began to march very carefully down the twisting path into the valley's heart.

"It is an abomination," said the person walking alongside me. "It is an affront before the house of the Lord."

I glanced at him and recognized the all-too-familiar collar. I sighed. "No-one's forcing you to tag along, you know."

"Be silent, venomous spittle of the Doom Serpent!" he barked, dodging the issue. "You are a servant of evil. An affront to God's will, a corpse reanimated of devilry that man should not wot of."

"Wot?"

"Indeed."

"Hey. You're just as much affront to God's will as I am. We've all got the same kind of black magic up our arses."

"You are wrong. I was returned to life by the blessing of the LORD, for He would have me continue my good work of spreading His name." He stared down at me with both nostrils.

"You are a demon taking human form, a silver-tongued tempter to draw the righteous from the LORD."

"Look, I've got nothing against the LORD," I protested. "I just didn't see him rushing to intervene when that jerk up ahead started bringing us back to life."

"You were not worthy of His gift!" he barked, a hint of mania dropping into his voice. He grabbed my face in one hand and almost knocked me off my feet. "Out, demon! Leave be the body of this poor wretched soul!"

I shook him off. He was obviously taking an extended holiday from reality, an option that I had to admit I was finding more and more tempting.

We had reached the outer wall of the fortress, and the portcullis that filled the entrance slid upwards like retractable fangs into the gigantic skull-shaped archway. The horde shuffled into the main courtyard, where two little desks were set up. Behind each was one of Dreadgrave's armored human minions, glumly sitting beside stacks of enrollment forms. A third minion, an undead girl who couldn't have been older than 20 when she had died, stood in the middle, earnestly hugging a clipboard to her chest. Dreadgrave nodded to her briefly, then disappeared into the shadows.

"Okay!" exclaimed the girl, her voice loud and high-pitched enough to make the maggots in my eardrums wriggle crankily. "Welcome to Greydoom Valley, and your wonderful new career as one of Lord Dreadgrave's undead minions! My name is Meryl, and I am the company settlement officer, so if you ever have any problems or if you just want to chat, my door is always open!" Quite a lot of the assembled dead were exchanging confused glances. "Now then, most of you will be working as security or maintenance personnel, but we do have some openings in middle and upper management, which we will assign once we've gotten all your names down and worked out your individual qualifications. But don't worry, there's a place at Greydoom Valley for even the least qualified, least physically intact zombie!"

A nearby torso gurgled appreciatively from its neck stump.

"We've got quite a lot of people to process," she continued, "so if you could form two orderly queues in front of the desks, we'll have magic users on the left—that's all you mages, priests, conjurers, anyone in the magic industry, on the left— and everyone else on the right. If you're not sure where you fit, just go on the right, there."

The horde began dividing into two grumbling columns. I couldn't help noticing that the priest had joined the queue directly in front of me. I tapped him on the shoulder.

"Feel free to leave at any time," I whispered. "This being a den of Satan's progeny and everything."

"I will not leave."

"And why's that?"

"I see now that this is the holy mission with which the LORD has blessed me," he said, through his teeth. "I am to destroy this den of evil from within."

"Well, at least give us time to settle down," I said gloomily, losing interest in the conversation. He glared at me for an instant, his lips stretching as far away from his teeth as he could manage. Then he fixed his gaze upon a point somewhere inside his own head and started speaking in dry croaky tongues.

Further interaction was impossible so I took the opportunity to steal his place in line, and soon enough it was my turn to be interviewed. I stepped forward.

"Name?" said the hairy man behind the desk, who was wearing a very authoritative spiked helmet.

"Jim . . . " I began, but then my rotten memory banks failed. "Jim something."

"James Smith," wrote the officer aloud. "Occupation in life?"

"Magic student."

"Ah. College boy. Were you thinking of a job as a mercenary, or just some support role?"

"Support, I suppose."

He nodded. "Good. Seems like everyone else in that cemetery was a mercenary, we're up to our eyeballs in the buggers. Must've been a lot of wars around there, I guess. What we really need is a cook. All the human guards've been eating tinned beans for months. You know anything about cooking?"

"I used to tend bar part time," I tried. He crossed something out on my form and I felt a little disheartened.

"Any idea how advanced a magic student?"

"Not very. Firebolts, that's about it."

"Well, there's nothing quite like on-the-job experience for a young corpse's education. You're on the security team. That basically means you hang around the fortress and kill adventurers."

"Just adventurers?"

He didn't look up as he wrote. "Anything that doesn't work here, but it's mostly adventurers, yeah."

I glanced around at the crowded courtyard. "Do you really need this many zombies just for adventurers?"

This time, he did look up. His helmet made it hard to tell but I think he was giving me a very funny look. "Call it erring on the side of caution," he said, with loud sarcasm. "Anyway, it's easy work, I'm sure you'll pick it up quickly. Now, I just have to ask a few personal questions for our equal opportunity policy. Country of origin?"

"Borrigarde," I said.

"New Pillock," he wrote.

"Ooh, you're Borrigardian too?" said Meryl the company settlement officer, who was floating around in an uncertain supervisey sort of way. "I'm Borrigardian! Did you die in the Pillock Wars?"

"Er, no. Before then. I think. College rivalry thing."

She was suddenly very interested. "A pre-integration Borrigardian? Both your parents, too?"

"Yeah, tenth generation," I said guardedly, wondering what she was getting at. "My family didn't get around much."

Her eyes were shining. Or rather, while they were still glowing with the sickly yellow light of necromantic magic like everyone else's, she was now gazing at me like a starving man gazes at a grilled cheese sandwich. She laid a hand on the officer's shoulder and glanced at my application. "Security? Great. Put him on my detail. I really look forward to working with you, mister . . . Smith." She scampered off about her business, leaving me and the officer, baffled.

"What was that all about?" he asked, like I would know.

"Cough," went the incredibly long queue behind me.

"Oh, right, let's keep this moving." He pointed to a nearby archway leading into the fortress. "You're in the main tower, that's the third turning on the right. Keep heading upstairs until you find a free bunk. Welcome aboard, look forward to working with you, etcetera. Next!"

# THREE

In the tower, the atmosphere was convivial. As I ascended the perimeter staircase I paused on each floor to take in the sights. Undead minions sat around on the straw mattresses and sackcloth sheets they would never actually sleep on, chatting, laughing, joking, all prejudices in life forgotten. Idly I kept an eye out for any of my crypt-mates, but one case of decomposition looks pretty much like another after a while.

I paused at the staircase to watch some corpses dance country-style to the earnest fiddling of a minion in the corner. Seeing their wide smiles—rather unsettlingly wide, in the case of the faceless ones—I very nearly considered staying. But no, I thought, shaking my head. This was not the life for me. Death for me. Unlife—whatever it was, it wasn't for me. I continued up.

It really was a very tall tower, and the sun had set by the time I reached the very top, and I emerged from the stairwell to the biting cold breeze of a Greydoom evening. I reflected that neither the sensation of cold nor the enormous climb had caused any degree of discomfort in my new, undead form, and my magic-powered glowy-eye vision let me see to the very edge of the horizon. None of it was any comfort.

Somewhere along the last fifty years I'd acquired a new perspective. Maybe it had been my horrific death, or vision of the afterlife, or seeing all the countries of the world unfolding below me, but having witnessed it from the outside, I realized just how futile my life had been. And now I had been living a second one for about four days in a far less functional body and didn't feel there had been any improvement in the key problem areas. So I decided I was done with it. My life had failed its field test. I would leave it for some other sucker.

I stepped onto the parapet and glanced sadly down the full height of the tower. Far below me the last few minions were still queueing politely in the main courtyard, like tiny, mutilated, foul-smelling ants. I snorted. It was easy to feel superior, looking down from this height. Perhaps this was why necromancers were always trying to take over the world.

There was a full moon, and even the drab landscape of Greydoom Valley seemed beautiful as it rolled away into the horizon. The very beginnings of dawn were bringing a spectacular tint to the sky. I drank it all in for a few seconds, then jumped off before I could change my mind.

The second time I died started off pretty similar to the first. My body hit a gargoyle on the way down with a sickening crunch, then cartwheeled to a bone-splattering finale on the solid stone far below. My grateful soul was immediately ejected like a blast of air from a bellows.

But from that moment, I could tell that something was wrong. There was no glorious light, and no sensation of being lifted through the air. I was still on the ground, standing over my shattered corpse in a world without sound or color. In the living world, minions as intangible as smoke were rushing over to inspect the damage, and still the universe was making no attempt to elevate me to a better place. I tried jumping up and down a few times, but I remained distressingly fettered to the earth.

The thought occurred to me, with a lurch of my astral tummy, that the priest might have been right. Maybe, having been raised by black magic, I was now a tainted thing in the eyes of the glorious golden presence that had welcomed me before. Maybe I was excluded from heaven, condemned to walk the earth as a lost soul, wailing and shaking chains and knocking things off shelves to scare the willies out of nervous losers whom no-one would ever seriously believe.

"Oh well," I said aloud, my voice sounding distorted and muffled as if I were talking underwater. "I'll take that."

I suddenly became aware that there were figures standing around me. They must have been part of the ethereal landscape, because the zombies in the living world were bumbling right through them undaunted. They were angels, but they bore very little similarity to the golden ones that had escorted me during my first brief visit to the hereafter. These were white, wearing flowing white robes that glowed with amazing brilliance, and their wings were little more than brief triangles poking poutily from their backs. Like the angels I had met before, they had no faces, but I felt none of the waves of love and acceptance that the golden ones had radiated. Eight of the white angels were standing around me in a tight circle, staring down like they were waiting for me to do something. High above, I could see endless legions of the same beings, flying across the gray sky at impossibly high speeds, each apparently fixated on some vital personal errand.

"Hello," I said, suddenly very intimidated.

I could hear a strange sound just on the edge of earshot, like a constant high-pitched gibbering in some incomprehensible tongue. At first I thought it was coming from the angels, but then I realized it was somehow entering my mind without needing anything as mundane as ears. The angels didn't move, but they still seemed to be closing in on me, still glaring eyelessly and ceaselessly. I was rooted to the spot, terrified.

As one they extended their arms, trailing billowing sleeves, and pointed at my body. By this point it was being shoveled into a wheelbarrow by two whistling ghouls. I wondered what the angels were getting at until I felt myself being pulled towards it.

"Er, no, that's OK," I said, displaying my hands. "I'm done with it, you can have it if you want—" a sudden roar of astral wind drowned my voice, and the pull strengthened, yanking me off my feet. I scrabbled wildly for a handhold, but the astral realm proved as insubstantial as it looked. The angels watched without movement or pity as I was yanked back into the land of the living.

For a few panicky hours I was trapped without sensation in a yawning blackness, until my vision suddenly sparked back on as Meryl carefully re-inserted one of my eyeballs. I immediately put it to good use by taking in my surroundings. In any sane doom fortress the room I was in would have been called a "stable." In this one it was apparently filling the role of infirmary. If it had ever housed horses they were now either stolen, escaped, or eaten.

I was lying—to use the word creatively—on a wooden workbench with a number of vicious-looking medical instruments. There certainly seemed to be substantially less of me than I remembered. And what did remain was twisted into some very unpleasing shapes. I should have been thankful that I no longer felt pain, but I was in no mood for gratitude.

"Well, that was a silly billy thing to do, wasn't it?" said Meryl, screwing in my other eye.

"Eye aah aah eye," I replied.

"Hang on." She clicked my lower jaw back into place. "There you go."

"Why can't I die?"

Her permanent smile extended a little. "You're already dead."

"Dead, but not dead enough."

She giggled. "That's awesome. I'm going to embroider that. You should write it down. If you wrote a book it'd be a good tagline for the back cover."

She picked up one of my legs and gave it a sharp twist until the bone reset with an eye-watering crack. "Ow," I said.

"That hurt?"

"No, but it looked like it should have done."

"Isn't he marvelous? Dreadgrave, I mean. Not like those lazy necromancers who just make zombies that fall apart the moment you trip them up. When he raises the dead, they STAY raised."

I was dubious. I still had very clear memories of those angel things and they didn't seem like Dreadgrave's work— they were certainly overdramatic and pretentious, but not in the same way. No, there was definitely something fishy going on. I wasn't in the mood to try and deduce anything further, though, because I had a hefty backlog of despair to offload.

"When I died, it made me realize something," I mono- logued, as Meryl continued putting me back together like a putrescent jigsaw. "I might have been surrounded by stupid people and arrogant people and fat people, and the natural world might have seemed to be be out to get me a few times, too, with rains and hurricanes and big steep hills that you have to walk all the way up on your way home from school. But you don't need to put up with any of that crap forever. You just die, and it all just shrinks away into nothing, and you wonder why any of it ever mattered. You're finally at peace. But now you're telling me that that's been taken away from me, for keeps. How am I supposed to feel about that?"

"Give it a rest," said a voice from somewhere off to the side. I swiveled my eyes—one of the few body parts I could currently move—as far as they could go and saw another severely mangled minion piled up on the next bench, and another on the bench after that. "We're all having to deal, sonny."

"What happened to you?" I asked.

"Jumped off the tower, didn't I? Like everyone else."

I had always considered myself a unique, special sort of person who didn't cave in to things like fashion trends, and this was a bit galling. "Do a lot of people do that?"

"All the time," said Meryl cheerfully. "Some people really have trouble accepting that they can't die." I heard a loud SHLOCK sound from somewhere to my rear, and sensation spread through my body like a diamond rain. "Welp, that's your spine back in. See if you can sit up and I'll test your reflexes."

"Hey, how much longer is this going to take?" said one of the piles. "I was here before that guy—"

"Shut up!" snapped Meryl, flashing a vicious scowl in his direction before turning back to me and softening. "You're all getting done in order of importance."

"I'm Dreadgrave's new personal assistant!" he protested.

"I mean, severity of injury."

"My thighs are in my lungs!"

She ignored him. My nerves were back to their usual, slightly numb selves. I sat with my legs dangling over the side as she prepared a small chisel, then stroked one of my knees like a small child petting a beloved family dog.

I took a good look at Meryl for the first time. As I had earlier noted, she was a couple of years younger than me, or at least had been at the point of death. Her hair was surprisingly full and red for a corpse and was arranged into two cheerful pigtails pointing diagonally upwards from her skull. She was wearing the kind of revealing leather singlet popular with female warriors who probably didn't get enough attention at childhood, but she was also wearing a plain brown dress underneath, which struck me as missing the point somewhat. As I took her in, she dug the chisel as hard as she could into the space just below my left kneecap.

"Have you seen a priest anywhere around here?" I asked, while we waited. "Tall and old, with a face like he's been sucking vinegar off a stinging nettle?"

"Well, you could be describing quite a few people I know, there," she said, watching my knee intently. Suddenly, my right foot kicked forward. "Yep, seems normal."

"This one keeps yelling about how we're all servants of the devil and how righteous he is."

"Funny how the whole resurrection thing has that effect on priests, isn't it?"

"So have you seen him?"
She pointed to the bench to my left. "He's over there."

His knees were hooked over his shoulders and half his ribcage was sticking out his back, but the face was unmistakable, as was the way his eyes were rolled back into his head as he tried to speak in tongues.

"Hey," I said, getting his attention by knuckling his forehead. His eyes swiveled toward me, and the hatred coming off them was almost physical. "I'm kind of considering options right now and I wanted to ask you something."

"Ask your question, demon of ignorance," he gurgled manfully, through his discomfort.

"Yeah. I was just wondering how long it takes to be saved with your religion. 'Cos I tried dying and it wouldn't take, and I'm wondering if it's anything to do with me being a heathen."

He seemed surprised for a moment, then took on the triumphant look of an evangelist with an in. "The road to becoming a Seventh Day Advent Hedge Devolutionist is a difficult but rewarding one," he said, with the labored air of the pulpit. "After the baptism of halibut oil, you must recite from memory the eight hundred Great Teachings of the Most Holy Brother Randolph the Incomprehensible. Only then, and after you have run the Sacred Hundred Leagues with the Stone Tablets of Blessed Hernia strapped to your back—"

A thought occurred to me. "Did you jump off the tower?" I interrupted.

"Twice now have I been plucked before my time," he said, his eyes glistening with rapture. "And twice now have I been returned by the LORD, to continue my great work. His angels came to me as my soul did move to depart, eight in number and without face, to usher me back to this world."

"Sou-nds fam–il–i–ar," interjected the corpse that Meryl was now attending to. She was beating him back into shape with a lot less of the tenderness she had shown me.

My mood shriveled even further. From what I could interpret, the priest had received the exact same treatment as I in the dead world. Seventh Day Advent Hedge Devolutionists, at least, were probably barking up the wrong tree. Still, the theory of the scheme was sound, and called for experimentation. "Is there a library in this fortress where I can look up religions?"

"Look," said Meryl kindly. "Why don't you stop trying to find ways to die and start finding ways to live?"

The line sounded very well-rehearsed. She'd probably used it on several patients today. "Pardon?"

"People keep coming through here after jumping off the tower, and they're all too busy moaning about not being dead enough to really step back and see what a wonderful thing has happened to them. There are people walking around here with their legs replaced with broomsticks and tea towels instead of faces, and most of them have much better attitudes than you.

I didn't think a Borrigardian would be like that." She paused and looked at me in a way she probably thought was authoritative, before going back to massaging a disembodied brain with the air of a baker kneading dough. "You've been brought back to life. Back to life! You're free to experience all the things you missed first time around."

"I'm dead!" I said, arms akimbo. "I'm a zombie! I stink and half my body doesn't work!"

"So life's become a challenge. Makes things more interesting." She looked at me pityingly. "Look. Give it a chance, all right? Working for Dreadgrave is a cushy gig. Give it a few weeks, and I'm sure you'll soon be getting up with a bright shining face every morning to meet the new day."

Not for the first time, and definitely not for the last, I sincerely missed the ability to throw up. "Fine."

"You'll do that for me?"

"Sure, whatever."

"Off you go, then. I'll let you know if your nose turns up."

# FOUR

So, I became an undead minion in the fortress of Necromancer Lord Dreadgrave. And after three months of trying, I was no closer to a dignified death.

Religion certainly didn't help. By the end of the second week, I was spending every lunch break converting myself to a new religion and every evening being scraped off the quad under the main tower. I became a practicing New Reformist, Lesser Somnambulist, Greater Pedant, Follower of Astromelon, Follower of Mongbotty, Follower of The Smaller Of Two Acorns, Soggoth, Bimbelle, Choppler, and Git. And I would have been a Seventh Day Advent Hedge Devolutionist if my bulk order of halibut oil had ever come in.

But no matter what freakish chants or arcane dance moves I displayed after death, none of it seemed to impress the angels—or whatever they were—who made no reaction besides batting me back into the living world like a cosmic ping-pong ball. After two weeks I'd grown disillusioned with the scheme. It didn't seem like any Gods worth their salt would be fooled by such lightning-quick conversions, and I was sick of Meryl's daily reminders to keep a sunny disposition and not stink out my dormitory with incense and rotting animal sacrifices.

I still didn't quite get Meryl. She spent almost all her time vying for my attention. At first I'd been entertaining the possibility that she had a crush on me—as had several of our mutual acquaintances, to their considerable amusement—but when she wasn't stitching me back together, all she ever wanted to do was talk about Borrigarde and how much I could remember about my family history. After being trapped in conversation for an hour trying to remember the names of all my family pigs, I took to avoiding her whenever we weren't sharing what was laughably termed "guard duty."

I had to admit, though, she had been right about one thing: working for Dreadgrave was a pretty cushy gig. "Guard duty" usually involved sitting around in a room or hallway chatting and playing board games with the other minions in the detail. There was no need to work out official patrols. There were so many undead scattered throughout the fortress that intruders tripped over several the moment they arrived—literally, if they arrived via the quad beneath the main tower.

Intruders, there were plenty of. I soon understood why Dreadgrave needed so many of us. It seemed like everyone in the adventuring industry was drawn to the fortress like moths to a flame, and with roughly the same results. Swordsmen, archers, mages, rogues—we found all sorts skulking around trying not to be seen, and none of them were a match for our numbers, especially since we couldn't stay down. I also found that being a magic-infused undead creature gave my spells a boost, and my firebolts could now actually singe an enemy, rather than just give them a touch of sunburn.

But I did wonder at the sheer number of adventurers trying to raid the fortress. More traveling mercenaries and bounty hunters passed through our dungeons every week than I had ever seen in my entire pre-undead life. We must have put the equivalent of three medium-sized villages through the rotating knives, and there never seemed to be any less of them around.

"There are a lot of people out there who seek to know my secrets," Dreadgrave had said, when I raised the issue one morning as he made his daily rounds. "Apparently they feel that sending these poor fools to their deaths would be much less trouble than, say, paying me lots of money."

Dreadgrave had turned out to be an amazingly good employer. He had learned from the examples of too many necromancers and dark lords who had ruled their minions with whips and iron fists and who had ended up friendless and dismembered the moment the chips went down. He followed through on his promises. The light musical theatre events took place regularly as scheduled and were pretty enjoyable, even if the traveling theatre groups that were brought in tended to perform with a certain wild-eyed terror. And we were allowed to keep whatever we looted from invaded villages. This rarely amounted to more than a few armfuls of potatoes and the occasional sheep, but we didn't hold it against him because he was just so considerate. One time I made an off-hand comment about how hard it was to hurl prisoners into the rat pit without getting nibbled, and the very next day there were nibble-proof overalls waiting in the rat pit antechamber. For three months, I had nothing to complain about, besides the fact that I existed at all.

On the morning of the day when things took an achingly severe turn for the worse, Meryl and I were on guard duty in Dreadgrave's office. He was sitting behind his enormous desk (carved with the prerequisite grotesque skulls and demonic faces), working on the accounts for the last village raid. Meryl was at the door and I was at the window, leaning on a pikestaff.

"Riders approaching," I said, watching clouds of dust rise from the horizon.

Dreadgrave glanced up. "Wearing?"

"Leather underpants, bandoliers—definitely adventurers," I reported. As a general rule of thumb, the likelihood of someone being an adventurer was directly proportional to the amount of exposed flesh on their person. (This was with the exception of magic-users, in which case it was directly proportional to the width of their sleeves.)

Dreadgrave came over for a look. "Huh. Bigger group than normal." He gave a little laugh—not his elaborate screaming cackle, but his understated evil schemey snicker for less formal occasions. "The fools will soon learn that no-one trifles with Lord Dreadgrave." He banged the speaking tube that led up through the ceiling. "Archers fire at will."

"Righty-ho," came the tinny response.

We watched the first volley of flaming arrows rain down. One of the horses started having second thoughts about its commitment to the galloping project. "So anyway," said Dreadgrave, "How're things going, Jim? Any more problems with nibbling?"

Dreadgrave had the gift of the good manager in that he always remembered your name, no matter how generically horrific your appearance. "Oh yeah, that's fine now. We're still having a little trouble with the bodies, though."

"Send in ground infantry," he said into another tube, before turning to me again. "Oh?"

A mob of axe-wielding undead guards rushed out the front portcullis to meet the remaining unpunctured heroes. "The rats don't seem to be nibbling the victims down fast enough," I said. "They usually stop after a while, and then you're stuck with dirty skeletons cluttering up the bottom of the pit."

"Mmm. Good for the intimidatory factor, though." A severed hand flew up and bounced off the window pane with a wet splat.

"Maybe, but it's getting pretty ridiculous. There'll be more skeleton than rat soon."

"Hm. Maybe we should cut down on the rat pit for a while." There was only one adventurer still on his feet, and he was running around trying to fend off minions with one hand and pat out his burning beard with the other.

"I don't think you need to do that—I mean, it's a really effective torture-slash-execution device. I just thought, maybe we could order a couple of boat hooks and drag some of the bodies out, maybe stick them on spikes in the front garden for the crows to have a go at."

He patted me on the shoulder. "Now that's good thinking, Jim. The gardeners have some of those . . . oh, what do you call them? Curvy blade things on the end of poles for trimming leaves on trees? You could probably use those."

By now, the last warrior was out of sight, and judging by the way the axes were falling and the wet sticky things were rising, it was probably safe to call the victory decisive. Dreadgrave rubbed his hands, and turned from the window. "Well, that was fun. Back to work."

"Lord Dreadgrave!" came a yell from a speaking tube labelled "Tower Quad."

"Yes, Frank?"

"There's another of 'em, lord. Rogue. Snuck in while we were distracted, got into t' quad. 'Sokay, though, Edward was jumping off tower and landed on 'im."

"Is he alive?"

"'Course not."

"I mean the rogue."

"Oh. Yeah. Bit conked out. Shall we throw 'im int' rat pit?"

Dreadgrave glanced at me. I shook my head.

"No . . . bring him up here. I haven't had a good villain gloat in a while."

We moved the desk out of the way so that Dreadgrave's throne stood alone in the middle of the room, then unfurled a narrow blood red carpet leading from the door to his feet. Dreadgrave put on the carved skull helm he only wore for visitors, while Meryl and I donned faceless minion helmets and stood either side of him, pikestaffs in hand.

After all that the effect was lost, because the rogue was still unconscious when Frank dragged him in and deposited him on the carpet. Like warriors with their lack of clothing and mages with their sleeves, the signature for rogues is their fondness for black. This specimen, for example, was wearing a black open-necked shirt, black hose, black boots, black cap, and great big black bruises where he had been struck by Edward's flailing limbs.

He was a small and wiry man, built like an acrobat, as rogues tend to be. Frank gave him a kick and rolled him over, and I furrowed my brow, puzzled.

There was something familiar about the man that immediately began digging at my mind. He was wearing the kind of small black mask with eyeholes that does less to conceal the identity than a pair of spectacles, and a stupid curly mustache so thin that it could have been drawn on, and I could have sworn I'd seen it all before.

"Wake him up," ordered Dreadgrave, slipping into his stern growl. Frank responded by gobbing viscous green phlegm onto the rogue's face, adding a much-needed bit of color to his outfit.

"Waaagh!" went the rogue, suddenly awake with suspicious rapidity.

"Who sent you here?" went Dreadgrave, steepling his fingers like a pro.

"Slippery John will never talk, Dreadgrave!" The rogue was clearly enlivened by the notion that someone considered him important enough to interrogate. "Torture Slippery John all you want, Slippery John never betrays his client!"

"Take him to the grinding wheel," said Dreadgrave, bored.

"Whoa whoa whoa!" added Slippery John quickly. "You didn't let Slippery John finish. Slippery John never betrays his client during peak work hours, but otherwise Slippery John is a free spirited renegade and owes allegiance to no man!" A long, awkward pause. "It was the Magic Resistance in Lolede City. They want your big book of necromancy."

Dreadgrave treated us to one of his best booming laughs. I nodded appreciatively behind my helmet. "The Magic Resistance have my terms! If they would know my methods, they must prove their commitment with gold, payable in installments! None will wrest that which is Dreadgrave's by force!"

"Yeah, that's pretty much what Slippery John said to them," muttered Slippery John. I definitely recognized him. The thought nagged at me like a bored schoolboy repeatedly kicking the back of my chair.

"Did you really think you could outsmart one such as I?" boomed Dreadgrave, returning to the matter at hand. "Slip past my invincible undead legions?" He gestured to Meryl and me—the sort of acknowledgement that was another of the many little things that made him such a great person to work for. "Many adventurers have attempted to best my fortress, but never one as pathetic as you."

"Well if you're trying to hurt Slippery John's feelings, then mission accomplished," muttered the rogue, not quietly enough.

"Cast this sniveling wretch into the Acid Fountain," ordered Dreadgrave.

"Emptied for cleaning," I hissed rapidly into his ear.

"Wait," he added, without missing a beat. "On second thoughts, throw him into the dungeons. His fate will be all the more agonizing if he is left to contemplate it for a while."

"Do you mind if I pop down and . . . interview him, after my shift?" I asked, after Slippery John had sniveled his way down the corridor. "There's something I'm curious about."

"Ah, yes. *Interview* him," said Dreadgrave, knowingly. "Just don't let him die yet. The acid's more fun to watch. Especially their faces when it reaches crotch level."

# FIVE

Dreadgrave's dungeons were a treacherous labyrinth of twisting passageways, devious traps and slavering monsters, which had claimed more lives than a decent-sized plague. I, however, had taken the employee induction and knew the secret: Turn right at every circular floor grating and left at every chained-up skeleton.

Fifteen turns later, I arrived at the main cell block and exchanged nods with the slavering monster on duty. Slippery John's cell was easy to identify. It was the one from which could be heard the sound of a flimsy lockpick rattling ineptly around inside the massive cast-iron lock. I peered through the barred viewing window, and could just about see the top of his head as he labored away. I wondered if it was worth mentioning the three deadbolts on my side of the door.

"Hey."

He glanced up elatedly, then his face fell as he took me in. "Oh. Thought it might have been a real person."

I let that slide. "Can I ask you something?"

"Interrogation, is it? Well, know this, demon: Slippery John is an incredibly easy nut to crack. Torture is completely unnecessary with Slippery John. He will sing like a canary at the slightest raised voice." His hands flew to his mouth. "Oh, crap, you're probably going to torture Slippery John now anyway since Slippery John brought it up. Well, fine. Just start with the water torture, it's pretty hot in here."

Torturing Slippery John was certainly looking tempting. "I don't want to interrogate you. I'm just curious about something."

"Oh," he said, sounding almost disappointed.

"Do you have a twin?"

His thick brow descended into an avalanche of a frown. "Nnnnno, not that Slippery John knows of."

"It's just that we had a bloke break in last week who looked, spoke and acted exactly like Sli—like you."

"Yeah," he said, nodding. "That was Slippery John."

"That was you."

"Yeah."

I tapped my foot for a moment, staring at the floor, wondering how best to phrase my next question. "Didn't we kill you?"

"Yeah, you did." He squinted, assessing my features. "Slippery John remembers you now, creature of twilight. You were the one who kicked Slippery John in the goolies and threw Slippery John into that big pit with all the rats."

"The Rat Pit."

"Yeah, you should probably think about clearing some of the bodies out of that thing, Slippery John saw five of his old ones down there."

I rubbed at my temple. "How many times have you been killed?"

"In this fortress? Coming up to about twelve, Slippery John guesses. Turning out to be a really hard quest, Dreadgrave's book."

"So . . . wait a minute, every time you die you come back with a new body?"

He was looking at me as if I was asking him if he knew how to breathe. "Don't you?"

"No . . . I mean, I do come back to life after I die but it's always in the same body."

"Whoa, that'd make things a lot easier." He thoughtfully smoothed his tiny mustache with a fingertip. "Much more convenient than going all the way back to the nearest church. Slippery John guesses that's because you're undead. Slippery John can't believe you wouldn't know about this. You'd have to be really out of touch."

"Well, yes, I've been dead for fifty years, and I haven't spent much time outside since."

"Oh. I guess you wouldn't know, then."

"Know what? Is anyone else not dying?"

"Nobody's dying. Nobody's died in fifteen years, not anywhere in the world. Not plants or animals, either. Every time anything dies, it reappears with a new body. Could you pull your jaw back up? There's a spider in your throat and it's really turning Slippery John's stomach."

I closed my mouth with an audible clack. I had suspected that the angels weren't anything to do with Dreadgrave's magic, but this new intelligence wasn't exactly reassuring. "Wouldn't this cause massive overcrowding?"

"No-one's being born. Everyone's gone sterile. No-one seems to be aging, either. It's like time's been standing still, but everyone gets to still move around and talk and stuff."

"But . . . how? Why?"

"Look. Slippery John is just a debonair master thief," said Slippery John. "Slippery John doesn't know any particulars. All Slippery John knows is that about fifteen years ago people stopped dying. The Infusion, it was called. The population of the world hasn't gone up or down since then—up until a few months ago, o'course."

"What happened a few months ago?"

It was difficult for him to look at me condescendingly when he was a foot shorter and stuck behind a cell door, but he managed it somehow. "You should know. Dreadgrave found a way to raise the corpses of people who died before the Infusion. The Magic Resistance are trying to figure out how he did it."

"Hence all the adventurers, I suppose."

"Oh, sure. This is the hottest quest right now. Big rewards."

"If any of this is even true, I don't see how raising more dead people is going to solve anything. It certainly didn't make my life any easier."

"Slippery John wouldn't know anything about that. Slippery John doesn't ask questions. Slippery John is just the kind of master thief who fetches things that no-one else can fetch. Slippery John doesn't let things like reason get in the way of—"

He was interrupted by a loud THUMP coming from directly above us. It was followed by a steady rumble, and orange dust drifted down from the ceiling. We both looked up very slowly. "Is it supposed to do that?" he asked, his voice very quiet and high-pitched.

"Erm . . . "

A crack snaked across the ceiling of the cell, spitting dust and pebbles as it went. Slippery John had just enough time to say "Er," before the ceiling gave and he was crushed by a hundred tons of wall, floor and foundation.

When the last few scraps had finished rattling to a halt and the dust had cleared somewhat, I stood stunned and frozen for a while, as the small non-terrified part of my brain tried desperately to encourage some motion into my muscles and remember the the emergency escape procedure.

"Aw, crap, Slippery John's spine is powderized," came a voice from somewhere around floor level, with the nonchalant tone of someone discovering a hangnail.

"Oh dear," I said, then felt pretty stupid about it. "Do you need any help?"

"Nah, that's okay, Slippery John's lungs are filling with blood, so Slippery John'll head right on out after he dies. You should probably make a run for it, though, if you're not going to be growing a new body after this."

Somewhere in the distance I heard another section of the dungeon become intimately acquainted with the room directly above it. "Right," I said. Slippery John's corpse had no further comment.

The ground was shaking, now, and dust was falling continuously from cracks that criss-crossed the ceiling of the cell block. The duty slavering monster had apparently shown greater intuition than I and scarpered. A slab from overhead landed with a dirt-scattering thud a few feet away. Instinct took over and I legged it.

The last three months of undeath had done a lot to clear up the stiffness in my joints and nervous system, and while I couldn't keep pace with, say, a high school athletics club, I could work up a decent speed. It didn't help, though, because half-way through the labyrinth I turned a corner and bounced off a fresh cave-in.

I changed direction and took a random turn to see if I could find another way around—something which, in retrospect, was probably a mistake. Within two seconds I had tripped a pressure plate, and within three I had an arrow sticking out of my chest. I glared down at the vibrating shaft, exasperated.

Another rumble shook the fortress, and the distant sound of rocks falling put another dent in my already battered hopes. "What the hell's going on?!"

"J," said a nearby wall.

"What was that?"

"Im," added the floor.

Something was scrabbling around in the infrastructure, searching. "Over here!" I cried.

"Jim!" cried a sewer grating set in the bottom of the wall to my right. It was, of course, Meryl. Her hair was stained brown with dust and was quickly disentangling itself from her pigtails.

"What's going on up there?!" I yelled.

"I dunno! The whole fortress is collapsing! Some . . . things are flying around zapping it! Everyone's running away but I came to find you!"

"Why?"

She made a few incoherent frustrated noises before pulling her vocal chords back into line. "I don't want you to die, all right?"

"I can't."

"Oh, you know what I mean! The way back's caved in as well but if we can get into the sewer system we can ride it out of here! Together!"

"Where's the sewer system?"

She disappeared from view for a second. "Take a side-step to your left."

I did so.

"Okay, now move about two feet forward."

"Now what?"

"You see that torch bracket? Not that one, the one just by your elbow."

"Yeah."

"Give it a little push like you'd accidentally brushed past it. And try to keep your body completely straight."

Taking a deep breath, trying to avoid thinking about exactly to whom I was entrusting my unlife, I reached out and nudged the bracket with my fingertips. The entire floor immediately gave way. I fell in a pencil dive down a one-foot wide gap between two gigantic troughs of boiling acid. Directly beneath my feet a rather heavily corroded drain cover was set in the floor. By the time I realized it couldn't possibly take my weight I had already plunged straight through.

I landed with an almighty splash in a fast-moving current, which immediately snatched me and yanked me into an underground stream. It was pitch dark, but judging by the smell, I probably didn't want to see what I was swimming in anyway. It had presumably been water from the river at some point, but the doom fortress had a lot of sewage, rubbish, noxious chemicals, and dismembered bodies to get rid of so by the time it was ejected from the fortress it had transformed into a rather lively soup of hazardous waste.

Whatever it was, the plumbing system was trying to get rid of it as fast as possible. I was hurtling down the canal at bewildering speed. I bounced from wall to wall, swearing involuntarily with each impact, before the canal narrowed into an outflow pipe and things became even less comfortable. A few tosses and turns later I completely lost my sense of direction and could no longer even tell the difference between vertical and horizontal.

Finally, I rounded a corner and saw a circle of murky daylight rocketing towards me. I was almost relieved, until I remembered that the sewer outflowed directly into the deepest, darkest crevasse in the south of Greydoom Valley, in strict accordance with Dreadgrave's "out of sight, out of mind" waste disposal policy. So I was heading towards a two hundred foot drop onto spiky rocks, where there would be no-one to stitch me back together but plenty of vultures to entertain.

I pushed all four limbs against the sides of the pipe to try and stop myself, but the fast-flowing sewage all around me had other ideas. I could barely slow myself down, the staples in my joints groaning and twanging in protest, and I was fast running out of pipe.

Moments before popping out of the outflow for my date with gravity, I saw a lip at the top of the opening. A small one, but solid enough to take my weight. I held out both hands and braced myself for impact.

No amount of bracing could have been adequate. The ridge struck like a scimitar to the palms. The jarring blow tore off my left arm at the elbow and flung it away. Somehow my right arm held, although two of the staples pinged free. My entire body below the shoulders kicked forward like a mule's hind legs. But I had stopped. I was safe.

After getting my breath back, I was forced to revise my hasty use of the word "safe." I was dangling from the edge of a hole in an otherwise smooth cliff wall, getting a faceful of biological waste. I had lost one arm and the other was being stretched to breaking point. The edge of the cliff was ten feet above my head, and to cap it all—

"Man, that was intense."

I sighed through my teeth. And to cap it all, Meryl was there. "What are you doing here?"

"I jumped in after you. To rescue you." A pause. "Sorry. Didn't really think. But hey, problem shared, right?"

The voice was coming from somewhere around the region of my crotch. I looked down, tried not to notice the yawning abyss directly below, and focussed on Meryl. "What are you hanging from?"

"The arrow in your chest. Sorry. I caught your arm, though." She waved it. "So there's no need to worry."

Another staple flew out of my other shoulder and my reach extended by an inch. Only three staples remained, and then I'd be relying on the knots Meryl had used to tie my tendons together. "I can't hold on much longer," I said, in case it wasn't obvious.

"Can't you climb up?"

"Not with one arm, no. Can you?"

"Oh, no, I'm completely hopeless at that kind of thing. When I was a kid I could never get all the way up to the treehouse because I was afraid the boys would look up my skirt."

Another staple flew off and lodged itself in my forehead. "We're going to die," I said.

"No we're not."

"All right. I might have deserved that. But we're going to be pretty inconvenienced."

"Okay. We need to think of a plan."

"How about this," I said. "I'll let go, then when we hit the ground, you hit the ground first. Then maybe your carcass will cushion my impact to keep me functioning long enough to stitch you back together."

"Why don't you just grab that rope?"

"What rope?"

"That rope that someone's letting down for us."

I didn't think I'd ever be so grateful to see spun hemp. I planted my foot on the pipe, let my hand go, felt a terrifying moment of peril that made me grateful my heart had already stopped, and grabbed the rope with all the limbs I had left.

Our rescuer took the strain with some difficulty, and I braced my feet on the cliff face. Meryl made her way from me to the rope and did the same. I edged my way gradually up to the top, employing my teeth in place of my missing arm, and with safety fragilely restored, I had time to thank whoever had come to our rescue.

"Save your thanks, consort of monstrosities," came a familiar voice. "For was it not written by the Most Holy Dmitri the Fishmonger, 'Let not all the demons die, or those they lead astray, so that tomorrow ye may continue to smite them righteously.'"

"Oh, pack that shit in," I said, helping Meryl up.

Something was very wrong. I could tell, because the priest seemed to be smiling. "Your snake's tongue will not penetrate me today, Godforsaken wretch," he said, with relish I found very unsettling. "I have succeeded in the glorious task the

LORD has given me, and now His perfect hand has fallen down upon the fortress of devils!" He made an unnecessarily dramatic sweep of the hand, and I took in what was left of Greydoom Valley.

Dreadgrave's horde was scattered across the plain like cockroaches ousted from beneath a piece of furniture, in various states of flight, terror and undress. They were all desperately trying to get away from Dreadgrave's doom fortress. I glanced up, and saw why.

"What the hell are those?!" I yelled, pointing.

Four or five glowing white orbs were circling the main tower. Each one was connected to a long, thin tentacle of greenish energy that whipped around the fortress, erasing everything it touched. It was nothing like any demolition I'd ever seen; a better word would have been "deletion." One by one, walls, beams and gargoyles became outlined in green and vanished into thin air, leaving no trace of dust or rubble.

Large portions of the fortress had already been deleted, causing others to collapse into the space they left behind. The place I had called home, that had seemed so solid and impregnable and reassuring only that morning, was being systematically erased. I could feel milky gray tears brimming in my sunken eyes and oozing down my face.

"Who's doing this?!" choked Meryl.

"Look closer," said the priest.

I squinted, trying to make out the shapes of the things bringing down the fortress. When I did, I felt an ice-cold needle of recognition rattle down my spine like a stick along a metal fence.

"The angels," I whispered.

There were the same faceless heads, the same robes, floating through the air without even flapping their ugly wings. The moment I recognized them I had to fight off an impulse to immediately burrow into the ground like a rodent fleeing from an owl.

They seemed to be saving the main tower for last, and when I looked again, I could see why. There, on the topmost platform—the very one from which I had hurled myself so many times—was a silhouetted figure, wrapped in a magic shield and apparently trying as hard as he could to keep it up.

"Dreadgrave!" I yelled.

The angels were gradually stripping the tower away from around him. I got the very strong impression that Dreadgrave was being toyed with, a mouse against five glowing astral cats. He was sending out magical missiles as fast as he could summon them, each one more powerful than the last. He threw everything from football-sized green fireballs to the gigantic roaring ones with dragon faces on the front, the ones that take years to learn and are banned from everything except the mining industry because they're used to drill holes in mountains. The angels didn't even try to dodge, just soaked them all up without so much as a flinch.

After a while, when the floor around Dreadgrave had been mostly picked away and he was trapped on a tiny unstable pedestal about six feet across, the angels lost interest. All five of them focussed their beams on his kneeling form. The shield didn't stop them for an instant. Within a second, Dreadgrave was gone. Within ten, so was the rest of the fortress. All that remained was a barren plain of flattened rock. It wasn't even smoking.

"Oh, god," I moaned.

Meryl patted me on the shoulder with my missing hand. "It's what he would have wanted."

"What?!"

"Okay, so maybe it's not what he would have wanted. I was trying to make you feel better."

"God's emissaries have done their work," said the priest, like a proud father. "The evil one has been vanquished by the eternal power of the LORD."

"Oh, eat a dick!" I snapped, shoving him. "Shut up about your LORD! The LORD's got nothing on Dreadgrave! The LORD never puts on musical productions! The LORD never lets us wear casual trousers! All the LORD ever does is get pricks like you to yell at me for not kissing his arse all day!"

"Er, Jim," said Meryl, pointing upwards with my disembodied arm, which she was getting a bit too attached to. "How worried do we need to be about that?"

The angels had been hovering over where the fortress had stood, perhaps silently gloating or contemplating a job well done, but now they were spreading out across the valley. The ends of their deletion beams were sniffing around at floor level, hunting for something. It didn't take long to figure out what. Those members of the horde too dozy or too decayed to get out of the way in time were erased before they could even scream.

"My God is coming to take me!" went the priest, but his voice cracked with uncertainty on the last word.

"Run," I suggested.

Meryl and I instantly broke into the closest thing we could get to a sprint. So, I noticed, did the priest.

The tendrils could move faster than we could run, but none of them seemed to be specifically chasing us, only sweeping randomly around to catch as many undead as possible. It would only be a matter of time before most of them were gone and the deleters concentrated on the last few stragglers. But one of the few advantages of being dead was never getting tired, presumably because we'd already slept as much as anyone could ever need, and it was an advantage we were making great use of as we made for the path out of Greydoom Valley.

A green line swept past behind us, close enough to peck the backs of our heels. I heard the noise they made, a sort of wavering buzz, like someone grumbling into a kazoo: a deeper, more hostile version of the gibbering I had heard during my visits to the dead world.

I risked a look over my shoulder. The angels were heading in the opposite direction. Most of the horde had been annihilated, and the angels were leisurely picking off the last few desperate sprinters one by one. It seemed we had been the only ones to run in this particular direction, which was probably the only reason we were still on our feet. But there were only a handful of runners left, and once they had been dealt with the angels would come right back for us.

Running didn't seem to help, so I started looking for somewhere to hide. We were near the edge of the swampy area in the south of the valley, the one from which Dreadgrave used to have us harvest deadly Prawn Frogs for his Doom Pond. More importantly, there were hundreds of stagnant green-brown pools covered by overhanging spiky weeds and misshapen trees. I dived into the nearest one and added swamp slime to the lengthy list of pollutants already in my robe.

I swept pondweed out of my eyes and arranged myself under the roots of a twisted black tree, where I could watch proceedings through a narrow gap in the foliage. A splash of viscous swampwater behind me, and Meryl appeared at my side, swiftly followed by the priest.

"Cowards," he hissed. "The LORD is calling back his children with the Light Most Holy and you cower in a bog!"

"Hey, after you," I muttered, in no mood for his crap.

The last zombie straggler—I recognized him as Ted, a bloke from our guard detail who used to rip pages out of mucky magazines and sell them behind the stables—faltered and was torn from existence. That seemed to be the last of them still out in the open; now, the angels turned for one last sweep around the valley. A green glow passed over our tree more than once, and each time we dropped our heads back into the swamp with a trio of plops. Finally it moved on for the last time and faded away. We were safe.

It was clearer than ever that the creatures were angels in appearance alone. "Deleters" seemed like a more appropriate name, or possibly "Bastards." The Deleters had regrouped in the center of the valley, where only a spattering of shattered black bricks indicated that Dreadgrave's fortress had ever stood there. Somehow it would have been less horrifying if they'd seemed smug or triumphant, but their body language showed nothing but emotionless professionalism. With military discipline, they arranged themselves into a tight square and disappeared. No flash of light, no fancy effects—they simply winked out.

After that, a thick, cloying silence descended upon Greydoom Valley, far denser and more noticeable than the chatter of minions or the squeals of torture victims had ever been. I carefully climbed out of the swamp, boots squelching unpleasantly, and absent-mindedly dug the prawn frogs out of my pockets.

"They'll be all right, won't they?" said Meryl, wringing out her hair. "They'll just come back like they always did, right?"

"Not without bodies," I said, gazing out over the valley. "Anyway, something tells me that wasn't the kind of death you come back from."

She nodded sadly, hugging herself. An intense feeling of loneliness settled on our shoulders as the panic faded away. She peered at me curiously as I drank in the empty landscape. "Why didn't you let yourself be taken?"

"What?"

"You were always so obsessed with killing yourself, looking for a proper way to die. I was expecting you to run out and let them do it." She smiled shyly. "I'm glad you changed your mind."

I stared at her for a moment. Then I smacked myself in the forehead so hard that my eyeballs rattled. "Oh, SHIT!" I smacked my head a few more times and jumped up and down for good measure. "SHIT! SHIT! SHIT!"

I ran out into the empty plain, waving what was left of my arms. "COME BACK, YOU BASTARDS!!" I screamed. "You missed a spot! Look! OVER HERE! UNDEAD MINION RUNNING FREE! Get off!" By now, Meryl and the priest had grabbed me under my armpits and were running towards the valley exit. "I'M OVER HERE AND I'M BIG AND FAT AND JUICY AND NOT DELETED COME BACK AND DELETE ME YOU PRICKS DELETE ME DELETE ME DELETE ME . . . "

# PART TWO

PART TWO

# ONE

We'd barely walked for half a day before the influence of Dreadgrave's doom fortress started to dissipate. It was as if all the color and vitality that Greydoom Valley had once drawn from the surrounding countryside was now rushing back. As we made our way along the path through the forest the sun was shining through gaps in the clouds, some of the flowers were tentatively opening their buds to check if it was safe to bloom, and the birds were making the first strangled attempts at singing again.

It was all rather ghastly. I'd been stuck in an impenetrable sulk all day, only half-aware of my trudging feet as they carried me along the road. The birdsong sounded like smug, twittery laughter, mocking my fall from grace. Barely hours ago I'd been secure, respected, with good prospects for senior rat pit management, and conveniently close to a nice high tower to regularly throw myself off. Now, everything was gone. Destroyed. Deleted.

I thought of that mysterious conspiracy of faceless apparitions in the dead world that refused to let me die, but who were apparently considerably more obliging when they appeared in the land of the living. There was no doubt in my mind that the dickheads that appeared in the astral realm were the very same dickheads who had destroyed my home. But why?

"How's the arm?" asked Meryl.

She had sewn it back on after we had escaped the valley, the first time we had made camp. Actually, "made camp" is too grand a term for it; we didn't need to rest or eat, so we had just sat on a log for an hour, thinking about things. I flexed my newly-repaired elbow and felt the stitches creak. "Angle might be off a quarter inch."

"Enjoy your good health while you can, spawn. Even the worst of the earthly maladies will seem like paradise after thy return to the blaze of the Inferno."

What patience I had had for the priest had evaporated with Dreadgrave. "Why are you still following us?"

"That I may smite you with righteous vengeance and rid the world of your putrescence."

"Well, go on, then," I said. I advanced until he and I were nose to nose, then pulled my robe and undershirt apart to reveal my scarred chest. "Right in the scar. Half the work's already done for you."

He hesitated for a moment. The lower half of his face was still scowling hatefully but the rest of it was being very careful to not look me in the eye. "No," he said, eventually.

"Oh, leave him alone," scolded Meryl. "You know full well he just doesn't want to admit that we're his only friends and he's got nowhere else to go."

The priest's nostrils flared so widely I fancied I caught a glimpse of his brain somewhere in there. "I am awaiting my next divine assignment from the LORD." He didn't deny anything, though.

We continued walking, and before long, the trees thinned out to reveal a small brick building in the middle of a fenced-off clearing. It was only when I spotted some crumbling grave-stones peering out of the grass that I realized aloud what we had stumbled upon. "A church. Let's take a look inside."

Meryl tutted. "Are you going to convert yourself again?"

"Slippery John said that when people die, they get new bodies at churches. I just want to see if that's true."

I could think of nicer places to come back to life. It had probably once been a pleasant little country church, one of those undersized and quaint chapels where the actual religiosity is secondary to the jumble sales and the summer potlucks and letting the local scout troop use the hall on Thursdays. It had evidently gone through some trying times since those days. Some of the windows were smashed, and large portions of the brickwork were scorched or held together by makeshift wooden scaffolding. I was trying to remember if I'd ever come here with the rest of the horde.

"I will not enter," said the priest, stopping dead at the churchyard entrance and folding his arms.

"Why not?" asked Meryl.

"I am a priest of the Seventh Day Advent Hedge Devolutionist Castlebridge Reformists," he said, with reverent pride. "This is a church of the Seventh Day Advent Hedge Devolutionist Castlebridge Classicists. I will not set one foot within this den of heresy."

I shrugged. "Whatever. I'm going in. Feel free to go off and get on with your life while you're waiting."

"You will not be free of me so easily, fiend," he called after me. I let him have his precious last word and continued towards the church.

The cemetery surrounding the church was half overgrown and half ruined by the hooves of the large number of bored horses that were parked on the grass. The most recent tombstone was from two decades ago, which supported Slippery John's story. Mourning the dead was probably a rather futile process if they'd be right back the next day complaining about their eulogy.

I paused at the church door with my hand upon the polished oak. There was a fresh piece of paper pinned up at eye level. *No pets / familiars*, it said. *No pipe smoking. No spellcasting.*

*Any business other than that related to the resurrection of self
or colleagues is not permitted. Patrons are not required to
say thank you, but it is always appreciated!!!*

I quietly pushed my way in, Meryl nimbly slipping in after
me just before the door drifted shut.

It didn't take long to see that there were a lot of things
wrong with this church. Most of the pews had been cleared
away, and the few that remained were arranged at 90 degrees
to the norm, giving the chapel more the impression of a
waiting room than a place of worship. This ended up being
quite appropriate, because the room was full of—

"Crap," I muttered, dragging Meryl behind a pillar.

Adventurers. And not just any adventurers, but adventurers I
clearly remembered torturing and murdering in Dreadgrave's
staff entertainment center. The long-haired barbarians who had
besieged the fortress that morning. The elves I'd last seen nailed
to the trees in the orchard with bunches of dead flowers lodged
in their throats. The dwarves I, personally, had been feeding into
the furnace conveyor just yesterday. For some reason, several
of them were wearing identical white bathrobes.

Fortunately, none of them had noticed our entrance. They
were all sitting rather tensely on the pews, with their eyes
fixed on the pulpit. The atmosphere reminded me strongly of
the examination room at my old college.

Standing in the pulpit was a man in the garb of a country
vicar. He was surprisingly young for his position, in that he
still possessed most of his own tightly-curled hair and it was
only just beginning to gray. A pair of steel-rimmed reading
glasses sat upon his nose and he was holding open a generic-
looking leatherbound copy of the local bible.

"Verse seven. 'And Craig did scatter his seeds randomly
upon the ground,'" he read aloud, with subdued passion.
"'And his attitude did displease the LORD, and nothing did

rise in the flowerbeds of Craig but weeds and forget-me-nots.'" He delicately dabbed his thumb and forefinger to his tongue and turned the page. "Verse eight. 'But Daniel sowed his seeds carefully, in a neat row, and the LORD did smile upon his labor, and there sprang forth a beautiful leylandii that did compliment the pond verily.' Now, can anyone tell me what these verses teach us?"

All the adventurers suddenly took a great interest in their showily impractical boots.

"Come on!" barked the vicar. "I run this service out of the goodness of my heart, and the least you can do is pay attention. It tells us that order must always defeat chaos. Order is what puts us above the beasts and the monsters. There must always be rules, and there will always be a just reward for those who keep order." He waited for a moment for it to sink in, then sighed and turned to a smaller ledger to his left. "And of course, things must always be done *in* order. Number 107." He turned his eyes heavenwards. "Number 107. If you are with us, please move to the front of the altar. Beware that if you fail to do so you forfeit your place in the astral queue."

He muttered some priestly doggerel under his breath, flicked his fingers as if there were something nasty on them, and a few magic sparkles fluttered out.

Suddenly, I saw a curious shimmer in the air in front of the altar. It was like sunlight reflected off a waterfall, constantly changing and shifting. After a few moments of random gyrating, it flew together, resolving into a heavily-built human skeleton. Organs, muscles and skin appeared, rolling onto the bones like a series of window blinds crashing down. Finally, an oily-skinned barbarian stood before the altar, tottering dizzily.

"Bathrobes on the left," said the vicar distastefully. The barbarian dutifully took one from a pile and made to cover his wobbling barbarian bits. "Collection plate just to the side. Donations are comPLETEly optional." It was impressive how the vicar was able to insert an entire subtext into one syllable.

"I know him," whispered Meryl, as we watched the barbarian don his bathrobe with deliberate casualness, to the absolute disinterest of nearby female adventurers. "I pulled his spine out."

"I told you," I replied. "People don't die anymore. We go back to the same body because we're undead, but people who're properly alive have to come to a church to get a new one. I thought he might have been having me on, until I saw it for myself."

"Who might have been having you on?"

"Him." I pointed.

The next resurrectee was, of course, Slippery John. He was hard to recognize without his black ensemble until his stupid little curly mustache burst forth onto his upper lip. He took a seat opposite his friends, two of which I recognized from among the warriors whose suicidal frontal assault had permitted Slippery John's equally suicidal infiltration of Dreadgrave's back door.

"Where's the book?" whispered a dwarf out the corner of his stringy black beard, as the vicar resumed sermonizing. The dwarf was typically thick-set, and he was busily trying to re-braid his beard as he spoke.

"Ja, yoo'd better haff some good noos, thief," hissed the barbarian, a big blonde bastard with an accent reminiscent of one of those snowy countries up north. "Dose vur damt expensive horses."

"Book?" asked Slippery John, still woozy. "Oh yes! That thing."

"Ja. Dreadgrave's book. De whole reason ve chust had our spines pulled out by de valking dead?"

Meryl nudged me in the exposed ribs. "Why did you want to see this?"

"I want to talk to that Slippery John guy a bit more," I hissed. "I want to know who hired him. They might know more about the Deleters than we do."

"You're not going to make this some kind of quest, are you? Why don't we just forget about it, go and find some other nice evil overlord to work for . . . "

I shook my head. "I'm going to find the Deleters. You can do whatever you like."

"Don't be silly. You need someone to keep your bits sewn on. So what happens after you find them? Revenge?"

" . . . Possibly."

"You hesitated. Promise me you're not just looking for a way to kill yourself."

I contemplated the ideal non-committal reply, before settling on "No."

We were crouched behind the bench on which Slippery John's three cohorts were sitting, so I carefully poked my head above the backrest to take a closer look at them. Sitting between the dwarf and the barbarian was a female warrior wearing ridiculously ornate spikey armor with tantalizingly large sections cut out of it.

There was something terribly odd about the woman. Not the armor—that was standard adventurer fashion. Many armor shops specialize in that sort of thing; as a teenager I had had an extensive collection of catalogues which I'd often read under the bedclothes late at night. No, what was odd was the way she sat: ramrod-stiff, legs together, hands clenched around the knees, never shifting her weight or fidgeting. Her face was fixed in an expression of mild concern, which she seemed to be directing at a wall.

"So where's the book," she said. I couldn't place her accent, either. It was petulant and airy, possibly from one of the rich coastal kingdoms with all those infuriatingly nice beaches. I also couldn't detect any trace of a question mark on a statement that was clearly hungry for one.

"Slippery John practically had it in Slippery John's hands," continued Slippery John enthusiastically. "Everything was going perfectly. Slippery John had skilfully avoided the mindless stares of the undead hordes and Dreadgrave was at Slippery John's mercy. Then—" To his credit, he only paused for a second as he noticed me and Meryl behind his comrades. "Incidentally, if anyone tells you a different story to Slippery John's at any point you should probably dismiss them as filthy liars."

"Let's just head back for the fortress," sighed the dwarf.

"Er, actually, Slippery John was just getting to that. Fortress isn't there anymore."

"The place for chatting is outside!" yelled the vicar irritably, but it was futile. Every adventurer in the place had suddenly cocked an ear at Slippery John's revelation.

"Yoo vot?" asked the barbarian, succinctly vocalizing the question on everyone's mind.

"Some angels came along and rubbed it out. Good thing we don't ever have to attempt that quest again, right?"

No one seemed to share Slippery John's feelings. In an instant everyone was on their feet and yelling at each other at the tops of their voices.

"All that for nothing?!"

"How're we supposed to get our armor back?!"

"Huh," went the female warrior without emotion, apparently addressing an empty pew.

"Stop shouting!" shrieked the vicar. "This church is a place of quiet dignity and respect!"

"Anyway," continued Slippery John quietly. Most of his former party were hotly complaining at each other so Meryl and I were the only ones paying attention to him as he began to slip off in his characteristic way. "Slippery John has to go buy some new black pants and hand in some quests over at Yawnbore, so perhaps Slippery John will get out of your way."

Now was my chance. As he attempted to speed-walk past us without making eye contact I stretched my arm across his path and pulled him smartly into the shadows. "We need to talk," I said.

"Ha ha!" he cried, smiling derangedly as I held him against the wall. "You fell for Slippery John's cunning trap, undead slime! You have wantonly stepped onto holy ground, and are now utterly powerless!"

A pause. "No I'm not."

"No, you're not. Slippery John was banking on a bit of an outside chance, there."

"What are the Deleters?"

"The angels? Saw them, did you? They fly around and they make things disappear."

"Yes, we gathered that. I need more detail."

"Hell, you know about as much as Slippery John does. They hang around in the dead world and only show up in the land of the living when they want to get rid of something. Slippery John saw them a few times clearing rocks out of the mountains north of Lolede. And whenever they delete a person, that person never comes back, not even to a church."

"Is that right," I said, rubbing my chin. Meryl was watching me with narrowed eyes.

"Can Slippery John go now?"

I adjusted my grip on his lapel. "Where do we find them?"

"Well, the last place anyone saw them was Dreadgrave's fortress, but Slippery John doubts that that helps you much.

You remember Dreadgrave's fortress. The place where you used to live. That is, you, the individual standing directly in front of me with his back to the rest of the room." His voice was gradually raising in volume, and he was staring meaningfully at something over our shoulders. "Slippery John isn't surprised that you'd be a little upset with them, especially since they deleted all your fellow undead and everything. Slippery John says 'fellow' because YOU, THE PERSON SLIPPERY JOHN IS ADDRESSING, are an UNDEAD, who was until recently ONE OF THE UNDEAD GUARDS FROM DREADGRAVE'S FORTRESS, THE SAME PLACE THAT HAS BEEN GIVING US ALL A LOT OF TROUBLE LATELY!"

I was wondering what he was getting at, and why he was urgently jerking his head at me, until I felt something warm and oily close around my shoulder like a big meaty vise. I was gently but firmly spun around and found myself face to pectorals with that big bastard of a barbarian.

"Excoos me," he said. "Didn't yoo look after dat big pit vid all de rats?"

There were rather a lot of adventurers staring at us, now. The barbarian holding me had arms like sackfuls of angry melons. Things looked grim. But these were only mercenaries, after all, ranking on the intelligence scale somewhere between fish and gravel. "Not at all," I tried. "You're thinking of Jim. That guy was a dick."

"Und didn't yoo pull my spine out?"

"No, that was me," said Meryl eagerly, getting between us. "I've been meaning to ask about your diet and exercise regimen, because you don't usually see a spine come out so cleanly and in one piece. I was really impressed."

"Oh. Tank yoo. I guess it comes dahn to plenty off protein und horsebahck riding."

"I demand that you return to your seats or take this outside immediately!" came the voice of the vicar from somewhere behind the wall of muscle. "I will not have squabbling in the house of the Father!"

I coughed. "Could you let go?"

"No."

The situation was becoming increasingly claustrophobic. I considered options. Surrender, perhaps, let them work off their frustrations on my undying, non-pain-feeling body, then get sewn back together later. But I could think of too many disquieting purposes they might find for my body parts before growing bored. The only other option was to hope that a distraction would come up within the next few seconds. That was an even worse plan, and no less so for the fact that it worked.

The hostile murmuring came to a sudden stop as the largest stained glass window shattered loudly and spectacularly and everyone reflexively ducked (except for the dwarves, who were way ahead). A heavy rock wrapped in flaming cloth bounced off the floor and embedded itself in the torso of an elf with poor reaction time.

There was one of those big, stodgy silences that follow a shock, punctuated by the tinkle of settling glass and the meaty thud of shards embedding themselves in flesh. From outside, we could hear choral singing.

"UGH," exclaimed the vicar, reddening with frustration. He squared his shoulders and marched stiffly down the aisle, crunching glass savagely underfoot. "This is so TYPICAL." He flung wide the main door, and the singing abruptly stopped.

I pulled a large chunk of glass out of my face with a dry chlock and tentatively peered outside. "Is that a catapult?"

Meryl poked her nose around the doorframe. "I think it's a trebuchet, actually."

"Well, excuse me. Siege weapons weren't my department. I was mainly rat pit." I looked around, but the barbarian wasn't listening. All the adventurers were jostling for space around the doorway, trying to get a good view of the scene outside in case opportunities for questing came up.

There, a small group of extremely wholesome-looking young people in flowing white garments were standing around the trebuchet. Two blonde men were resetting the mechanism while a freckled girl with flowers in her hair was trying to get another missile lit.

"What the hell is this?!" barked the vicar furiously.

"Hi, Barry," said the ringleader, a middle-aged woman in round spectacles, nervously gripping the trebuchet's trigger rope.

"Don't you 'Hi, Barry' me! You know full well this is the busy part of the day!"

"Forgive us for our trespass, but we, the Enlightened Church of the Earth Mother Youth Group, could not stand idly by anymore. All these misguided souls being resurrected with your false teachings and tainting the spiritual essences of the ether, well, we couldn't have lived with ourselves a moment longer." One of the youths dinged a small finger bell in response to some unspoken signal.

"Don't talk such rot," said Barry nastily. "You want the prime spot near Dreadgrave's fortress like everyone else. The Emancipated Church of Mongbotty tried it yesterday, and those sun worshippers were at it the day before." I glanced at him and noticed that he had produced a very large and very un-pious-looking crossbow.

"Your aura darkens, Barry. Your spirit rejects the falsehood of your words."

"Oh, piss off."

The woman pulled on the trebuchet rope with her heavily beringed fingers and another missile plunged into the church roof. The youths rang their finger-bells again. Most of the adventurers took this as the signal to start running away.

"Look," said Slippery John, squeezing around Barry. "Slippery John would just like to be off and let you get on with it, if that's all right. Not much point in hanging around now the fortress is gone, anyway."

"See how your crude building welcomes the hand of the All-Mother," sang the youth group leader, fluttering her fingers. "The womb of life envelops . . . what did he say?"

"What were you saying earlier?" said Barry, grabbing Slippery John's collar as he attempted to sneak off. "What do you mean, it's gone?"

"It's been deleted," said the surly dwarf from Slippery John's party. "No more fortress, no more quest. No need for us to hang around here."

"The deranged menace of Dreadgrave is vanquished!" said Slippery John in a suitably epic tone of voice. "The people of Greydoom Valley are liberated from his dark rule of oppression!"

Barry's teeth were clenched so hard that I could almost hear his jaw creaking like an old wooden gate. "What wonderful news," he said.

"The, er, children of the Earth Mother see now that there is room in her bountiful fields for all faiths," said the woman as her acolytes began packing up the trebuchet. "So we'll just be toddling off . . . oh." One of her youths was whispering something in her ear.

"What?!" went Barry.

"Er. Juniper tells me that that last missile might have been—"

Her words were unexpectedly hyphenated by a dreadful earth-shaking boom. An extremely large chunk of Barry's church flew off in several different directions. A great belch of oddly-colored flame unfolded into the air, and then, with a terrible sense of inevitability, what remained of the building toppled over and crumpled into ruination.

The silence became more and more awkward as it rolled on. One of the youths rang his finger bell uncertainly.

Barry dropped to his knees in the rubble. "Gone," he said, quietly. "I've lost it."

The youth group lady coughed. "Sorry."

"I've lost it all," he continued, burying his fingers in the powderized brickwork. "It was all I had. I spent all my money forcing Emmett out of this place. I've got nothing. And it's all because of—"

His accusing finger stabbed at the air where the youth group had been, but they and the trebuchet had tactfully slipped away into the trees while Barry had let it all out. He looked around, and I met his gaze. His face was a terrifying thing to behold— and I'd been hanging around zombies for the last three months.

"You," said Barry, getting slowly to his feet and taking up his crossbow again. The tone of his voice lowered dangerously as he decided he could vent his frustrations on me. "You're one of them. Undead. Aren't you! From the fortress!"

"What on earth makes you think that?" I said, quickly.

"You're gray as ash and you've got no nose!"

The few remaining adventurers, remembering what had attracted their attention before the trebuchet incident, were gathering behind Barry the vicar. I coughed. "Yes, well, I have a condition. And I must say I find your prejudice against the physically disabled quite upsetting."

"Heed not the lies that slither from the black tongue of Darkness," boomed a familiar voice. "They are the prostitutes of the Adversary, who fell to their knees and drank deeply of the vile liquids that ooze from his grotesque member."

Our friend the priest was standing at the back of the crowd, having reappeared at the first opportunity to make my life difficult. A long silence followed.

"Whoa," said Meryl. "What doom fortress were you living in?"

# TWO

"I'll tell you what I want to know," said Meryl, a little later. "I want to know where they found a big cage on wheels at such short notice."

I was systematically pulling at the bars, looking for one that wasn't completely rigid. "I can't say that's my biggest concern right now."

"Struggle while you can, beast," intoned the priest smugly. "Soon divine retribution will visit you!"

I head-butted the nearest bar, frustrated. "You're in this cage as well, you know."

"I have been nominated to deter your escape," he replied, folding his arms. "The minions of demonkind are slippery with the foul butter of dreadful cows."

I really couldn't think of a response to that, so I went back to looking for a weak spot in the cage. Fat chance. Wherever Barry the vicar found his equipment, they clearly had good workmanship standards.

He had spent the last hour or so negotiating with the small group of adventurers who still cared enough to hang around. Desirous for vengeance they may have been, but most of their type wouldn't even do their own washing-up unless you called it a "quest" and paid in cash. Finally he came back over and glared at us through the bars.

"I've been listening to some of the stories of what you used to get up to in that doom fortress." His scowl of righteous indignation cranked up a few notches as he spoke. "Pollution.

Playing God with life and death. Torture. Murder. Spines getting pulled out. Rats. It's all so . . . *untidy*." He spat the word like a sour apple.

"It is the LORD's truth," went the priest, glaring at me.

"But that I could have overlooked," continued Barry. "This is the life that adventurers accept. They were the ones intruding and you were expected to retaliate, even if your methods were obscene." He picked through his words slowly and carefully, trying not to let his anger explode. "No, it's the innocent people of the county villages who must be avenged. The endless pillaging. Killing people. Setting fire to things. Raping—"

"We weren't raping," I interrupted. "We're dead. And we're not into that."

"There was that one sheep," said Meryl.

A shudder ran through me. "We never figured out exactly what happened to that sheep. But it wasn't raped."

"Well, whatever happened, it definitely wasn't consensual . . ."

"Shut up!" screeched Barry. "You three are all that remain of a regime that terrorized every decent churchgoer in Goodsoil so you're going to provide the closure everyone clearly needs. We are going to roll you into the main square in Applewheat. Then we are going to light you on fire, and the townspeople will see their tormentors brought to justice. And then this county can begin the long road to recovery under the caring eyes of God."

"Amen, brother," said the priest, nodding.

"Will you stop agreeing with me!" yelled Barry, knuckles whitening around the cage bars.

"What do you think this is going to prove?" I said. "It won't kill us or hurt us. We'll just grow another body at a church."

"Dat's not troo," came the voice of the northern barbarian. He appeared at Barry's side, leading a glistening brown horse that appeared to be constructed from bowling balls and old leather. "Slippery Yon told me it vorks differently for de undead. Dey alvays haff to coom back to de same bordy."

"Is that right," said Barry unpleasantly. "That's what happens when you turn your back on nature, is it? The Almighty cuts off your second chances? Well, let's see how many farms you can despoil when you're piles of ash."

Within moments the horses were harnessed and being nudged into a gentle trot. Our cage began its shaky journey through the countryside, a thick mass of mercenary bodies on all sides filling the air with the stink of meat and steroids. Barry walked in front, self-righteousness practically leaking from his ears. I leaned against the front of the cage, gloomily out-staring a gyrating horse's arse.

"I know what you're thinking about," said Meryl in a sing-song voice.

"Do you."

"And no, being burned to ashes won't kill you properly. Remember Paul?" I did: another lost member of Dreadgrave's horde, a short bloke with a wonky eye and an exposed brain. "Fell into the acid fountain. They brought him to the infirmary in a chamber pot. He was still conscious. Talked by blowing bubbles in morse code."

"Not the most encouraging thing to bring up right now, Meryl."

"No, I guess not. But don't worry, we've got plenty of time to think of a way out of this. Meryl's on the case!"

"Fight not your righteous fate in the fires of Good," went the priest, still standing in the opposite corner with arms folded. His voice didn't seem as loud and obnoxious as usual, so perhaps reality had begun to slowly seep through. I was beginning to get the hang of interpreting him.

Something burst wetly against the back of the cart. The remains of a rotten peach rolled to a stop near my foot. Behind us, three rascally farmer's sons were keeping pace, giggling and clutching armfuls of expired produce. It was nice to see that some traditions remained alive.

A pomegranate bounced off the cart and exploded against the face of the female adventurer from Slippery John's party, who was walking along on the left. She didn't so much as flinch, but continued walking at a perfectly maintained pace, swaying her hips in exactly the same motion with each step, juicy seeds dripping off her fine upturned nose. Experimentally I leaned out of the cage and waved a hand in front of her eyes. Not a blink.

"Slippery John wouldn't bother if Slippery John were you," said Slippery John from the other side of the cage. "She's got the Syndrome."

"She looks healthy to me," I said, watching her tea-colored thighs rotating like synchronized metronomes.

"That's the thing. Syndrome only affects the good-looking ones. Drylda over there used to be an adventurer like anyone else. Quested part-time to pay her way through college, y'know. Then the Syndrome hit her. Out of nowhere, that's how it always goes. They stand around like they've got a broom up their arse, start talking weird, lose interest in everything except quests and having the best armor. Sometimes they stop moving altogether for days at a time. Don't even wake up no matter how many times you fondle and sniff their pert bodies." A pause. "Or so Slippery John hears."

"So it's a disease?" said Meryl. "I used to help out in Dreadgrave's alchemy lab now and then; it's a little hobby of mine."

"Dunno. Magic Resistance have been looking into it. They could just be depressed from all the Infusion business. But then, show Slippery John someone who isn't. And it's only adventurers that get the Syndrome, and only the most skilled and best-looking ones at that. And then there's the last stage, of course."

He put on what he probably thought was an enigmatic smile. I sighed. He clearly wasn't going to continue until I asked and made him feel important. "What's the last stage?"

"After a while, they go into their little trances for longer and longer. Then they just go into one and never come out. Eyes open. Still breathing. But they don't move. All they do is stand there. And . . . pose."

"Pose," I repeated.

"Weirdest thing. There're special gardens set up in the cities where you can bring them to stand around all day. Nice place to bring a date, actually. You know, Slippery John's enjoying this little chat. Isn't it good to actually talk and get to know each other without bringing torture and murder into it? Shame we're gonna burn you to death. Burn you to life. Well, we're gonna burn you to something, at any rate."

I sensed an opening. "You wouldn't have to burn us to anything if you'd just let us go."

He winced and pursed his lips, as if I had offered to sell him a dodgy horse while he was in the middle of eating limes. "Slippery John's kind of committed to this quest, now. Slippery John's put it in the log and everything." He produced a little black book on whose cover the words "QUEST LOG" were daubed in correctional fluid, and turned to the penultimate entry, written in an extremely neat, careful hand. *Escort vicar and lynch wagon to Applewheat, burn contents*, it said. The final entry on the opposite page read, *Find out if anyone in Applewheat sells black pants*.

"You could consider this a slight update to the objective."

"Slippery John finds it hard to understand you when you

clench your teeth like that. So what would you have Slippery John do?"

"Escort us to Lolede," I said, inspiration striking. "You keep talking about some Magic Resistance. They're interested in how Dreadgrave brought us back to life, right? They'd probably pay a lot of money to get their hands on us."

"You're probably right, dead man. But here's the thing. Lolede City, wherein lies the Magic Resistance, is three hundred miles away by sea. Whereas the village of Applewheat is . . . where's the village of Applewheat?"

"We're here," called Barry from somewhere in front of us.

"So you can see how Slippery John's original quest is a teensy bit more straightforward."

Among the villages of Goodsoil County, Applewheat was probably the closest thing to a capital city, in that it actually had a village square and more than one tavern. It was also the closest village to Dreadgrave's fortress, and as such had been a frequent target for pillaging when we'd had a long day or just didn't feel like walking very far. I had been impressed every time by how quickly the buildings would be reconstructed after a good razing, generally just in time for the next one.

It was a typical market day. Yokels clustered around the village square, skillfully circumnavigating the regular piles of horse plop. Wives in gray wool shawls stood around in small groups, gossiping and ignoring the merry apple-cheeked children who dodged between their skirts. And yelling at all of them from behind rows of stalls were the operators of the many surrounding farms.

The hubbub of shoppers and cries of traders repeatedly advertising the luvverliness of their spuds died down as our miniature wagon train rattled into the middle of the square. We very quickly drew everyone's attention, since we weren't root vegetables or covered in manure and as such stuck out like sore thumbs. The adventurers started taking hay from the nearby feeding trough of a very put-out-looking horse and started heaping it into the cage and around the base.

"Come up with a plan, yet?" I hissed in Meryl's ear.

"I've got it all worked out. As soon as the fire's hot enough to melt the metal in the bars, we bend them out of the way and run."

I let my shoulders sag. "Brilliant."

"Seriously? I thought it was rubbish."

"If I could have everyone's attention," went Barry, adopting the pulpit stance and unconsciously groping for his holy book. It was a needless statement; his voice was the only sound, save the cawing of distant carrion birds with extraordinarily good foresight. "We have great news to bring you."

"Is that my hay?" came a voice from the crowd.

"The dark cloud that once hung over this land has been vanquished once and for all," continued Barry. "And these minions of evil are all that remain of-"

"Is that Meryl?" said one of the shawl-clad wives at the front of the throng.

"Hi Mrs. Bindlegob," said Meryl, waving.

"Will you be wanting pastries delivered tonight, dear? Only Colin's in bed with a sniffle."

"Tell him not to worry about it, Mrs. Bindlegob."

"You're a tresh, Meryl."

Barry coughed indignantly. "As I was saying, all that remain of that dread regime . . . "

"Hey, Jim!" called Anthony the blacksmith. "We found the problem with your cranial press, there was a piece of skull stuck in the screw. You want to take it back now?"

"Er . . . I'm kind of in a cage right now, Anthony."

"Oh, so you are, lad."

"Dreadgrave is gone!" yelled Barry, clenching his fists. "Rejoice, good people! The dark overlord will never again practice his blasphemous necromantic arts in this world!"

A shocked silence followed his outburst, broken by that unimportant person's voice again. "Where'd he go?"

"He didn't go anywhere! He's been annihilated! Angels did it!"

"The white angels?" said Anthony. "Those things that disappear stuff?"

"That's awful!" went Mrs. Bindlegob. "Has anyone told his mother?"

"She'll be inconsolable, the poor dear," said one of Mrs. Bindlegob's cohorts. "She was so proud when Dreadgrave bought the doom fortress and moved out of her loft, she must have boasted it to everyone this side of the river."

"And who's going to look after his horde?" said someone else.

"Oh, we're all that's left," said Meryl. "Everyone else got deleted too."

"What? Even Ramsay?" said Mrs. Bindlegob.

"'Fraid so."

"You poor ducks. If you need anywhere to stay while you find a new overlord . . ."

At this point I became aware of the air gradually rising in temperature, and glanced at Barry the vicar. I'd only seen a face like that once before, when one of my classmates confused his firebolt and water conjuration spells, resulting in his head being inflated with boiling hot steam. Barry's reddened lips were clamped tightly together and his fists were vibrating in sync with his nostrils. Any second now he would probably either explode or rocket into the sky on a column of flame.

"What is wrong with you people?!" he exploded, silencing the rabble. "These creatures razed your homes! Pillaged your crops! Did . . . things to your sheep! Now they've been brought down and the peasantry is free!"

"Who are you calling peasantry?" said Mrs. Bindlegob.

"Yeah, we're lower middle class!" cried someone at the back. "At least!"

"You want peasants, you can just roll your wagon over to somewhere like Bumbleston."

Barry spluttered. "I'm from Bumbleston!" This, he quickly realized, had been exactly the wrong thing to say. The crowd groaned as a collective.

"Oh, that's just typical," said one of the farmers. "Some peasant from the sticks comes in here with no idea of anything trying to tell us how to live."

"Dreadgrave's horde pillaged us every Saturday after lunch, like clockwork," continued Mrs. Bindlegob. "We all got out in the fresh air for a run around and a good scream. Did us the world of good."

"And then on Sunday we'd all get together as a community to rebuild the houses, then have a great big picnic on the green," said Anthony, eyes moistening. "It kept our entire construction workforce in employment."

"My house has been burnt down and rebuilt every week since Dreadgrave set himself up," said Giles the elder, waving a gnarled walking stick. "It's great! I never have to clean the bloody place!"

"But I'll tell you the one bad thing about being near Dreadgrave's fortress," said Mrs. Bindlegob, and you could tell from her tone of voice that she was working towards a devastating point. "All the adventurers you have to put up with."

A grumble of agreement rippled through the crowd. One or two of the shrewder adventurers started fondling their sword hilts.

"Yeah, bloody adventurers, swanning about like they own the place," mumbled Giles.

"Knocking on your door at all hours of the day and night, wanting to rummage through your drawers for potions and loose change," said Mrs. Bindlegob's friend.

"Buying up all the best armor," said Anthony, scowling. "We had absolutely nothing for ourselves for our last fancy dress party."

"Don't forget the robes," added Chris the tailor. "Bloody wizards buy up all the dressing gowns and everyone freezes half to death come winter. And they always expect me to sew magic essence into the fabric. Stuff makes me sneeze."

"And they hang around the inn all day drinking all my stock, breaking furniture and flinging axes at lady's pony tails because they think it'll impress someone," said Graham the innkeeper. "I'm trying to diversify into a family eatery and here're these berks smashing up the barroom yelling for ale and whores."

Barry visibly gave up appealing to the populace. "Just light the damn fire," he growled. One of the nearby swordsmen was now holding a flaming torch—the sort that spontaneously generates whenever a mob gets big and angry enough—and he obediently threw it onto the hay. Meryl, the priest and I all scrambled for the corner, trying to occupy the same square foot of cage. A cry of outrage swept over the townsfolk.

"And now they're picking on Jim and Meryl!" cried Mrs Bindlegob.

"They tortured and killed us! Several times!" wailed the dwarf from Slippery John's party.

"Oh and I suppose two wrongs make a right, do they?" said Mrs. Bindlegob, drawing herself to her full height and planting her hands on her broad hips to signal the winning of an argument. "Put that silly fire out," she added, as she and several members of the front row advanced forward.

One of the confused adventurers did something that he probably wouldn't have done had he had more time to think and consider the possible consequences. He drew his sword.

The events that followed would come to be remembered by the locals as the Battle of Applewheat. The adventurers had more experience with fighting, obviously, but the peasants had greater numbers and were eager to demonstrate how a lifetime of soil-tilling puts the edge on your muscular strength.

It was quite instructive to watch a rowdy punch-up take place between people who had grown used to the fact that death no longer held any meaning. Barry the vicar was the first to fall, skewered by a pitchfork. He might have survived that, but it was hard to tell, because the battle closed in over him as he crumpled to the ground, where a hundred pairs of angry stamping feet quickly reduced him to a blood-smeared mass that was one inch thick and eight feet wide.

Meanwhile, I was chanting Level 1 Water Conjuration spells as fast as I could manage, but they were designed for hikers with poor planning skills who needed to fill a waterskin in a hurry, not firefighting. Most of the water evaporated before it could make an impact, so all I was really doing was creating a small, inefficient sauna.

"Try stamping it out!" yelled Meryl over the hullabaloo outside.

"Yes, *you* could certainly try that!" I corrected.

"The flame of righteousness is upon me! I feel my Father calling!"

"Jim? I'm sort of burning."

"Roll around on the floor!"

"It's not helping, Jim . . ."

"I meant part of the floor that isn't on fire!"

"There isn't any . . ."

Her sentence was aborted as the cage began to tip. The peasants had firmly pushed the battle back into the village square, where they seemed to have gained a clear advantage. They were poorer equipped but had far greater numbers, and weren't bound by the adventurers' unspoken agreement to aim for the armor rather than the fashionably large sections of exposed skin.

I'm not sure who, exactly, pushed over the cage; the battle had become so difficult to follow that it could have been either side, by the peasants to aid our escape or the adventurers to hasten our destruction. All I know is that we and the cage tumbled heavily onto Ian the carpenter's workbench, where a vise handle lodged itself in my brain.

I died again. A few moments of total confusion followed as my soul burst out of my body, tumbled end over end through a storm of flailing limbs, then flew right out of the battle and into the street. I lay on my back in the washed-out dirt, with the usual post-mortem thoughts running through my head: chiefly wondering if it was really worth standing up again.

"Well, thanks a bunch," came a voice, reverberating with the usual hollowness of sounds in the dead world.

I glanced up. I wasn't surprised to see him. I had discovered very early on, back in Dreadgrave's frequently crowded main quad, that the temporarily disembodied spirits of the dead can interact. But there had never been enough time to do anything besides exchange nods and sympathetic shrugs. "Hello, Barry."

His shimmering astral body was unmistakable. It even had its own dog collar. "Don't you 'Hello, Barry' me. What did you do to these townspeople?"

I shrugged. I was too tired to be confrontational. "Pillaged them. Burnt their houses. Stole things. Dunno what to tell you."

"Have you any idea how inconvenienced I am right now? I was the only resurrectionist for miles! I'm going to have to float all the way to Bumbleston. Emmett is never going to let me hear the end of this."

I stood up and resolved to ignore him. The fire seemed to be going out and Deleters were starting to notice me, so I resignedly began to make my way back towards my body. I noticed Drylda the Syndrome-afflicted warrior, mechanically performing the same sequence of thrusting and slicing over and over again. Then I looked again, and I couldn't stop looking.

There were two shimmery semi-transparent wings emerging from Drylda's back like a bad angel costume. They definitely hadn't been there in the living world. I floated closer.

No doubt about it. Little white wings. Far too small and non-corporeal to be of any use for flight, but there they were. Curious, I reached out and poked one of them. I was fairly certain she wouldn't react even had we not been on different planes of existence, which is why it came as such a surprise when she did.

Her whole body flinched, causing me to do likewise and fall onto my astral arse. She stopped fighting, stiffened, then toppled over backwards with perfect comic timing, eyes glazed and mouth still fixed in mild disdain. Her attacker, a leathery thatcher, accepted this as a victory and moved on.

When her body lay still, a curious astral sheen appeared over her head, like a veil of fairy dust. Then a shimmering white oval rose up from inside her face, emerging from between her nose and mouth. I felt my astral stomach turning in protest, but I still watched, paralyzed with horror. The little white shape moved a little further out to reveal that it sat upon a pair of sparkling shoulders, and the sudden shock of recognition allowed me to find a voice.

"Deleter!" I shrieked. "There's a Deleter inside her!"

"I am not listening to you!" called Barry.

The Deleter looked surprised, insofar as one can with a featureless face. Then it started shaking spasmodically, almost as if it were trying to pull itself free. Drylda's body shook similarly, like a disobedient horse trying to throw off its jockey, before both gave one particularly violent lurch and fell back down, still. The Deleter sank back inside her, apparently in defeat.

I looked around to see if anyone else had noticed, and jumped with shock a second time when I saw that the entire street was absolutely swarming with Deleters. There were far more than the usual committee that routinely hustled me back to my body. They were like a crowd gathering at a road accident.

"I didn't touch your friend!" I said automatically, putting my hands up. Then I thought about it for a little longer. "Actually, I did! Very inappropriately! You'd better delete me before I do it again!"

I was talking to myself. They weren't the slightest bit interested in me. In fact, every single one of them was standing with their rigid, blank faces angled towards Barry the vicar.

He realized it at the same time I did, with a terrified flinch. Being wordlessly judged by hundreds of shimmering celestial beings would be enough to strike religious dread into the staunchest atheist, so I could only imagine how petrifying it must have been for a career godbotherer.

"Er . . . it's OK," he was saying. "I was just on my way to find a church . . ."

He tried to back away, but they had surrounded him, blocking every escape route.

"I'll walk faster!" came his final, desperate cry, as he disappeared from view behind a wall of shimmering white wings. I heard a few distorted screams and a glimpse of a thrashing limb, then both disappeared completely beneath the mass of white bodies. They formed themselves into a vaguely ball-shaped mass and flew off into the sky, vanishing from sight.

Barry the vicar was gone. I stood frozen in place, pondering my next move, before a handful of the remaining Deleters turned their attention to me. They pointed dismissively in the direction of my corpse.

"Oh, come on," I said, as I felt myself being pulled back. "What makes him so special?!"

# THREE

The battle had been decisively concluded by the time I came back to life. The victorious peasants had repaired to one of the inns to finish off the last few barrels of ale in preparation for its grand reopening as a family eatery. Only the merry apple-cheeked children remained on the battlefield, kneeling on the chests of the dead adventurers to force potatoes into their mouths and punch them in the face.

I sat on an upturned donkey cart, cradling my chin in one hand while a slightly singed Meryl filled the hole in my head with spackle. "Then they just whisked him away," I concluded. "Nothing left. I don't know what to make of it."

Meryl was smoothing off the spackle job with a small trowel. "Maybe they deleted him for the same reason they did it to Dreadgrave?"

I frowned. "But they didn't delete him. Not the same way. And besides, they deleted Dreadgrave because he was messing around with the new life and death rules. That Barry guy was just a bit of a prick." I turned to look at her. "How did we get out of the cage, by the way?"

"Well, after the bars got hot enough, we were able to bend . . ."

"I am once again saved by the guiding hand of the LORD," barked the priest, sitting nearby. His arms had been dislocated when the cage had turned over, and he was waiting for Meryl to reset them so he could get back to pointing accusing fingers in my face. "Praise His name for your good fortune, unbeliever."

"Did you hear that? He's down to calling us unbelievers, not the courtesans of hellspawn or whatever," said Meryl. "I think he's really starting to loosen up."

"Yeah," I said. "Maybe after a few more months he'll be merely rude. Listen, about the Deleters. They're not just deleting things. They're doing things to adventurers. One of them had one inside her. I saw it. It was horrible."

"Yeesh," said Meryl with disinterested concern.

"They've got to be doing it all for a reason, right? The deleting and the Syndrome. But why?"

"I don't know why you think you need to get so involved," said Meryl through a sigh.

"Forget it," I muttered, deliberately avoiding her point. I lapsed into glum silence, waiting for her to finish.

A few minutes later I saw Mrs. Bindlegob and Anthony coming towards us, carefully picking their way around the recent resurrectees busily looting their own corpses. "Hello, dears," said Mrs. Bindlegob. "How are the patients?"

Meryl patted the back of my head fondly. "All plugged up and ready for action," she said cheerfully, before turning her attention to the priest.

"Shame about young Dreadgrave," said Anthony, shaking his head. "If there's anything we can do to help you back on your feet, just ask."

"We're not staying," I said quickly, as Meryl opened her mouth. "A few things we have to take care of elsewhere. But I would like to borrow a wheelbarrow."

"Least we can do," said Mrs. Bindlegob, fidgeting and stirring the bloodstained dirt with her foot. "It's just . . . we were talking, and we know Dreadgrave's gone and everything, but we wondered if you loves would be kind enough to pillage us every now and again, for old times' sake?"

"We'd pay you by the hour," added Anthony, as the silence dragged on.

"Why don't you just . . . pillage each other?" I said.

Everyone fell silent. Somewhere, a bird called. The wind whistled through the trees. A dying adventurer spat out potatoes. And Anthony and Mrs. Bindlegob slowly, slowly turned to look at each other.

We were afforded a spectacular view of Applewheat as we made our way up the road out of Greydoom Valley. It was evening now, and the burning houses added a picturesque column of smoke to the pinkish sunset. When we were far enough away that the dancing peasants were no more than specks in the village square, Meryl finally spoke.

"Why are you bringing her with us?"

I stopped to shift my grip on the wheelbarrow handles and tuck Drylda's legs back in. "Would you believe I feel a little guilty for her being like this?"

"Well . . . no, actually, I wouldn't."

"Why not?"

"Because you're undead and completely without empathy? You used to throw people to be eaten to death by rats?"

"They didn't die permanently . . ."

"Yeah, but you didn't know that."

"Will your tongue ever cease to twist foul lies, heathen?" spat the priest, who had been walking ahead, but now turned and joined the conversation as it moved to the subject of my shortcomings.

"All right, fine. She's got the Syndrome and the Syndrome is something to do with Deleters. That's about the size of it."

"That's still not a good reason to lump her around."

"Look, it's not that complicated! Something weird happened when I touched her in the dead world and I want to figure out what. Why are you being so yappy about it?"

"I am not yappy!"

I stopped, and eyed her for a second. "Are you . . . are you jealous?"

Embarrassment and immediate denial said volumes in these situations. So it was rather disheartening when Meryl seemed genuinely bemused by the question. "Nooo . . . Why would you think that?"

I attempted to make a gesture that encapsulated her, me and our close proximity. "You've been following me around since the moment we met."

"So you thought that I was . . ." She tried to repeat the gesture. " . . . With you? No. God, no. We don't have glands. How would that even work?"

I took up the wheelbarrow again. "No, right. We're going to stop talking now. This conversation is heading for ugly places."

"The bonds of marriage are the scalding hot chains of the fornicator," muttered the priest, apparently lacking a more appropriate verse.

We rounded the top of the hill. The forests of the valley had given way to the grass of the plains. For a couple of hours we proceeded through a picturesque vista of rolling yellow fields broken up by green hedges and the occasional brown-and-white rank of snoozing cows. After that the sun went down, so we followed the path in pitch darkness for a while before reaching a crossroads. A three-way directional sign was erected in the middle, illuminated by a standard light-bearing sprite.

I inspected the signs. Going back into Goodsoil via Applewheat was out of the question, at least until they rebuilt it again, which narrowed the options to Yawnbore and New Pillock.

"Slippery John said he was going to Yawnbore," I recalled.

"So?"

"Still some things I want to clarify with that thieving prick. And Yawnbore's on the coast. We can get on a boat to Lolede from there."

"Why do you want to go to Lolede?"

"Den of iniquity!" contributed the priest.

"To find the Magic Resistance. That's what I want to talk to Slippery John about. He said they're trying to find a way to restart normal life and death, so they might know more about the Deleters. And they can help figure out what I did to Drylda and what it means. Is that enough reasons?"

"But we have to go to Borrigarde," said Meryl.

I looked at her. Up until that point, I had thought I was on the verge of understanding Meryl's motivation; she happily went along with whatever I was doing like an eager puppy who knew how to sew, and could occasionally be relied upon to hurl herself between me and danger. Now it seemed something had excited some kind of independent thought inside her skull and she was going on about . . . what?

"There is no Borrigarde," I said, slowly and carefully. "There is only New Pillock."

"It's always Borrigarde in spirit," she said, her voice becoming unexpectedly testy, but after a deep breath she was all smiles again. "Come on, after fifty years dead there's got to be some part of you wants to see the green, green grass of home."

"If there was, I coughed it up ages ago. Are you sure you're not thinking of somewhere else? The only green I remember was the local beef."

"What about your family?"

"Why do you think I died so far away? I was at mage college because it was either that or work my arse off at home, sharing a bed with Granddad and both his wives. I'm not what you'd call attached."

Her lower lip was definitely quivering. "But . . . it's Borrigarde!" she stammered. "Your country is lying crushed beneath the heel of Pillock oppression! We're probably the last pureblood Borrigardians in the world and it's up to us—"

"What did you say?"

"I said . . ."

"Pureblood?" A number of previous conversations with Meryl lined up in my memory, and her use of the word suddenly knocked them over like a row of dominos. "Oh god. I get it now."

She was avoiding my gaze and toying with her fingers. "What do you 'get', lapdog of the Damned?" asked the priest.

"She's a Binny. The Borrigardian Nationalists. The most pathetic bunch of rural xenophobes to ever declare themselves the master race."

That did the trick. Meryl's bottled-up rage burst out of her in a single blast, along with some unidentifiable gray liquid from her nostrils. "We are not pathetic! And we did not declare any master races! It was just about having pride in your country!"

I couldn't help laughing bitterly. "Pride? In Borrigarde? Home of the King Derek the Third Memorial Compost Heap? And besides, you do know that all the kingdoms in Garethy descended from the same tribe? Every country is the same! And Pillock even has a nice lake district. What possible reason is there to go back to Borrigarde now?"

"We can end the occupation!" she cried, a revolutionary gleam in her glowing eyes. "The time is right! All they need is a push, and that's us! The vengeful spirits of the dead, returning to take back our nation's glory! The people have lived under Pillock oppression for long enough! Stop sniggering!"

"I can't help it! You're like a little revolutionary piglet! You want to know what life is like under Pillock oppression? It's exactly the same as it always is: brown and full of live-stock. Only difference is Derek the Fourth has to piss off and live in his beach house."

"Don't talk about His Divinely Appointed Majesty like that! Can't you see what's at stake? We could be heroes!"

"Heroes," I repeated, sneering.

"Isn't that what all this chasing Deleters is about? Saving the world?"

"It's about finding a way to die."

She put one hands on her hip and made a sweeping gesture in Drylda's direction. "Don't give me that. No-one goes to all this trouble just for suicide. You died defending your school from invaders. You told me. You died a hero."

I stopped sniggering. My grin faded. "Die a hero, die a coward," I said, bitterly. "Same grave either way."

"Come off it. Why were you even going to magic school if you didn't want to be a hero?"

I glanced at the priest, who was watching us silently with wide, disapproving eyes. Then I looked at Drylda, curled up in the wheelbarrow and pouting alluringly at a tree.

"You want to know why I was studying magic?" I said. My voice sounded strange and distant.

She frowned. "To be a hero?"

"I was going to open a shop. My very own little magic shop in a nice gullible town somewhere. With velvet blue curtains on the ceiling and shelves covered in weird-shaped jars full of colored liquid and body parts. That's what kind of people we are, Meryl. We're shopkeepers. Passers-by. Undead minion numbers thirty-two and thirty-three. We're not the heroes.

"But . . ."

"Heroes are the kinds of people we used to torture. Those dicks who lit us on fire this afternoon, they're heroes. They swagger into a village, sort out any problem that can be solved by whacking it a few times, make out with the blacksmith's daughter, then bugger off long enough for the problems to come back. They load themselves down with armor and weapons and treasure because inside they're very empty, sad little people. In the long run they've never achieved anything, ever."

"I'm talking about being heroes to the people of Borrigarde," she said, tapping her foot.

"And I'm telling you that it wouldn't matter even if your plan wasn't retarded! Your brilliant plan—to barge into a country you haven't even seen in decades to try and talk some pig farmers you don't even know into beating up another bunch of pig farmers so that life can stay exactly the same!"

"And you're seriously saying you'd prefer being dead? I don't get what you saw in that! I've been dead too, you know! It was just boring!"

The fog of rage faded from me. The rush of angry blood that had rushed to my head began to gooily slide back down my neck. Somehow Meryl and I had found ourselves yelling nose-to-nose. I took two careful steps back.

"This world," I said, "is stagnating. Every inch of it. The timbers are rotten and the plumbing's full of frogs. Even the bloody heroes are broken." I kicked the wheelbarrow. "I don't give a toss about what comes after anymore. All I know is that it's got to be better than this."

"So that's all you care about? Dying for good?" Her voice was quavering. "Not thinking anymore? Not remembering?"

"It's overrated. Grandad's hands used to wander in his sleep and I've been trying to stop remembering it for sixty-five years. Point is, if you think I'm going to spend the rest of my li—" I paused for thought, then threw up my hands. "I'm just going to call it 'life' from now on, all right? If you think I'm going to spend the rest of whatever it is dithering about in this poor excuse for a world, you're obviously as stupid as you look, sound, act and are. I'm going to Lolede and I'm going to find the one thing that apparently has the power to pack all this in."

Something felt terribly unusual about the silence that followed,until I realized that Meryl and the priest were both lost for words. I enjoyed it while it lasted.

"I'm going to Borrigarde," said Meryl, finally. Then she turned and strode off down the road back to Applewheat for a moment, before smartly rotating on a heel and heading for New Pillock.

I watched her until she had disappeared into the darkness, then turned to the priest. "Well?"

He drew himself to his full, impressive height and set his mouth and nose into the usual disapproving grimace, but there was uncertainty in his eyes. "I will go with her," he announced after some thought. "Be watchful of thy womenfolk, for their wombs are forever welcoming of Sin's mighty flesh." He marched stiffly after Meryl before I could think of a response.

The sprite on the sign must have been motion-sensitive, because after I hadn't moved for a while, it winked out. There I stood, abandoned by my fr— by my collea— by some associates, alone at a darkened crossroads with only a wheelbarrow full of catatonic adventurer to keep me company.

It was fairly obvious what was going to happen next. Somewhere in the distance, a wolf would howl. A cold wind would blow across the hills. The sudden unpleasant knowledge of being totally alone would creep over me like fast-growing fungus. Within a minute I'd realize that for all my talk I really had valued the company of Meryl and maybe even that dipshit priest. Within two minutes I'd be pelting down the road to New Pillock after them.

In the distance, a wolf howled. A cold wind blew across the hills. I picked up my wheelbarrow and took the road to Yawnbore, whistling.

# FOUR

After a few days uneventful journey—for there is no other kind in Garethy—I reached the coast. The sun was rising again, the reflections on the calm ocean providing it with a temporary scarf. And there, at the bottom of the hill, lay Yawnbore, a crescent-shaped forest of brick houses jealously hugging the bay.

"Here we are, Drylda," I said. She was much more agreeable to talk to than my previous party members. "Are we ready for the shithole of the day?"

Yawnbore was a retirement hotspot and tourist destination. It featured the closest thing to a beach in the entire continent of Garethy, a bank of razor-sharp shingle that had taught many a child's feet to dread the traditional family holiday. It had the largest density of inns of any town in the country, some of which were even classified as "hotels" because they put a few mattresses in the stables and a diving board over the horse trough.

It was stupidly early in the morning, even for old people. As I headed down the main road through the outskirts of town, nothing was stirring except a few poorly-secured garden gates, squeaking back and forth in the chilly morning breeze. The only other noises were the grinding of my rusty metal wheelbarrow and the jingle of Drylda's accoutrements.

"So we just have to find something heading to Lolede," I thought aloud. "Charter ship. Fishing boat. A buoyant piece of wood will do. I'll have to lash you on with a bit of rope, Drylda."

I looked down. The wheelbarrow was empty, but for a faint whiff of fake tan.

A number of unpleasant scenarios ran through my mind before I turned around and saw that Drylda was lying ten feet behind me in a scantily-clad heap. I sighed, backed up the wheelbarrow, and piled her back in.

"You're a bit too light for your own good," I muttered, proceeding with the barrow. "Suppose that armor can't weigh much, hm?"

Again, I looked down. Again, she was gone, although the fake tan smell was diligently holding the fort. She had fallen out of the barrow at exactly the same place as before. The next time, I pushed forwards as slowly as I could, and watched her closely.

There. Right as we were crossing the imaginary line border that separated the town of Yawnbore from the surrounding countryside, her body moved. She bent at the waist, her head and upper torso diving for the ground. It was rather like she was being wrenched out of the barrow by an invisible rope. Or . . .

I took up Drylda's limp wrist and pushed her hand towards Yawnbore. Something pushed back, as if I was trying to hold two repulsing magnets together.

" . . . Or pushed by an invisible wall," I realized aloud. "But why can I . . ."

An idea occurred to me. Leaving Drylda and the wheelbarrow where they were, I walked back to a little pond a short way back down the road and rummaged around in the vile algae-covered water until I discovered a sleepy frog, grown fat and complacent from an abundance of flies and lack of predators. I took him back to the barrow, bounced him up and down in my hand once or twice, then flung him overarm.

He bounced off thin air with a wounded croak, leaving a splatter of reddish-green stuff that hung unsupported for a moment before raining down upon the gravel. His little warty body twitched in death throes for a few seconds, then I carefully picked up his body by one spindly leg and flung it forwards again. This time, it sailed uninterrupted through the air before coming to a squidgy rest in someone's flowerbed.

So there was a magical barrier around the town that blocked living things. It wasn't a completely absurd concept. Many towns had walls to shut out all the gnolls, goblins, and football hooligans that roamed the countryside looking for things to fight or pour beer over. And magical force fields were cheaper than walls, although they were less reliable and tended to result in one or two local babies with seven heads or lycanthropy a few generations down the line. The fact that this one was invisible was a little harder to understand. The raw form of the spell was invisible, but coloring agents were usually added before distribution, so that they couldn't be used for nefarious (if entertaining) purposes.

"Hello!" I called. "Is someone in charge of this wall? Medical emergency!"

The only sound was the distant rumble of the ocean and a very faint wet noise of frog innards sliding down flower stems.

"I'll just see if I can find a watchman, Drylda," I said over my shoulder.

I left her at the barrier and made my way into Yawnbore proper. This early in the morning she was probably safe from slavers—god knows what they'd even expect her to do.

I was surrounded on all sides by quaint retirement cottages, and looming over them was the clock tower that marked the town center. I shielded my eyes from the watery glare of the rising sun and checked the time.

"Nine twenty-five," I read aloud. That couldn't possibly be right. Barely half an hour had passed since sunrise.

I turned a corner into another pristine row of thatched roof cottages, and became aware of a metallic sound. I'd finally found someone: an elderly woman standing behind a picket fence, trimming her bush with a pair of heavy duty clippers.

"Hey," I said, jogging up, but anything I had to follow that up with died in my throat as I took a closer look.

She was holding clippers and standing in the vicinity of a bush, but there seemed to be several inches of clearance between the two. Nothing about her dreamy smile or the contented, flouncy way she handled the clippers made any indication that she didn't know exactly what she was doing.

"Er, hey," I repeated with a little less confidence. "Do you know where I can find someone to open the barrier?"

"Yes, mister?" she said, in a cheerful tone of voice. She didn't look at me, but continued her work while staring vaguely at something above and to the right of her hedge.

I waited for her to elaborate, but she seemed to forget I was there. I coughed. "So . . . can you point me in the right direction?"

"I don't know what she was thinking!" she replied.

She still wasn't looking at me, so I took a quick glance around to make sure there wasn't anyone else in the street. Then I waved my arms around for a moment to check for invisible ones.

"Good morning," she said suddenly and loudly, as if calling to someone from across the road.

I jumped in surprise. "Good . . . morning?"

"What a wonderful fabric," she added, before sliding to the ground and continuing to happily clip at a fence post.

"We don't like your sort around here," said a gruff male voice from behind me. I turned around, and saw a bald man in a checkered shirt lying stomach-down in the road, glaring at me with open hostility. We regarded each other for a few moments, then he attempted to stride briskly off into the ground.

At that point I decided that a brisk jog to the town center would be prudent. I met a handful of townspeople on the way, but none were in any position to be of use. Most of them didn't even respond to my presence, and just walked around in small circles in the middle of the street. A small boy was standing catatonically on a curb with his arms outstretched at his sides, and a small girl was punching a dog.

The town center was a large circular space that separated a row of shops and hotels from the laughable beach, with the clock tower in the center. At the base of it an unshaven man in the clothes of a town official was staring intently at the winding handle while turning it extremely slowly.

My first thought was that the magical barrier around town had been in place for a few too many generations, but that didn't seem to add up. There wasn't any mutation going on; instead, it felt more like the people of the town were working from some kind of script that had had all its pages mixed up and stamped on a few times by an aggressive horse.

Driven now more by morbid curiosity than my original search for assistance, I continued along the seafront, where my eye was drawn to the largest hotel, a tall, white, grand affair with a pair of impressive classical pillars around the entrance. It looked like it had been the victim of some kind of invasion; all the ground floor windows were smashed in and the main doors were both swinging on one hinge. On the nearby wall, someone had daubed little symbols of male anatomy all over the *No Riff Raff* plaque.

This was new. Every other building in the town was displaying signs of neglect, presumably because the caretakers were all busy punching livestock or banging their heads against walls. This one showed all the hallmarks of deliberate vandalism, and I'd done enough looting in my time to recognize the work of a fellow enthusiast. That meant sane people had been here. I stepped gingerly over the ruined doors and into the lobby.

The interior wasn't any tidier. Anything that was potentially valuable was missing, and everything else was damaged. The reception desk lay in an ugly pile of splintered wood and pages from the check-in book. The manager was propped up against a wall with a lampshade on his head and his torso wrapped in velvet curtains.

"Lovely ocean view," he repeated like a mantra.

I passed under a broken timber into what I suppose must have been the dining room, because the splintered remnants of tables lay near crumpled tablecloths and shattered flower vases. An elderly, posh-looking couple were sitting on two of the few upright chairs. They were dressed only in underwear and the woman was running a comb through the man's impressive handlebar mustache.

Behind the bar across the room a podgy man in a pirate outfit held an upended bottle of wine to his lips as the contents were transferred to his gullet with a series of rhythmic "glook" sounds. He hefted the bottle as if to hurl it across the room, but froze when he noticed me flinch. His gaze tracked back and forth from my head to my feet a few times.

"What's wrong with yer face?" he said.

I blinked. "What?"

"WHAT'S WRONG WITH YER FACE?!!"

"No . . . I heard you, I was just caught off guard."

"Yeh've seriously never been asked that before? Bugger me. Where the 'ell are you from?"

"It wasn't the question, it was . . . why has everyone in this town gone all weird?"

"Aye, we noticed that. Same question crossed our minds."

"We?"

"Aye," he said. Then he added "Aaargh," because at that point an extremely large and heavy rock came crashing down through the ceiling, and his headscarf did very little to slow the fatal destruction of his skull.

I tried to think of something to say, but all I could come up with was "Waagh." A second boulder crashed in and came to rest an inch from my foot, drizzling splinters of ceiling onto my shoulders.

At first I made to bolt for the door, but then I heard a siege weapon being activated right outside, so I spun on my heel and went for the stairs. Another missile struck the building as I reached the third floor and almost threw me off my feet. I knew then I'd probably made a mistake, but there was no time to re-assess. I ran into the nearest room. A middle-aged man was trying to write on the window pane with a fork. I pulled him gently away and took a look outside.

The source of the missiles stood in the middle of the street on four mighty wheels. A large, sturdy catapult being operated by a gaggle of meatheaded mercenaries. *No, wait*, I corrected myself. *Not a catapult, one of those sling things. A trebuchet.*

I flinched as another payload slammed into the building, and felt the floor slant forward an inch. The hotel wasn't designed to withstand much of anything more stressful than an energetic honeymoon couple, and the trebuchet had apparently moved past warning shots and was ready to get down to some good old-fashioned total destruction.

I had to get out of this building, preferably via a back door of some description. I should have made my move then, but a sudden cessation of movement out in the street caught my attention.

As one, the adventurers manning the trebuchet had suddenly snapped to attention, thrusting their pectorals out like bricks mounted to cupboard doors. I poked my head carefully out the window, and saw, coming down the road, the very same big cage on wheels I had gotten to know intimately in Applewheat, still blackened from our previous meeting. Its new occupants had probably been picked off the streets of Yawnbore, because they were talking to themselves and acting out a variety of incongruous mimes like some kind of mobile performance art troupe.

The carriage was being hauled by a pair of overworked horses, and there was a row of individuals walking along either side of it. Some of them were adventurers, but most I recognized as the white-clad members of the youth group that had destroyed Barry's church. And leading the procession was Barry himself.

Even from a distance he was easy to recognize. I'd seen more than enough of that jowly, self-righteous face when it had been glaring at me through the bars of a cage, not to mention disappearing beneath the wings of ravenous Deleters. Something had changed about him, though. There was something new and confident about the way he carried himself. Three inches above the ground.

"Things ticking along nicely over here?" he said, levitating over to the trebuchet. He was in an unusually good mood, and maybe it was my imagination, but his voice seemed to possess more of an echo than everyone else's.

"We are beginning the demolition as ordered, your Divine Majestic Holiness," said the adventurer holding the trigger rope, an elven fellow in a girly purple doublet.

"And you've already checked the building for people, yes?"

The elf swallowed hard, and even from the window I could hear the thick wad of nervous sputum thumping down his gullet. "I . . . not just yet, my glorious lord."

Barry looked up at the hotel with mock confusion. "I don't

see how you'd be able to search the place after it's been destroyed."

"He forgot, son off de most High," said another member of the trebuchet party. It was the oily northern barbarian. "I didn't vont to say anyting 'cos he vos supposed to be in charge."

"Oh dear," sighed Barry.

"My lord, if I forgot it was because GAAAAAGH," said the elf, as he burst into white flame. My skin prickled in sympathy as his body convulsed with agony before collapsing into a heap of crumbling ash.

Barry withdrew his pointing finger. "I ask one simple thing from my employees: that you follow all my instructions and not deviate from them. You've only got yourself to blame. Oh yes, and—" He paused to point at the barbarian, who immediately flared up with a heavily accented scream. "—Nobody likes a tell tale. You can both go and think about it by the clock tower. I'll resurrect you later if there's any time left in the schedule."

I had learned about the level 60 Righteous Smitation spell in my first year of magic school. Only the highest-ranking priests in the most ethically flexible religious sects are allowed to learn it, and even then there's a whole pile of forms to fill in before someone can be authorized to cast it. On top of that, it uses up their entire magic reserve for the day, leaving them in need of a lengthy lie down and a few decent swigs of communion wine. Barry the vicar had just cast it twice in one minute and wasn't even swaying.

"Right then," he said, rubbing his hands. White energy crackled around his palms. "The rest of you, get inside and clear everyone out before you throw any more rocks." The three adventurers at the trebuchet—a dwarf, a swordsman and a battle mage, who had been standing with the frozen but relaxed look of students when the teacher is picking on someone else—suddenly snapped to attention and jogged smartly into the hotel.

Barry called after them. "Our target is to get everyone rounded up and at least half the demolition work done by the end of the day. Quickly, people!" He clapped his hands.

The very last thing I wanted to do was fall into the clutches of the new and improved Barry. I slipped out into the stairwell. I could already hear muffled bumps and scuffling on the ground floor, and a couple of pairs of boots began tromp-tromping their way up the stairs.

I flattened myself against a wall—I wasn't sure if it helped, but it felt like an appropriate thing to do—and made my way through the halls, wincing with every creak of the floorboards. If I could find a window, perhaps I could escape before they found me, even if it meant jumping down three stories and having to sneak out of town with my legs partially embedded into my torso.

I found an unlocked door quickly enough, and ran through it into a large double room. The occupying family were all sitting cross-legged on the bed around a plate of half-eaten breakfast. As I pulled the door shut behind me and shoved a chair under the handle, one of the children took a fried mushroom, shook it in her hand, then cast it back onto the plate like a die.

I crossed the room and pulled the window open. There was a lovely view of the brick wall opposite and a picturesque cluster of bins in the alleyway below. Nothing that could possibly offer a soft landing, and I was amazed by how frighteningly high up the third floor was when looked down from like this. I looked left and right for a nice quiet corner where I could rethink my plan, but the sudden crunch of a door being kicked open down-stairs brought things back into perspective.

I had hooked two legs over the windowsill and prepared to lower myself gently when the entire hotel began to shake violently. One of those early trebuchet shots must have done something to the building's integrity. I was left dangling from the windowsill by my fingers, feet frantically scrabbling against the wall and elbow staples creaking with displeasure.

The father of the occupying family suddenly appeared at the window. He looked left, then right, then down, straight into my eyes.

"I told you to keep this window shut," he said, face totally blank.

"Oh, you bastard," I replied, unsure whether I was referring to him, Barry, or God.

He smartly slammed the window closed. I snatched my hands away before I could add ten broken fingers to my list of problems. Then gravity, that smug jerk, tapped me on the shoulder and asked me how I thought I was going to stay up. I didn't have an answer to that. I fell.

After an arm-flailing, stomach-lurching fraction of a second, I managed to grab the ledge above the second floor window. My feet found solid purchase on the sill. My life abruptly stopped flashing before my eyes. I was safe.

I was also staring right into a room containing a very surprised-looking dwarven mercenary, one leg still frozen post-door-kicking. He was wielding a battleaxe about the size of a small tree, and my landing seemed to have left me thrusting my hips towards the window in what could be misconstrued as an invitation.

"Hi," I said. Then, because that didn't seem like enough, "This isn't what it looks like."

"It looks like you're trying to sneak out of the building," he replied.

I was wondering how to word my response when the entire hotel lurched dizzyingly. Beams and girders from all over the building joined together in a chorus of groans. Then the architecture gave in and began its final, inevitable journey to the ground.

I and the dwarf only had time to exchange a single terrified glance before everything began to shift ninety degrees from the norm. I tumbled through the window into the room, slamming into the dwarf as he struggled to remain upright and sending the pair of us rolling down the tilting hallway.

I was deaf and blind with a faceful of beard, and only became aware that we had been heading for another door when I felt it smash open beneath my spine. Fortunately we had rotated by the time we hit the window, and the dwarf went through first. He might have survived even that, had he not then landed on the cobblestones outside, driving thick glass shards into his important parts.

I, meanwhile, found myself sitting upright on his corpse, whose many broken bones had made it a surprisingly soft landing pad. I looked around, astonished at my good fortune, and my eyes met those of an equally astonished Barry.

Then a building fell on me.

I attempted to stand up, and succeeded, but my body didn't come with me. I pushed myself upwards, passing through several layers of rubble and unfazed guests before I emerged into the thin, grimy air of the dead world.

Barry and most of his minions had had more sense than I and retreated far enough to avoid injury, pulling the trebuchet with them. Barry floated with hands on hips, foot tapping upon thin air and mouth set into a thin line of irritation.

When I drew closer to him, I felt my spectral stomach lurch. In the dead world, his body was bathed in a dazzling incandescent light. And just like Drylda, he was full of Deleters. I counted five pairs of Deleter wings poking out of him, and three Deleter heads jutting out of his upper back. Deleter hands were caressing his scalp, magic sparkles bursting in showers from their fingertips and settling in his hair.

He was possessed. Taken over by some kind of magical monstrosity. No, I corrected myself; not possessed. It was still Barry's own personality under all that power, which meant he'd joined forces with the Deleters. And that was a hundred times worse.

# FIVE

Being trapped under rubble actually wasn't so bad. One or two of my bones needed resetting and I had to manually bash my skull back into shape against a bit of pipe, but after that I was fully functional, with nothing to do but relax and kill time counting the bricks. Several hours passed rather quickly before I was discovered by the latest incarnation of the dwarf I'd been lying on, no doubt looking to retrieve his equipment.

"Blimey, this one's a real mess," he exclaimed, as he and several of his colleagues lifted the largest piece of debris off my face.

"Hi."

"Oh. It's you." He grabbed me by the legs and pulled me out into the open air, the back of my head rattling unpleasantly against jagged rocks all the way.

Once I'd been laid out in the street for all to see, I heard a tongue clicking with the resonance of a hammer hitting a steel barrel. "Ugh," said Barry. "I'm starting to see a pattern. You and those walking blights you call friends always seem to be around whenever I'm being inconvenienced by a town full of corrupted innocents."

"It was like this when I got here," I muttered, but no-one was listening.

"Secure his arms behind him." He nodded to the dwarf, who pulled me up onto my knees and busied himself with binding my wrists. "Didn't think you'd ever have to face me again, did you? That's how you operate, isn't it, always running, never facing the consequences for the evil that you do?"

"You were the one trying to incinerate me," I pointed out.

My logic failed to impress. "Bind his legs, too." Barry watched the dwarf at work for a second before something occurred to him. "Is that normal rope?"

" . . . Yes, your majestic highness?" said the dwarf, in the half-questioning tone of someone who suspects that he's in trouble but can't fathom what for.

"He's a mage, you idiot!"

"Is that going to be a problem, lord?"

Barry groaned audibly and rubbed at his temple with a curious crackling sound. "Benjamin?"

"My lord," went the battle mage in the party, a swarthy, well-built human with one of those tragic black goatees that people grow when they have some kind of grudge against their own chins.

"Remind us what the first spell they teach you at Mage School is?"

Benjamin folded his arms smugly, the teacher's pet being given a chance to shine. "Removal of smell from a wet dog's fur."

"I meant the first offensive spell."

"Oh! Firebolt."

"Exactly. And what does a firebolt do to normal ropes?"

"It . . . lights them on fire?" went Benjamin slowly, watching Barry's expression.

"Yes, that's exactly what it does. Do you see the issue, Groyn?"

"I don't think I've got any other rope, your holiness," mumbled the dwarf named Groyn, twiddling the hemp between his sausagey fingers.

"Just cover his mouth so he can't say the incantation," sighed Barry.

"I thought you wanted to interrogate him, lord of wonder?"

A dangerous silence passed before Barry replied. He was clearly debating internally how many more minions he could atomize and still keep to schedule. "Okay then. We won't cover his mouth. Just shut him up if he tries to say the words."

"What words?"

"Benjamin?"

The mage held up a hand. "Arcanus Inferus Telechus," he incanted, making the appropriate finger waggles. A flaming sphere rocketed into the sky, scattering the seagulls.

"So if he starts saying that, cover his mouth."

"Yes, sir."

"Have you got your hacksaw?"

"Right here, lord," announced the dwarf, whipping one out from inside his jerkin.

"Good. Now, I'm going to ask you some questions, undead. And every time I hear an unhelpful answer, you're going to lose a body part."

I scoffed. It was a good scoff, too, probably one of my best. "I still don't feel pain, you know. You can't threaten me with torture."

To my surprise, Barry actually looked offended. "Torture? I bet you'd like that, wouldn't you. Me sinking down to your level. I wouldn't sully my hands with such barbaric tactics; it would undermine everything I believe in." He bent down until his face was inches from mine. I could feel heat radiating from it. "I know you don't feel pain. I know you think being undead gives you some kind of get-out clause for danger. But you've only got one body, and you're not even supposed to be in that one. This isn't torture. This is more like confiscation of stolen goods."

I'd rather hoped he'd forget about those undead resurrection rules. "Just ask your bloody questions," I said, sulkily.

"I shall. Now then, it's actually quite fortunate that you're here, since you were next on my list after this town. But there're another two of you deviants around to deal with. Where are they?"

"They went to New Pillock," I admitted. It was a betrayal, but Meryl and the priest were somewhere far away and unable to complain, while the hacksaw was right in front of me and very happy to be of service.

"New Pillock. I see." He tapped his chin. "And don't tell me. If we start running now we could have caught up with them within a few days, yes? Please don't think I was born yesterday."

"Does that mean you didn't like the way he answered your question, lord?" said the dwarf, eager to be back in the good graces.

"It most certainly does. Start with the leg. Just the foot and half the shin for now."

My exasperation reached vocal levels as I watched the hacksaw worry at my tibia. "Why are you doing this?!" I cried. "You're not getting justice for anyone! All the adventurers we killed just came back to life anyway! The villages we sacked . . . have you been to Applewheat lately?"

He scoffed. "This isn't about justice. This is about doing a job."

I didn't like the sound of that. "For the Deleters?"

"The angels are just servants. Handmaidens to a divine power you couldn't even begin to comprehend." He turned his eyes heavenwards and took up his pulpit stance mid-air. "The angels carried me to Him. He spoke to me from within a beautiful, shining form. He said His world has grown corrupt, and must be fixed. And if I help Him repair the corruption, then I will be given the glorious task of forever keeping the world in line with His divine vision."

For a moment I wished that the priest hadn't opted to go with Meryl. It would have been nice to have some competing lunacy on hand. "But . . . why you?"

"Because of my unwavering faith, I suppose."

"You suppose? So you don't know?"

"Of course I know! Shut up! Because I share his vision! A true utopia! Where every righteous man, woman and child will live for eternity, free from death and chaos and the fear of getting their spines pulled out!" He pointed a finger in my face. "You do not fit into that vision, and neither do your friends, and neither does this town!"

"Er, why does he need you to demolish Yawnbore?" I asked. "Why doesn't he just make his Deleters delete it? Come to think of it, why don't they just delete us?"

He rolled his eyes and made a frustrated noise, to cover up the fact that he was stalling for time. "Bec . . . we . . . ugh . . . why don't you just shut up?! This is supposed to be an inter- rogation! That means questions come from me! Ah, good." The dwarf handed him my left foot, still inside my favorite boot. "Benjamin?"

"*Arcanus Inferus Telechus*," chanted Benjamin, taking aim at the foot as Barry chucked it towards him. After a burst of orange flame both foot and boot were raining down upon us in little black specks.

"You say 'Ar-car-nus'?" I said, putting on what I hoped was a brave face. "I always pronounce it 'Ar-cay-nus'." I wiggled my fingers behind my back.

Benjamin's scoff was a lot better than Barry's, but I think still needed a bit of work to be at my level. Perhaps it was my no-nose thing. "Maybe that's how they teach it in the hick schools."

Barry glanced at him for a second, then cast a lightning bolt at his feet. Benjamin immediately screamed and collapsed, attempting to beat the flames out of his robe with his wizard staff. "Oh, for Si-Mon's sake," said Barry, bewilderingly. "He's trying to cast the spell, you idiots! Now he's got the first word out! Groyn!" Groyn started at the sound of his name. "If he starts saying any word that begins with 'inf', shut him up! Now tell me where your friends are!"

"All right, all right," I said hastily. "I'll tell you. It's not like I'll be the one cryin'. Us undead don't really stick together, you know?" I wiggled my fingers again.

"Tell me!"

"They're in very close vicini-ty," I said.

"Vicini-ty?" His brow furrowed. Then he froze, twice; firstly with realization, secondly with ice.

What Benjamin had failed to mention was that while Arcanus Inferus Telechus (firebolt) is indeed the very first offensive spell they teach you at mage college, the first *defensive* spell they teach you is Arcanus Cryonus Vicini (ice blast). It's a handy little workhorse that temporarily freezes everything in a small radius around the caster, invented three hundred years ago by the noted frost mage Frigham as a means of teaching his dog how to "stay."

I broke the frozen ropes off my wrists and knees. The ice encasing Barry and the few adventurers he hadn't slaughtered out of irritation was already cracking and breaking off in the pleasant seaside temperatures. The ice blast wasn't intended to be a devastating fight-winner; its purpose was to allow a mage enough time to either scarper or line up some of the bigger weapons in their arsenal. Since the ice blast *was* the bigger weapon in my arsenal, I went for the first option.

———

Running was difficult with one foot missing, but I figured if I could re-learn how to work an entire body after fifty years dead, then I could get the hang of this. Of course, the disorienting forty-five degree angle didn't help, and might have explained why I ran in the wrong direction and ended up on the beach.

This was the northern half of the beach, the part set aside for holidaymakers, separate from the docklands to the south. A rather morose-looking donkey stood hoof-deep in shingle next to a sign advertising rides upon his mangy back. An ancient wooden pier stretched out over the sea for moony-eyed lovers to walk along and discover there was nothing interesting on the other end, either.

From the town behind me I heard Barry smacking his minions around. The spell had lasted even less time than I'd hoped and I was fast running out of avenues. Trying to sneak back through the town to the main road would be analogous to dangling my dried-up knackers over a lion's mouth. I looked at the donkey, but it wasn't offering any other suggestions. So that was it, then. I was trapped between God and the deep blue sea.

I watched the deep blue sea roll patiently up and down for a second and eventually a little light came on in my head. Of course. I was still thinking like I was alive. For once, being undead was an advantage; I didn't have to cling to retro fashion trends like breathing.

I grabbed a few handfuls of shingle and stuffed every pocket in my robe, then waddled under the pier and into the water. I kept wading until the sunlight-dabbled surface was a good six feet above my head. Then I wrapped myself around a suitably heavy rock and waved off a couple of fish that were trying to nibble scraps off my face.

The adventurers were already there, running back and forth along the beach, searching for me. One of them, probably Benjamin, thundered his way along the pier. He stopped, flustered, at a railing directly above me, and glanced down.

I screwed my eyes shut and chanted inside my head, hoping he would move on. *I am a crab. I am thinking crabby thoughts. I am tightening my grip on this rock with my big red pincers.*

Eventually I heard him stomp sullenly back the way he came, and I relaxed the crab mindset. As I did so, a new thought arose: why didn't I just give myself up? Things had been so hectic lately that I'd almost lost sight of my actual goal. If Barry was working for the Deleters, and the Deleters were enforcing some glorious plan for the world that demanded my removal, they might just rub me out.

But then there was the question Barry had refused to answer—why were they making him demolish Yawnbore, rather than deleting it themselves? I still couldn't begin to grasp what, exactly, Barry and his ethereal sponsors were playing at. And then there was the fact that he had sawn my foot off.

The point was quickly becoming moot, as the adventurers had regrouped on the beach, abandoning the search. They came to some worried consensus, then disappeared back into the town.

I was in no hurry to surface. I rearranged myself on my rock, brushed off some confused and amorous female crabs, and tried to come up with a plan.

# SIX

Seven plans later, I noticed with a start that the sun had gone down. The thing about being undead is that without the usual human naggings of sleep, food and air, it's easy to lose track of time when you're deep in thought—doubly so when you're being distracted by cold seawater and naughty fish.

All I'd come up with was that I had to get to Lolede. And since there were no ships docked in Yawnbore, I'd have to swim. It wouldn't be a very stimulating trip, and there would probably be a lot of sharks that might understandably confuse my body for chum, but there was no other option. The Magic Resistance would know what to do. I'd lost Drylda, so uncovering the mystery of her condition was on hold, but that was hardly my top concern at that point.

No sense wasting time. I sat up. Then I kept right on going. At first I thought my pockets had split and disgorged their stones, but then I realized that the rock I had been sitting on was in fact a stout treasure chest, which was now connected to a grappling hook being hauled up from above.

Overhead was the underside of a rowing boat, a stark black turd shape against the moonlight. I tried to get away, but by the time I figured out that the grappling hook had also snagged a big handful of my robe, my head was already breaking surface.

In the darkness, I couldn't make out the occupants of the boat, but they didn't look like adventurers, or at least not like any of the ones I'd seen with Barry in Yawnbore. I decided to hope for the best and play dead, a role for which I had unmatched qualifications.

"Don't remember this lad bein' 'ere when we sent the chest down," said a gruff voice in a strong sailor accent.

"Did we kill anyone last time we hit town? I can't remember. I was pretty drunk," said a slightly more refined voice.

"Hey, Slippery John knows this guy!" said an extremely familiar voice. "How've you been? Slippery John was wondering where you ended up."

I kept my tongue firmly lolled.

"'E's dead, Slippery John, 'e's not gonna talk back," said the first voice.

"Nah, nah, nah. He's not dead. Well, Slippery John means, he is dead, but he still talks and moves around. Look, you can tell he's not properly dead 'cos the corners of his mouth are twitching."

I gave up. "Look," I said, prompting a yelp of fright from the two pirates. "You could just throw me back and forget this ever happened. It would make all our lives a lot less complicated."

"Slippery John was hoping Slippery John would run into you again," said Slippery John. He looked the same as always, but now he was wearing an eyepatch, as was each of his two new friends. "Wondering if that quest idea of yours is still open?"

"What quest idea?"

"That quest where Slippery John escorts you to Lolede City. Slippery John's been onto some of Slippery John's contacts in the Suicide Squad and they're really into the idea."

"What Suicide Squad?"

"You know, the Magic Resistance. The secret council of magicians who are investigating ways to end the Deleter plague and restore death and entropy to the universe." He looked at me in silence for a moment. "Slippery John is wondering if he should have said all that."

"Wait." I jerked a thumb vaguely in the direction of the cacophony of demolition work coming from Yawnbore. "You're not working for Barry?"

By now the two pirates flanking Slippery John were over their initial shock at my reanimated status and had drawn themselves to their full sitting height to look down at me through their nostril hairs. "The Bloated Rats don't work fer no man but Cap'n Scar," said the one on the left. I was adjusting to the dark, now, and could make out that he was in fact a bloated pirate with a ratty beard.

"Or first mate Dodgy Bill if Captain Scar's sick," added the other pirate, who was thin and probably from a higher class background, given that his blond hair looked like it occasionally came within earshot of a comb.

"Or second mate Smilin' Phil if they're both out of it."

"Slippery John wouldn't work for Barry again," said Slippery John. "Maybe it's one of those strange thief-senses at work but I swear there's something a little bit odd about him now."

"A little bit, yes," I said irritably.

"Slippery John was trying to buy passage with these boys when he brought that barrier down."

"Yes, about that, we should be getting back to the ship," said the posher pirate. "Will you be coming along, mister?"

"I suppose so," I said, with a sigh.

"First the fishin' trip, now this," muttered the stout pirate as they took up the oars. "Why do we always get stuck with the smelliest loot?"

The Black Pudding was a small but well-armed affair with large numbers of cannons poking out from the top deck like seasick tourists. It was painted entirely black and was concealed from the eyes of Yawnbore in a cheeky little cove just around the bay.

The moment I clambered up onto the deck, Slippery John's two escorts grabbed me by the shoulders and flung me onto my face. A gap-toothed cheer went up among the assembled crew.

"Aharr!" went a booming voice from above. "What 'ave we 'ere, my lads? Not much meat on 'im, is there? Maybe we should throw 'im to the sharks!" The crew cheered raucously, raising their cutlasses to the sky.

Slowly, I looked up. A pair of gigantic black boots came into view. They were followed by the tattered hem of a black woollen dress over a dense network of petticoats. My gaze continued traveling upwards until I could look the wearer in the eye.

"Ew," she said involuntarily as she took in my face. "Looks like someone already did."

"We dredged 'im up from the bay, Cap'n Scar," said one of my handlers. "'Parently he's some new kind of dead where yer get to be a bit alive an' all."

Captain Scar was an enormous, matronly woman, whose tattered, old-fashioned dress appeared to be held together by a swordbelt and bandolier. She reminded me very much of the senior dinner lady from my old school, who had once took on the entire school cricket team at Tug o' War. She hadn't won, obviously, but no-one could deny that the woman had balls.

Her pirate crew—every single one of whom were sporting eyepatches—was certainly in awe of her. There were twenty of them clustered around the sides of the deck, giving her a wide berth as she stood with hands on hips. They watched with the terrified but respectful eyes of trapped zoo patrons watching an escaped gorilla decide whose children to eat first.

"It's cool," said Slippery John, smiling fearlessly from behind his impenetrable shield of stupidity. "He's with Slippery John."

Captain Scar relaxed, and most of the crew began to sheathe their cutlasses. All that jeering and threatening business had apparently been some kind of formality. "Er," I began. "Are you the ones who looted the hotel?"

"Saw that, did ye?" said Captain Scar proudly. "Did a nice bit of work on it, aye?" She pumped her fist obscenely. "Weren't very satisfyin', though, like. Everyone just lay flat on their back an' took it, and the spark just weren't there, ye know? Sort of like me first marriage." Up until then, I'd never been sure how one laughs "uproariously," but Captain Scar demonstrated it beautifully.

"I'm looking for passage to Lolede," I said, rising up to my knees.

"Aye, well," said Captain Scar, before firing from the corner of her mouth a mass of chewing tobacco the size of my fist. "Ye're gonna 'ave trouble there. Firstly we're not a soddin' taxi service. And secondly there's a barrier stoppin' us from leavin' the bay."

"The magic barrier?"

"Aye, it extends a few 'undred yards out to sea. We can sail right up to it but at the last second we jus' get pushed away. Sort of like me second husband!" She slapped me between the shoulder blades hard enough to rattle all my remaining teeth. "We sail in fer some shore leave and find everyone in the town's come over all weird. So we're about to pack up and go when that Barry lubber arrives with 'is catapult and puts 'is magic barrier up."

"It's a trebuchet," I said.

"No it's not, it's a magic barrier. Don't be stoopid. So 'e put it up and we've been stuck 'ere fer about a day. Hidden in the cove, mind. 'E doesn't know we're 'ere, yet."

"If I help you get past the barrier, can I get a ride to Lolede?"

Captain Scar stroked her chin. It was like watching someone caress a brick with a ham hock. "Ye know anythin' about magic?"

"I'm a mage," I said, deciding not to reveal that I'd never technically graduated mage school and only knew four spells: two for combat, one for conjuring water and one for dog grooming. "Also, I can pass through the barrier."

"Oh aye, and what makes ye so special?"

"Because . . . I'm undead. I'm dead as far as the rules of nature and magic are concerned."

"Sounds like me third marriage." I nimbly ducked as laughter broke out again and a hand like a bagful of steaks swung through the air. Then she thought in silence for some time, stroking her impressive chin as her mental cogs turned. "So," she said, finally. "How would yer go about switchin' off the barrier?"

I put on my best expert voice. "Magic fields only turn off if the caster wills it, runs out of mana, falls unconscious or dies."

"We could've figured that out, lad." She snapped her fingers with a sound like a sausage striking a kettledrum. "Nah, I've got a better idea. Why don't yer just make us all undead?"

"Er," I said. "Er . . . er."

"Aye," said Scar, grinning excitedly and chewing a black thumbnail. "If yer make us all undead like you, we'll all be able to go through the barrier!"

"But we'll be undead forever," piped up a nameless pirate.

"We'll be ghost pirates!" cried Scar. Some of the pirates looked at each other in confusion for a moment, then the realization sank into their brains with a burst of childlike joy.

"We'll become legends!" cried first mate Dodgy Bill, leaping to his feet. "They'll be scarin' each other with stories of the ghost pirates across the seventeen seas!"

"We'll set up base on an island with a big mountain shaped like a skull!" went Vacuous David.

"I'll cut the sails up so they look all shredded and scary like!" added Corpulent Neil.

"We'll invade coastal towns and walk through walls and look at all the teenage daughters in their underpants!" added Smilin' Phil. This brought on a round of particularly lusty "aharr"s.

"I can't walk through walls!" I yelled over the growing chorus. It only silenced them for an instant.

"I thought yer said yer could," said Phil.

"Magic barriers! I said I can walk through magic barriers!"

"Then we'll walk through magic walls and look at all the wizard daughters!"

Captain Scar silenced her excited crew with a single clap of her hands that violently blasted air into my face. "Right then, it's decided." She pulled her lacey collar away from her massive neck. "Me first. Give us a quick bite. Not too 'ard. And don't worry, I won't get too attached." She nudged me in the ribs.

I stared at a large and prominent vein on her throat, which was thumping as if playful kittens were rolling around inside. "No . . . no, this is extremely wrong."

A noticeable darkening of mood signaled that I had just put my remaining foot in it. A subtle hiss of disapproval was running through the audience. Captain Scar covered her neck and drew herself up, nostrils flaring. "Do ye know what 'appened to the last man 'oo said 'no' to the Bloated Rats?" she said, levelly.

"You gave him a ride to Lolede?" I said, being a stupid bastard.

"No."

"We did, technically," said Dodgy Bill helpfully.

Captain Scar grinned. "Oh aye, yeah, we sent him to Lolede. Also we sent him to a few other places. Simultaneously, like. So ye might want to reconsider yer position before we reconsider it for yeh."

I reconsidered, but my position wasn't showing any improvement. "I can't . . . make you undead, I just—" I had to stop talking because a cutlass the size of a surfboard was pressing on my vocal chords. Instantly the rest of the pirates followed Captain Scar's lead and drew their swords with a deafening scrape of metal, until twenty lengths of sharpened steel were pointing at my heart. Slippery John sat on a nearby keg, cheerfully watching the drama unfold.

"So undeath's too good fer the likes of us, is it, fancypants?" said Captain Scar touchily.

"It's just not transmittable by bite," I said, trying to move my adams apple as little as possible. "It doesn't work like that."

"Aye, all right," said Scar reasonably. "Maybe we'll just chop yer into bits and see if we can figure out how it does work."

I could see that honesty wasn't doing me any favors in this company. "All right, all right," I said, attempting to nudge the cutlass away with a fingertip. "You have passed the test. Your insistence and base threats have proven you worthy of my, er, wondrous dark gift."

"That's more like it," grumbled Scar, withdrawing her sword. The pirates reluctantly followed suit, but kept their blades unsheathed in case I tried being difficult again. "Where do yer want us?"

"Well, that's sort of the thing. It's a complicated process. I need to get hold of some reagents, some, uh, dragon . . . moss. And the . . . eyes of a . . ." I took a desperate glance around. " . . . Seagull."

"Men!" bellowed Captain Scar. "Take arms! We're goin' into town to loot the magic shops!"

I displayed my palms and shook them before the "aharr"s got too loud. "No no no, wait wait wait. If you do that, Barry'll know we're here!"

"That's another three 'no's, laddie. Ye're walkin' a pretty fine line. It won't matter if 'e figures out we're 'ere. We'll swipe what we need, leg it back to the ship, you work yer oogie boogies and we'll be off."

The audience were getting more and more unruly the more times I tried to pull them back from a state of beard-chewing overexcitement. "N— I mean, yes, but we still wouldn't be able to pass through the barrier."

"Why not?"

"Because," I looked down. "The floor."

"What?"

"I mean, the ship. The ship wouldn't be able to pass through, because . . . it's . . . made of wood. Organic. It's technically life, the barrier wouldn't let it through."

They seemed to buy it. They put their pillaging sacks down and scratched their heads, thinking.

"I suppose," said Scar, "we could kill that vicar, then, while we're there."

Relief flooded out of me like a burst of gas from a volcanic vent. I nodded as fast as I could, causing something to dislodge inside my skull and rattle around. "And then you'll take me to Lolede?"

"Suppose so. We were 'eadin' there anyway for Slippery John. And the music festival's comin' up there soon."

"Slippery John wants to take a quick look around the countryside before we go," piped up Slippery John, hopping onto his feet. "Slippery John wants one last chance to look for Drylda."

"Drylda? I left her in a wheelbarrow on the way into town," I said, because my guard was down and I couldn't stop myself in time.

"What?! She was with you?!" It was the first time I'd ever seen Slippery John genuinely angry, rather than just stupid or pleased with himself. "What perversity have you been inflicting upon Slippery John's woman, villainous lich?!"

I put my hands up as the swords came out again. "I didn't do anything! I was just taking her to get her looked at! Since when is she your woman?"

"She's Slippery John's fiancée! Slippery John asked her to marry him just before the Battle of Applewheat!"

"And she said yes?"

He looked momentarily guilty. "Sort of. In a fashion. Didn't say no, at any rate." He turned to Captain Scar. "Slippery John has to go get her."

"Oh come on," I said, determined to not take at least one person's bullshit today. "We don't have time."

"Maybe yer don't know who yer dealing with," said Captain Scar, the cutlass finding my throat again. "That's Slippery John, that is. King o' the Lolede Thieves. Slayer of the Necromancer Lord Dreadgrave." Slippery John coughed. "An' if 'e says we're goin' back for 'is woman, we're goin' back for 'is woman. Or to be more specific . . ."

# SEVEN

To be more specific, *we* were going back for his woman. As in, Slippery John and me, alone, in the rowboat. Barry and his cult were distracted by their demolition work, so at least we wouldn't have to worry about them, assuming they had all recently undergone severe brain injuries.

This was the plan: We'd land at the very end of the beach, far away from Barry and his crew, reunite with Drylda, and push her barrow around the force field to the cliffs north of town, where the Black Pudding could stop to pick it up once the barrier was off. When she was in position, I'd cast a fire-bolt into the night sky as a signal for the pirates to begin the assault. Unfortunately, it would also be a fairly obvious signal for the newly-empowered Barry.

"So, creature of darkness," said Slippery John, after several minutes of rowing in awkward silence. "When they were stitching your corpse back together, did they put the lungs in backwards?"

I treated him to a long, glowy-eyed stare. "What?"

"Slippery John was just wondering if that's how you got so good at talking out of your arse."

The first stare went down so well I gave him another. "You've been working on that for the last twenty minutes, haven't you."

He was puffed up with triumph. "You might be able to fool those grog-addled corsairs, but nothing slips past Slippery John." He leaned back, repulsively pleased with himself.

"Which is ironic, when you think about it."

The rowboat landed not far from where I'd first submerged myself, near the pier. In the distance the creaking of a trebuchet alternated with the crunches and rattles of masonry in distress. Barry's crew were hard at work in the soon-to-be-not-so-high-rent suburbs in the south end of town.

I immediately hopped out of the boat and began scraping up a fresh supply of shingle for my robe pockets.

"What're you doing, undead?" said Slippery John.

"I'm going to swim to Lolede."

"Why? There's a ship going there."

"Yes, and when the crew figure out that I can't make them into ghost pirates they're going to fire all my body parts out of different cannons."

"Ah, that's just pirates. All mouth, no pantaloons. They'll forget all about it by the time we're out of the bay. Slippery John thinks you're being too hard on them. After they fitted you with that nice wooden leg, too."

I kicked at the shingle bitterly. "They broke it off of a stool, for god's sake. There's a splinter sticking right in my stump."

"And anyway, what about my quest? You said Slippery John could escort you to the Suicide Squad in Lolede."

"I'll find them myself."

"And how're you gonna do that, dead man? Ask directions? Saunter up to the front door and ask to speak to the manager? Think about it. If they gave their address out to any old time-waster, the Deleters would just find them and rub them out, yeah? They never use the same meeting location twice. When they want you to do quests for them you have to put a bag on your head and have the details whispered to you from inside a toilet cubicle."

There he was, standing smugly on the darkened beach, little arms folded, one little beady eye shining gleefully from behind his little mustache and pirate eyepatch. It would have been so easy to stove his little chubby head in with a rock. "All right," I said, sighing the dust out of my lungs. "Let's just find your stupid catatonic girlfriend."

The streets were deserted. Barry's thugs must already have picked up all the townsfolk. We made our way west through the maze of alleyways towards the main road where I'd entered the town. Slippery John insisted on darting stealthily from cover to cover while I sulkily tromped down the middle of the roads.

"So she just stopped moving?" he asked as we neared our destination.

" . . . Yeah," I said, deciding not to mention my part in Drylda's current condition.

He clicked his tongue. "The final stage of the Syndrome," he said, sagely. "Did I tell you about that?"

"You did, yes. So this whole mission is totally pointless. She's not going to be of any use to you."

"Slippery John doesn't see the point in explaining this to you, corpse. You'd need things like feelings and actual human decency to understand. True love is blind to petty flaws like total catatonia."

"I get the impression you're hoping it'll be blind to a few other things, too. Anyway, there she is."

We were back at the border of Yawnbore, and the feature-less, hilly, utterly-devoid-of-lunatics grasslands that surrounded the town had never looked more enticing. Drylda was exactly where I'd left her, half-in and half-out of an Applewheat grocer's rusted wheelbarrow. Slippery John bounded up to her excitedly, smacked straight into unexpect-edly solid thin air, and fell flat on his back.

Meanwhile, I strolled through the barrier and idly took up the wheelbarrow handles. "Shall we?"

Slippery John sat up, feeling his jaw for loose teeth. "Something's not right. Why's she all limp?"

I picked up her wrist for a second. It dropped back down with a jangle of bracelets. "I thought that was the last stage of the Syndrome. Isn't it?"

"The last stage of the Syndrome is supposed to make them stiffen up. They stand in a nonchalant macho pose with their legs apart and their chest thrust out forever. You want to make them sit or lie down, you have to break their knees with a mallet. They've never gone all floppy like that. Are you sure she's not just dead?"

I felt her. "I dunno, she's pretty warm."

Slippery John flinched, his hands pressed up against the invisible barrier like a gesture of placation. "Slippery John would prefer it if you didn't put your hand there."

I glanced down, then back up. "What's Slippery John going to do about it?"

He scowled from behind the invisible wall. "Why do you feel you have to antagonize me, servant of evil?" A beat. "Actually, Slippery John sort of answered his own question, there."

A loud crashing noise rang out from somewhere behind us, a safe distance away and yet upsettingly close. We spun around just in time to watch the historic town hall collapse into a pile of historic timbers. Barry was ahead of schedule. I ducked into what I assumed was a stealthy crouch and pushed Drylda away from the ongoing destruction, Slippery John keeping parallel pace on the other side of the barrier.

When we reached the cliff edge at the top of the hill, we were afforded a slightly acrophobic bird's eye view of Yawnbore. I needn't have worried. Barry was still occupied with the southern half of the town, most of which was already little more than an unusually large gravel driveway. The tallest remaining structure south of the clock tower was Barry's trebuchet, poking out above layers of ruins like a curious gazelle peering over tall grass.

From here I could even see the pirates' cove, right past the town at the other side of the bay, and if I strained my undead eyes, the glint of Captain Scar's spyglass at the ship's prow. Or stern. Or whatever the front bit is called.

"You going to send up that firebolt, then, villainous wraith?"

"Seems a shame to interrupt such a peaceful evening," I muttered, as another building collapsed. I waited for the cover of a suitably large demolition, then held my hand aloft and set my fingers a-waggling. "*Arcanus, Inferus . . .*"

I stopped. I had suddenly noticed movement on the outskirts of the town. Slippery John followed my gaze. "Hey, aren't they friends of yours?"

"Oh, god, no," I whispered.

Two distant figures were walking up the main road into Yawnbore, exactly the same one I had took. The first figure was wearing pigtails that looked like two guinea pigs were trying to escape from its head, and the second one was walking with its hands behind its back, pretending to have nothing to do with the first.

"Hey, Slippery John thinks you might want to finish off that spell."

I looked at my upraised hand just in time to see my sleeve catch fire. I snapped it off my robe and stamped on it, then stared at Meryl and the priest again. They were only blocks away from Barry's operation. I broke into a run.

Then, two steps later, I broke out of it. A lot of conflicting thoughts were having a shouting argument in my head. If I couldn't reach Meryl in time, she'd stumble right into Barry, true to idiot form.

But I didn't give a furious flying toss about Meryl. She was a big enough girl to take responsibility for her own stupid actions.

But then I looked down at my wooden leg. I imagined myself hundreds of years down the line, still pursuing my quest for deletion, my non-regenerating body gradually being worn down by repeated damage and wear and tear until there was nothing left of me but half a skull dragging itself along by its eyebrow.

"Slippery John wishes he could get away with your kind of indecisiveness in Slippery John's fast-paced life of adventure and peril," said Slippery John pointedly.

Meryl had been the only thing holding me together since my rebirth. She might have been offensively chirpy and a rabid nationalist, but at least she knew how to sew. I ran. Slippery John remained where he was, leaning on the barrier and making comforting small talk with Drylda's indifferent carcass.

By the time I reached the main road, they had already moved on into the inner suburbs. Fortunately, the priest had been scattering pamphlets on people's driveways. I followed the trail, trying to keep as quiet as possible with my new leg clacking woodenly against the cobblestones.

I was passing by a cottage home with a particularly well-kept lawn and an inept attempt at topiary, when I heard noises from the adjoining street.

"—Ust wondering if you'd seen our friend anywhere," came Meryl's voice. "You remember? Thin, no nose, talks like a complete miseryguts all the time?"

"Yes, I remember him." Barry's voice sounded irritated. "I'm just surprised that you're coming to me about it."

I hopped over the fence. My foot caught on the crossbar and I fell on my face into the immaculate grass, turning it into an impressive stealth roll as I freed myself. Then I gathered myself up onto hands and knees and crawled past the cottage to the rear garden, where I took up position behind a conifer, gently pushing the leaves aside with one hand.

I was looking out onto a street that seemed to mark the border of Barry's demolition work for the day. Every building in my field of vision had now been leveled. The timeshare holiday homes of an entire continent's middle class lay in a thin layer of shattered bricks and plaster.

Barry and his squad of mercenaries were nearby, gathered around the trebuchet with their backs to me. Meryl and the priest were a few yards down the road. It was like a stand-off between two miniature armies, one of which had apparently forgotten it was at war.

"It's never too late to bury the hatchet, that's what Dreadgrave taught us," said Meryl proudly.

"I remember that hatchet," muttered one of the adventurers.

"So I just wanted you to know I forgive you for trying to burn us and ask if Jim passed through here."

Barry scratched his head. He seemed more confused than malevolent. "Well . . . actually, yes, he did. We had him destroyed."

Meryl's smile froze. "You what?"

"You said you destroyed him, Benjamin?" said Barry to the mage in his employ.

The pack of mercenaries passed around a few panicky glances, then all of them made a brave attempt to simultaneously hide behind Benjamin. "Er, yes, that's right," said their reluctant spokesman. "Trapped him on the beach, blew him up. Pow! Just like we said. Nothing but ashes left."

"Ya, and dey orl bloo out to sea," said the freshly resurrected northern barbarian bloke. "And dat's vy dere's no body and joo can totally stop tinking about it."

"We destroyed him because he defiantly refused to reveal your location," said Barry. He was trying to be triumphant about it but Meryl's puppy-dog stare and oozing tears were making him visibly uncomfortable. He gave an embarrassed cough that resounded like a thunderclap. "So . . . now we're going to destroy you, and you've rendered his sacrifice moot. Sorry."

A very awkward moment of silence passed as Meryl took this in, mouth quivering.

"Behold, I have brought this minion of heresy to undergo your proper judgement," barked the priest suddenly, who knew a turning of the tide when he saw it. "May her smitation be deservedly swift, my brother in God."

"But . . . what did we ever do to you?" said Meryl, her cheeks swelling up and something burbling disgustingly in the back of her throat.

Barry puffed himself up, clearly preparing to deliver the same line of bullshit he'd fed me. "I am the avatar of a divine power," he said, grandly. "The undead are aberrations to His . . ." His enthusiasm died, withering away against Meryl's pathetic stare like butter under a level 60 Infernal Destructoblast. He turned his back on his targets. "Oh, just blast them."

"Yes, blast her," said the priest smugly, folding his arms and taking a step back.

"Blast both of them."

"Yes, blast both of her legs," said the priest as fast as he could. "Her sinful, whorish legs."

I was waiting for Meryl to don her usual set of reality blinkers and say something chipper and blasé in the face of annihilation. She didn't. Her shoulders were slumped and her head was hanging glumly. Her pigtails seemed to be drooping like the ears of a dog cornered by a master with a rolled-up newspaper. The moonlight shone off globdules of gray, viscous tears on her cheeks.

Benjamin held a hand out towards her and began to twiddle like a pro. "Arcanus, Inferus, Maxima . . ."

"Maxima" is an all-purpose word added to an incantation to amplify the spell's effect, generally to the point of leaving the caster completely exhausted for a good ten or twenty minutes. There wouldn't be enough left of Meryl's head to spread on toast.

A second passed.

Suddenly, I was standing out in the street, off balance. My wooden leg had somehow found its way into my hands, which were still reverberating from an extremely powerful impact. Benjamin lay on his back, a comically large lump rising out of his hair and arcane fire still crackling about his fingers.

All eyes were upon me in a frozen tableau of surprise. The only sound was the bush behind me gently rustling back into place. Barry, who had been floating disgustedly away from the scene, stopped and spun around. Any moment now, I thought, someone is going to take the initiative and get the action going again. And it would probably be better if it were me. I crouched, grabbed Benjamin's sparking hand, and pointed it skywards.

"*Telechus*?" I said.

I hadn't been sure how advanced a mage Benjamin was, but judging by the power of the blast he must have at least been a post-graduate. My vision whited out, and a deafening roar flooded my ears.

My vision cleared after a few moments. Benjamin and I were unharmed, of course. It's a legal standard for spells to come pre-installed with a complex system of sub-spells that protect the caster or casters from harm. Otherwise there would have been a lot of mages running around with blackened stumps where their forearms should have been.

The adventurers had taken the worst of the blast. Every single one of them was flat on their back, arms and legs protectively curled up like cockroaches, groaning like rusty garden gates. Thin columns of smoke were rising from where their hair and eyebrows had been.

Meryl and the priest, who had been furthest away, were stunned, but standing. Meryl snapped out of it first and ran to my side as I hastily lodged my wooden leg back into the stump with a sickening thump. "They said you were dead!"

"I am," was the obvious response.

"They said they destroyed you!"

"Well, they didn't. Let's go."

My first instinct was to get the hell away from the scene before the adventurers could regain their senses. I had my fists clenched and one leg raised in preparation for breaking into a run when a wall of holy white flame burst forth from the ground, surrounding us.

"You said you destroyed him!" said Barry, floating into view from his hiding place behind the trebuchet. Little white sparks were bursting from his furious eyes. "Clearly you didn't! And yet you said you did! That's just . . . not professional!"

I could have run through the fire and hoped for the best. I could also hypothetically have existed with all my skin burnt off. But it still seemed like a better plan than standing and waiting for Barry to start smiting . . .

Something crashed to the street nearby. Everyone turned to see a brick rattling to a halt on the ground.

"Er," said Barry. "Where did the sunlight go?" He looked up, and was immediately answered by a piece of plaster bouncing off his nose. He opened his mouth to say something along the lines of "ow" when there was a horrible wet crunching sound and a hefty chunk of cornice was suddenly sitting where his head had been.

Barry and his team had been working to bring down a sturdy two-story post office before Meryl's interruption, and the impact of Benjamin's blast had encouraged it to finish the job by itself. Now it was bending slowly towards the ground as if it had been punched in the gut, sprinkling loose objects and architectural features as a prelude to a spectacular collapse.

"Run," I suggested.

Holding our arms over our heads like evening commuters caught in the rain, Meryl, the priest, and I made it past the stricken building moments before it smashed to the ground. A great cloud of brown dust billowed out, discouraging the few adventurers who were on their feet and trying to give chase.

"Weren't you in New Pillock?" I asked Meryl, as we ran towards the coast. "Given up on the revolution?"

"On the contrary!" she said, thrilled by my question. "The people of Borrigarde have risen up! A mighty fist of guerrilla resistance swept across the land, and the reins of power were seized from the Pillock occupying forces in a historic battle by dawn!"

I jogged thoughtfully in silence for a few steps, trying to process this. "What."

"An interim government has been formed and a new age of hope and liberty has begun. Our people's spirits have been carried through these difficult times by the stories of a man, a pureblood Borrigardian, who rose from death itself to carve out a legend!"

I was certain she'd been repeating that to herself the whole way here. "Please don't say you've been telling them about me."

"The stories of your exploits inspire our fighting men!" A pause. "I might have exaggerated a little. But they're really impressed with how you rose to the rank of Executive Rat Pit Administrator so quickly. Everyone wants to meet you, Jim! There's talk of a seat in the government! You're a hero to the people!"

By this point we'd arrived back at the coast. "I already told you I don't go for the 'hero' thing," I said distractedly, looking for an escape route.

"Ho really? So what was all that business back there if it wasn't leaping to the rescue?"

From somewhere behind us came the crunching of heavy adventurer boots coming across freshly-created gravel. I ran into the beach and started scraping up shingle. "That was sort of a reflex action," I said, stuffing my pockets. "Come on. Pick up some stones."

"What for?"

"We need to hide under the sea."

"Right." She stirred the pebbles uncertainly with a toe. "So what're the stones for?"

"To weigh you down."

"Oh I see! Of course. Sorry." She turned to the priest, who was watching disdainfully with arms folded. "We need to pick up some stones!"

He sniffed. "The day I scrabble in the dust for my gratifications is UNGH."

I looked up just in time to see Meryl and the priest felled like bowling pins by a flying donkey before its musty flank hit me full in the face, knocking me off my feet. I spent a disoriented second struggling to push the hairy, foul-smelling mass away before it hurtled off into the sky with a single despairing hee-haw.

Benjamin the mage walked slowly towards us, hands still raised from casting Level 12 Animal Levitation. "Found you," he said, with murder in his eyes.

"Barry's dead," I pointed out. "You can stop doing his bidding now."

"Oh, no, you misunderstand me, old boy. *Arcanus*. This is entirely for me. *Inferus*." Bolts of fire magic crawled up and down his forearm. "Finishing another man's spell, by god, the cheek of it. *Maxima*. Is that another thing they teach you in peasant school?"

He'd gotten his magic reserves back quicker than I thought; that little cudgel-induced nap had apparently been very restful. I wondered if there was anything I could say between now and the next magic word that would cause Benjamin and I to become firm friends.

"Tele . . ." he began, before something behind us caught his eye. "Is that a pirate shi—" He quickly left the scene, horizontally and on the business end of a cannonball.

The Black Pudding was doing a pretty good job of making the pathetic Yawnbore coastline seem epic as it creaked and "aharr"ed its way along, firing again and again at what remained of the town and Barry's cowering army. Three rowboats on the near side of the ship were steadily filling up with cutlass-waving corsairs, looking forward to a good old pillage.

"Friends of yours?" asked Meryl.

"Oh, balls," I said, quickly getting to my feet. I sprinted along the pier towards the ship, waving my hands for attention. "STOP LOWERING THE BOATS!" I yelled over the cannon fire. "WE HAVE TO GO NOW!"

The massive bulk of Captain Scar stepped up to the ship's prow. She held her hands to her mouth and her equally massive voice boomed out across the water. "WHY DO YER ALWAYS HAVE TO BE SUCH A BUZZ KILLER?!"

"BARRY'S DEAD! BARRIER'S DOWN! WE HAVE TO GO NOW BEFORE HE GETS HIMSELF RESUR-RECTED!"

"WHAT ABOUT THE DRAGON MOSS?!"

I thought quickly. "TURNS OUT I HAD SOME IN MY POCKET THE WHOLE TIME! STOP LOWERING THE BOATS AND WE'LL COME OUT TO YOU!"

"ARE YE SURE BARRY'S DEAD, MATEY?!"

I paused on the verge of diving off the pier. "YES!" My throat was beginning to feel very rough.

"ONLY 'E'S LOOKING PRETTY FRISKY TO ME!!"

Somewhere behind me, I heard the angry lurch of a slightly damaged trebuchet, followed by the sound of a heavy payload whistling through the air. I glanced up just in time to see a loose collection of half-bricks batter the Black Pudding's crow's nest, whose occupant had the presence of mind to stop waving his cutlass around and dive into the sea.

Barry was alive again, his head none the worse for its ordeal. His anger had become a tangible force, crackling around him in a semitransparent white sphere.

"I," he hissed, sparkling white energy bursting from his mouth and eyes, "have a SCHEDULE!"

A collection of heavy bricks rose unbidden from the ground and collected themselves in the trebuchet's sling. Barry waved his arm, and the trebuchet flung another payload across the bay, this time leaving the top part of the Black Pudding's middenmast hanging at an unhealthy angle.

There was a blast of cannons, and the Pudding returned fire. Two cannonballs were aimed at Barry and seemed to be dead on target until they reached Barry's shield, whereupon they halted in mid-air and split into droplets of molten steel.

"You can't stop me!!" he roared. "I have GOD on my side!"

I looked around for the priest, feeling certain he'd have something to say about that. He was still on the section of beach where he'd been knocked down, watching Meryl, who appeared to be desecrating Benjamin's latest corpse. I watched, baffled, as she gathered his top half into her arms and waddled towards an oblivious Barry, holding out the dead mage's still-sparkling hand like . . .

Like some kind of handheld cannon. I swore so loud that the spiders in my lungs had to cover their childrens' ears, then started running back towards Meryl. I knew what she was planning and I knew what would happen if she tried it.

"No!" I cried, muted by another futile cannon blast at precisely the worst moment.

"Tel-ech-us," I heard Meryl announce, pointing Benjamin roughly in Barry's direction.

Several complicated things happened. Or rather, one very simple thing happened for several complicated reasons.

Magic can go wrong in so many fascinating ways you have to spend six months at mage school copying out the rule book before they'll even teach you the wet dog spell. It's certainly possible to cast a spell with the fresh corpse of a man who's already said most of the words, because the magic stays stored up in his body; it's just that doing so is really, really stupid. Magic is a living thing, inclined to all the same bloody-minded pettiness of other living things, and there are two things it really doesn't like: being cast by a dead guy (properly dead, not the inferior Dreadgrave brand) and being cast by an amateur.

The result of either was generally what we in the trade call "a voyage to the cock-up peninsula." Meryl was attempting both. By the time she finished saying the word I had almost reached her, so I was around just in time to take a full-scale magical blowback right in the mush.

After my eyes started working again and my ears stopped ringing, I discovered that I was in the air and the entire town was traveling away from me at great speed. I made the mistake of wondering how I'd gotten through that intact, at which point I made intimate contact with the Black Pudding's figurehead spine-first. I heard a sound like a wooden ruler breaking over someone's knee, then felt my limp carcass flop down into the water.

I tried to start swimming, but my limbs were obstinately refusing to respond. I floated on my back for a while, staring up at the night sky and slightly misaligned figurehead, listening to the distant sounds of Yawnbore: the crackling of massive fires and a succession of little follow-up explosions trying to leech off the success of the first.

Then I heard the splashing of an inept swimmer coming up to my side, and Meryl's face moved into view. "Jim! Are you all right?"

"My spine's broken and I can't move. You?"

"One or two liquefied internal organs. Nothing I was really using."

"I, too, am once again spared, that I would complete my God-given destiny," added the priest, like anyone cared.

The pirates let a rope down, so Meryl tied it around my legs and I was hauled upside-down to the deck. On the way up, I had a chance to get an inverted look at what remained of Yawnbore after the disastrous magical hissy-fit. Most of the seafront buildings were burning merrily, and I hazarded a guess that the thin layer of ash and blackened body parts around the splintered remains of a trebuchet were all that remained of Barry and his crew. Perhaps he would appreciate Meryl's blunder keeping the demolition on schedule.

"So things're getting a wee bit confused," said Captain Scar after her men had laid me out on the deck. "'Ave yer what yer needed fer the undeadifyin'? Are we killin' the vicar or what?"

"No, no, he's dead. We can get past the barrier now."

"Well, all right then." She made a complex hand signal, and a couple of her men rushed off to haul up the anchor. "We'll skirt by the cliffs to pick up Slippery John and be on our way. Is there a reason why ye're lyin' down like that?"

Meryl appeared over the side. "Hiya," she said, flapping her hand madly in what was probably supposed to be a greeting.

Captain Scar looked at her, then back to me. "'Oo's she?"

"An associate," seemed like the most honest answer.

The priest arrived next, taking a good long look down his nose at the company he was now keeping. Captain Scar sighed and folded her arms. "Ye only ever seem to raise more and more questions, don't yer, laddie?" said Captain Scar, rubbing her chin again. "We're pleased as punch to be gettin' away from that shithole town, though, so I won't make too much of an issue of it if yer 'and over all yer valuables and promise to look like 'ostages."

"Deal," said Meryl, rolling me onto my front and messing with my tormented robe. "Shall we have a look at this spine, then?"

With my face flat against the splintery wooden floor, I was given chance to reflect. "Barry," I said. "He was killed when that bit of rubble fell on his head, right?"

"Probably. A bit of his brain hit me in the eye."

"But he came right back, is my point." I gestured upwards with my eyebrows. "Pull me up. I need to check something."

Obediently, she hauled me up by my shoulders and propped me up on the side. The site of Barry's most recent death was getting further and further away, so I focused my magic undead vision as hard as I could.

There was movement around the trebuchet's ruins. A little dust eddy was swirling, moving the ashes around. A tiny little whirlwind with an artistic leaning seemed to be engaged in creating a little ash sculpture of a man.

"Shit," I exclaimed, disturbing my lung spiders a second time. "I knew it'd be something like this. He regenerates! We have to go faster!"

"Not 'til we pick up Slippery John," went Captain Scar from the main deck. "Not much prevailin' wind, anyway."

"But the barrier could come back up any sec—"

"Tally ho!" came a voice from above us. We were passing by the cliffs now, and Slippery John took the opportunity to leap heroically onto the deck, Drylda, wheelbarrow and all. The cast-iron wheelbarrow landed squarely on me, pinning me to the floor. "Oh, sorry, monstrous cadaver. Slippery John got a bit caught up in the moment, there."

"Go faster!" I yelled, as loudly as I could manage with a mouthful of deck varnish. "The barrier . . ."

"Yeh've got this nasty 'abit of thinkin' yeh can order us around," said Captain Scar irritably.

Then the barrier returned, at precisely the moment when the Black Pudding was part-way over it. And everyone who hadn't listened to me had only themselves to blame for what happened next.

When I'd foretold that the barrier wouldn't let the Pudding through, I'd been pulling things out of my arse. The fact that I had apparently been horribly, inconveniently correct, did not bring any feeling of triumph. With a quick but incredibly loud CRUNCH of distressed wood, the ship was neatly sliced in two.

The larger part was the one still within the barrier, occupied by a stunned Captain Scar and her crew. Outside was the prow, occupied by Meryl, the priest, Slippery John, Drylda, Drylda's wheelbarrow, and me. And we quickly discovered that there's a good reason why ships don't get launched onto water when they're only one-third finished.

The deck dipped sharply, and the wheelbarrow did what wheelbarrows do and began to roll forward, pulling me with it, catching my robe in the axle. Unable to stop or free myself, all I could do was glide towards the foaming sea and hotly curse both my choice of career and its impractical dress code.

"Jim!" cried Meryl, diving towards the runaway wheelbarrow, missing, and slipping right off the deck into the sea. I added her to the cursing list.

"Slippery John to the rescue!" cried Slippery John, who had been a fixture of the list for quite some time now. He bravely leapt forward, grabbed Drylda's ankles, and hauled her into his arms with a jangle of wristlets and concealed daggers. Relieved of most of its ballast, the wheelbarrow immediately slid right into the sea, where it upended and remained buoyant just long enough for me to yell, "You bastard!" before the water closed in over my face.

# EIGHT

Firelight from the burning town fluttered prettily off the waves as the wheelbarrow dragged me rapidly away from the surface. I could see the two halves of the Black Pudding disintegrate as they sank, the creaks and crashes of falling masts mingling with the grumbling of wet pirates fighting each other for floatation devices. Then the sound faded, and all was silent.

I strained until my brain bulged, but I couldn't make so much as a finger twitch. Everything below the neck was so much dead weight. The most I could do was bug my eyes out and blow bubbles full of swear words.

Chests of loot and chunks of black-painted wood were raining down around me. And there was something else, a madly-shaped black silhouette coming straight at me. My imagination conjured all sorts of betentacled undersea disasters of nature before I realized that it was Meryl, swimming down towards me, her tattered dress billowing out.

In the semi-darkness I couldn't make out her face, but I could see the desperation in her movements. The wheelbarrow was heavy, and pulling me down fast. The laws of physics were making it very clear that they'd prefer her to be going back up, now, and she was thrashing against them with all her strength.

My arms and legs were limp but outstretched towards her. She was close enough that I could make out every greasy strand of her fluttering pigtails. She made a savage burst of extra effort, and her fingertips came within inches of mine.

I probably shouldn't have tempted fate by wondering if she'd actually reach me, as one of the cannonballs from the Black Pudding effortlessly overtook her at that point and planted itself squarely in my throat. I sank, and Meryl disappeared into the gathering darkness.

The blurry shadows of the deep became even blurrier and shadowier, then suddenly disappeared altogether. I couldn't see or hear, and all I could feel were the pecks of bored fish and my body being occasionally shoved aside by something extremely big and distressing that made me grateful for the darkness.

The wheelbarrow bounced off some kind of reef, and I spun end over end for a while, intermittently scraping against jagged rock. The water pressure had been bad enough ten feet below the surface, but now it felt like an angry gorilla repeatedly slamming my skull between a pair of cymbals.

A grotesque slimy sensation trailed up my forehead and away. *Perfect*, I thought. On top of everything else, my eyes had just exploded. *Anything else you'd like to throw at me while we're on a roll, God? Giant squid, perha—*

I dropped out of the water.

One second the pressure had been trying to compact my entire body into a perfect sphere, the next I'd fallen through some kind of ridiculous upside-down surface into . . .

. . . Air? It had to be. But it wasn't like proper air. Proper air didn't hang around at the bottom of the sea, for one thing. And this felt . . . thicker, somehow, like moving through clouds of dust. I was fairly certain I was still falling, but there was no wind, and not a single sound.

I looked around, confused and terrified, momentarily forgetting that my eyes were currently diffusing rapidly into the water somewhere above me. When I recalled that my confusion multiplied, because I could see something.

At first, it was a glimmering line far below me, a diamond-white string reaching across the abyss. As I fell closer, I saw that there were several of the lines. Then hundreds. There was a whole web of flowing white shoelaces hanging in blackness, stretching away endlessly in both directions.

Then I fell a little closer, and I saw that they weren't just lines. They were queues. Queues of Deleters, every single one rushing along at an alarming speed to some mysterious errand, flapping their wings in perfect, silent unison. I wondered if I should have been panicking, but my attempts to scream made no noise, so I settled for being dumbfounded.

Then I fell closer still, and saw that I was falling straight towards one of the Deleters. My flailing hand had already scythed straight through it without stopping. Tendrils of lightning scuttled up my arm and drilled their way through the center of my forehead. Something ran across my brain in spiked running shoes. A spasm jerked my entire body, finally dislodging my robe from that damn wheelbarrow. My twitching foot kicked a second Deleter in its featureless face, sending another bolt of fizzling unpleasantness into my body.

The sensations passed, but something was left behind. There were words in my head, burnt into my brain in big, thumping letters, as clear and lucid as the memories of my first catastrophic fumble with Jemima from the healer school next door.

**From:** "Simon Townshend"
<thenewguy@loinclothentertainment.com>
**To:** "Donald Sunderland"
<mugginshere@loinclothentertainment.com>
**Subject:** Re: Re: Re: Population numbers?

Relax - im on top of it
-S

**From:** "Donald Sunderland"
<mugginshere@loinclothentertainment.com>
**To:** "Simon Townshend"
<thenewguy@loinclothentertainment.com>
**Subject:** Re: Re: Population numbers?

Simon, I'm REALLY angry right now. I already told you you can ONLY use deletion protocols on minor npcs, NOT quest characters and DEFINITELY NOT world architecture. Everything in the world is TIED TOGETHER on a VERY COMPLEX LEVEL. Rubbing out important things willy-nilly does BAD THINGS to other things in the world. Now the WHOLE of Yawnbore's bugged out. We have to get rid of the WHOLE town and EVERYONE in it before too many npcs notice and then rewire ALL the associated quests.

From now on, DO NOT use deletion protocols. EVER. Get rid of Yawnbore within WORLD CONTEXT. Get some npcs to use demolition spells or siege weapons, break up the buildings, round up the inhabitants and we'll put them in quarantine on murdercruel. DON'T **** THIS UP SIMON IF WE DON'T KEEP TO BETA SCHEDULE I'M TELLING BRIAN IT WAS ALL YOUR FAULT.

-Don

> **From:** "Simon Townshend"
> <thenewguy@loinclothentertainment.com>
> **To:** "Donald Sunderland"
> <mugginshere@loinclothentertainment.com>

**Cc:** "William Williams"
<dub@loinclothentertainment.com>
**Subject:** Re: Population numbers?

Found what was causing the numbers—some quest character was bringing minor npcs back to life who died before the entropy protocols were shut off, don't know how he was swinging that but oh well, I solved the problem already, aint you lucky to have me around???
-S

> **From:** "William Williams"
> <dub@loinclothentertainment.com>
> **To:** "Donald Sunderland"
> <mugginshere@loinclothentertainment.com>
> **Cc:** "Simon Townshend"
> <thenewguy@loinclothentertainment.com>
> **Subject:** Population numbers?
>
> Hey guys,
>
> I was just goig over the world statistics over lunch and I noticed something wierd. NPC population is 2451991 at the moment, right? But the logs say when we killed entropy it was 2451958. That's like 33 extra and Im pretty sure that's not possable. Should probably look into whats causing it, could be an  error in the calculation module.
>
> -Dub

. . . Went the first set. I caught the word "Yawnbore," and the word "deletion." Was this some kind of Deleter communication? I hardly had time to even begin digesting it before a second set of gibberish muscled its way into my mind's eye.

**IM sign on 09:14AM**

**doublebill:** hey man

**sunderwonder:** dub, what are you doing

**sunderwonder:** we are sitting across from each other

**sunderwonder:** you can just talk to me verbally

**doublebill:** i wanted to talk about simon

**sunderwonder:** ah fair enough

**doublebill:** i maybe compleatly out of line here but just here me out

**doublebill:** weve been working with him for a coupel of weeks now and theres somethnig about him that needs to be said

**sunderwonder:** you're referring to the fact that hes a complete dickhead

**doublebill:** i wo

**doublebill:** yes

**doublebill:** i am

**doublebill:** and he is

**sunderwonder:** i know

**sunderwonder:** it'd be fine if he was crap at his job and a nice guy

**sunderwonder:** or if he was a dickhead but good at his job

**sunderwonder:** but he's the worst case scenario

**doublebill:** maybe brian would transefr him if we askd

**sunderwonder:** you know hes already been transferred twice right

**sunderwonder:** he put ham fighters 3 behind six months

**sunderwonder:** it was in the newsletter

**doublebill:** so why hasnt he been fried

**sunderwonder:** brian thinks there's still something in there somewhere

**doublebill:** well intersteller bum pirates was pretty awesome i thought

**sunderwonder:** so did brian

**sunderwonder:** word is it was tommy mason who did most of the actual work on that, dickhead took the credit

**doublebill:** oh

**sunderwonder:** i think the whole bum aspect was dickhead's idea tho

**XxSuperSimonxX signed in at 9:24AM**

**XxSuperSimonxX:** hay there cool cats

**XxSuperSimonxX:** you know we're all sitting in the same office right

**XxSuperSimonxX:** helloo anyone there?

**sunderwonder:** hello simon

**XxSuperSimonxX:** just letting you know im completely on top of the yawnboar situation

**XxSuperSimonxX:** ive got some npcs onto the job

sunderwonder: which npcs

**XxSuperSimonxX:** there was this one nearby whod already hired a bunch of adventurers

**XxSuperSimonxX:** hes on top of it

**sunderwonder:** when you told him to do this

**sunderwonder:** you did it as an in-world avatar, right

**XxSuperSimonxX:** whats that

**sunderwonder:** were you in the form of a human character or a moderator angel when you spoke to him

**XxSuperSimonxX:** oh yeah the second one

**XxSuperSimonxX:** also i upped his stats to the highest levels so he could get the job done quicker

**XxSuperSimonxX:** thats cool right

**XxSuperSimonxX:** anyway cant hang around chatting all day

ive got to get on top of my progress report for brian
**XxSuperSimonxX:** chow for now cool cats
**XxSuperSimonxX signed out at 9:33AM**
**sunderwonder:** its spelt 'ciao'
**sunderwonder:** you stupid dickhead
**sunderwonder:** i hate you so much
**doublebill:** why does he keep saying things are on top of things

I was snapped out of my bewildered trance by a sound like a tuning fork being mangled under the hoof of a speeding horse. It was followed by an irritable gibbering, as a few more Deleters broke off from their lines to circle around me. My vision was filled with white light, which would probably have been blinding if I hadn't already had that covered, and then I was falling again.

This was back to nice, familiar, decent falling, complete with the violent rushing wind that rippled my clothes and looser flaps of skin. A pleasant warmth beating down upon my scalp implied a bright noonday sun. I had been ejected from the Deleter realm, which came as an extremely temporary relief. The freezing wetness of what I guessed was the cloud layer engulfed me for a second, then gravity was free of distractions and rolled up its sleeves for my final, horrible descent.

I landed on an ocean surface that might as well have been made of cobblestones. All four of my limbs immediately shattered. Thankfully the wheelbarrow was lost to the Deleter realm and my pockets had split, so I was no longer weighed down. I felt my limbs splay out upon the water, and I began to drift.

I had no way of knowing how long I was like that, blind and paralyzed, floating face down, exuding so thick an aura of misery that even the sharks steered clear. It could have been days. Weeks. Possibly years, but probably not. What I do know is that I was finally stirred from my daze by the sound of crashing surf. I felt my forehead carving a furrow in the wet sand of a mysterious shore.

Seawater sloshed at my useless legs, fluttering my shredded robe as my face gently settled into the mud. I let a deep sigh of relief bubble through the silt. I was blind, immobile, alone, and face-down in the dirt. Finally, something I could deal with.

# PART THREE

# ONE

There are people who think that blindness and paralysis would be some kind of deathlike existence. If that was true, it wasn't deathlike enough for my tastes. But then, I couldn't really get into it because I had to keep swearing and blowing really hard to shoo off the crabs that came to poke around my nose hole and assess my orifices as living quarters.

As the days went by, my thoughts turned frequently to those bizarre visions of Deleter communication I'd intercepted in the strange realm beneath the sea. I could feel something left behind in my head, the mental equivalent of a seed caught between my teeth. On the occasions when boredom took hold and I began to daydream, a few letters and sprinklings of punctuation marks would break off and become visible in the corner of my mind's eye.

Lacking any other project to pass the time with I began to experiment with coaxing it forward. It was uphill work; the moment it realized I was looking for it it seemed to dart shyly back behind some dusty childhood memories. I theorized that if I could enter some kind of trance-like state, perhaps its guard would drop for long enough to for me to sneak a good look at it.

When I was a child, my dad used to take us out badger-watching sometimes; we'd sit in a wooden box staring at a hole in the ground in the hope of catching a glimpse of nature's most boring animal. All buggering night. But dad's twisted idea of a good time could finally prove useful.

One night, after successfully dissuading the evening wave of crabs, I took a useless deep breath, and visualized every inch of that badgerwatching hut. The insipid smell of sawdust. The heat radiating from tightly-packed family members bickering over sandwiches. The distant hoot of an equally bored owl. I felt ennui setting in, and with it, something dislodged from

ube.com/watch?v=TANd-_Z_UZA
**sunderwonder:** that's disgusting
**doublebill:** you mean awesome
**sunderwonder:** stop sending me these stupid videos
**doubleb**

I was broken from my trance by a shrill wail, slowly rising in volume. The implanted memory ran back to its badger sett. The source of the noise became loud enough to be right next to my ear, and something else pulled me into a sitting position and wrapped itself around my torso.

"Unf," I said.

The high-pitched screeching noise eventually separated out into actual words. "Oh my god I thought I'd never see you again but I knew you'd be on the same currents as us so I knew you'd get washed up on this shore sooner or later and oh my god you're all right!" I felt her shift back. "How come you've got no eyes?"

"Hello, Meryl."

"Stay right there." She propped me up onto my knees and I heard her run off up the beach. She was gone quite a while, long enough for me to lose my balance and faceplant back into the sand. Finally she returned, rolled me onto my back, then did something cold and slimy to my face.

Suddenly, I could see again. Meryl gave my new eyeballs a quick polish with her sleeve. "Can you move?"

"Yes, Meryl, I can move. I've just been lying on this beach for the last few weeks because I can't resist the great taste of wet sand."

"Aw, it's so nice to hear that sarcasm of yours again. Let's take a look at the damage." She plopped me back down and produced her first aid bag: a combination of sewing equipment, carpentry tools and butcher knives.

"Something . . . happened to me," I said, as she pried muscles apart to get at my skeleton. "I think . . . I've been to the realm where the Deleters come from."

She paused in her work. "And you didn't get them to delete you?"

"There wasn't really a good time to ask, I was only . . . what the hell are you wearing?"

The question was rhetorical—I could see damn well what she was wearing. It was a tight-fitting sleeveless black leather jumpsuit with the zip unfastened to the navel, revealing the remains of her filthy old brown dress underneath. "You noticed!" she said, thrilled. "Slippery John took us adventure shopping. He said this is what all the female rogues wear in Lolede."

"Did he mention exactly what kind of female rogues he was talking about?"

"You were saying something about a Deleter realm?" she said, carefully splinting my femur with a handy piece of driftwood.

"Yeah. They put something in my head. I don't know what, exactly, but it's been telling me stuff. A lot of it doesn't make any sense, but . . . uh . . ." I blinked a few times. "Where exactly did you get these eyes from?"

"Octopus," she said, as casually as she could.

"Octopus."

"Closest thing to the human eye found in nature, octopus eyes. I wouldn't look at people like you're looking at me now, though. It's a bit weird and gross. You were saying?"

"Actually I don't think you're the sort of person I want to talk to about this."

"Fair enough."

I was wracked by a sequence of electric spasms as Meryl knotted my spinal cord back together, and sensation returned to my limbs. I flexed my arms and legs, stood up, fell over, then stood up again, slower.

We definitely weren't in Garethy anymore, because it was a nice day. There wasn't a cloud in the sky and the beach was a warm, inviting bank of fine white sand. As we moved away from the sea, tufts of stringy vegetation began to poke up through the sand like hair on a teenager's face, and before long we were in a plain of long, windswept grass. It was a far cry from the Garethy grasslands I had known, which for most of the year have to be technically classified as extremely large puddles.

"Follow me," said Meryl, wading through the waist-high grass. "Not too far to walk. I said I'd meet the others at Cronenburg."

"What's Cronenburg?"

"It's a town. Come on. Shouldn't be too . . ."

I ducked as a growl thundered across the grass. The worst kind of growl: loud, deep, and filtered through several layers of sharp teeth. And it was coming from very close by.

Meryl scratched her head as the echoes boomed away. "Huh. Bit early in the day for that." She looked down. "Why are you on all fours?"

I grabbed her by the zip fastener and pulled her down until we were both concealed in the grass. "It's a gnoll."

"You're not afraid of gnolls, are you?" said Meryl goadingly.

Another lung-splitting roar sailed overhead. "Yes," I replied, unashamed. "Fear is a healthy and natural response to things like gnolls. They used to ambush farmers on the way to market. We had to run and hide up a tree while they were busy biting the heads off all the horses."

"Oh, come on. Let's watch!" Before I could stop her, she scuttled off in the direction of the sounds. I hurried after her before I could remind myself not to care.

The gnoll's roaring continued as I crawled after Meryl, and it was soon joined by the sound of several pairs of armored boots disturbing a gravel path, followed by the agitating squeal of metal against metal and the considerably more agitating squelch of metal against flesh. By the time I caught up with Meryl, the noises were mere feet away. I poked my head out the grass to look.

It was, indeed, a gnoll. It looked the way gnolls do: like a cross between a bear, a dog and a pictorial textbook on dentistry. But this was a much larger and more terrible specimen than the comparatively quaint Garethy gnolls.

The two adventurers fighting it seemed unafraid, despite both sporting a lively collection of oozing teethmarks. They continued to swing their ridiculously large swords around in the perfect unison I recognized as one of the hallmarks of the Syndrome.

The gnoll, rapidly losing blood from several perfectly straight slash wounds, had sensed the turning of the tide and was running in a wide circle to escape its attackers. The swordsmen were at its heels, but every time they got close enough, they stopped dead and attacked using the same Syndrome thrust and slash I'd seen Drylda employ. It was perplexing, but it did lend credence to my theory that adventurers couldn't walk and think at the same time.

Eventually the weight of numbers and the gnoll's faster blood loss ended the battle decisively, and the monster collapsed to the ground and breathed its foamy, blood-flecked last.

"Gee gee," said one of the swordsmen, without emotion.

"Ell eff gee cron," replied the other.

"Kay kay."

The two adventurers carelessly tore off all the beast's foul-smelling armor and equipment—a mixture of randomly-scavenged tools, kitchen utensils and roadkill tied together with string—stuffed it unsorted into a large sack, and sprinted off towards the horizon, leaving the corpse where it lay.

I stepped dizzily out into the open, watching them go. "What the hell were they saying to each other?"

"That's just Syndrome-speak," said Meryl, a curious authority in her voice. "All the Syndrome adventurers talk like that to each other. Slippery John says you see a lot of it on the Adventure Trail."

" . . .What's the Adventure Trail?"

"This is. Duh." The patronizing click of her tongue was like a pair of nutcrackers being clenched around my skull. "It's the main road around the continent all the adventurers take, looking for quests. We're going to follow it to Lolede City, as soon as we meet up with Slippery John, Drylda and Thaddeus."

I flailed my arms in frustration. "Who's Thaddeus?!"

"You know, the priest. He told us his name while we were clinging to the boat. He's really excited about going to Lolede, too. Printed off a whole new run of pamphlets and everything. He was just saying this morning what a shame it'd be if we had to go on to the big city without you."

Meryl was beginning to give me a headache. "I get the impression you're extrapolating."

We walked in silence for a few moments, which turned out to be more than Meryl's excitable brain could handle. "I've never been to Lolede City before," she said, bouncing her pigtails. "You know it's the biggest city in the world?"

"Yes, I knew that. So does everyone else who did primary school geography. Why are you so excited?"

"Aren't you?" She was practically skipping.

"I thought you wanted to go back to Borrigarde. I thought you had a post-revolutionary government to worry about."

She stopped practically skipping for an instant, and probably hoped I wouldn't notice. "Yes, but, there's still a lot of breathing room with these things. Plenty of time to take a little holiday, expand our horizons a bit. Never mind. What are you going to do when we get there?"

I didn't let her change the subject. "Meryl, did you honestly spark a revolution in Borrigarde?"

"What do you mean?"

"I mean, did the revolution actually occur, in the real world, with real actual people involved?"

All the parts of her face remained perfectly still, but I could see the façade of good cheer rapidly draining away. Then she mentally injected a little more of whatever it was that kept her going. "Of course! It's not something I could lie about for long, I mean . . . revolutions are big things. This one certainly was. Swords and ploughshares all over the place." She was trying not to meet my gaze. "But anyway. Lolede City! Yay!"

"Because if there was a revolution, it probably set a record for speed. I mean, you were only there a day or two."

"We took them by surprise, didn't we? The oppressors weren't expecting insurrection from a bunch of ignorant pig farmers who don't know what's good for them."

She wisely fell into silence, but there was considerably less of a spring in her step. I watched her for a few moments with my head tilted. "Meryl?"

"Yes?"

"What are you going to do when we get to Lolede City?"

She didn't reply, but I took her poisonous glare as a victory.

# TWO

"Slippery John said he'd meet us at the inn," said Meryl, when we arrived at Cronenburg later that day.

"Any particular inn?" I asked.

"Slippery John just said 'the inn.'"

I put my hands on my hips and took in the endless racks of shingles that lined what a flamboyant signpost identified as the Street of Inns. "Slippery John is a fatheaded, useless berk."

"Oh, come on. He's not useless."

The day was wearing thin and the sun was making exaggerated yawns and meaningful looks at the horizon. We'd been trudging through the plains for a few hours before Cronenburg appeared, and it didn't take long to be underwhelmed by the place. It had once been a tiny hamlet, the kind of town where yokels in big hats leaned against barrels in the middle of the street, chewing straws and making filthy cross-eyed looks at anyone who wasn't the product of rampant inbreeding, but (as Slippery John had told Meryl, who had in turn told me) the Adventure Trail had turned it into a popular traveller's rest for wandering mercenaries.

We'd passed a lot of those on the way. Barbarians, dwarves, battle mages, elves, healers—the road was permanently serving as an unusually large catwalk for absurd battlewear.

Syndrome sufferers were commonplace and easily spotted; they were the really attractive people who jogged robotically along the road, awkwardly swung weaponry at the endless wandering monsters that adventurers attract, or just stood perfectly still in fixed heroic poses in the middle of the highway, to the immense frustration of their non-afflicted friends and peers. I'd never seen so many of them packed so densely in one place.

"Well, no need to start fretting," said Meryl. "We'll just have to check all the inns in turn. You want to take that side of the road and I'll take this one?"

"How about you take both sides of the road, and I'll go do something else."

"Ah. Gotcha." She tapped her nose. "Reconnaissance."

"No." I tapped the place where my nose used to be. "Shopping. I want to find a new robe that isn't about to rot off with water damage."

"Fair enough."

She began poking her head into the inns and I kept walking to the town center. This didn't take long. Cronenburg only had three streets, which formed a Y around what I would have called a village square had it not been perfectly circular. The Street of Inns was the southerly branch of the Y, and the two arms were the Street of Magic and the Street of Combat. Every single building in Cronenburg appeared to belong to a business of some kind.

The streets were absolutely packed with human traffic, everyone shoving their way through the crowds in hasty pursuit of their individual shopping needs. After being swept relentlessly around the town center for a few laps I made a burst of effort and stumbled out into the comparatively sedate central plaza. I stood on a bench to get a clearer look around.

There evidently had been a bit too much surplus in the town planning committee's annual budget, and the very air seemed to sparkle with the setting sunlight reflecting off brand new

shop frontage and polished cobblestones. The centerpiece of
the town was a huge, silvery ornamental fountain depicting a
wild-haired barbarian with one furry boot planted on a defeated
gnoll. Crystal-clear water ran from its stab wounds. And just
to underline the message, a six-foot long plaque at the bottom
read *CRONENBURG WELCOMES ADVENTURERS* in big
serifed letters.

They'd certainly taken the message. Adventurers were everywhere. Loitering in the plaza chatting about nonsense, emerging
from the shops wearing tacky multicolored armor fresh out of
the wrapping. You could tell who had only just arrived, because
their outfits were filthy with blood and gnoll guts.

The gore-spattered new arrivals were all queueing up
outside a building at the very point where the two northern
branches of the Y intersected, a prime position where I'd
expect to find a town hall. It was an unadorned building of
well-polished black glass that seemed almost embarrassed by
the elaborate façades that rubbed its shoulders. The adventurers in the queue were clutching armfuls of dented gnoll
equipment and clumps of foul-smelling offal. They would file
into the main entrance and emerge moments later, relieved of
their gnoll garbage and holding clinking bags of coins.

I shrugged. I was new to the land, and there were no doubt
a lot of weird local customs I was unaware of. Maybe gnoll
offal was the primary ingredient of some popular local deli-
cacy. I took a deep breath, shouldered my way back into the
throng and, after a few more trips around the circle, managed
to get onto the Street of Magic.

I quickly found the kind of shop I was after: a pleasant little
tailor's with garish star-patterned fabrics prominently featured
in the window. Just outside the door stood an oily teenager in
a smart, professional robe. His fixed smile looked like it was
becoming painful.

"Drelmere and sons, fine outfitters for the discerning magician!" he was shouting, his voice barely carrying over the hubbub. "Robes! Pointy hats! Beard grooming supplies! Yes, you sir, how can OH GOD HURRAAARRGLAB."

I waited patiently for him to finish decorating the pavement with his stomach contents. "Sorry," he said, bent double and gulping. Impressively, he immediately continued his sales pitch from that position. "Looking for a new robe?"

"Yes, this one's starting to whiff a bit."

"Yes, I . . . gathered that, sir." He took a few deep, groaning breaths into a star-patterned hanky and seemed to gather himself. "What sort of price range were you OH GOD YOUR EYES HURRAAARRGLAB."

I tapped my now bile-sodden foot. "Shall I come back later?"

"No!" he said very quickly, straightening up. "No, it's fine. We have a lovely selection of robes for a discerning . . . person, from as little as 49 talans."

"What's a talan?"

He chuckled condescendingly. It would probably have been more effective without the sick all down his front. "The currency of Lolede, sir." When I didn't reply for a moment he added, "You need them to buy things."

I resisted the urge to put on a show of searching my pockets, because I was afraid of what was currently living in them. "Excuse me a moment," I said. "I left my wallet in my carriage."

I drifted back towards the village square, considering options. I didn't even know what a talan looked like. Most of the rural communities in Garethy got by on the barter system, and the closest thing to currency there was the turnip. And then, of course, as part of Dreadgrave's horde I'd gotten used to the "give us all your worldly goods or we'll set fire to you" system of economics.

Slippery John would probably have some money, I thought. If he was reluctant to part with it I could always stand within smelling range until he changed his mind.

"Name," said a voice.

I turned. An elven hunter was staring at a point just to the side of my head with the unmoving intensity of an obvious Syndrome victim. Absolutely nothing about his manner indicated that he was addressing me, so I attempted to walk away before we caught something horrible from each other.

He wasn't to be dissuaded. He burst momentarily into a dramatic sprint until he'd closed the four yards between us and pressed his nose against my forehead. "Name," he said again.

"Jim," I admitted. I'd made the mistake of getting backed into the fountain, and now there was no path of escape. "How do you do?"

"Job."

His voice had no emotion or intelligence behind it. It was less like communication and more like expressionless throat noise that coincidentally formed words, like a dog saying "roof." "Freelance," I said eventually. "If I could just get out of your way, I'm a little bit freaked out . . ."

"Quests?" An ever-so-slight upturning of pitch towards the end of the statement led me to conclude that it was a question.

My gaze immediately swung over to a nearby sign that I'd noticed earlier and been somewhat baffled by. It read, *NON-ADVENTURERS WITHOUT QUESTS ARE ADVISED TO NOT STAND IN ONE PLACE FOR LONG PERIODS.*

Now that I knew what to look for, I saw them dotted throughout the crowd. Questgivers. Armored knights in the pay of lords and barons stood around the areas of highest traffic, soliciting cheap muscle for dirty jobs, shoulder to shoulder with farm workers looking for someone to shoo the gnolls off the pumpkin patches. I'd stumbled into some kind of quest exchange.

My first thought was to shrug him off and leave, which was backed up by my second, third and fourth thought. But it was my fifth thought that somehow got control of my voice.

"Yes, I have a quest for you," I said, placing two fingertips on his sternum and gently pushing him out of my personal space. "Lend me fifty talans."

Our gaze met for a few seconds, or rather, I looked into his eyes and he focused vaguely on something behind my head. Then he produced an understated but roomy purse from his britches, shook out five freshly-minted coins, and thrust them forwards.

"Your quest is complete," I announced, jingling them in my palm. "Well done. You are truly a hero."

The tiniest glimmer of understanding flashed momentarily in the center of his dead eyes, then he turned a smooth 180 degrees and jogged off into the crowd, swinging his hips.

Fifteen minutes later I emerged from the tailor in an inexpensive but hard-wearing outdoor robe intended for long-distance trekking and battle magic. My old robe had already been peeled off, wadded up into a foul-smelling blob and dropped down the deepest storm drain the tailor's assistant could find. With my own personal quest completed, I headed back towards the Street of Inns.

Something was going on in the town square. The elf I'd "hired" for my "quest" was being interrogated by a small throng of adventurers. I wondered if I should be concerned until the elf saw me and removed all doubt by pointing a stiff, accusing finger in my direction.

The head of the little group, a blonde dwarf, bore down on me with anger bristling to the ends of his absurd mustache.

"Are you the one who OH GOD YOUR EYES HURRAAARRGLAB." He picked some half-digested morsels out of his beard and tried again. "Are you the one who gave Erick the 'lend fifty talans' quest?"

"Er . . . I have a condition," I tried.

The dwarf's eyes narrowed. "You didn't sign his quest log." He snatched a little black book from Erick's unresisting hands and pushed the latest page under my nose. It read, in an impossibly neat hand, *Quest 127815, Undead Minion, Cronenburg: Lend me fifty talans*.

"You . . . what?" I stammered.

"You didn't sign it off, genius! How's he going to register it at the Guild if it's not verified?"

The rest of the page was filled with a small grid of little boxes to fill in. One for a signature, one underneath that was headed *points awarded*, and another reading *performance: adequate / good / outstanding*. A pen was pressed into my hand and I decided that rolling with it was the safest option.

"Right," said the dwarf, when I'd finished writing. "Pink copy's yours." He made to give me the receipt, then something fired in his head and he snatched it back. "Holy iron, did you just give him 100 points for that?"

"Er, yeah." I'd flipped back over a couple of pages and it seemed like an average amount. "I was impressed by the speedy service."

Now my receipt was being passed around the gathering crowd of adventurers and creating excited murmurs in its wake. I could feel the hot breath of incoming disaster on my neck. "I wanna do this quest too," announced the dwarf, digging out his own dog-eared quest journal and wallet. "Fifty talans, right?"

"Here's my 50 talans!" came a female voice, probably belonging to the slender fist that hung overhead, spilling coins.

"I do money quest," droned a Syndrome-afflicted mage.

Somehow I'd gotten backed up against the fountain again. I displayed my rotten palms in futile protection from the coins being thrown in my face. "Whoa!" I yelled over the developing hubbub. "I don't need any more! I needed fifty talans and he was convenient! It was a one time thing!"

The many fists that clutched money and quest logs went away sadly. Then the fists rematerialized clutching swords and battleaxes.

"Well okay then," I said. "Can I get that pen back?"

"Where the hell have you been?" said Meryl, when I caught up with her in the Street of Inns at about three in the morning. "Where did you get that huge bag of money?"

I dumped it on the pavement, sick of hefting the weight around. "Is there a word for the exact opposite of a mugging?"

"You've got a coin in your nose hole." She pulled it out helpfully and inspected it. "What happened, exactly?"

I told her.

"So wait, they all gave you fifty talans each just so you'd sign a piece of paper and write down '100 points'?"

"Exactly."

"How does that even work?"

I held my hands out. "I don't know! They wouldn't stop giving me money! And I was actually holding out hope that this continent would be slightly less insane than the last one. This isn't very encouraging."

She raised an eyebrow. "Yeah, you look devastated. That's a nice new hat, by the way. Gold leaf?"

"No, Elfweave. Looks like gold leaf, about three times the price." I adjusted the brim. "Give me a break, I've been rotting on a beach for weeks, I'm cheering myself up. Invested in a couple of new mage spells, too."

"Oh really? Such as?"

She promptly vanished in a burst of glittery particles. In her place sat a stunned little black-and-white bunny rabbit, twitching its nose in adorable wonder for a few seconds before the transformation reversed. There was a brief surreal in-between moment when the rabbit momentarily had breasts and a head four times too large, then there was the *crack* of a universe falling back into line and Meryl returned.

"The rabbit spell," she said, bored. "Yeah, it was a funny prank the first ten or twelve times I fell for it at Dreadgrave's."

"It is not a prank. It's a combat control strategy that also happens to be incredibly hilarious."

"Thaddeus is here," she announced, pointing to the nearest inn, *The Good Innvestment*, whose shingle was optimistically decorated with the image of an innkeeper waist-deep in coins. "Slippery John went scouting ahead, said he'd be back by sunrise."

"Did he take Drylda?" I asked as we entered the Good Innvestment.

"Yeah, why?"

"I'm thinking that the only thing that's going to get scouted is the inside of her bodice."

"Why don't you like Slippery John? You seem to spend your whole unlife following him around."

"He set us on fire."

"Oh, that was just adventurer stuff. You wouldn't understand. You shouldn't take it so seriously."

Another thing that was difficult to take seriously was the interior of the Good Innvestment. The designers obviously knew what adventurers expected from a wayside inn-scowling battle-scarred innkeeper in eyepatch and apron, unvarnished tables, smoky torchlight and ale served in the biggest flagons your restaurant supplier could find–and they were trying so hard to be that kind of place you could practically hear the walls straining with the effort. The tables had had their varnish sanded off, then scratches and imperfections had been carefully added with a chisel. The flaming torches were normal magic-powered lights with fluttering bits of orange cloth attached. The barman had the eyepatch and apron, but he was thin and permanently beaming, and his battle scars were drawn on with eyebrow pencil.

"How much, exactly, has the priest lightened up?" I asked, as we dodged the innkeeper's attempts to wish us a nice day.

"Thaddeus? It's like talking to a different man. I really think you'll be amazed."

I'd seen him now, his lanky, gray-skinned form easy to spot among the rippling bronzed musculature of the other clientele. He was sitting by himself at one of the unvarnished tables, arms folded, intently watching a nearby table of dwarves and narrowing his eyes every time any of them started to raise a glass to their lips.

"Hey, Thaddeus," said Meryl. "Look who I found."

Thaddeus sneered so hard that his nose became sandwiched between the two halves of his upper lip. "My soul weeps blood to know that your putrescence blights this realm still, suckler of evil's horny nipple."

I glared at him, then at Meryl, who shrugged. "Well, Slippery John really seemed to be getting through to him, anyway."

I sat down and buried my face in my elbows. "Will you please stop going on about Slippery John?"

"What have you got against him? He's trying to get along with you, you know."

"Leaving aside—"

"—Leaving aside the burning thing—"

"Also the fact that he's an adventurer, and therefore a self-obsessed money-grubbing moron in severe denial about the fact that he's not the handsome prince in his own personal fairy story?"

A smug little gleam flashed in the glow of Meryl's eyes. "I know what this is about. You hate adventurers because you were originally killed by them."

"No I wasn't. I was killed by students. The adventurers just didn't help. And anyway, I've been killed by lots of things. Jumping off towers, tools in the skull, falling buildings . . ."

"Yeah, but the first time's special. You never forget it." She cupped her chin in her hands and her gaze went somewhere else. "I remember mine. I was a burgeoning flower of womanhood. He was the weird kid who kept playing with his switchblade. We were both so nervous, but we figured it out together." She sighed. "I think they hanged him for it."

"Anyway," I said, changing the subject as fast as possible, "why shouldn't I hate adventurers? I think we're both entitled to at this point."

"Are you kidding? They dedicate their lives to helping people. They're heroes."

I rolled my eyes. "You have this thing about seeing things in black and white, don't you? Good and evil. Heroes and villains. Probably comes from that Binny upbringing. Life's more complex than that. There are no heroes or villains. There's just people who want money and people who want a bit more money."

"What about you?"

"What about me?"

"Wouldn't you say you're on a heroic quest?"

I looked at her, eyebrow raised. "I wouldn't call getting myself killed a particularly heroic goal."

"It's still a quest. And you've already had epic battles and stuff."

"Having a quest doesn't mean anything. Everyone's on a quest. I want to die. You've got your Borrigarde thing. And Thaddeus hasn't alienated everyone in the world yet."

"Your prattle will impress not the agents of the Almighty, creature of the deeps."

I sat up. "Actually, Barry's the one who's apparently got the backing of the Gods. And he's a lot more passionate about things than we are. Maybe he's the real hero."

Meryl blinked a few times. "Are you serious?"

"Of course not. You started an absolutely retarded conversation and I'm making fun of you. Do try to keep up."

The debate ended when someone ran down the street outside, loudly ringing a handbell, and every adventurer in the room immediately bolted for the door. Within seconds the three of us and the innkeeper were the only people left in the inn. All was silent but for the sound of abandoned chairs and barstools gently rocking on their back legs for a moment before falling over with a clatter.

"What was that all about?" wondered Meryl aloud.

"Gnolls are attacking," said the innkeeper, as nonchalantly as one would announce that the buns were being delivered.

It was my chair's turn to fall as I leapt to my feet in alarm. "Gnolls?"

"Mm, yes," the innkeeper nodded. "Whole tribe of the things live just outside town. This happens every few nights. Good thing all these stalwart adventurers are around, hmm?" He winked. The eyepatch spoiled the effect somewhat.

"Let's get out of here," I suggested.

"Scared of gnolls, are we, champ?"

"They're gnolls!" was the best argument I could come up with. This was the second time I'd been asked to justify being afraid of gnolls, and I still couldn't fathom why. It was like being asked to explain why old people should wear clothing.

"Maybe you should watch tonight's battle," suggested the innkeeper. "You can get a good view from the window."

I crossed over and peered around the shutter, preparing to slam it closed at the first sign of tusks. A crowd of around forty adventurers were gathered around the tasteless fountain, near a couple of opportunistic refreshment stands and some spectators with less sense of self-preservation than I.

An overweight man with a preposterously huge mustache and a massive, jewel-encrusted mayor's medallion strode confidently into the center of the plaza. He stepped onto a wooden platform and addressed the crowd. "O noble warriors of fortune," he boomed, his grand country accent clearly audible even from this distance. "The vile Hairybum tribe are on their way to do all manner o' indescribably awful things to our village. We beseech you . . ."

"Skip the intro." A dwarf pushed his way to the front of the crowd. It was the blonde fellow who had accosted me earlier. "We've all heard it a million times. What's the reward?"

The mustache wobbled back and forth in irritation for a moment. "Twenty points for every dead gnoll. The usual arrangement. Hang onto yer receipts and hand 'em in at the town hall to get your logs signed . . . what's the matter? Why all the consternation, sirs?"

"There was this beggar earlier on," continued the dwarf over the displeased muttering of his fellows. "Handing out hundred-point rewards for lowest-level quests. There hasn't been some kind of boost in the town budget, has there?"

"Of course not! That individual was most certainly not sanctioned by the town Quest Committee! We cannot afford to hand points out like that!"

"Come off it, Dubbly," said the dwarf. He gestured suggestively at the mayor's glittering accoutrements, then the fountain, then the gaudy shop fronts that were lit up with multicolored glowing signs and advertising boards now that night had fallen. "You've been raking it in with both hands since the Trail started. Now I'm thinking our patronage has got to be worth a bit more to you than twenty points a gnoll." This provoked a chorus of "yeah"s and "preach on"s from the assembly.

At that point a chorus of roars like the angry moos of a herd of demon cows echoed through the town. From the other end of the Street of Inns I saw a stormcloud of activity rise up, moonlight reflecting off many crudely-fashioned axes and hand blades.

The gnolls were charging towards the village square, an army of snarling monsters in unmatching piecemeal armor. Like the one we'd encountered earlier, these were a formidable bunch: hardened desert scavengers, black of fur and a good foot taller than Garethy's forest gnolls. The leader of this pack could probably have crushed a Garethy gnoll to death between his pectoral muscles.

"Now wait one minute!" bellowed the mayor. "We ain't quite ready yet!"

The gnoll charge slowed and stopped, lowering their weapons and scaling back their war cries into mildly perturbed grumbling.

"You've got to understand," said the mayor, turning back to the adventurers. "Guild tax is climbin' up again. We've already moseyed our way through most of the town plannin' budget for the year."

"So how do you explain that beggar?"

"I ain't got no explanation for that, sirs, I told you, that fella musta been some kinda independent operator. Now, are all these gnolls gonna have to kill themselves or are you gonna be adventurers tonight?"

His passionate appeal utterly failed to do the trick. Many of the adventurers were already drifting away, along with most of the bored spectators.

"Now hold on!" yelled Mayor Dubbly as more and more of his audience deserted him. "I could be persuaded to go up to twenty-three points a head?"

"It's too late for that now," said the dwarf spokesman, following his colleagues. "You waste our time, we lose the spark."

All Dubbly and the gnoll horde could do was stand, open-mouthed and crestfallen, impotently watching the stars of the evening's entertainment wander off into the night.

"Gruffug khakhaf gafflekaff?" rumbled the head gnoll, having difficulty pushing his words through the hideous forest of pointy teeth that filled his mouth.

"Yes, I suppose you can still have your free meal coupons," sighed Dubbly. "Collect 'em from the town hall."

"Groff."

Excitement rejuvenated, the gnolls dispersed. I suddenly noticed that I'd unconsciously ducked when they'd arrived, and was now watching the street with my non-existent nose hooked over the windowsill. I stood, attempting to gather my dignity.

"What was that all about?" asked Meryl, as we rejoined the priest. Several adventurers had already returned to the bar to resume drinking.

"I dunno," I said, "but I have a horrible feeling that it was my fault. We should probably get out of here and back on the road. We can meet Slippery John on his way back."

"What, right now?" She clicked her tongue. "Look, I know a lot of people have been trying to destroy you lately but that's no reason to be paranoid."

As if to punctuate her sentence, the entrance door suddenly broke off its hinges and flew horizontally across the room, erupting into bits against the body of a poorly-placed rogue. Two of the invading gnolls entered, squeezing themselves uncomfortably through the human-sized doorway like hairy, murderous toothpaste.

"What the hell, guys?!" shouted the innkeeper, furious. "You know you're not supposed to damage property! This was covered at the meeting!"

"Gruffuk," went one of the gnolls apologetically. He was the slimmer of the two, which meant he could probably only bench-press two or three horses at once. "Groffty grukkuffug," he added, pointing a filthy black claw directly at me.

"Oh, balls," I retorted, not the slightest bit surprised.

The only way out was through the advancing wall of fur and muscle that was now dividing the bar and reception area. Choices and consequences raced through my head. Every single one of them ended with at least one part of me getting chewed on. A particularly large dollop of foamy spittle landed next to my foot and my brain desperately accelerated.

"New quest!" I heard myself yell. "Save me from gnolls! Big rewards!"

"Ugh," muttered Thaddeus, still calmly sitting. "At least accept fate with a little dignity, child of damnation."

It had done the trick, though. The monsters froze. At some point between my utterance of the words "big" and "rewards," every adventurer in the bar had finished their drinks, stood up and begun fondling their weapon hilts.

There passed a significant moment of stillness. Nobody in the room wanted to be the first to make a rash movement that could snowball into large amounts of property damage.

"Gruk," went the slimmer gnoll, no doubt also the more erudite of the pair. "Graffogok koggogok roffgroff."

"What was that?" I hissed.

Meryl's mouth materialized next to my ear. "I think he said, 'new quest, help us capture undead, even bigger rewards.'"

"You speak gnoll?"

"No, but the gist was pretty obvious." She gestured to the adventurers, who had all turned from the gnolls to us like heavily-armed weathervanes. "What now? Offer even more rewards than that?"

I sighed. "We'll be back and forth all bloody night. No, I think I'm just going to go with the flow." I folded my arms and bowed my head as a shiny new elven mace slammed across the back of my skull.

It was the first time I'd been killed since my dalliance with the Deleter realm, and as my spirit was pushed out into the dead world I realized that I hadn't escaped from that bizarre place unscathed. Something had changed.

I could still see the washed-out physical world around me. I saw my body, along with Meryl's and Thaddeus's, being slung over a gnoll's bulging shoulder. I could see my companions' souls being cast out to join me in the dead world.

But everything else was different. My mind felt sluggish and dull. My astral form was slanted at a strange angle, and one of my arms was hanging uselessly.

"J-m?" said Meryl's ghost, concerned. "W-a-'s –h- m-t-e-? Y-u-e f-i-k-r-n- i- a-d –u- . . ."

The dead world was flickering in and out like a broken light. It was like two worlds were trying to occupy the same space. One was the standard ghostly dead realm, and the other . . .

Physically it was the exact same place, but everything was formed from glowing lines against a black void, like thin brushstrokes on black velvet. The terrain beneath my feet was a network of green triangles, as were the walls and fittings of the Cronenburg buildings. My corpse was a body-shaped yellow cage, while the gnolls and adventurers tormenting it were a vibrant red.

The souls of Meryl and the priest were white. No, I realized —they were gray. They only looked white because of the millions of tiny Deleters that swarmed over their astral forms like ants.

I looked down at my hands. They were all over me, too, scurrying all over my ghostly flesh with skinny white arms and legs. Like the other Deleters, they were white humanoids with blank white heads, wings and robes, but these were the size of cockroaches, and scrabbled insanely about with none of the emotionless deliberation of their larger fellows. They were all over my limbs, my torso, even my face, teasing my eyelids and climbing down my nose hole. I opened my mouth to scream, and felt hundreds more of them pouring out of my throat . . .

**XxSuperSimonxX signed in at 9:44AM**
**XxSuperSimonxX:** whats cooking cool cats
**XxSuperSimonxX:** its cool that im working from home 2day right
**sunderwonder:** yes
**sunderwonder:** please work from home as often as you like
**XxSuperSimonxX:** sweet
**XxSuperSimonxX:** what are we on top of today
**doublebill:** populatoin numbers thing again
**XxSuperSimonxX:** I took care of that already
**XxSuperSimonxX:** do keep up son
**sunderwonder:** yes I remember you saying
**sunderwonder:** but there are still three resurrected npcs unaccounted for

**XxSuperSimonxX:** pff

**XxSuperSimonxX:** just three wont matter

**doublebill:** they kind of will actually

**sunderwonder:** anything that doesn't belong in the world can corrupt the build

**XxSuperSimonxX:** okay fine

**XxSuperSimonxX:** ill get barry onto it

**sunderwonder:** barry who

**XxSuperSimonxX:** hes the npc I put on top of the yawnbore job

**XxSuperSimonxX:** ive been talking to him a bit

**XxSuperSimonxX:** its amazzing how intelligent the npcs are. I think we should all be very proud of what weve done on this project

**doublebill:** you only just joined

**XxSuperSimonxX:** anyway gotta run

**XxSuperSimonxX:** got important work to get on top of, cant sit around chatting like you two slackers

**XxSuperSimonxX signed out at 9:58AM**

**doublebill:** do you think hes actually going to do any work

**sunderwonder:** god I hope not

**sunderwonder:** that's the only reason I suggested it

**sunderwonder:** with any luck hes wanking himself raw as we speak

# THREE

I woke to find myself back inside the body for which I was developing a deep antipathy. Particularly for my eyes, because a heavily laden gnoll loincloth was bouncing and swaying directly in front of my face.

Blood was beginning to ooze into my head so I had probably been upside-down for some time. My wrists and ankles were lashed to a gnoll spear, carried between the well-endowed gentleman behind me and presumably another gnoll outside my field of vision.

The air had the hot and stifling quality of midday. Looking up, or down, I saw a sandy desert trail rolling along. A few old stories I had heard regarding desert gnolls and their customs chose that moment to start haunting me.

"I feel I should mention I taste absolutely bloody awful." I croaked. It was almost certainly true, but my captor's thundering thighs weren't convinced. "Seriously. If you've ever poured really old milk on your breakfast cereal by mistake, multiply that by a few million."

"Jim? Is that you?"

I tried to look around, but only succeeded in rocking myself back and forth sickeningly. "Meryl? Where are you?"

"I . . . don't know." The voice was coming from my right. "I'm looking at a gnoll's bottom."

"You got lucky."

"Take your suffering in silence," came a voice from my left. "For it is the meek who will inherit the LORD's bounty."

"Grokkuf," snapped a gnoll. I assumed the word meant "Silence!" because there are certain traditions between captors and captives. I complied; talking wasn't easy from this angle anyway.

As the gnolls carried us God-knows-where I tried to digest what I'd seen in the dead world, but those thoughts were all being supplanted by thoughts on what it would be like to be stuck inside an undying body as it was split into mouthfuls and frogmarched single file through a monster's digestive tract. Spending eternity as a dollop by the side of the road was not an appealing prospect.

Eventually whichever gnoll was taking the leadership role went "Grok!" The procession halted, and I was treated to the hypnotic sight of a gnoll's posing pouch quivering to a halt.

"Are these the ones we discussed?" said a new voice. It didn't belong to a gnoll, but I took very little comfort in that. There was a strict headmaster-y tone to the voice that only gets used when someone is about to get in serious trouble.

"Gruff."

"Cut them free but leave their wrists bound."

"Kaffagraff?"

"No, reimbursement of combat materials will not be authorized until total completion of this assignment."

The gnolls did as they were bid. The nearest one to me swung its massive makeshift blade at my bonds, freeing me from the spear and very nearly some of my fingers. I collapsed into the dust.

I took the opportunity to sit up and determine where we were. A vast desert continued endlessly and unhelpfully in every direction. We were on a wide stone road that I guessed was part of the Adventure Trail, but there wasn't a single sign of civilization on the horizon. I realized with some distress that this was the kind of place you'd go to dispose of a corpse.

Our rescuers, for want of a better word, were an elf and a dwarf. Their neatly-pressed black suits and ties really didn't seem like practical desert wear, but if they were in any way uncomfortable they were hiding it incredibly well.

The elf was painfully skinny—not unusual for elves—and seemed incapable of standing still for even a second. He was constantly pacing, flicking his head around, and twirling a large butterfly knife between his bony fingers. His perpetual grin was wider than any I'd ever seen, and that included several guys I'd known at Dreadgrave's with no skin on their faces.

The dwarf could be called stout, but not the same way you'd call an innkeeper "stout" because you're too polite to call him "fat"; he was like a broad barrel full of pure, rigid muscle. He stood, meaty little arms folded, copious black mustache creased into a businesslike frown with the merest sneer of contempt. He was wearing a battered iron helmet that didn't go very well with his suit, but then neither did the rest of him.

Meryl, Thaddeus, and I were arranged in a row before the black-suited couple, then forced to kneel by way of deft kicks to the backs of our knees. The elf sauntered over to me, nearly hypnotizing me with the endless circling of his knife. His eyes were two harsh white marbles in dark, sunken sockets. "So, my little pickled eggs," he said in a wheedling voice, lifting my chin with a finger like an ice pick. "Expect you're wondering why URGH HURRAAARRGLAB."

I winced. "Yeah, I get this a lot."

Somehow, vomiting only served to heighten his maniacal glee. With an excited giggle, he slowly stood back upright, gangly limbs audibly cracking, then re-acquired his grin, now a little stained with bile and bits of food. The dwarf hadn't moved. "Expect you're wondering why you're here, aren't you, my three little pigs?"

"It matters not," exclaimed Thaddeus suddenly. "I answer not to your crude pagan threats, only to the perfect enlightenment of—"

"Grokkuf!" snapped the lead gnoll, shoving the back of Thaddeus's head with the shaft of an axe. Something snapped audibly and the priest fell face-down into the sand, limp.

"Expect you're wondering why you're here, aren't you, my two little ducks," repeated the elf, tone of voice unchanged.

Meryl glanced back at the gnolls momentarily. "To be . . . eaten?"

"It was not our intention to have you consumed by our workforce," barked the dwarf in a monotone.

The elf sat cross-legged in front of me and leaned forward, staring in fascination. "So it's true," he said, reaching out and tucking a stray length of hair behind my ear. "The dead walk among us! What was it like?"

I was leaning back as far as I could manage and his nose was still piercing my personal space. "Whuh?"

"Being dead. What was it like?" He sounded like a schoolboy interrogating a friend about his first sexual experience. "Was there a God? Why'd you come back? Are you immortal now, too? Do you feel pain? Do you feel this?"

His arm was a blur for a fraction of a second, then he wasn't holding his knife anymore. I looked down and saw the hilt quivering into my chest. "N-no, we don't feel pain," I said, not wanting my terrified silence to bait him any further.

He rolled his eyes. "Didn't think you would." He withdrew his knife with a *chunk* and stood up.

"The post-mortem condition of the three suspects appears to leave them largely unfazed by physical torture, Mr. Wonderful, and as such you will be deprived of your chief source of fulfillment on this occasion."

Mr. Wonderful let the knife complete a few more revolutions, then thrust it straight through his right palm. He watched his own blood drool down into his sleeve for a moment like a cat watching the birds. "Fulfillment," he repeated, finally. "I can't remember the last time I got fulfillment out of this gig. Is it true you lot died before the Infusion?"

Meryl and I nodded wordlessly, staring at his hand.

"God, those times were rich. I could take pride in my work back then. I could cut a lovely little smile into a pretty face and know it'd have it for life. I could feel a man's dying breath upon my sleeve and know he wouldn't be back up and writing formal letters of complaint the moment I took my eyes off him." His tone of voice remained level, but his face was screwed up with hatred and his fingers were drumming the knife hilt like hyperactive woodpeckers.

"Who are you?" asked Meryl politely.

We jumped as the elf suddenly tore the knife out of his hand. His face instantly became calm and serene, before he resumed grinning and the corners of his mouth strained back towards his ears. "My name is Mr. Wonderful. My lovely assistant is Bowg."

"We are employed as agents of the Adventurer's Guild," said Bowg stiffly. "Our official job description is 'troubleshooting,' but we are chiefly called upon to administer violent coercion."

Mr. Wonderful's grin remained, but his eyes weren't joining in. "Bowg, my little comrade in arms, did we not have a pleasant chin-wag last week about you revealing our intentions too early in conversation with everyone we meet?"

"I recall our conversation, Mr. Wonderful, but I dismissed your request on the assumption that your notoriously short attention span would cause you to do likewise."

"Well anyway, my little sanitary towels," went Mr. Wonderful, turning back to me and gently caressing my scalp with his blade. "Stop me if I'm off the mark. Judging by your quiet little faces, you might have a little inkling suspicion that you know why we brought you here?"

"Doubtless the instruction of the fallen ones," came the muffled voice of Thaddeus, still face-down in the sand. A nearby gnoll dutifully stood on his head, and he was silenced.

"Something to do with Cronenburg?" I hazarded.

"Well, sit this boy on a piggy bank and call him right on the money. Picture the scene, my little toothbrush. A little birdie tells us that there's some nobody questgiver in a nowhere town raking in coinage in return for adventure points. That doesn't seem like a tenable state of affairs, now does it?"

"What makes you think it was me?" I asked.

"Our contacts in Cronenburg furnished descriptions of the perpetrators," said Bowg.

"How do you think we think it was you, you sepulchral retard?!" went Mr. Wonderful angrily. "How many animated corpses do you think there are walking around in Cronenburg?" He jammed his knife into his other palm and tottered a little as the pain flooded his mind with hormone soup. "So tell me, my little stinkwort. Where can be found the magical portal to the fairy realm from which you came, where money grows on trees and economic crises can be averted by clicking your heels together and wishing with all your might?"

I'd known from the moment it happened that my windfall would return to bite me in the arse tenfold, but even so this was a bit much. "Look, I'm sorry," I said. "I'll give the talans back. It was just a little joke that got out of hand and in retrospect wasn't very funny."

"The talans?" Mr. Wonderful seemed highly amused, which I decided was an extremely bad sign.

"It is your bestowing of fraudulently large amounts of points, not your theft of talans, that are of concern," said Bowg.

"But . . . they're just numbers on paper," I said.

Another grisly CHLOK echoed off into the desert as Mr. Wonderful cleanly impaled his own thigh. "Oh dear," he said, as if he'd merely dropped the toast. "Another foreign hick right off the boat who didn't bother to read the brochures. How does it work where you're from, you bung adventurers half a crate of turnips and a pair of your dad's old pants to chase the foxes out of Squealy McBumrape's pig farm?!" The volume of his voice was slowly rising, but plunged back down after he pulled the knife out. "Things work differently on a sophisticated continent, my ugly little rural friend. We got ourselves a little organized."

"Did you know you use the word 'little' an awful lot?" said Meryl. Mr. Wonderful ignored her, but I saw his lower eyelid twitch.

"The Lolede Adventurer's Guild has an arrangement with city councils, town authorities, mobile collectives, and licensed, independent quest providers," said Bowg. I hadn't seen any part of him but his mouth move since the moment we'd met. "Each month they pay the Guild appropriate fees and are given a suitable points rate to be divided between their appointed questgivers and bestowed to adventurers upon completion of quests. Points can be redeemed at Adventurer's Guild branches for bed, board and training, paid for by the quest provider fees."

"This, my li— my small jellied eels," said Mr. Wonderful, "is what we call a balanced economy. And forgive me for going out on a particularly blackened and uncomfortable limb, but I don't think you've coughed up questgiver dues, have you, my tiny cream puffs? So." He steepled his fingers so hard that his knuckles looked about to burst. "How would you propose we remedy this unfortunate bubble in the Adventurer's Guild's wallpaper?"

"I have a big bag of money," I said.

"Not anymore you don't, manky pants. But it's not going to be enough. You used up the points allotment equivalent to about twelve of those bags. Have another . . . stab at it." He twirled his knife meaningfully.

"You could ask the adventurers to . . . give the points back," said Meryl.

Mr. Wonderful's eyes widened, and he slapped his forehead with a bony crack. "WELL, Bowg!!" he screamed. "There was me under the impression they hadn't given this any thought!! But witness how the lady BOWLS me over with her logic!! ASK THE ADVENTURERS TO GIVE THE POINTS BACK!! I'M QUITE LIVID AT MYSELF FOR NOT HAVING THOUGHT OF IT!!"

"Presumably you did not think of it because the points are virtually untraceable and it is highly probable that they have already been redeemed for unreturnables such as room and board," said Bowg.

Mr. Wonderful leaned on Bowg fondly. "Irony goes completely over his head, doesn't it? BECAUSE HE'S VERY SHORT!!"

"What do you want from us?" I asked.

"Ah, that's better. I like you. Well, my diminutive leaping salmon, my first idea was to grind you all up into powder and sprinkle you over my herb garden. Which would have certainly brightened up my day and probably my rosemary also, but that wouldn't bring the money back, would it?"

"The usual punishment for quest fraud is forced service in the work rehabilitation center in the royal palace at Lolede City," said Bowg.

"Work rehabilitation center," mimicked Mr. Wonderful, holding Bowg's head in both hands and flicking his mustache ends up and down. "I always preferred the old name.

'Dungeons.' But no-one pays attention to an old-fashioned murderer." He stared sadly into the middle distance for a second, then reassembled his grin. "So, my microscopic hatstands, how quietly do you intend to come?"

I took a moment to reflect. Our hands were tied, we were in the middle of hostile desert, there were two professional murderers in front of us and an entire gnoll tribe was stinking up the rear. It seemed odd that he'd even ask, but then, there seemed to be a lot of odd things about Mr. Wonderful.

"We'll come quietly," I said.

"My life just sets up a series of disappointments, doesn't it," said Mr. Wonderful, twirling his knife back inside his suit jacket. "I'm sick of all these ignorant foreigners. Wish we could have another decent deliberate fraud like Mr. Churley."

"Mr. Churley himself cannot be relied upon to provide you with such stimulation because the excruciating trauma his body underwent in our last meeting will no doubt remain fresh in his memory."

"Oh, shut up." Mr. Wonderful made a bored gesture with his fingers, and then one of the gnolls must have bashed me around the back of the head, because I died again.

**From:** "Brian Garret"
<briang@loinclothentertainment.com>
**To:** "Donald Sunderland"
<mugginshere@loinclothentertainment.com>
**Cc:** "William Williams"
<dub@loinclothentertainment.com>
**Subject:** Re: Re: Simon

I do understand your concerns, I did hear some similar things from Peter and Gavin after the Ham Fighters 3 debacle. But have you ever considered that you just haven't been creating the right environment where Simon can have a chance to shine? There's clearly a lot of talent there, I mean, you all played Interstellar Bum Pirates, it has to take something special to create the WTC's game of the year, right? Let's all try to be team players and maybe this year will be ours.

Regards,
Brian Garret
CEO, Loincloth Entertainment

> **From:** "Donald Sunderland"
> <mugginshere@loinclothentertainment.com>
> **To:** "Brian Garret"
> <briang@loinclothentertainment.com>
> **Cc:** "William Williams"
> <dub@loinclothentertainment.com>
> **Subject:** Re: Simon
>
> Hello Brian. There's really no way of putting this diplomatically, but I strongly believe that progress is only looking good BECAUSE Simon is spending so much time away. You know that I usually have something nice to say about everyone, and even when I don't I'll usually be quiet and passive aggressive about it, but Simon Townshend is an incompetent boob. PLEASE take him away from us and put him somewhere where he can do no harm to our project or the human race.
>
> -Don
>
> > **From:** "Brian Garret"
> > <briang@loinclothentertainment.com>
> > **To:** "Donald Sunderland"

\<mugginshere@loinclothentertainment.com\>
**Cc:** "William Williams"
\<dub@loinclothentertainment.com\>
**Subject:** Simon

Hi boys,

I'm a little concerned by some reports I'm hearing
that Simon has worked at home for four days out
of the last week. We should be stepping things up
for crunch time and it's important that the whole
team be on hand at all times. Don, as his supervisor
you should be putting your foot down on this.
Progress is looking good on mogworld at the
moment but things are only going to get tougher.

Regards,
Brian Garret
CEO, Loincloth Entertainment

# FOUR

"Oi!" said Mr. Wonderful, as a ringing slap across the back of the head brought me back to consciousness. "You awake, my little plump cherry? We're here!"

I opened my eyes to find myself lashed to the back of a horse, face-to-face with its huge, muscular arse. The gentle rocking from its measured up-down motion almost lulled me back into the doze before a second smack brought me to full awareness. I looked up.

Lolede City was clearly a great and powerful center of civilization. The buildings were fine white stone and loomed several stories high. The streets were wide and actually paved, with separate sections for pedestrians and carriages. Back in Garethy, you just had to develop the instinct to dive to the side whenever you hear horses coming.

And yet, there was something wrong about Lolede City, even from what little I could see over the horse's arse. Considering it was mid-afternoon there didn't seem to be many people on the streets. There were a few adventurers running around on their paid errands, half of them with the determined hip-swinging lope of the Syndrome. The only civilians I could see were small clusters of three or four loitering on a couple of street corners.

They didn't look like they were in a hurry to do anything or get anywhere. They walked around dragging their feet like sulky children on the walk to school, or made disinterested conversation while staring at their shoes. I found myself remembering the conversations I'd had in the dead world with my fellow zombies, after another round of futile leaps off Dreadgrave's tower: people brought together by mutual misery, trapped together by something they couldn't see or understand.

"Oi!" yelled Mr. Wonderful, smacking me again. "I said YOU AWAKE?!"

"Yes, yes, I'm awake."

"WHAT?!!" Another smack.

"I said I'M AWAKE!"

"GOOD!" He smacked me three more times in quick succession. All my remaining teeth were swaying back and forth like seasick sailors. "Put your curtseying skirts on. We're meeting the king."

"We're what?" came Meryl's voice.

"Use of any city's work rehabilitation center requires approval from the resident executive officer," said Bowg.

"Procedure," said Mr. Wonderful, pronouncing the word like he was trying to dislodge something from his teeth.

We rode up the main street and through a set of massive gates into the grounds of what could only have been the royal palace, because the guards outside were wearing preposterous furry hats and purple tunics, and royalty are the only ones who seem to be able to get away with making people wear that sort of thing.

The palace itself was a glorious building, all high towers and classical arches, constructed in pricey white marble. Its shape was utterly ruined by a much newer extension that hugged the side of the main building like a barnacle. It was constructed almost entirely from black glass, just like the guildhouse from Cronenburg, with a matching queue of adventurers lined up at the entrance.

We rode past the queue and up to the main doors of the

palace proper. They were wide open, and a few men in black suits were lounging about, dragging on cigarettes.

"Let's keep it moving, my little pineapple fritters," said Mr. Wonderful. He smartly undid my bonds and pushed me off the horse with his foot. Meryl and Thaddeus were similarly removed from the back of Bowg's horse, and the three of us were prodded meaningfully towards the grand palace entrance with Mr. Wonderful's butterfly knife.

Our hands were still bound, but at least we could walk on our own. We trudged past a number of the flamboyantly-dressed ceremonial guards, who stood motionless at regular intervals against the walls clutching halberds. They were watching Mr. Wonderful and a couple of other black-suited Adventurer's Guild thugs and radiating so much repressed anger that they could have served as a central heating system. Mr. Wonderful held out a hand and gently slapped each one in the face as we walked by.

We passed through a pair of ornate oak doors and into the great hall. The whole of my family's farm could probably have fit in it, including the fields. Maybe even the Blumkin farm next door, which would certainly have made the feud more interesting.

The sheer size of the place was underlined by the fact that there was only one piece of furniture in the room. The king's throne stood at the end of a magnificent mosaic that covered the entire floor, once pristine, now horribly scuffed by the expensive black shoes of the Adventurer's Guild agents who swaggered around like they owned the place.

We took up position off to the side while we waited for business to be concluded with the person ahead of us in the queue. He was an immensely unhappy-looking man in the dirt-spattered clothes of a farmer.

"Forward," commanded the king, bored.

Quivering all over with nerves the farmer approached the throne, cap in hand, as a Guild agent on either side loosely but firmly held his shoulders.

"Your majesty," he said, his fingers drumming uncertainly on the brim of his hat. "My farm just isn't making enough to pay the questgiver fees. People aren't buying as much corn as they used to."

The King of Lolede was surprisingly young and handsome, or at least had been when the Infusion hit, with a black beard and the kind of deep tan that can only be achieved with serious money and the frequent exotic holidays it can buy. He sat slouching in the throne in a bright red military uniform with polished gold buttons, with a coldly angry look on his face, as if he were upset at being the only one who bothered to dress up.

Before replying the king glanced at the Guild agent in loosely-cut suit and narrow-brimmed hat who was leaning casually on the throne's ridiculously tall backrest. To the king's relief, the agent seemed to have nothing to add. "What do you need the quests for?"

"Snuffle bats keep interfering with my crop. I have to keep hiring adventurers to drive them away. Your majesty, please, I have no alternatives. My sons are all away at college and my wife is too fat. I can't be watching my field all day and all night. I tried it for a while but after three days I started hallucinating and set my field on fire."

The man standing by the throne finally spoke, inspecting his fingernails throughout. "What did you do that for?" he asked, with no apparent interest in the answer.

"Er . . . I don't really remember. I just knew that whatever it was, it had to be killed by fire. Anyway, I'm here to ask that we be given just a little more time to pay. I'm getting a postal order from my relatives soon . . ."

The King opened his mouth to speak, but his advisor got there first. "Of course you can have time to pay. You've always diligently paid your dues until now, and we're always keen to reward loyalty. Give this month a miss, and just pay double next time. Okay?"

There was nothing but absolute warmth and sincerity in his voice, which seemed to trouble the farmer even more. His eyes flicked left and right. "Is that all?"

The advisor still hadn't looked at him. "I don't know, is it?"

"Yes! Yes, that's all. Thank you, your majesty."

"Run along, then."

The farmer was deftly spun around by his two minders and escorted from the room. I couldn't help noticing the ghastly look on the farmer's face. He had clearly been running a lot of worst-case-scenarios through his head, and the fact that none of them had occurred had only amplified his dread.

"Next," went the king's advisor. The king gave him a dirty look of royal proportions.

"State your HURRAAARRGLAB," went the monarch.

"Mr. Wonderful," said the advisor, daintily wiping the king's mouth with a hanky. "What do we keep telling you about your interrogation methods? The information's never reliable and it really hurts our image."

"It's all right," I sighed. "This is my actual face."

"I haven't found a good nose replacement," said Meryl cheerfully. "I had my eye on a doorknob at one point but I didn't think he'd go for it . . ."

"We have extrapolated that the suspects expired pre-Infusion," said Bowg, just behind me, "and currently exist in a state of mobile expiry fueled by necromantic magic."

"They're undead?" said the king, sitting up.

"They are undead," said Thaddeus, who had been uncharacteristically quiet for the walk up. "I am a reborn spirit in service to a higher cause. I will accept no further interrogation, for I am exempt from the petty judgement of Man. Only to the highest authority of Heaven will I bow."

His statement didn't impress as much as he'd hoped. A few nearby agents exchanged confused glances, as if a mouse had just marched into a cat restaurant and demanded to see the manager.

"I am a priest of the Seventh Day Advent Hedge Devolutionists," continued Thaddeus. "Answerable only to a jury of the High Pruners, in accordance with the seventy-third Judicial Treaty."

"Seventy-third," repeated the king's advisor. "I know that's ringing a bell somewhere." He stroked his chin theatrically.

"The seventy-third treaty was revised in the re-appraisal of national policy in the week that followed the beginning of the Adventurer's Guild's partnership with the Lolede government," said Bowg. "The document was included in the second bonfire of the third day."

"List the charges," droned the advisor, bored again, after Thaddeus' confident expression dissolved.

"Quest fraud," said Mr. Wonderful. "We'll just give them the standard holiday package and go."

"Now now," said the king, suddenly taking a lot more interest and sitting up as straight and noble as he could manage. "Our judicial system prides itself on its merciful nature. I'm sure it was just a misunderstanding."

This king was certainly an improvement on Derek IV of Borrigarde. I nodded as emphatically as I could.

"The costs of the suspect's fraudulent selling of Guild Points totaled over 12,000 talans," said Bowg.

For a moment, all was still but for the sound of the king's drumming fingers echoing loudly through the hall. "Yes, well," he said, finally. "Mistakes are made. Newcomers to our land often have trouble grasping the points system. We should be understanding."

"Their actions are also believed to have been a direct cause of the current economic crisis in Cronenburg," added Bowg.

The advisor looked up. "Really? Is that why there've been so many riots there lately?"

"Small communities always bounce back from these things," said the king, through his teeth.

"How many buildings burned down this morning? Seven?" said the advisor.

"Twelve, including a Guild facility." corrected Bowg. "There were also eighty-seven confirmed fatalities."

"Yes, and we missed them for this," said Mr. Wonderful spitefully. "Can we take the graveyard triplets downstairs now? They're as guilty as all buggers."

"Let them go," insisted the king. Every agent in the room instantly twisted their faces like they had a sour taste in their mouths.

"One month work rehabilitation for every hundred talans," droned the advisor, waving us away. "Usual arrangement, every five days of good behavior can be exchanged for free restaurant coupons upon release. Next."

The king suddenly surprised everyone by standing up, pulling himself to his full regal height and smashing the end of his sceptre into the ground with a conversation-silencing crash. "I," he roared, "am the KING!"

The advisor coughed, unimpressed. "Yes, your majesty, you're the king. A noble, wise king."

"Y—"

"So noble and so wise that he understands exactly the importance of the relationship his kingdom has with the Adventurer's Guild." His tone remained bored and civil but there was a lilt in his last few words that brought to mind a concealed knife flashed momentarily in a sleeve.

His royal wetness sat back down. "Just take them to the damn dungeons," he muttered.

"Work—"

"Work rehabilitation bloody center!"

# FIVE

Mr. Wonderful led us through a labyrinth of opulent chambers and down the well-worn steps of a broad spiral staircase. As we descended below the surface the magnificent décor gave way firstly to the fat-streaked swelter of the kitchens, then the pungent haze of the wine cellars and the giggly squeaks of drunken rats, and finally the torchlit stone passageways of the dungeons.

In adherence to some kind of unspoken rule among architects, the dinginess of the dungeons was in direct proportion to the opulence of the upper levels. The tunnel walls switched intermittently between ancient brickwork and natural cavern, and were too narrow to allow anything but single file. The fetid stench of corpserot and sewage drifted through the air alongside the anguished cries of tormented souls. Occasionally we passed occupied cells and filth-spattered skinny arms would reach out to scratch at us and tug at our clothes.

On the whole, it was rather homey. It took me right back to the good old days of dungeon duty back in Dreadgrave's fortress. These lacked Dreadgrave's professional touch, though, as if the architect had been ashamed of himself.

At the very deepest point of the dungeons, the tight corridors opened out into a huge underground chamber. The ceiling was too high to see, and most of the floor had given way into a deep black chasm. We edged along a narrow ledge that ran along a rough-hewn wall honeycombed with misshapen cell doors.

"This one looks like your color, doesn't it, my physically reduced chocolate biscuit?" He slapped me ringingly on the back and I stumbled into the cell. Barely waiting for the last of my limbs to cross the threshold Mr. Wonderful slammed the bars shut behind me.

"Comfy?" he said, his omnipresent grin glistening in the torchlight. "Don't hesitate to tell the guard if you need anything, he comes around once every few months. Well, have a nice decade." He disappeared for a moment, then came back. "That was supposed to be ironic. I wasn't sure if you picked up on that."

The sound of his pointy-toed shoes flapping musically against the rocky ground drifted away into silence. I sat down upon the mattress, which was about as thick as a folded piece of toilet paper, and took in my new home.

The cell was little more than a hole carved out of Lolede's unyielding red foundation, probably by lowest-bidder contractors working with cheap excavation spells on a lousy deadline. I could only have stood up straight if I'd sawn my head off from the ears upwards. The walls were so uneven I could have used them for grating cheese.

I lay back on the mattress. With my head against the back wall, my feet extended through the bars in the cell door. A sneaky rat nibbled a scrap from my toe, then dropped dead after a squeaky coughing fit.

It was almost perfect. The sheer distance between me and the lunacies of the surface world was as tangible as a big, comfortable quilt. I wasn't dead, but being locked away in my very own hole, in no danger of getting any more bits sawn off, maybe that could be enough.

"Jim?" came Meryl's voice from the cell to the left. "I just realized. You were the only one doing the frauding. But they threw all three of us in here. What's with that?"

"Your every touch leaves stains of blackness," added Thaddeus from the cell to my right. "You drag even the purest souls down into the maelstrom of slime from which you crawled."

A little air escaped from my puffed-up mood. "You could have mentioned you were innocent at any time."

"I was kind of expecting you to."

I didn't respond. I lay back on the mattress and closed my eyes—

"Jim?"

My entire face twitched. "Yes, Meryl?"

"I'm a little bit upset, actually, Jim."

"Well, I'm very sorry, all right?!" I snapped.

"See, sorry was all I wanted. Didn't hurt, did it?"

"Could you shut up for a while, please? I'm trying to think."

More accurately, I was trying to explore my implanted memories. Dying was the easy way to bring them out in a rush, but the dead world's new look gave me the willies. Fortunately, the more Deleter communication I saw, the easier it became to access it. I just needed to lie back, shut out all stimuli, think of the badgers, and slowly it would . . .

eally exciting project to be working on. I think this is the first time a game has featured total procedural generation in every aspect. Obviously we've had to nudge its evolution here and there to create the world we and the players want, but otherwise the planet basically built itself.

**HMorris:** certainly sounds exciting

**HMorris:** Of course another thing that has caused some excitement is the news that Simon Townshend has joined the team, who readers will know as the visionary genius behind Interstellar Bum Pirates

**HMorris:** What has he brought to the table?

**HMorris:** hello?
**sunderwonder:** sorry could you hold on a second, I'll brb
**IM sign out 2:28PM**

**IM sign in 2:29PM**
**sunderwonder:** dub, help me out
**sunderwonder:** im doing an interview and i need something nice to say about the dickhead
**HMorris:** uh
**HMorris:** i think you're typing in the wrong window
**sunderw**

"Jim?" called Meryl again, her whining voice spearing through my trance.

I kept eyes and mouth firmly closed, as futile as it would be. Refusing to respond would only give her more silence to fill.

"Jim, I can't get the bars open."

I gave up. "It's a cell! It's not supposed to open!"

"I know, but . . . how are we going to get out?"

"I don't want to get out! I like it here! It's nice and safe and a few seconds ago it was quiet!"

A pause. "What about the quest?"

"Bugger the quest!"

Meryl paused. Then the pause stretched on a bit, and upgraded itself to a stunned silence, and then to a sulk. At that point, I opened one eye. "What's the matter now?"

"Nothing," she said, quickly. "I just hate it when you make that giving-up talk."

"You know what? Me too. It always seems to jinx it."

Something tweaked my foot. "Hey," said a new voice. "Wake up."

I gritted my teeth. You'd have thought I'd be able to find some peace and quiet in a sodding oubliette. "Who is it?"

"A friend."

I doubted that. The only things I counted as anything close to friends were currently scuttling about laying eggs in my liver. A figure was crouched just outside my cell, dressed in a black cloak with a cowl that concealed most of their features in shadow. "Who are you?"

"I trust you didn't believe yourself entirely without allies in Lolede City," hissed the newcomer. "I'm a friend of the Magic Resistance. They are still very keen to meet you and your associates."

A faint Slippery John-shaped bell rang somewhere in my memories. "Oh."

"Take this." A little yellow shape rolled into the cell. "There's a key to your cell inside that scone. You'll have to find your own way around the guards, but keep to the servants' tunnels and you shouldn't have a problem. Good luck."

"Just one thing," I said.

"Of course."

"You're the king, aren't you."

A long pause. "What on earth makes you think that?"

"You aren't even disguising your voice. And you're still wearing your crown under your hood."

He pulled his hood down tighter, and his voice suddenly dropped an octave. "I am a mysterious stranger. That's all you need to know."

"Oh, come on. You buggered it up and you know it. Man up and move on."

Somewhere in the darkness of his hood two deeper pools of darkness implied flaring nostrils. "Do you know who you're talking to?!"

"Yes. The king."

Another long pause. "Shut up!"

Then he disappeared.

I remained where I was, watching the key-filled scone, making no attempt to pick it up. The key represented freedom, but freedom to do what? Get blasted to ashes by Barry, or sliced to ribbons by Mr. Wonderful? Failing that, just wander around until every single person in the universe wanted to grind me into paste? At least nothing in this cell was trying to light me on fire. Perhaps, for now, it would be prudent to stay.

"Jim?" came Meryl's voice. "Who was that? What did he say?"

I picked up the scone. "Just the room service," I replied, tucking it under my mattress.

Everything was blessedly peaceful again. And there was still information in my brain to be extracted. I carefully lay my head back, waited five minutes for good measure, then finally allowed myself to relax.

"Hey!" said a new voice, as something tweaked my foot again. "Long time no see, dead man!"

I opened my eyes and slowly looked up. "Hello, Slippery John."

"Hi, Slippery John!" said Meryl happily. "We're in prison!"

"Slippery John sees you've made an enemy of the Adventurer's Guild. That was Slippery John's fault. Should probably have known you needed Slippery John around to protect you from them. Slippery John puts his hands up to that one." He did so.

"Who are they?" asked Meryl.

"A big guild that organizes adventuring."

"Well, we figured that out from the name," I muttered.

"Slippery John means, they organize it ALL. Questgivers register with the Guild and pay dues. The Guild tells the heroes where to go. Questgivers hand out points. Monsters drop loot. The heroes do the quests and come back to the Guild to cash in loot and exchange points. The Guild sells the loot back to the monsters. Good scam they've got. There've always been adventurers, of course, but demand for us skyrocketed after the Infusion."

"Why's that?" asked Meryl.

Slippery John was clearly relishing a rare chance to sound intelligent. "'Cos monsters don't stay dead, do they. Right after the Infusion Slippery John got a regular gig clearing witch-harpies out of a mine up Skitterbritch way. Nice bunch of girls, actually, very professional, never wore any . . ." He made a motion over his chest with both hands, and seemed to go into a trance for a few seconds before shaking himself out of it. "Anyway, long story short, the Adventurer's Guild started putting pressure on the mine's owner, so he got sick of the whole business and Slippery John had to sign up for the Adventure Trail. The harpies set up a gentleman's club a few leagues east, Slippery John heard. Slippery John hasn't been, but apparently it's nice if you're into that."

"But where did the Guild come from?" said Meryl.

Slippery John shrugged. "Someone had to look after the money. And then absolute money corrupted absolutely, o'course. They're everywhere, now. Can't move for agents and guildhouses. Slippery John heard they're setting up offices in Garethy and Anarecsia next year."

"Can't someone stop this?" said Meryl, pointedly.

"What, like a hero?" I snapped.

"A-nyway," said Slippery John in a sing-song voice. "Getting back on track, the whole fugitive thing does add a bit of a spanner in the whole plan with the Magic Resistance, but Slippery John reckons they won't be too much of a problem. They're only an organized army of ruthless psychotics with limitless resources, but no worries. Slippery John's licked fatter problems than this." A croissant skidded through the bars, and his voice dropped into a whisper.

"There's a key to your cells in there. Most people just escape by killing themselves and getting another body outside, but obviously that's not on your menu. Slippery John can't help you any more than that, 'cos Slippery John suspects he was spotted by every guard in this place on the way here."

"There he is!" screamed a gruff voice.

"Whoops, gotta go. Meet up with you later." Then he scuttled off, followed closely by a clattering group of armed soldiers in furry hats.

"What did he say?" said Meryl from the next cell. "I didn't catch his last bit."

I put the croissant next to the scone. "He said to hold tight," I said. "He's going to go off and organize an escape but it might take some time."

"Oh, cool!"

"He also said it's very important that we all be absolutely silent for a while. It's because of . . . reconnaissance or something."

"He can count on me!"

Having ensured that Meryl wouldn't distract me for a while, I folded my arms and waited for the cries of pursuing guardsmen to fade away. Then I lay back, closed my eyes again, clamped my arms around my head and visualized a badger until I could almost taste it.

**onder:** oh fu

My cell door clanged open. A stout figure seized me by the legs and threw me over his shoulder, knocking the wind from me before I could say "waagh" or "ow" or "what the bloody hell are you doing." I spent a few confused minutes staring down my captor's back at the dungeon floor as I was carried through the tunnels, then a threadbare carpet came into view and I was dumped onto a squat three-legged stool.

The room I'd been transported to looked like a warden's office. It had apparently been in a state of advanced disuse for some time, but had recently been recommissioned. An ornate antique desk was lying pushed up against a wall with the legs broken off, while a much more modern replacement took pride of place in the middle of the floor.

Behind it sat Mr. Wonderful. He seemed right at home, resting his feet on the desk and testing the point of his knife with a fingertip. Bowg, for it was he who had carried me from the cell, took up his usual position nearby.

Mr. Wonderful was holding a small thesaurus open on a marked page. "Settled in yet, my . . . my . . . embryonic troublemaker? Enjoying the cell?"

"Yes, it's nice, thank you."

"Really." He sucked a bead of blood from his finger. "So what if I said we might have found a use for you, hm? Something that might involve getting out into the open again? Would that not interest you?"

"Um. No. Not really."

Mr. Wonderful froze, smiling thinly. Then in two sudden movements he slapped his hand on the desktop and cleanly severed it at the wrist. "WELL THEN, TOUGH TITTIES!" he screamed, squirting blood directly into my face, before calming down and daintily wiping his gushing stump with a small hanky. "I've still got a very lovely plot in my herb garden I've got in mind for you."

I closed my eyes for a few seconds until I could be ready to face the universe again. "What do you want from me?"

"See, now that's the kind of attitude we like to see. Some nice clever knuckling under. You have to really work at a fellow's knackers to make him knuckle under these days."

"It has been observed that you are associating with a renegade who operates under the moniker Slippery John," said Bowg.

"Er, yeah," I said uneasily. "We've crossed paths."

"It is also known to us that the individual who calls himself Slippery John is operating on behalf of a clandestine organization officially referred to by our intelligence as the Magic Resistance and known colloquially as the Suicide Squad."

For a few precious moments in the dungeon it had seemed like things were looking up, but now events were trickling back down towards uncertain and uncomfortable territory. "Yeah, he, er . . . mentioned something about that."

"Our lug-holes have also picked up some mutterings on the grapevine about those jerks being very keen to get their hands on some pre-Infusion post-alive carcasses that were stirring up trouble in Garethy," said Mr. Wonderful, dreamily poking his exposed ulna with the tip of a knife and watching the pool of blood expand across the tabletop. "And sorry if I'm flying high above the mark here, but your accent struck me as rustic enough to fit the metaphorical bill."

"Look, I don't know anything about them," I said, unable to look away from his mutilated wrist. "I'm not bothered about finding them anymore. I just want to stay in the cell."

"Oh, but I think there is something you . . . want . . .," said Mr. Wonderful. He was swaying and getting rather pale, probably from the blood still streaming gaily from his wrist. "You want to die. You were . . . lucky enough to be killed before the Infusion hit and now you think you deserve your good . . . fortune back. Don't give me that look. We . . . make it our business . . . to know things about people, my . . . little . . . something that's not really leaping to mind right now . . ."

"Can you kill me for good?" I asked, probably too quickly.

"Total existence suspension has been successfully executed only by U.A.L.B.s in the period following the Infusion," said Bowg.

"You eh what?" I asked.

"Unidentified Angel-Like Beings."

"Oh right. Those."

"But, but, but," said Mr. Wonderful, now unable to lift his head from the desk. "Squadicide Sue are doing some . . . stuff . . . interesting stuff . . . probably not far from a throughbreak with all that . . . dying . . . thing . . . gloshdy blergh." Then he collapsed off his chair and disappeared behind the desk.

"The Magic Resistance have been closely researching the Infusion phenomenon and are rumored to be making progress in discovering a means to remove its effect from the world," said Bowg, taking over Mr. Wonderful's seat. "Their information will lead you closer to your goal. In return for your release and the non-infliction of bodily mutilation you will re-establish contact with Slippery John, earn the trust of the Magic Resistance leaders, then supply us with their identities and location."

"You want to stop the Resistance," I translated aloud.

He didn't give a straight answer. "Circumstances deriving from the Infusion have created harmonious conditions for the Adventurer's Guild's growth. Our desire is for these circumstances to remain, enabling us to continue offering services for the wellbeing of our clients and customers."

Talking to Bowg was like talking to a garden gnome with slightly less personality, but I felt much less intimidated with Mr. Wonderful gone. "You're afraid that the Magic Resistance are going to find a way to restart entropy, and if they do that, demand for adventurers and quests will go through the floor. You know, I've only met one other person who thinks the Infusion was a good thing, and he was an insane vicar with Deleters instead of a brain."

I heard the sound of running feet coming down the hall towards us, then the door flew open and the latest incarnation of Mr. Wonderful entered, wearing a white bathrobe and heaving air in and out of his lungs like an old bellows. "Must be nice living in a palace," he announced, catching his breath. "Having your very own chapel on site. I miss anything fun?"

"The prisoner has been informed of the task we have in mind for him and our reasons for assigning same," said Bowg. "He has been analyzing our motives in a tone I would describe as unsympathetic."

Mr. Wonderful fixed me with a hateful glare for a second before it shifted back to his maniacal grin. "You know what? I can relate." He ousted Bowg from his chair and recovered his knife, experimentally twirling it around his freshly-restored fingers. "You'd have to be some kind of frothing lunatic not to want the Infusion to go away. Ooh, my old body's still here. Anyone else hungry?"

"I . . . don't eat."

"Really? But you look so well-nourished." He worked away with his knife for a second before tearing the stiffening left forearm off his old body. "Now, I'd love for murder to go back to having the same impact it used to have, but I'm the kind of psychopath who understands the importance of loyalty." He took a bite out of the bicep and resumed talking with his mouth full, blood running from between his teeth. "So basically you're gonna do what the Adventurer's Guild want you to do or we're going to cut you into thin slices, wrap you around pickles and sell you at a delicatessen counter. Fair?"

"W—"

"No, not fair at all. Of course it isn't. Don't know why I even phrased it as a question, really." He sucked some unmentionable stains from his fingertips. "Carry that with you at all times. Try to lose it and we'll track you down, stuff it down your gob and sew your lips shut."

It was a lump of amber containing half a Reetle, a magical regenerating insect. I'd learned about them in mage school. They were used as tracking devices, because one half of it would always indicate towards the other in a fruitless quest to reconnect. It was probably cruel, but Mr. Wonderful—still busily consuming his own limb—clearly didn't let that bother him.

"You will be returned to your cell," said Bowg. "Shortly a guard will hang the key loosely on their belt and feign sleep just outside the door. Escape and re-establish contact with Slippery John. Your progress will be monitored."

Bowg spent most of his time standing perfectly still, but when called to action, he tended to execute several movements in extremely quick succession, as if he'd been queueing them up. Now, he threw me over his shoulder again and strode out of the room. Mr. Wonderful waved the severed arm and grinned madly. "BYEEEE!!"

Once he'd hurled me back into my cell and slammed the door, Bowg took up a carefully-calculated position where he could be seen from both Meryl and Thaddeus's cells. "My goodness me," he said loudly in his usual monotone. "You certainly are a tough nut to crack. I've never seen a prisoner undergo such horrific torment and not reveal a single thing. I am bowled over with newfound respect." Then he marched stiffly away.

A few moments later an extremely fat and inept-looking guard lumbered into view, carefully set up a little stool on the ledge outside my cell, sat himself down, and began making loud, exaggerated snoring noises.

"Keys," I reminded.

He got halfway through a swear word before stopping himself. He brushed his belt a few times, pretending to be dusting himself off, until a ring with three large keys slid down to jangle freely from a hook on his belt. Obviously you can't buy belts with hooks on, so he'd just stuck a cheap coat hook on with some masking tape.

I leaned on the bars, drumming my fingertips, watching his belly rise and fall with "sleep." Making any kind of agreement with Mr. Wonderful would be a bad idea of legendary proportions. Someone like him couldn't possibly be trusted to keep his word. He apparently couldn't be trusted to walk across a room without getting blood all over the carpet.

*Plus, it would be wrong.*

I froze. That had been an odd thought for me. It sounded more like something Meryl might say, and that's why it was rather disturbing to find in my head.

No, I was fooling myself if I thought I had a choice. The only alternative was the herb garden: spending half the time being crammed speck by speck through tiny roots and the rest being farted out into the soil. Blind, deaf, conscious and excruciatingly bored for the rest of eternity.

I sighed. "Don't bother," I said to the guard. "I'm okay for keys. You like scones?"

"I really can't get over how easy escaping from that dungeon was," said Meryl, once we were back in the daylight. The sewage tunnels had opened out into a pathetic excuse for a public garden somewhere in the scummy side of town, the kind of area where the upper class have been shitting on everyone for so long that a little more couldn't hurt.

"Personally, I'm just glad to be out of there," I said. "Did Slippery John mention an address we could find him at?"

"Seriously, they must have really poor standards for guards in this part of the world," she continued. "That fat one outside your cell just kept sleeping while you were letting us out. And you were slamming the doors really loud."

"It's all this big city living, probably. Makes you tired. Let's . . ."

"Actually, I'm wondering if we shouldn't go back and tell someone." She took an uncertain look back at the tunnel entrance we had emerged from. "I'm starting to think he might have had a heart attack or something."

"No, really, it's fine. I saw him wake up just before we left."

"Oh. Okay. Actually, come to think of it, all those unlocked doors were a bit weird, too . . ."

"Our quest is watched over by a higher power," said Thaddeus, who was just behind us. "Through me, the guidance of Heaven steers your rank and unworthy feet."

I glanced at him for a second, then extended a hand and muttered a few words. He transformed into a grim-faced rabbit with a sternly twitching nose.

"What did you do that for?" said Meryl.

"As a witty conversational counterpoint. And to cheer myself up. I keep forgetting I have this spell."

Rabbit-eus bared his teeth, then ballooned madly, stretching back out into human form. "Make your merriment while you can, vile member of Azazel. The laughter will be mine when you toss forever in his flaming sink trap."

"Why the hell did I let you out?"

"Because it was the right thing to do," said Meryl firmly.

I stopped and hung my head, exasperated. "Please don't start that shit. We've been over this."

"Now, come on, even you have to admit that risking everything to bravely escape from unjust imprisonment, spring your friends, and fight your way out of the dungeon is pretty traditionally heroic course of action."

"I wouldn't call it 'fighting our way out.'"

"Well, even so, going through a few doors someone left unlocked and crawling out through an unguarded sewer tunnel still isn't completely outside of hero town."

"Meryl, for god's sake. I'm not a hero. I just want to go to sleep."

"You're going to keep saying that, and you're going to keep saying that to the Magic Resistance when we find them, and you're going to keep saying it all the way through finding the Deleters and removing the Infusion and saving the world, and maybe then you'll realize how wrong you were all along."

I imagined myself shaking hands with Mr. Wonderful as a Deleter beam slowly evaporated everything that was me from the feet up. I saw a fifty-foot Mr. Wonderful hand-in-hand with Deleters skipping gaily across the land, spreading misery and despair among the immortal populace, trapped forever in unchanging bodies and centuries of permanent slavery to a corrupt, omnipotent Guild. I saw them curse my name between every heaving wail and sob as the betrayer who destroyed mankind's only chance of escape from the insidious power of an otherworldly evil.

"Oh, fine," I said. "I suppose I must be the hero, then."

# SIX

We made our way further into the slums of Lolede City. It really was a wretched district. The streets were painfully narrow. If a carriage were passing through here, its windows would be pressed right up against the houses—not that anyone rich enough to hire a carriage would be interested in such a grim sightseeing tour of society's bottom rung. Thaddeus hung back a few feet behind us, distributing from his limitless supply of pamphlets.

We turned a corner and found ourselves in what I'm fairly certain was the red light district. It had the usual hallmarks; painted women in impractical stockings, furtive-looking gentlemen pretending to ask them for directions, and a curiously large number of discreet alleyways and "massage parlors."

"This seems like a good place to start looking for Slippery John," I thought aloud.

Corpses were everywhere, but no-one seemed to be bothered by it. The living simply picked their way around the stiffening bodies. A converted garbage cart was making its way slowly down the street while two men in flat caps loaded the corpses onto it. A sign on the cart read *Omalley's Dog Food*. Ahead of them, a handful of recent resurrectees wearing the standard church-issued white bathrobes were hunting through the piles, trying to recover clothing and possessions from their former selves before they became the property of Mr. Omalley.

We passed through a pedestrian precinct, where my attention was drawn to a trough in the middle of the footpath. It had probably once contained plants, but they had been torn out and replaced with a bed of bloodstained three-foot spikes. I was puzzling over this choice of landscaping when I heard a scream of defiance from overhead and a woman in casual office attire flung herself from a rooftop, somersaulted several times in the air, then landed heavily on the points with an effect not unlike a generously-filled jam sandwich being stamped on. Meryl broke into spontaneous applause, which earned her a few dirty looks.

"Funny how we never saw this sort of thing back in Garethy," she said, watching a man slumped against a wall attempting to strangle himself.

"I suppose Garethy wasn't that big on creative thinkers," I theorized aloud.

We passed by a large brick wall that was part of the local jailhouse. The authorities had put up a large instructional poster depicting a wholesome-looking woman with a finger to her chin and a noose around her neck, beside the words *Be responsible with your deaths! Don't let suicide addiction become your life!* Once they'd put that up, though, the local residents had taken it as an invitation. Most of the details were covered by smaller, more lurid posters advertising a variety of services. *BORED HOUSEWIFE FOR BLEEDOUTS AND DECAPITATION. HOT HOT CANNIBALISM. ACID BURNS FOR DISCERNING GENTLEMEN.* Each one had an address underneath, followed by the address of the nearest church.

I was taking a closer look at a particularly colorful advertisement that asked me rhetorically if I'd ever tried lead poisoning when Slippery John turned up. I spotted him out of the corner of my eye as he darted stealthily up the pavement towards us, his black outfit providing no camouflage whatsoever in the daytime sun. He was diving from cover to cover, repeatedly glancing back the way he'd come. I watched him roll back and forth between a postbox and a pile of corpses a few times before I lost patience and walked up to him.

"Hi."

"WAAAGH!" he cried, startled, before flattening his hands and pretending that his terrified jump had been some kind of martial arts move. "Shouldn't sneak up on a master rogue like that, dead man! It's a good way to do yourself an injury!"

"I'll bear that in mind." I said, with a level of deadpan that you have to be dead to get right.

"Right on, minion of foulness. We'd better get moving, we're supposed to be meeting Slippery John's contact in the underground tunnels."

"Weren't you being chased by guards?"

"Witness how Slippery John effortlessly evades his pursuers at every turn!" He took another lightning-fast worried glance behind him. "Yes indeed, there's not a dungeon in the world that Slippery John hasn't strolled through as if the very walls were vapor. Except the one in Dreadgrave's fortress, obviously," he added quickly, as one of my eyebrows began to climb up. "You creatures caught Slippery John on an off day there. And there was that place in Anarecsia where the guards all wore low cut tops . . ."

I turned him into a rabbit. Moments later, a small platoon of armed guards from the palace dungeons jogged past, kicking their knees high and chanting "hup."

Meryl hastily picked up the rabbit and stroked it until they'd gone past. "Good timing."

"I didn't know they were there. I just wanted him to shut up for a second."

"Oh, pshh. It was the heroic instincts hastening your arm, right?"

This time I pictured Mr. Wonderful dancing a tango with Bowg on the ruined, undying body of the human race as it cried out for me to save it. For a moment the human race looked a hell of a lot like Meryl. "Sure, whatever."

She grinned, and lovingly bobbed Slippery Rabbit in her arms. I watched as he cleaned his ears and wiggled his whiskers up and down. I congratulated myself for going for the optional upgrade that also provided the rabbits with adorable little bowties.

"Uh," said Meryl. "Shouldn't he have changed back by now?"

I stared at him. He twitched his nose.

Some time later, as the sun was going down, we were sitting around a table in a nearby bar. The establishment was operating under the shallow pretense of being an entertainment venue, because there were a couple of boards set up on barrels in the corner as a makeshift stage, on which a trio of underdressed women were gyrating around strangling each other.

Meryl was still clutching Slippery John the rabbit to her chest. Some of the dancers, who had spent several minutes squealing and scratching behind his adorable ears, had managed to find him some carrots, and he sat in Meryl's arms toying with one of the uneaten stalks.

"How long has it been now?" asked Meryl, again.

"Two hours," I said.

She rubbed her chin. "How long are these spells supposed to last?"

"Seconds."

"So what does this mean?"

"I have no idea."

"I thought you were a magic student."

"It is because I was a magic student that I am completely without an explanation for this. As far as I knew the world record for prolonged bunnymorph was around two minutes."

"So it is possible to make the spell last longer?"

"Yes, if you're a top level mage trained for competitive spellcasting."

She rested her chin on her folded arms and thought for a moment. "So what does this mean?"

"Could we please stop going back and forth between the same questions? I keep saying I've got no idea."

"But don't you have some kind of cure spell that turns rabbits into humans?"

"No! It does not work like that! Do you know how hard it is to turn one living thing into another living thing for longer than a second? The universe just doesn't tolerate it! The spell basically works by pointing over reality's shoulder and saying 'Look over there!' It's not designed to last! The only possible explanation for this is that I have somehow become more powerful than God!"

"Your blasphemy never ceases!" blurted out Thaddeus, in what I'm pretty sure was some kind of reflex action. Experimentally I turned him into a rabbit again, and sure enough, seconds later he was right back to his grimacing self. "Witness how the LORD deflects your corruption from my blessed form!"

"Just for once it'd be nice if you defied character and made some kind of helpful suggestion."

"The solution is to PRAY, heretic. Only the LORD may name who shalt person and who shalt bunny rabbit be."

I watched Slippery John some more. Praying seemed to be the last thing on his mind. He had lost interest in the carrot and had apparently defaulted to the other main instinct of rabbits, his little head alertly tossing left and right on the hunt for female bunnies.

"Perhaps if we killed him he'd come back as a human?" said Meryl.

I shook my head. "Polymorphed rabbits are indestructible."

"Why?"

"Well, think about it. If you had a spell that could instantly transform any foe regardless of size into a convenient fragile bunny rabbit, why would you need any others? It'd completely destroy the offensive magic industry."

"Then I guess there's nothing we can do but wait."

I heard a powerful, authoritative cough. Behind me, I saw two black-suited Adventurer's Guild agents in a booth, reading newspapers. One of them caught my eye for an instant, then slowly licked his finger and turned a page portentously. Clearly Mr. Wonderful was expecting fast results, and it probably wouldn't be long before his extremely limited patience gave out and he decided that the wellbeing of his herb garden took priority.

"No," I said, making sure everyone heard. "We can't waste any time. Come on, think. He must have said something to you about how he contacts his people."

"Well, yeah," said Meryl. "While you were on the beach he mentioned that he got up to all kinds of secret business in the men's toilets in the park."

A few moments of silence passed as I considered this. "Did he mention . . . exactly what kind of secret business he was talking about?"

"Not really. Magic Resistance business, I guess. He said there's some kind of tunnel entrance in there."

I drummed my fingers for a second, then stood up. "I guess we'd better take a look, then." I turned my face partly towards the agents behind me. "A look in the toilets in the park, that is.

The toilet where we suspect might be found a tunnel. A tunnel that may lead us to the Magic Resistance. Which we are still diligently looking for."

One of the newspapers rustled in a gesture of acknowledgement.

"That's the spirit!" said Meryl, encouraged. "Let's go."

"Okay then," I said. "You bringing the bunny?"

"Sure am."

"Could you . . . stop him from . . . doing that?"

She looked down. "Oh, come on. He just wants somewhere warm to hide."

# SEVEN

The park turned out to be a network of bright green lawns and beautiful flower gardens, taking up a large chunk of the city's west side and bisected by the river. Of course, the knowledge that plants were as immortal as everything else spoiled the effect somewhat. The place would look forever beautiful no matter what the groundskeeper did, which explained why he was sitting motionlessly on a bench near the park entrance, leaning on his rake and no doubt contemplating suicide for the umpteenth time.

The area around the toilets was one of the zones set aside for adventurers suffering from the final stage of Syndrome: a small forest of men like sweaty bipedal horses, women like hip-thrusting shop window mannequins, wispy elves like windswept ornamental trees, and dwarves like scowling piles of suet pudding. They stood in the usual Syndrome poses, the men with hips thrust forward, the women presenting their chests and posteriors like barnyard hens. The only motion was the slight up-down movement as they filled and emptied their magnificent heroic lungs.

The effect could have been eerie, and if there had been an ounce of perceptible humanity remaining in any of the buggers it probably would have been, but as it was, the display was actually rather appealing. Children chased each other between the rows and a young couple was sharing a sandwich and a bottle of wine between the legs of a particularly tall barbarian warrior.

The toilets were located in a small, pleasant, cottage-like building, with a sign reading "Relief Center," because there is a certain kind of local authority who will reluctantly concede that toilets must exist but feel there's no harm in dancing around the issue. Once again I could tangibly feel the massive distance between me and Garethy, where hanging actual toilet paper in the shithouse as opposed to old newspapers was considered hoity-toity.

The interior of the gents' was much closer to home. The custodian obviously hadn't dragged himself through here in a while. The stink was foul, the mirror was broken, and the corpse slumped against one of the sinks had probably injected himself with fatal amounts of illicit substances weeks ago—and no doubt a few more times since then.

"So what are we looking for, exactly?" I said.

There was a long silence.

"Redemption for your ungodly sins," barked Thaddeus opportunistically. "Fall to your knees and plead for a righteous evaporation, foaming urine of demonic puppies."

I sighed and poked my head outside. "Meryl, just come in."

She blushed yellowly. "It's the boys' toilets!"

"No-one's around."

"Don't lie. You're around and Thaddeus is around."

"We're not having a pissing contest, Meryl, we're looking for a tunnel. Get in here."

"Oh, fine." She stepped gingerly into the room as if she were commencing a bout of firewalking, and her eye was immediately drawn to the corpse. "Ooh. You know, I did always wonder what goes on in here. Any idea where the tunnel entrance could be?"

"Not yet." I was investigating one of the cubicles as well as I could without actually touching anything. "Wait. Scratch that."

She came in for a closer look. "'Slippery John's secret tunnel entrance,'" she read aloud. The words were nestled in the middle of several items of graffiti detailing who woz ere and what kind of good times they could provide.

I noticed that the rabbit was reaching out a paw, trying to touch the graffiti. "I guess this is it. Unless it's a trick, but Slippery John doesn't strike me as the sophisticated type."

"So this must be the secret switch," said Meryl. She leant forward and decisively pushed the brick inwards. It fell out the other side of the wall.

"No, I think you just open it by the big ring in the floor," I said, crouching. The trapdoor was old and rusty and the hinges squealed like a grief-stricken violin, but the rust had flaked off around the edges and the handle, so it had obviously been opened and closed many times in the recent past. A set of worn stone steps led down into the foul-smelling underbelly that the unrelenting beauty of the park was doing its damnedest to compensate for.

We descended into a sort of disused basement-sewer type chamber, then the stairs ended and were supplanted by a sloping tunnel that must have been magically bored into the rock. The walls were an archaeologist's wet dream; as is usually the case with cities as old as Lolede, most of the buildings had been regularly destroyed over the years by wars and barbarian invasions, so building contractors throughout history had saved time by laying foundations over the ruins and starting again. We descended through countless generations of broken architecture and fossilized artifacts, sandwiched together in layers like a descending diagram representing the development of weapons technology. At the top, magical superweapons. Then gunpowder. Then crossbows. Then swords. Then sticks. Then rocks. Then magical superweapons again.

We finally reached the bottom of the tunnel somewhere around the third crossbow layer and found ourselves in the middle of a centuries-old alley, the cobbled paving stones now inseparable from the petrified bones of the lucky bastards who died permanently while futilely defending these streets in some long-forgotten turf war.

I summoned a small fireball and held it aloft to light the way. The rocky ceiling was barely a foot above our heads, and some of the stalactites almost reached the floor. It was like some colossal granite hedgehog had rolled onto the city and died.

"Old, isn't it," said Meryl.

I stopped walking. "Surely even you ran that through your head before you spoke and realized how inane it was."

"All right, all right. Let's just keep going."

"Which way?" We had arrived at a junction. A great number of petrified skeletons were here, half-sunk into the floor and now inseparable from each other or the surrounding rock—the site of either a particularly bloody ancient battle or some very dangerous traffic.

"Don't ask me," said Meryl, beaming at her own lack of sense. "You're the one who wanted to come down here."

"You scheme to lead my unsullied being to the corrupting satanic depths from which you spawned," interjected Thaddeus. "Truly your rejection of the LORD has left you cursed with demonic ignorance."

I tightened my lips, counted to ten, then turned to Meryl. "Does Slippery John know?"

"You . . . want me to ask him?"

"You got a better idea?"

We stared at each other, and her gaze dropped first. She sighed, pulled her neckline out and spoke loudly and clearly into her dress. "Which way do we go, Slippery John?" The wobbling mass in her clothing jostled around for a second. "He's indicating the right."

I didn't move. "How, exactly, is he indicating the right?"

"None of your business."

"The right." I bounced the fireball thoughtfully up and down for a moment, looking back and forth at the two identical dark passageways. "Okay then." I took the right.

It swiftly led into a narrow network of alleyways in the ancient city's red light district. Long-forgotten flyers and posters were still hanging on the walls, some still bearing faint images of exposed breasts and buttocks whose owners had long since gone to dust, evidence of a saner, pre-Infusion era. We were passing through the parking area behind a prehistoric strip club when my firebolt reached its preset lifespan and fizzled out, plunging us into darkness.

Instantly, I heard the stumbling skitter of something big and insect-like moving nearby. Slippery John gave a high-pitched wheeze as Meryl tensed up, hugging him tighter.

I'd never had a problem with the dark, even less so now that the three of us were probably the most disquieting things in it. Still, there's something instinctively terrifying about hearing what sounded like the skittering of either a six-foot cockroach or five hundred regular-sized ones marching in eerily perfect unison.

I summoned another fireball as fast as I could, just in time to see something on a nearby wall hastily disappear. I had only caught a glimpse, but it had vaguely resembled a drying rack wrapped in bone-white skin. I found that Meryl and I were suddenly standing back-to-back, while Slippery John had disappeared into the deepest recesses of her dress again. Thaddeus was a few feet away, watching us contemptuously.

Maintaining fireballs for so long was rapidly draining my meagre magic reserves. The new one was already dimming.

I could hear the scuttling noise from all around us, now, and many pairs of milk-white eyes were peering at us from the surrounding blackness.

"Thaddeus," said Meryl from the corner of her mouth. "Maybe you should come a bit closer to the light?"

The priest was at the edge of the illumination my magic could offer, arms proudly folded. "Ask me not to warm myself at the sputterings of demonic conjuration. I am already closer to the Light than you abominable—"

He had to stop, then, because a skinny white arm had snapped across his mouth. Several more seized his limbs and torso. The arms were stick-thin and pure white, but unmistakably humanoid. They hauled Thaddeus back into the shadows and out of sight, but we heard him loudly and determinedly singing hymns all the way until he was out of earshot.

"They took Thaddeus! They took Thaddeus!" whined Meryl.

"I noticed! I noticed!"

By then I was already running through the tunnels, holding the fireball in front of me like a relay runner, our pursuers scuttling close behind. I barely made fifty yards before I tripped on a bit of kerb and fell catastrophically onto my chin.

I was pulled onto my back and restrained by countless pairs of skinny grasping hands. Somewhere nearby I heard Meryl yelp as she, too, was taken down. But I kept concentrating on the fireball and was able to keep it going about a foot above my face for long enough to finally get a proper look at our captors.

They were human, or at least had been once; now they looked like asylum patients who had been coated in plaster dust and had all their body fat sucked out. Their eyes were pale and squinted against even the pathetic light my magic could provide, but as my reserves dwindled and the fireball shrank, they drew closer with increasing audacity and brazen lack of concern for personal space.

The face of a particularly wizened albino appeared upside-down in my vision. His cracked and paper-thin lips parted, and after the usual spontaneous heave at the first sight of my face, he spoke.

"W-will you turn off th-that bloody light," he whispered.

"Sorry," I said automatically, snuffing it out. Only then did I think to refuse, but it wouldn't have mattered; my magic reserves were depleted anyway.

"People are—*hup*—trying to s-sleep," he hissed. He spoke with tremendous difficulty, as if he'd only just learned how to talk from a narcoleptic chain smoker—or, indeed, that he'd spent most of his life in an underground cave. He also had a tendency to quickly intake breath at odd points in his sentences. "You w-will not—*hup*—steal the treasure!"

"We don't want to steal your treasure!"

"S-seriously?"

"Yes!" I offered a silent prayer of thanks that Slippery John was in no position to talk.

"Then w-why did you—*hup*—come down h-here?"

"We're just looking for some people! We didn't even know you had a treasure!"

"We don't."

I wondered when someone was going to hand me the script for this scene. "What?"

"We don't h-have any treasure. *Hup*."

"Then why would you assume we're looking for it?"

His voice suddenly rose from a hiss to an angry squawk. "We don't f-friggin' know! We—*hup*—have adventurer clots down h-here every f-friggin' week—*hup*—looking for trea-sure we don't f-friggin' have, hup. They think it just g-grows down here or something."

He sounded very put-upon. "Can we just get out of your way?" I asked.

"Wh-who are you—*hup*—looking for, anyway?"

"The Magic Resistance."

It was like dropping the local cat's name at a mouse festival. The crowd of underground dwellers collectively gasped, like five-year-olds responding to the sound of mum's favorite vase smashing to the floor. I'd become accustomed enough to the dark to see that the elder me was staring so hard his eyeballs were about to plop out and bounce off my face.

The little grasping hands rapidly pulled me to my feet and withdrew. I felt a couple of them return to hastily dust down my robe.

"W-well, it would be re-remiss of us to not—*hup*—point you in the right direction," said the leader. "Less said, soonest mended. S-sorry about handling you like th-that and—*hup*—accusing you of . . . w-would you like to kick me in the stomach a few times to m-make up for it?"

The elder and his associates gently led us back through the darkened streets to the junction where we'd made what had turned out to be the wrong decision. I summoned another small fireball, and they jumped back with little surprised yelps.

"J-just head along th-this way and follow the—*hup*—signs," said the elder, his pointing finger the only visible part of him.

"Where's Thaddeus?" asked Meryl.

There was some frantic whispering in the dark. "W-would it be okay if we—*hup*—hung onto him for a while? Apparently he's telling us some really—*hup*—intriguing th-things about our relationsh-ship with the LORD."

"Yes," I said immediately. "Hold onto him for as long as you want."

"Y-you're too kind, sir. *Hup*. Good luck."

He attempted to scrabble away from us, but there was some more urgent whispering from his fellows and he was pushed back into conversation with us. "S-sorry," he said. "W-we just need to know. *Hup*. On the s-surface. The infusion of-of immortality. *Hup*. Is it s-still going on?"

"Er, yeah."

His glowing eyes disappeared for a moment as he hung his head in sorrow. "Okay." He turned. "B-back ins-side, everyone. Hup. We'll give it an-nother ten years."

The scuttling sound scuttled away. I glanced at Meryl, then opted to start along the underground street before she leapt on the opportunity to say something stupid. We barely made twenty feet.

"Hey," she said. "Do you think those guys are scared of the Magic Resistance?"

I didn't look at her. "I wonder how you got that impression."

"It was the way—"

"RHETORICAL. That was a rhetorical statement."

She was only able to shut up for a few yards. "I do feel bad about Thaddeus. Maybe we should think about rescuing him later."

"He's useless."

"That's so cold. Would you just abandon me if I was useless?" A pause. "What's that look for?"

Before long we happened upon what I presumed were the signs the leader albino had mentioned. "TURN BACK" was the most direct of them. Others included "HORRENDOUS DANGER" and "TRESPASSERS WILL UNDERGO THE TORMENTS OF ALL THE DAMNED."

The further we advanced, the more urgent and tightly packed the signs became, until finally they all rather ominously disappeared and the narrow underground street opened out into a large plaza too vast for my fireball to fully illuminate. We were soon alone in a circle of yellow light, no walls to be seen.

I suddenly became aware that I was hearing not two, but three sets of footfalls. The third one was trying as hard as it could to sync up with mine. I stopped, and heard a faint stumble as they were caught off guard.

"Who's there?" I called.

"It's me," said Meryl. "Meryl. Hi."

"I meant . . ."

Suddenly, a cold breath of wind swept by, ruffling my sleeve. I spun around, and my fireball deformed madly and disappeared, as if some great and terrible magic force had simply absorbed it. Meryl grabbed my shoulder.

"Where are you?!" I yelled.

"I'm here!"

"Meryl, shut . . ."

Her voice had come from several feet away. The hand on my shoulder belonged to someone considerably closer.

"Erm," I said, carefully. "Do you know the Magic Resistance?"

Something dark and bag-like was pulled over my eyes, then something long and stick-like whacked me over the head.

**doublebill signed in at 22:13PM**
**doublebill:** hey man
**doublebill:** cant sleep
**sunderwonder:** I told you to stop trying to talk to me after work
**sunderwonder:** especially after 10
**sunderwonder:** that's my special me-time
**doublebill:** sorry
**doublebill:** were you jerknig off

**sunderwonder** YES

**sunderwonder:** what do you want

**doublebill:** are you as concerned abot simon as I am

**sunderwonder:** in the sense that im concerned hes going to suffocate with all those dicks in his face

**doublebill:** be serios

**doublebill:** you think hes been acting wierd lately

**doublebill:** more than usual

**sunderwonder:** yeah but since hes not talking as much im not complaining

**doublebill:** all he does is sit at his desk playin the build takling to that pet npc of his

**sunderwonder:** yes yes yes we all work in the same office you know

**sunderwonder:** ive seen him sitting there with his mouth hanging open like a retard

**sunderwonder:** guess he gave up on making any real friends

**doublebill:** that's the thing

**doublebill:** simon talks abuot barry like hes realy a person

**sunderwonder:** I know, its creepy

**doublebill:** no I mean

**doublebill:** maybe barry IS a person

**sunderwonder:** ok time for you to shut up and go to bed

**doublebill:** just listen

**doublebill:** if barry can converse with smion like a person then that means our ai passes the touring test

**sunderwonder:** oh wow your right

**sunderwonder:** what a truly momentous day in the history of technology

**sunderwonder:** is what I would be saying if AIs hadnt passed the turing test years ago

**sunderwonder:** weve been over this, passing the turing test doesn't mean anything

**sunderwonder:** even if it seems like a person its always just running on preset responses to preset stimuli on more and more complex levels

**doublebill:** yeah

**doublebill:** but maybe the human mind is no different

**sunderwonder:** oh god

**sunderwonder:** you've been watching star trek again havent you

**doublebill:** no

**sunderwonder:** you answered too fast

**sunderwonder:** you totally have

**sunderwonder:** it always makes you talk like captain picard

**doublebill:** fyi it was ds9

# EIGHT

The bag was yanked roughly from my head and my octopus retinas were immediately dazzled by a spotlight. I was sitting hunched forward with my arms tied behind a backrest and my ankles bound to chair legs. Even had it been a decent size the chair was too hard to come within earshot of comfortable, but it seemed to have been sized for a schoolboy. That fit, because there was an intensity in the room that evoked a meeting with the headmaster.

"Mr. Wonderful?" I hazarded, even though I couldn't smell the usual pungent mix of metal and sweat-drenched silk that usually marked his presence.

"Who are you?" They were speaking through a voice disguising spell. Their words sounded like a baritone singer with a sore throat was speaking them into a metal drum at the bottom of a well.

"My name's Jim." That didn't seem like enough. "Don't look into my eyes, you'll throw up."

"I am conditioned to be unaffected by such things."

"Oh, you liar," said another voice. It was also disguised but the pitch was higher. "You should have seen him earlier, dear. Your bag came off while you were out and he was hosing down the entire back passage."

"Why did you have to tell him that?" went the first voice, bravely retaining its dignified, powerful voice. "Do you do it just to get a rise out of me, is that it?"

"I thought you wanted to ask him questions, not me."

The first voice cleared its throat. It sounded like a sink being unblocked inside a broken church bell. "What is your last name?"

"I don't know," I said. "It's usually just Jim."

I heard paper rustling. "James Rufus Bottomroach," said the first voice. "Does that name ring a bell?"

I sighed. "Yes, that's me."

"Hey!" came Meryl's voice from somewhere in the darkness surrounding me. "You said you couldn't remember your last name!"

"It came back a while ago, back at Dreadgrave's," I said, miserably. "I was hoping if I ignored it it would go away again."

"Member of the Bottomroach family of pig farmers in Borrigarde, Garethy. Ran away from home in defiance of your father's desire that you follow his trade. Enrolled at St. Gordon's Magical College, and completed one year of a beginner's degree in applied combat magic. Killed at the age of twenty-three by an invading force of warrior students from Stragonoff, which event led to the warrior school in question being closed down by the legal action of several bereaved parents."

"Including my parents?"

The paper rustled again. "No. Your parents couldn't even afford to have your body returned to Borrigarde. It was anonymously interred in a cemetery in Goodsoil County. That was sixty-five years ago."

"Sounds like you've had it pretty rough, poor duck," said the other voice. "Mind you, I hope I look as good as you when I'm eighty-eight. Only with a nose."

"The details of your life are mere trivia," continued the first voice. "The interesting part is the fact that a young man who met a sticky end sixty-five years ago is currently sitting before us, fully capable of movement, thought, and articulate conversation."

"Always takes you so long to get to the point, doesn't it. It's like you can't get enough of the sound of your own voice."

"If you weren't my wife, woman . . ."

"And now you've given away that we're married. Now he could take that information, figure out our identities and do something devious with them."

"Well, it was pretty obvious," pointed out Meryl.

"You were returned to life by one Brutus Dreadgrave," continued the husband testily. "A privately funded necromancer who seized control of Goodsoil County apparently in order to experiment with the raising of individuals who died before the Infusion. Apparently his success was even greater than any of us could have anticipated."

"How do you know all this?" I said.

"It is simply the business of the Magic Resistance to know everything that interests us. How we gather our information is of no consequence."

"Oh, typical," said the wife. "This is just because we got all this from MY intelligence network. I bet if we'd found it out from that gaggle of drunks you call spies you wouldn't miss an opportunity to blow their trumpet."

"If we could return to the point . . ."

"Oh, you should have seen him, dear. When my girls dug up your death certificate, he went off and sulked in the attic with his silly train set for three hours."

"IT IS NOT SI—" The husband stopped himself and took a few calming breaths. "What we need to know is how Dreadgrave succeeded in resurrecting pre-Infusion fatalities with their souls intact."

"Why do you need to know that?" I asked. "Aren't there enough suicidal immortals around?"

"We don't intend to use it to resurrect our very own undead horde, if that's what concerns you. But Dreadgrave did what we had long thought impossible. He altered the status quo. He found a way to inflict the Infusion upon those previously unaffected. If we can reverse-engineer his methods, perhaps we can also find a way to remove the Infusion's effect."

"I don't know how he did it," I confessed. "He didn't tell us any of that. I just did guard duty, ran the rat pit and sometimes managed the heads on spikes."

"I know how he did it."

I stared at Meryl. Or rather, since I was still blinded from the spotlight, I looked vaguely in the direction her voice was coming from. A subtle movement of blurry shapes behind the light indicated that our two interrogators were doing the same.

"I was his first success. Worked as his lab assistant for a while. He didn't realize I had free will until after he raised all you guys in that cemetery. I was just easy-going and he seemed so pleased with himself I didn't have the heart to say anything."

"You know his method?" went the husband.

"Well, okay, I don't KNOW-know. But I know that it had something to do with Syndrome victims. He was always sending his men out to round them up from the big adventure towns. Then he'd make me chop them up and pick out the bits he wanted. That's how I learned anatomy."

"You knew about the Syndrome back then?" I asked, flabbergasted.

"All I knew was that we had to find attractive people in armor who ran everywhere in really straight lines and didn't talk much. And that he wanted me to cut out their eyes and brains."

"Hey, he was probably after those things you found," said the wife.

"Shft," went the husband.

"Don't you shush me. And why are we even keeping up the secrecy thing? They're obviously the right people."

"Maybe if you weren't so quick to trust everyone Carlos and Debbie wouldn't have been captured."

"Well maybe if you weren't so quick to not trust people more of them would want to work for us. I'm just going to turn the lights on."

"No!"

There was a crackle of magic and a set of lamps snapped on, replacing the spotlight. Now we could see that we had been brought into the main chamber of a vast cathedral, probably dating from around one of the swords layers. A massive stained glass window directly facing us had been broken in by the petrified roots of some massive tree from a slightly less ancient generation. A lot of the rubble and rotting furniture had been cleared away to make room for some magic-powered lighting, workbenches, cabinets, and the two chairs into which Meryl and I had been strapped.

A corpulent woman on the far side of middle age was standing by a lightswitch, wearing a black robe with something of the cult about it and a pair of gold-rimmed spectacles on a chain around her neck. Her husband was sitting on a large, high-backed leather chair just in front of us and had swiftly pulled his hood over his head as the lights had come on. In the shadowed recesses of his face, something was glowing a malevolent red.

"Oh, don't be such a baby," said the woman. She smartly stepped over and tugged his hood back down. I yelped and fell backwards in my chair.

"Hey, I know you!" said Meryl. "Dreadgrave had a poster of you in his office."

It was Baron Civious. He was easily recognizable from the picture of him I'd seen in the Children's Compendium of

Incredibly Traumatizing Bedtime Stories, which had colored many a troublesome childhood night (usually piss yellow). He was close to seven feet tall and had the kind of absurdly slim build that you can only get from a liquid diet. Half his face was covered in an expressionless metal mask, and the other half was so thin that the cheekbone was poking out through the flesh. His eyes glowed red, as did several veins that crawled visibly beneath his chalk-white skin. Under his black robe, he was wearing what looked like a woolly cardigan in warm autumnal colors.

"Yes, all right, I am Baron Civious," he said, noting my reaction. "Get up. You will not be harmed while you are potentially useful."

"He's all talk, really," said Mrs. Civious, helping me up.

"Argle barargle," was all I could manage.

"I thought you were the lord of the Malevolands?" said Meryl. "Dreadgrave was always talking about taking us there on a field trip some day."

Baron Civious's face was already like thunder, but her question turned it into a forty-eight-hour deluge with hailstones the size of cowpats. "The Malevolands are now Fortune Valley. I refused to work with the Adventurer's Guild and they used their influence to displace me. My treacherous minion Wormgob now rules in my place."

"Now now," said Mrs. Civious. "You were always the one who said the day Wormgob staked you in the heart would be the day he was ready to inherit your empire."

"If he'd done it out of his own initiative, I would have been satisfied. But the Guild paid him. He rules now as their puppet. Even then I wouldn't have minded if he'd had the balls to actually stake me in the heart, but this—early retirement!" He said the last two words in the same way my dad would say "those damn coloreds."

"Show them the things," said Mrs. Civious.

Baron Civious stood up from his seat, gathering his robe about him. Even the simplest of his actions was steeped in omen and dread; when he drew himself up to his full height it was like watching someone solemnly raise a flag depicting the end of the universe. He beckoned us towards two of the workbenches, upon which lay two autopsied corpses. One was an albino from the tunnels, his stiffened fingers stuck in horrified claws that were probably something to do with the massive hole in the back of his head. The other was an adventurer. It was human, male, as bronzed as polished copper, and probably handsome before his features had been peeled off his face, so he was obviously a Syndrome victim.

"We already suspected that there was a link between the Syndrome and the Infusion," said Civious, waving a hand across the body with the same kind of gesture he'd use to send a platoon of skeletal warriors into battle. "It was when we dissected the brains of the victims that we discovered something strange."

"There you go again, talking too much," said his wife, arms folded. "She already said Dreadgrave knew about the brains. This is why everyone was so bored at our last dinner party."

Civious shot a murderous glance at her. "I could have been rid of you when you grew too old, woman. There will always be youthful beauties who would willingly surrender to my dark power."

"Yes, but none of them know how you like your porridge, do they?"

The dread lord unflinchingly inserted an emaciated hand into the adventurer's exposed brain. It emerged holding what looked like a transparent rubber ball with a number of short, quivering tentacles. The inside was filled with green smoke that glowed softly from within. It was a similar shade of green to the crystals that had powered Dreadgrave's mass resurrection spell back in the cemetery, during those happy, innocent days that seemed so long ago.

"That's it!" said Meryl excitedly. "Those are the things Dreadgrave was messing with."

Civious held it to his uncovered eye, rocking it back and forth between thumb and forefinger. "This is a Chlorofon's Folly. It is an organ found within the brains of sentient creatures, but for centuries no scholar has been able to determine its purpose."

"I've seen those!" said Meryl, like a teacher's pet. "They don't usually look like that, though."

In response, Civious thrust his free hand into the albino's brain and pulled out another little sphere. This one lacked the tiny tentacles, and the green inside wasn't glowing. "Here is a Folly from an . . . ordinary individual. As ordinary as the cave-dwellers can be said to be, at any rate."

"Yeah, what's with those guys?" asked Meryl. "They say hello, by the way."

Civious sniffed in contempt. It put all of Thaddeus's best sneers to shame. "They oppose the world's new order but lack the courage to take up the struggle, instead living a pathetic life of cowardice, huddled in the dark. They are worthless."

"Still, nice to have some quiet neighbors for once," sighed Mrs. Civious.

"From the moment an adventurer shows the symptoms of the Syndrome, the Chlorofon's Folly inside their head mutates. It extrudes rudimentary limbs that lodge themselves in surrounding brain tissue. Any attempt to remove the object results in death."

Mrs. Civious brushed aside a few giblets and set down a tray bearing cups of tea and a plate of biscuits. "'Course, we're not one hundred percent sure if it's the removal of the thing that kills them or the state he leaves the brain in while he's trying to get it out."

"So it's some kind of symbiote?" asked Meryl, a former evil scientist's assistant talking shop with another evil scientist.

"'Parasite' would be a better word," said Civious, nibbling severely on a digestive biscuit. "My researches indicate that the Syndrome renders its victims permanently braindead upon contraction. The Folly then takes over their entire nervous systems, turning them into living puppets. When you interact with a victim of Syndrome, you are addressing the entity that controls them, not the person to whom their body once belonged."

"Urgh," I said.

"So the Folly takes control of them?" asked Meryl, taking the little sphere from him.

"No, not in itself. It has more in common with magical technology. It's my theory that it acts as a conduit for the instructions of the controlling entity."

"You liar," said his wife. "You know full well it was Carlos's theory."

He took that one in his stride. "It doesn't matter who came up with the theory. The point is I believe it's the right one to pursue."

Every time I looked at Civious another of the dreadful blood-soaked stories of genocide and grotesque experimentation screamed at me from inside my head. Instead, I concentrated on the tea and biscuit he was holding. "So . . . Deleters are controlling people?" I said. "What for?"

"With no way to communicate directly with the beings you call Deleters, all we can do is speculate. The possessed adventurers make no attempt to seize power or gather intelligence, so invasion isn't the motive. All they seem to want to do is adventure. But if we follow that line of thinking, it leads us to the inescapable conclusion that . . ."

" . . . That the Infusion was orchestrated by these beings for no better reason than to make our world ideal for adventuring," said Civious and his wife in unison. "A place where quests never end and everyone gets a turn to complete them."

"You make this exact same speech to everyone we enlist," said Mrs. Civious.

"So?" snapped the Baron. "It's a good speech. Does the job."

"I really don't want to get involved in any of this," I said, their horrifying use of the word "enlist" having only just sunk in. "I'm looking for the Deleters so I can stop having to live for any longer."

"Why are you staring at my teacup?"

I jumped. "Sorry, sir."

"If you merely wish to find the Deleters, that we can help you with. Magic analysis has led us to conclude that all of these spheres are sending and receiving invisible messages to and from a specific location in the world, the origin of all the Deleters' influence, which I have called the Nexus."

"That name was Carlos's idea, too," whispered Mrs. Civious into my ear.

"Assist us with our goal, and in return we will provide you with its exact location."

"Assist you . . . how?"

"Erm," said Meryl. "Is it supposed to do that?"

She held out her palm. The green color had vanished from the Folly, leaving a featureless black pearl. The tentacles hung off it like limp noodles. Civious snatched it from her. "What did you do?"

"Nothing! I was just holding it!"

Civious placed it under a magical analysis device he had set up on the workbench. It was the same model as the one from my old university lab, but presumably wasn't crusted with dried bodily fluids from years of creative hazing rituals. "It's dead," he announced. "It's lost connection to the Nexus."

"I'm sorry, I'm sorry," said Meryl fretfully. "Shall I pay for it?"

"Don't worry about it, love," said Mrs. Civious, patting her maternally. "We've got loads."

"The mutated Follies are unbreakable. I've never seen any stimuli cause them to change in any way." The Baron tapped his chin. It tinged metallically. "James. You take one." He grabbed a small bloodstained tray of the things from another workbench and held it out as if offering around nibbles at a party. I took one, and it almost immediately clouded over with blackness, like ink being dropped into colored water.

"Hey, it happened much faster with him," said Meryl, then she looked at me. "Jim, what's the matter?"

I couldn't look away from the little black ball. Something inside it screamed tinnily, as if from far away, then was cut off by a harsh crack. The tentacles stood on end. I could feel the Deleter thing inside my mind shuddering, as if in pain, before it gave in and flashed something new before my eyes.

**From:** "William Williams"
<dub@loinclothentertainment.com>
**To:** "Donald Sunderland"
<mugginshere@loinclothentertainment.com>
**Subject:** Re: Fwd: account probz

k stop worrying

> **From:** "Donald Sunderland"
> <mugginshere@loinclothentertainment.com>
> **To:** "William Williams"

&lt;dub@loinclothentertainment.com&gt;
**Subject:** Fwd: account probz

Dub, I'm at the airport on one of those coin-op internet
terminals. Look after this pleb's issue ASAP. And DON'T
let Simon do anything STUPID while I'm on vacation.
The doctor says I CAN'T have ANY STRESS.

> **From:** "Pus Monkey"
> &lt;wakboggart357@freemail.com&gt;
> **To:** "Support"
> &lt;support@loinclothentertainment.com&gt;
> **Subject:** account probz
>
> aight guyz 1 of teh chars on my accunt int workin
> nemore wuzup wid dat!!?!!
> login: wakbakboggart
> name: drylda
> peace
> - todd

I was stirred from my reverie by the unique sound of Meryl
snapping her half-skeletonized fingers. "Jim?" she said,
checking my pupils. "Where'd you go?"

Baron Civious was seated at a workbench, scribbling madly
with a large feather pen upon an ornate sheet of vellum scroll.
The man's commitment to tradition was nothing short of
applaudable. "I observed that the activated Folly reacts
extremely negatively to the touch of Dreadgrave's free-willed
undead," he read aloud as he wrote.

"You could use their actual names," said Mrs. Civious, who
was standing over him. "They're not adventurers, you know.
They're actual people with feelings."

"Comma, James and Meryl," continued Civious, pretending he wasn't listening and was going to add that anyway. "This calls for an opening of a fresh line of enquiry. I theorize that the spheres have some close connection to, perhaps powered by, the presence of life. The same corruption of life that powers the . . . that powers James and Meryl may be spreading to whatever magitechnology exists within the sphere."

"I don't really like 'corruption.' It implies that there's something wrong with them."

He smacked himself in the face in irritation. His signet ring clattered loudly against his mask. "They've both been dead for six decades and they're walking around. That strikes me as pretty damn wrong."

I, meanwhile, was debating with myself whether or not to reveal to the bickering Magic Resistance the details of the Deleter correspondence in my head. There was no way to convince myself that it wasn't vitally relevant to their goals. But then again, the blob of amber hanging heavily in my robe pocket reminded me that Mr. Wonderful was going to render the goals themselves irrelevant. All I had to do was hold on long enough to learn the location of the Nexus. In the meantime, though, the mention of Drylda's name in my last vision had helped me remember something I'd been meaning to bring up.

"Drylda," I said. "Drylda went all weird and floppy after I touched her in the dead world."

"You touched her?" said Meryl, horrified. "Where?"

"In the Applewheat battle."

Mrs. Civious chuckled to herself. "I've never heard it called that before."

I explained what had happened that eventful afternoon in Applewheat. How I had seen the tiny Deleter inside the Syndrome-inflicted Drylda, and how my touch had caused it to spazz out. I made a particular point of mentioning how I had lumped Drylda halfway across Garethy at my own pointless expense in the increasingly futile hope that she might eventually prove useful.

"Where is she now?" asked Civious. "It would be useful for me to examine her."

"I bet it would," said Mrs. Civious. I got the impression that she and Captain Scar would have gotten on extremely well.

"Slippery John knows where she is," I said.

"Yes, where is Slippery John?" asked Mrs. Civious. "He was supposed to be the one to bring you in." A pause. "Why are you looking at each other like that?"

Sensing that he could seize an opportunity to be the center of attention, Slippery John the rabbit peered out from Meryl's neckline, snuffling at the air. I meaningfully jerked my head towards it.

"Oh, sorry love, didn't know that was in there," said Mrs. Civious. "I thought you were just a bit fat."

"I don't understand," said the Baron. "Is that his rabbit?"

Once again I found myself exhaustively providing exposition, explaining exactly the circumstances by which Slippery John had been transformed into a rabbit. This time I placed particular emphasis on how it would be extremely unfair to describe it as my fault.

"You're saying," said Baron Civious in a deadpan voice that put all of mine to shame. "That a basic Bunnymorph spell acquired from a franchised magic shop has maintained a transformation for over four hours?"

"Ooh," said Mrs. Civious. "Well done, you. Have you considered taking it up competitively?"

I got the feeling that the Baron was having trouble believing me, and he was waiting for me to give him the actual justification for bringing an adorable fluffy animal into his presence and undermining his entire image. "I have noticed that being undead sort of amplifies the effect of my magic . . ."

"Yes, yes, the Civious Effect. I know of it; they named it after me. That wouldn't account for an extended transformation of this length."

"Hang on, loves," said Mrs. Civious. She had been poking around in a nearby filing cabinet and had produced one of those vellum scrolls. "I know something like this came by once. Tch. Why do you always write everything on scrolls? It's such a nuisance to sort through. What's wrong with pages?"

"I like everything to be neat and together," said Civious, drumming his fingers on a table.

"They have these things now called 'staples.' Wouldn't hurt to not be a complete luddite, would it?" She skimmed the contents of the scroll for a moment, then pointed triumphantly. "Here we go. There was no official record, but two hundred years ago Roggar the Invincible reported that he bunnymorphed his assistant in a pet shop north of Deborah. The assistant wasn't recovered for six hours, at which point he was found in a hutch with three female purebred show rabbits."

"Yes, well," said the Baron. "This is a tactic well known to competitive bunnymorphers. The willingness to remain a bunny can be strong enough to overpower the reversal of the spell."

"But what could . . ." I began. Then I noticed that Slippery John had disappeared back inside Meryl's dress, and was wriggling around in a manner that could only be described as "rummaging." "Oh."

# NINE

**XxSuperSimonxX signed in at 1:44PM**

**XxSuperSimonxX:** hey dub

**XxSuperSimonxX:** the dubster

**XxSuperSimonxX:** dubolicious

**doublebill:** hello simon how are you

**XxSuperSimonxX:** is don enjoying his holidays

**doublebill:** probably

**doublebill:** hes stoped calling every hour

**XxSuperSimonxX:** spot on

**XxSuperSimonxX:** hey speaking of don do you know how to work his thing

**doublebill:** what

**XxSuperSimonxX:** you know his thing where you type in an npc and it tells you where they are in mogworld

**doublebill:** uh

**doublebill:** yeah i know hwo to work that

**doublebill:** and so do yuo cos don showed you on yor first day

**XxSuperSimonxX:** oh yeah

**doublebill:** you do rememer how to use it right

**XxSuperSimonxX:** yeah totally

**doublebill:** you must have uesd it if you got rid of those three unded like you said you did

**XxSuperSimonxX:** oh yeah i totally did that

**XxSuperSimonxX:** never mind

**XxSuperSimonxX:** hey ive got this great idea for the game

**doublebill:** uh

**doublebill:** okay

**XxSuperSimonxX:** you know how theres all these different countries and factions and junk

**XxSuperSimonxX:** why don't we just unite them all into one big one

**doublebill:** why would we want to do that

**XxSuperSimonxX:** and have one big leader in chaerg of the whole shibang

**doublebill:** maybe yoy shold wait til don gets back

**XxSuperSimonxX:** come on man cant you make one decision without old tall dark and broom stuck up ass holding yor hand

**XxSuperSimonxX:** this is a great idea right??

**doublebill:** well not really no

**doublebill:** i mean don made it so thered be as many countreis and factions as possable

**doublebill:** the more conflict there is the more quests and battles and raids

**XxSuperSimonxX:** cmon itd be great

**XxSuperSimonxX:** ive planned it all out and ive even got an npc in mind for the world leader

**doublebill:** simon listen to me

**doublebill:** absolutly no this is not goig to work

**XxSuperSimonxX:** we ll see about that

**doublebill:** what does that mean

**doublebill:** simon

**doublebill:** hellooo

"Hey." Meryl snapped her fingers in front of my eyes. "Stop zoning out."

I shook my head to dispel the vision. "The stuff's coming out by itself now. I don't know how to stop it."

We were back on the streets of Lolede City—having

stopped by the albinos to ask directions back to the surface —and had spent a short while looking for somewhere to place a rabbit so that it would swiftly not want to be a rabbit anymore. We had eventually settled on the dog track.

The two of us leant on the barrier, looking down onto the field, waiting for the race to start. Slippery John was obliviously nibbling at a daisy.

"So, working with Baron Civious," said Meryl. "If Dreadgrave could see us now, eh?"

"I'm just wondering what his motives are."

"I'd have thought they'd be the same as everyone else's. Making everyone become mortal again."

"That's the thing, isn't it. He's always been immortal anyway."

"Then I guess he just misses being special. Anyway, we're really making progress now. We'll have that Infusion down before you know it."

Another vision of Mr. Wonderful flashed through my mind's eye. This time he was picking bits of children out of his teeth. "Meryl, there probably won't be anything we can do about the Infusion. Let's just focus on getting me deleted."

"Wouldn't you like to die with the knowledge you did something truly selfless to help your fellow man before you left?"

I imagined another possible future. This time I saw a colossal statue of myself with devil horns and a diabolical sneer. The pedestal had once borne the words *THE GREAT BETRAYER*, but was now unreadable beneath several layers of rotten fruit, dung and bodily fluids hurled by passers-by. I was the adversarial figure of a new global religion that would exist for the rest of eternity, possibly worshipping Thaddeus as the messiah.

"I won't care, because I'll be dead," I replied.

Somewhere off to the left a whistle blew and we heard the thunderous noise of many absurdly skinny dogs sprinting across the track towards us. Slippery John, meanwhile, had rolled onto his back and was twitching his paws, possibly in expectation of a cuddle.

"Well, that's about as undesirable a situation a rabbit could possibly be a rabbit in," I said, as Slippery John's animal form disappeared behind various shades of stubby fur and rangy muscle. A despairing squeal was just about audible over the barking, but it was hard to tell if it had come from a rabbit or a freshly restored Slippery John.

"Wait, I think it worked," said Meryl. "Look, a scrap of black cloth just flew out."

"Let's give it a few more minutes, just in case," I said, not looking away.

"Fair enough." She looked around. "Hey, what's going on over there?"

I followed her pointing finger. Around the entrance of the dog track the usual traffic of men in dirty tweed suits and flat caps was being smartened up by the presence of numerous people in bright white robes, the well-trodden muddy ground doing no favors to their pristine hems. They appeared to be handing out leaflets.

I swiftly lost interest and looked back down. "Ah, there we go. The dogs worked."

Meryl also looked. "A little too well, perhaps."

The dogs had quickly parted ways with Slippery John after he'd gone limp and unentertaining. They continued with the race, leaving behind what looked like an enormous, badly-made pancake mingled with a few random spatterings of raw mince and a selection of black rags.

"Anyone know where to find a church?" I asked aloud.

———

"Slippery John finds himself a little bemused by recent events," said Slippery John, later. "One second Slippery John was talking to you, the next Slippery John was being torn apart by wild dogs."

We were walking along a street in one of the lower-rent districts, where the corpse collection points were spaced a little further apart and the stink of rotting flesh was overpowering. Fortunately I didn't have a nose, Meryl was used to it, and it seemed to take some time for messages to travel from Slippery John's nostrils to his brain, so none of us were affected.

"So, Slippery John was a rabbit?" said Slippery John. "This is completely news to Slippery John. The primal rabbit mind must obviously have taken over and made Slippery John completely unaccountable for any embarrassing things Slippery John may or may not have possibly done while in that form."

"Well, thank god for that," I muttered dryly.

"Yes, speaking of, where's that religious friend of yours? Slippery John admits he was a little nervous about introducing Civious to that guy."

"He's being held hostage by underground cave dwellers," said Meryl.

"And it's your fault," I added.

"Don't fret. Rescuing hostages is Slippery John's forte. Slippery John'll get on top of that later. But in the meantime, priorities! We have to pick up the wife."

"I thought you were only engaged?" asked Meryl.

"Slippery John found a little chapel while you were playing around with the Adventurer's Guild. Really nice service. Held up Drylda with a broomstick and had someone work her mouth to do the vows. Slippery John would've invited you shades of nightmare but, you know, probably not your scene. No blood sacrifices to horrific cosmic deities or anything."

"So where did you leave her?" I asked, wanting to change the subject before Slippery John decided to tell us how he spent his wedding night.

"The usual place where you leave bodies. In a gutter."

Sure enough, Drylda was slumped in a gutter outside a small adventurer's hostel in a particularly unpleasant district, mingling with a pile of local corpses. Her tanned, technically living flesh easily stood out against the alabaster white and gray-green of the genuine dead, like a peanut on a pile of rotten macaroni.

"There you are, dear," said Slippery John, hauling her onto his shoulders and tottering only slightly under the weight. "Going to meet some interesting new people. You remember these servants of darkness?" He froze for a second. "Hey, do you smell something?"

"Well, I didn't expect to run into you chaps again," said Benjamin.

Those were precisely our sentiments as we saw who was standing behind us: the mage whom we had last seen having unruly spells cast from his incomplete corpse. Meryl stiffened. I immediately began summoning a firebolt. Slippery John dropped into something approaching a threatening martial arts pose with all the impact of a kitten arching its back and mewing dangerously.

"Easy there," said Benjamin. He displayed his palms in what was either a gesture of peace or the casting stance for a Level 52 Exploding Bones Curse. "I'm past all that mercenary adventuring nonsense. I've got a true calling."

He was wearing one of the pristine white robes we'd seen being modeled at the dog track. He'd shaved off his beard and sculpted his hair into the kind of oiled, presentable arrangement one assembles when being introduced to one's fiancee's parents. As I took this all in, his use of the word "calling" began to feel a little ominous. "What are you doing here?!" I said.

"Just wanted to say hello." He seemed perplexed by the notion that we'd hold a grudge, or expect him to hold one for our spectacular misuse of his body. "That's what you do when you see people you know, isn't it?"

"I meant . . . what are you doing here, on this continent?"

"As part of the recruitment drive. Look, have a leaflet." There was something spacey about him, like he'd been drugged, or finally found true love somewhere where there were a lot of gas leaks. "I was like you once, full of anger and tormented every waking second by inhuman desires to blast the flesh from the bones of my enemies." I noticed the corner of his mouth twitch before he continued. "But then I discovered the Truth, and dedicated myself to spreading the joy."

I inspected the leaflet. It was professionally printed on glossy paper, and was headed with the words, "IT'S TIME FOR THE TRUTH! IT'S TRUTH THIRTY!"

"What truth?" asked Meryl.

"Truth. Capital T. The Truth about the world in which we live. And by joining the world's fastest growing religion, you can learn exactly what that Truth is."

"You mean how it's being run by mystical beings who like possessing adventurers?" said Meryl. "'Cos we already figured that one out."

"Did we? Slippery John didn't," said Slippery John. "Huh. That's a bit of a downer, isn't it."

Benjamin seemed impressed. "I see you have been privy already to some of the LORD's teachings. But it is by no means a downer, my slippery brother. Hearing the Truth is what sparked this wonderful change in me. But I suspect you have more to learn, brothers and sister. If you knew the whole Truth, you would understand."

I picked through the leaflet. It seemed like the standard sort of religious rhetoric, the same kind of thing I'd made a small collection of back at Dreadgrave's fortress when I'd been trying to find the right religion for permanent death. As per usual, it made a big thing of the Truth it was peddling while revealing as little of it as possible, because this sort of group generally didn't try to feed you their really mythical nonsense until your first cheque cleared.

"Glad to hear things are looking up for you. We'll be off now," I said quickly, jerking my thumb over my shoulder in a very obvious gesture that went completely over his head.

"That's okay. You'll learn the Truth with everyone else as soon as the LORD comes," said Benjamin.

"Awesome. Well, this isn't really my scene but I'll pass this onto a guy I know who's into this kind of thing . . ." I made that gesture again.

"He should be coming any moment now. We went on ahead while He stopped at a rest stop for the night but He should be along soon if He didn't set off too late in the day."

That was a new one. I frowned in confusion for a moment before a sudden horrible realization pulled down on my stomach and pushed my eyeballs half out of my face. "This LORD of yours . . . you wouldn't be talking about Barry, by any chance?"

"He prefers to be referred to as the LORD these days," said Benjamin cheerfully. "That or Divine Holiness. Or Bazzer when He's had a few."

"This is a . . . bad thing, right?" said Meryl, taking a guess from the look on my face.

"When you say fastest-growing, how fast are we talking about?" I said, slowly and carefully.

"Within the last month we absorbed forty-five percent of all worldly religions," said Benjamin casually. "Most of the nations of Garethy have already turned themselves over . . ." I didn't catch the end of his sentence because I was running away as fast as my ratty wooden leg would allow.

Now I remembered where I'd seen those white cultist robes before. That youth group that had blown up Barry's church, and who'd been working for him by the time I got to Yawnbore. I'd assumed it would have taken him longer to get the world domination thing going.

"Where're you going?" asked Meryl, when she and Slippery John had caught up and matched pace. "Civious's place is back that way. We have to tell him about Barry."

"Yes, yes, I know," I said quickly, slowing to a stop. "But . . . if he's coming, then I have to . . . make some preparations."

"What sort of preparations?" said Slippery John.

"You know. Gathering reagents. Upgrading the robe. Mage-y sorts of preparations." I grabbed Meryl around the arm. "And Meryl has to get some stuff for her sewing kit."

"I do?"

I looked her in the eye as hard as I could. "Yes, Meryl. You've used most of it up keeping us all repaired and if there's going to be a big fight then it'll be better to be fully stocked."

"Oh. Yeah, I guess that makes sense. Slippery John, you go back to Civious and we'll meet you there."

Slippery John didn't move. One of his eyes narrowed and he gave me a sidelong look. "Wait a minute. How does Slippery John know you're not thinking of running away before Barry gets here?"

"Oh, come on," said Meryl. Slippery John ignored her, keeping eye contact with me.

I hesitated for a painful few seconds, then a sudden thought ticked a few boxes in my head and my hand flew to my pocket.

"Here," I said, handing over my half of Mr. Wonderful's tracking Reetle. "If you have something of mine, I'll have to come back." I watched as he gave it a silent inspection, possibly assigning a monetary value in his head. "Otherwise I might lose it," I added.

"Well, all right then," he said finally, pocketing it and shouldering his wife. "Doesn't hurt to give a little now and then, does it, dead man."

I watched his little black form scamper off into the shadows, open-mouthed with surprise at how easy it had been. Then Meryl plucked at my sleeve, and I immediately began fast-walking in the opposite direction.

The fast-walk slowed down by several orders of magnitude as we neared the city walls. The streets were becoming matted with crowds. It was the first time I'd seen so many people in one place in Lolede City; people who weren't either adventurers or dead, that is. They were squeezing themselves around a snake-like train of tightly gridlocked carriages that led all the way to the western gate. And moving through the gathered populace only became harder when Meryl started pulling on my elbow.

"Hey, hey, hey," said Meryl. "Shops are this way."

It was probably time she knew. "We're not going to the shops."

"Well . . . where else do we buy things?"

"We're not going to buy things. What we're going to do is go out the city gates and start walking."

"And then what?"

"Actually we're pretty much just going to keep doing that. Probably until we reach an ocean. Or a big hole in the ground."

Understanding finally crashed into place behind her eyes, erasing her vacant smile. "You're going to run away. So Slippery John was right."

"I know—isn't that a frightening thought. But we don't want to be around when Barry gets here."

"There's no reason to be so scared."

"Do you even listen to yourself? You remember what he was like in Yawnbore!"

"But now we've got Civious to protect us! He's more than a match for Barry!"

"Have you seen how he looks at us? He's trying to think of the best time to get us on a slab and figure out how we work."

"Oh, he is not. And anyway, what about getting deleted?"

"I've weighed it up and I'm prepared to put that goal on the back burner for now. Look, we'll hang out in a cave some-where nearby and wait and see what happens, and after Barry leaves we'll just come back and tell Civious we had trouble figuring out the one-way system, all right?"

While I was babbling I was edging my way through the throng towards the gate. No-one in the crowd seemed to be particularly concerned; most of them were just waiting to be let by. I jumped up and down a few times to try and see what was blocking the traffic, and caught a glimpse over everyone's heads of a much livelier commotion just outside the gate. There was a mass of white clothing, and I could just make out the faint "ting"s of finger bells. Then I jumped into someone's rear axle and bounced off onto my arse.

Meryl shook herself free of my grasp. "I'm going back to them."

I deflected numerous pairs of legs and pulled myself upright. Meryl's bobbing pigtails were already disappearing from view between the bored, sweaty peasants. I took another look towards the gate, but the crowd had formed a solid wall, blocking my escape.

I came to a quick decision, then ran off after Meryl. Behind me, I heard the crowd moan in dismay as the western gate's portcullis thundered down.

# TEN

> **From:** "William Williams"
> <dub@loinclothentertainment.com>
> **To:** "Brian Garret"
> <briang@loinclothentertainment.com>
> **Subject:** Simon
>
> Dear Mr Garret,
>
> This is Bill Williams from the Mogworld project. I am writing to formerly ask that Simon be removed from the

porject. I saw him doing something wierd to the moderator toolsets he isnt supposed to be using and I think
he might be up to somthing. Also I cant prove it but I
looked over his sholder yesterday and I'm pretty sure I
caught him trying to access the internal net security
protocols. Im pretty sure you can fire him for that.

Yours sincerely

William Williams
Mogworld project
Office 418
This Building

"That was quick," said Slippery John, as Meryl and I sullenly
re-entered the lair of the Magic Resistance.

"Early closing," I growled, bitterly.

"This mortal, this Barry," said Baron Civious, standing at full
imposing height and going over a few scrolls while his wife and
Slippery John lay Drylda out on a slab. "Is he truly as powerful
as Slippery John claims? From whence did he come?"

"He was a nobody vicar for some nobody religion back in
Garethy," I explained. "He threw in his lot with the Deleters
and for some reason they gave him huge amounts of power in
return for doing little jobs for them." I explained about Yawnbore
and the level of magic Barry had been showing off, that had
allowed him to simultaneously float a foot off the air, regenerate
from any injury, maintain a magical barrier the size of an entire
town, and reduce human beings to piles of dandruff.

"The beings that conquered our world have chosen an
avatar, a spokesman," pondered Civious, stroking his
extruding cheekbone. "Could he be powerful enough to match
even me?"

"Well, if you're concerned about that, maybe you could get a bit of exercise by lifting a finger to help," said Mrs. Civious, arranging Drylda's legs. "And stop stroking your extruding cheekbone, or it'll never get better."

"James, there is a line of inquiry I believe you can assist with. You have had your eyes replaced with eyes from an octopus, and they are fully functional, correct?"

"Ugh, there you go again with the stating the obvious," muttered Mrs. Civious. "It's not like he was bumping into walls the whole way here . . ."

"They're functional in the sense that I can see through them, but not in the sense of people being able to look at them without throwing up . . ."

"I am intrigued by what you told me earlier," interrupted Civious, looming over Drylda's body and carefully caressing her face, brushing her hair behind her ears. I noticed Slippery John pout jealously. "That Dreadgrave had an interest in the eyeballs of the Syndrome victims. I wish to see if there has been any change in the functioning of the eyes. Since we have both a live, vegetative Syndrome victim and an individual with replaceable body parts, we have the opportunity to fulfil my wish. And this, incidentally, was something Carlos never thought of."

"Oh, no-one's impressed," said his wife.

Slippery John, who had been sitting by Drylda's "bedside" fondly stroking her hand, looked up. "Hey, hey, whoa, whoa. Unless Slippery John's grabbed the wrong end of the stick, Slippery John thinks you're talking about scooping out his beloved's eyeballs and putting them into a stanky dead guy's face. No offense."

"We'll give them back when we're finished," said Meryl, already brandishing her favorite scalpel. "You can keep them in a little box or something."

Slippery John's eyes narrowed. "Slippery John is thinking that maybe Slippery John will take his wife away and let you find some other vegetable to mutilate."

"Slippery John should consider how many kinds of torment can be explored in a single afternoon," said Civious, without emotion.

"Slippery John has decided to be amenable," said Slippery John, without skipping a beat. "As long as you give them a bit of a polish afterwards and spray them with something that smells nice." He took a rather hasty step back.

"Wait!" I said. "You want to do this right now?"

"Is there somewhere you need to be?" asked Civious.

"But what about Barry? He could be here any day now! We have to prepare!"

His unmasked eye met mine, and I felt the bottom drop out of several of my internal organs. "I was the Lord of the Malevolands. The very essence of dark magic is a plaything in my grasp. If there truly is an individual in this world who can match my power, then no amount of preparation can save us."

"Well okay then," I squeaked.

I lay on the slab. Everything had been black since Meryl had levered out my octopus eyes with a pencil. I'd been listening to fumbling, grotesque surgical noises, and Mrs. Civious scolding her husband for close to half an hour.

"Nearly ready," said Meryl, close to my ear. "Sorry, Drylda's eyeballs are being a bit stubborn. You'd almost think they weren't designed to pop out."

"Ha ha," I muttered.

I heard a musical twanging sound, the crash of a metal implement being dropped on a tray, and Civious hissing a dreadful curse.

"And one of them just rolled under a desk. Sorry. You've got to expect some teething troubles when you're on the cutting edge of scientific discovery."

"There you are," came Mrs. Civious's voice. "Just brush the fluff off and we're ready to go."

I felt pincers worrying at my optic nerves, prompting a few sparks and whooshes before my vision, then a pair of warm, wet, blobs sank into my eye sockets.

"What do you see?" asked Meryl.

"The inside of my head."

"Oh, sorry." She carefully rotated the eyeballs. "How about now?"

My vision focussed quickly. The patchy, broken ceiling of the cathedral returned to view, along with the flaking paintings of beautiful, naked angels left by a long-dead artisan who didn't get out enough. Something had changed, now, though. My vision was absolutely perfect. The colors seemed to glow with increased vibrancy. Even Baron Civious seemed to have a bit more rosiness in his cheeks—

I looked at the Baron again. Then I sat bolt upright.

"What is it?" he asked, expertly disguising his startled jump as an incidental little tic. "What do you see?"

"Words!"

"Words?"

I waved at a point about one foot above his scalp. "There are words over your head!" I looked around. "Over everyone's heads!"

They were in bright orange serifed lettering, as if stamped by some great cosmic movable type. And it seemed that wherever I positioned my head the words rotated to face me, creating the disquieting impression of being scrutinized by language. Slippery John's words simply read "Slippery John." The Baron's was also his name, but underneath was the word

&lt;BOSS&gt; in smaller lettering. Mrs. Civious's label bore her maiden name, which I won't repeat, but gave a good indication of why she was eager to relinquish it. And Meryl's read "Lord Dreadgrave's Undead Minion."

I relayed all of this to my colleagues. "Fascinating," said Civious, as the others began carefully pawing the air above them. "The entities that control the Syndrome victims appear to be employing some kind of sophisticated intelligence-gathering magitechnology. What else is there?"

"There's this thing floating in the corner of my vision," I said, reaching out a hand and trying in vain to touch it. "It's like a red bar with words around it. And . . ."

I stopped. I'd just looked at Drylda. There was something wrong with the label above her head. It was meaningless gibberish, a string of flickering punctuation marks that constantly changed. Then it began to expand, growing beyond the confines of the space above her head, bleeding into the room.

I jumped back to escape the deluge of hyphens and question marks but they moved with me. They weren't in the room, I realized. They were overlaid onto my eyes, and there was no escape. Soon I couldn't see anything but oceans of meaningless orange punctuation. I felt myself trip on something and collapse to the ground, then a string of gibbering exclamation marks tunneled their way into my brain and the world fell away into void . . .

**doublebill:** you there
**sunderwonder is currently Away. He may not reply to your messages.**
**doublebill:** dude talk to me plaese this is really importent
**sunderwonder is currently Away. He may not reply to your messages.**
**doublebill:** I dont know how he did it but dickface has hakced the net security so I cant send emails

**sunderwonder is currently Away. He may not reply to your messages.**

**doublebill:** and now hes taekn away my mogworld admin tools

**sunderwonder is currently Away. He may not reply to your messages.**

**doublebill:** hes messin around with the build and I cant do anythnig to stop him and I think im about to start crying

**sunderwonder is currently Away. He may not reply to your messages.**

**doublebill:** yeah here I go

**####!Lord_Dreadgrave's_Undead_Minion signed in at 4:14PM**

**####!Lord_Dreadgrave's_Undead_Minion:** AAAAAAAAAAAAAAAAAAAAAAA

**####!Lord_Dreadgrave's_Undead_Minion:** AAAAAAAAAAAAAAAAAAAAAAA

**doublebill:** is that you don

**####!Lord_Dreadgrave's_Undead_Minion:** AAAAAAAAAAAAAAAAAAAAAAA

**####!Lord_Dreadgrave's_Undead_Minion:** what?

**doublebill:** doublebill: is that you don

**####!Lord_Dreadgrave's_Undead_Minion:** what?

**doublebill:** why do you keep saying what

**####!Lord_Dreadgrave's_Undead_Minion:** you can hear me?

**doublebill:** er

**doublebill:** yes

**doublebill:** who is this

**####!Lord_Dreadgrave's_Undead_Minion:** i don't know what's happening!

**####!Lord_Dreadgrave's_Undead_Minion:** my name's jim!

**####!Lord_Dreadgrave's_Undead_Minion:** they put dryl-da's eyes in my head and now i'm here!

**doublebill:** it says your coming from inside our main server

**doublebill:** are you a player

**####!Lord_Dreadgrave's_Undead_Minion:** no, I'm a mage!

**####!Lord_Dreadgrave's_Undead_Minion:** i'm an undead mage!

**####!Lord_Dreadgrave's_Undead_Minion:** i don't see any servers here or any kind of waiting staff!

**####!Lord_Dreadgrave's_Undead_Minion:** it's just a big black space!

**doublebill:** wait

**doublebill:** did you say drylda

**doublebill:** are you the guy who had the account probz

**####!Lord_Dreadgrave's_Undead_Minion:** i don't have an account!

**####!Lord_Dreadgrave's_Undead_Minion:** there weren't any banks near my farm! i kept all my money in a tin under my mattress!

**####!Lord_Dreadgrave's_Undead_Minion:** why are you asking these stupid questions?!

**doublebill:** what do you mean who are you

**####!Lord_Dreadgrave's_Undead_Minion:** oh god.

**####!Lord_Dreadgrave's_Undead_Minion:** i've figured it out.

**####!Lord_Dreadgrave's_Undead_Minion:** you're one of them, aren't you.

**doublebill:** what

**####!Lord_Dreadgrave's_Undead_Minion:** you're a deleter!

**doublebill: doublebill:** what

**####!Lord_Dreadgrave's_Undead_Minion:** you're one of

those things that take over the adventurers!

**doublebill:** whoa

**doublebill:** are u an npc

**####!Lord_Dreadgrave's_Undead_Minion:** why can't you talk properly?!

**doublebill:** oh man

**doublebill:** are you seeing this don i so called this

**sunderwonder is currently Away. He may not reply to your messages.**

**####!Lord_Dreadgrave's_Undead_Minion:** the hell was that

Reality came back in a disorienting burst. I was on the slab, once again viewing the world through octopus vision. Slippery John was carefully inserting Drylda's eyeballs back into her sockets.

Civious was at his desk again, scribbling on another scroll while his wife observed from behind. "A curious reaction was observed in the subject—"

"In Jim."

"—In James, the subject. After reporting the name labels and what he described as a red bar in front of his vision, the subject, JAMES, reacted with terror to some as yet unknown stimulus and became unresponsive for some time, although it is undetermined at this point whether this was induced by the vision or his having fainted through abject cowardice . . ."

"Are you all right?" said Meryl, mopping eyeball slime from my face with a bit of cloth. "You got into a bit of a tizzy there. We had to change the eyes back in case they were doing something horrible to your brain—"

"No, no, you have to put them back," I said, grabbing her wrists. "We were communicating! I was talking to one of the Deleters!"

"You're quite certain?" said Civious, quickly standing.

"It was speaking our language but it used words in ways that didn't make sense . . ."

"This is a major step," said Civious, standing over Drylda and caressing her face again. "First contact has been made with the controlling entities. Perhaps now that we have established communications we can find a way to make them listen to reason."

We gathered around the slab, all six of us, and gazed down upon Drylda's prone form, each pondering the implications.

Wait. Six? Me, Meryl, Slippery John, and the Civiouses made five . . .

"Oh, don't let me interrupt the scientific breakthrough, my little eager beavers," said Mr. Wonderful. "Finish the biology lesson, and then we'll move on to the dissecting."

# ELEVEN

"Baron Carnax Winchester Civious," said Mr. Wonderful, perching upon the autopsy slab, madly twisting a butterfly knife while staring fixedly at the baron. "It really does pain me to the bone to see you like this."

Bowg was doing what he did best by blocking the exit.

Civious, Mrs. Civious and Slippery John had been restrained by three members of Mr. Wonderful's private army of gnolls, whose comrades were diligently ransacking the place for anything that looked important or amusingly colorful.

"I'm given to understand the Guild offered you a primo package," continued Mr. Wonderful. He was practically vibrating with nervous excitement, as if he was being interviewed for his dream job by a ferocious tiger. "All you had to do was be a nice little evil overlord, stay in your assigned nation, oppress the peasants, and let yourself get killed now and then, and everything could have been delightful. Now look at you. Hiding in a cave with nothing to your name and a big gnoll drooling snot in your ear."

Civious shook out the excess. "The Magic Resistance is more than just me, Wonderful."

"Yeah, yeah, yeah, we know," said Mr. Wonderful, nodding keenly. "You sent an invisible messenger spell while you thought we weren't looking and signalled for your spies to go into hiding. You should have given them more detailed instructions; we picked most of them up at a bus-stop."

"Didn't we talk about this exact thing?" muttered Mrs. Civious to her husband, just quiet enough for everyone to hear.

Slippery John made a big show of twitching his face madly, then gazed rapturously into space. "It's a miracle! The Baron's evil mind-control spell has been lifted, just in time for Slippery John to escape prosecution!"

Mr. Wonderful's expression didn't change as he drew another knife and flung it in Slippery John's direction, without looking. It thudded neatly into a wall just under Slippery John's ear.

"And incidentally," continued Mr. Wonderful with barely a pause. "I love the hiding place. An abandoned cathedral underground. All it needs is a—oh, no, wait, it does have a pipe organ. Nope, wouldn't expect to find a dark lord here. What, you run out of snowy mountain fortresses with your face carved into them?"

"Smirk all you like," said the Baron, flaring his nostrils. Mr. Wonderful was happy to oblige.

"No, no, I kid, I kid, I have to admit, it was a pretty effective hidey-hole. Probably wouldn't have found you." I made the mistake of making eye contact with the lunatic. "If it weren't for my little wooden horse over here." He came over and fondly put his hand around my shoulder.

"Jim?" said Meryl.

"You!" went the Baron. I had never heard anyone inject so much hatred into a single syllable.

"Didn't even need that much persuading, the love," said Mr. Wonderful, pinching my cheek. "Led us right to you, give or take a few dodgy short cuts. I'd say he's got a bright future ahead of him, but I gather that's not what he has in mind for himself."

He was squeezing so tightly that it was becoming difficult to talk. "This wasn't the deal," I croaked, trying not to look at the others. "You said I could get the information I needed first."

He detached himself from me, losing interest fast. "Don't really remember bashing out the exact conditions, Jimbo, but what exactly did you want to know?"

"The Nexus. The Deleter source. I need to know where it is."

He elaborately waved a hand at Civious and took a step aside. "Well, he's right there. Feel free to interrogate."

Stupidly I met Civious's gaze, and it took all of my concentration to not immediately burst into flames. "Er . . ."

"I name you betrayer," he said flatly, voice quivering with suppressed rage. "You will be divided into your component parts, and every single one will know a new agony for a hundred lifetimes."

"We're very disappointed in you, young man," said Mrs. Civious. The Baron's words had been painful, but hers were like tent pegs being hammered into my knees.

"Tch, bad luck," said Mr. Wonderful. "Thanks for playing, have a nice un-life or whatever you call it."

"This isn't fair," I insisted.

"You were imprisoned in the work rehabilitation center on a charge of quest fraud," said Bowg. "You were offered your freedom and a pardon in return for cooperation with our enterprise. You and your colleague may now go free and our dealings are concluded."

"Oh, is that right," said Meryl. It was a tone of voice I'd never heard from her before. A sarcastic, jaded tone, edged with genuine anger. It was like watching a toothless puppy trying to fasten its gums around an intruder's leg.

"Your suffering will be eternal," said Civious, who hadn't ceased to glare at me for a moment. "In a millennia's time scrolls will still be written on the horrors you suffer."

"Now, I would think even you would have stopped using scrolls by then, dear."

"And you," continued Civious, rotating his entire body towards Mr. Wonderful as if being turned by a giant crank. "You can gloat while you can. My power cannot be contained by your petty methods."

Mr. Wonderful's smile faded. For a moment he almost looked regretful, then his expression slowly twisted into rage. He stepped towards Civious until they were nose to nose, then spoke slowly and bitterly, spitting each word into the vampire's face. "Who the hell's gloating, hm? You think I'm enjoying this?"

Meryl, Slippery John, and I all nodded.

"Well, I'm not," he retorted weakly, before jabbing a finger recklessly into Civious's chest. "You were my idol. I had a poster of you in my bedroom. I used to dream of meeting you and you adopting me and throwing me big birthday parties and pushing my real dad off a bridge, and . . ." He was staggering around now, sweating profusely. His gangly limbs shifted like a couple of deck chairs trying to pull themselves free of each other. "I don't like any of this. This Infusion rubbish. But there's no way to reverse it, is there? It's not a disease, it's . . . it's evolution. You might as well try to retract your own arms and legs by thinking really hard."

"Of course it can be reversed," said Meryl nervously. "It's just that no-one's found a way."

"Fifteen years!" squawked Mr. Wonderful. "Fifteen years of this plague! Fifteen years without proper killing! There comes a time when you have to give up!" He seemed to unravel more and more the longer he had to stand in front of Civious. His hands were at his ears and his face was horribly twisted with fear. Dark patches of sweat were spreading all over his suit. "Why can't . . . I just . . ."

"Mr. Wonderful," said Bowg, simply. For the first time, his voice displayed an ounce of inflection; a very slight emphasis on the first syllable of "Wonderful": a warning. Mr. Wonderful reacted with a terrified start, then he screwed his eyes shut and all emotion drained from him like water from an upturned bucket. He stood motionless for a moment before his eyes flicked open and his grin returned.

"Yes, well, can't stand around here nattering like a little mothers' meeting," he said, twirling his knife again. "The good Baron over here has an appointment with an interrogation room at the castle and my favorite box of nipple clips. If you're . . ."

"HAAAAAAAAAAAAAAAAI," cried Slippery John, hurling himself forward, limbs flailing and swinging in a magnificent display of martial arts training. His little mustachioed face ran straight into Mr. Wonderful's twirling knife and the result was not dissimilar to a bag of jam being thrown in front of a lawnmower.

"Anyway, as I was saying," said Mr. Wonderful, shaking what I think was a tongue off his wrist. "If you're very good, Jimbo, I'll let you sit in on the interview."

I screwed my eyes shut and hung my head, turning my back on Civious. I could still feel his gaze boring into my shoulder blades.

"Then let's all head for home, my little back stabbers."

"Despatch officers to nearby churches with orders to recapture the individual who identifies as Slippery John," said Bowg to one of the gnolls.

The gnolls filed out through the surface tunnel, Civious and his wife following, pictures of quiet, straight-backed dignity. Meryl tried to copy them as she followed, but looked more like a small child imitating her parents while out on the town.

She stopped at the door and looked at me. I expected there to be milky gray tears in her eyes, but they were dry. Her mouth was set into a flat, angry line. "You really aren't any kind of hero, are you."

"I did keep saying."

Then she was gone.

"Chin up, my little dog biscuit," said Mr. Wonderful, taking up the rear of the procession. "Once you get yourself killed properly there'll be plenty of loose chicks in the special hell for people who betray their mates."

I dug my hands in my pockets, hunched my shoulders and followed. "We're more like colleagues, really."

The sun was setting and the thick smog from Lolede's corpse incinerators was painting thick brush strokes of brown on a glowing orange sky.

"Sorry we couldn't get a proper procession to the palace worked out, your lordship," said Mr. Wonderful to Civious. "On longer notice you'd have gotten the full treatment. Stupid hat, donkey cart, pulled along through the streets for the kids to throw rotten peaches at. You'll have to make do with being manhandled by the smelliest gnoll we've got."

"Greef?" said a nearby gnoll hopefully.

"No, the gist of Mr. Wonderful's statement was that there would not be peaches available to your colleagues on this occasion, Terrorfax," said Bowg. "At the point when we pass through the market you will be debited one or more boxes of spoiled cabbages."

"Groff."

I risked a glance over at Meryl. She was walking along beside the Civiouses (Civii?), staring at the ground. The last I'd seen her impenetrable bubbliness vanish like this was in Yawnbore, when rumors of my disintegration had been greatly overstated.

*That's because she genuinely cares about you*, went a little voice in the back of my mind. *Not in the sense that you could potentially be useful at some point, or because they've got nothing better to do than tag along, the way most of your relationships work.*

*Look*, I replied, *Back off. Firstly I have enough voices in my head with all that Deleter rubbish I have in here, and secondly, you can stop trying to appeal to my human side, because that part of me is currently a layer of dust in the bottom of a coffin thousands of miles away. She's only been trying to keep me going because I'm from Borrigarde and she's a nationalist weirdo who wants me to join the pig farmer's rebellion. There's no reason to give a flying toss about her.*

*No, I guess there isn't,* said the voice. *So why do you?*

I took another glance at Meryl, but a crowd of fleeing peasants were got in the way.

The fatalistic population of Lolede had suddenly conjured up a lot of energy from somewhere. They were running at full pelt, the men clutching as many bags and boxes of possessions as they could muster, the women dragging screaming children by the hand. They were all fleeing in the opposite direction from where we were going, a detail I should probably have read more into.

"Stop!" yelled Mr. Wonderful. He had to yell it a few more times before the order osmosed through the gnolls' earwax to their brains. Then he stepped out into the middle of the street and held an arm out rigidly to the side. A few seconds later, there was a SMACK and a fleeing peasant fell back with a broken nose.

"What're you running for? Where's the fire?" asked Mr. Wonderful, holding up the unfortunate fellow by the hair.

"Over there," the peasant replied, pointing, before struggling free of Mr. Wonderful and sprinting after his fellows.

By then, the smell of smoke and the sound of roaring flames had reached us. The sky was suddenly orange with fire rather than glorious picturesque dusk. We looked up just in time to see the large upper window of the towering palace of Lolede burst outwards and vomit flame.

"So, I believe you were saying you were escorting us to the palace," said Civious, turning to Mr. Wonderful. The elf chose not to reply, but his habitual knife-twirling accelerated a few notches.

"Proceeding to the administrative center will resume as planned, pending further developments," said Bowg.

Further developments came when I saw a couple of those white robe-wearing types round a corner and drift towards us, ringing little finger bells and occasionally skipping. Certainly disquieting, but I still felt that the townspeople had overreacted somewhat.

"Oh, hello," said Benjamin, for the lead devotee was none other. "Happened earlier than we anticipated, don't you know."

"What did?" I asked, running forward.

"The coming of the LORD, of course. He arrived an hour ago with the rest of our happy little group."

"What's the hold up?" called Mr. Wonderful from the rear. "Just tell him we don't want any pamphlets!!"

"Barry's here?" I said. "Did he light all those fires?"

"Well, not personally, no. The LORD always calls for verbal diplomacy and authorizes violence with extreme reluctance, as I'm sure you know. It's just that the followers of the Truth can tend towards the over-zealous."

"But . . . all you're doing is skipping about ringing bells."

"Ah. That's the thing about learning the Truth, you see. It changes you, but there's no way of predicting how. I was one of the ones who made peace with themselves. Some people just stop caring altogether, become totally indifferent. And some people . . ." He rotated a hand and screwed up his face meaningfully.

"Some people what?" I could hear the distant thunder of charging feet. I'd assumed that it belonged to the peasants who had just run past, but now I realized it was getting louder.

"Some people go completely off their bonce. You remember Groyn? Short chap, beard, sawed off your foot?"

"Yeah?"

"Learnt the Truth the same time I did. Went on a voyage to blotto junction, I'm afraid. I don't think he's stopped biting the heads off children for a moment since then."

The rumbling was getting extremely close, and, I realized, was mingled with a bloodlusty roar of absolutely incredible fury, emerging from several well-muscled throats.

"Isn't it marvellous?" said Benjamin, looking back down the road towards the sound. "Soon everyone will know their own Truth."

The noise was suddenly joined by accompanying visuals when a horde of muscular fanatics in red-spattered white robes appeared at the far end of the street, bearing down upon us, brandishing massive bladed weapons overhead and screaming.

"Gnolls, adopt battle formation," droned Bowg, who had shrewdly maneuvered himself to the back of our group without anyone noticing.

"Grurf?"

"He means, wave a weapon around in front of you and run in that direction until the screaming stops," said Mr. Wonderful helpfully.

"Grafk."

The gnoll army's tactics were virtually identical to the cultists; they immediately charged forward holding weapons

aloft and bellowing all the air out of their lungs. But while
the gnolls were doing the same thing they did for most of
their waking (and sometimes sleeping) lives, the insane
acolytes were genuinely angry about something. So it may
have been complacency that led to the gnoll defeat.

One gnoll can easily kill one adventurer, even a foamy-
mouthed rabid adventurer drugged up to the eyeballs with
religious fervor. Indeed, a gnoll could comfortably kill six
adventurers simultaneously by employing all four limbs, teeth
and tail, but it's the seventh adventurer lodging axes between
their vertebrae that proves problematic, and there were more
than enough adventurers to go round. They were still pouring
into the battle even when the last of the gnolls was being
stamped into paté.

"It seems your forces have been found wanting," said
Civious.

Mr. Wonderful was breathing fast and his knife was
twirling so quickly that an occasional fingertip flew out of
the blur. "Just say 'we lost!'" he yelled. "TWO WORDS! WE!
LOST! YOU SOUND LIKE A PRICK!"

"Perhaps we should start running," I suggested, as the
victorious adventurers turned to us without even pausing to
wipe the pulverized gnoll off their boots.

"Why don't you just offer them a deal and sell us all out?"
said Meryl nastily.

Everyone else present was either too proud, too upset, or
too insane to see sense, so it was up to me to seize the initiative and run for the nearest side alley. My companions
followed one by one as the sight of the advancing horde broke
down their confidence.

While large armies of berserk warriors are fine with simple
instructions like "run down a street killing everything," they
have trouble when you try to program in more complex instruc-

tions like "follow stragglers down alleyways." The mob roared harmlessly past the junction behind us, and were slowly absorbed into the background noise of the stricken city as we ran roughly in the opposite direction, taking random turns.

We were temporarily safe, but that came with the tense realization that we had no idea where we were. We stopped in a little alley that opened into another main road and peered around the corner. The area was deserted but for discarded suitcases and a few stragglers.

"We must find access to the underground," said Civious. "In my lair, we can regroup."

"We don't have to regroup, we're already in a group," said Mrs. Civious. "You want to go back for your train set, don't you?"

"No," he replied, a little too quickly.

"Well, maybe we should find an Adventurer's Guild and hook up with OUR mates," said Mr. Wonderful, hands on hips. "Maybe that'd make you a little bit less inclined to think you're in charge, hmm?"

"We could just work together for a bit," I said nervously as the air between Civious and Wonderful began to crackle with hatred.

"Oh, listen to the noble bastion of friendship," said Meryl, arms folded.

"You know, Meryl, at some point you have to let being cross at me fall below survival as a priority."

"What do you care? You don't want to survive at all."

"Will everyone . . ." began Mrs. Civious in a loud, school-teachery sort of voice, before she was silenced by a crowd of screaming children fleeing past the alley entrance, closely followed by a very hungry-looking Groyn.

I poked my head around the corner and withdrew it as fast as I could when I saw another charging mob of white-clad murderers following him. "How many of them are there going to be?" I wondered aloud, exasperated.

"Logically however many are required to destroy or force submission from the largest city in the world," offered Bowg.

"You really think that's what they want?" said Meryl.

"Well, doesn't look like they're here for the theaters, does it?" snapped Mr. Wonderful. He was clearly feeling confused and redundant from no longer being the most dangerous thing in the room.

"This way," commanded Mrs. Civious, since all the other potential leaders were too busy glaring at each other.

We zig-zagged back through the alleys, switching direction whenever we heard screams and tramping feet, until we inadvertently took one too many turns and burst out of the slums altogether and into the commercial district, where the streets were wide enough to occasionally admit sunlight to the ground.

"I hear crowds," said Mr. Wonderful. "Back we go."

"Wait," said Mrs. Civious. "It's not the cultists. I don't hear screaming."

That was novel enough to engage everyone's interest, and we carefully made our way towards a nearby pedestrian precinct. The sound of a bustling crowd became clearer and clearer until I poked my head around the corner of a pie shop and saw the cause of the commotion.

Making its way down the street towards us was a makeshift army of townspeople. Burly builders and dockworkers in rolled-up sleeves and flat caps clutched sledgehammers and crowbars, forming a protective frontal guard in front of a few rows of office workers armed with staplers and chairs.

Leading them, holding aloft an expensive-looking ornate sword, was a familiar man in an equally familiar hooded robe.

He noticed us arrive and held up a hand for his army to halt, which they eventually managed after a few yards of pushing and swearing.

"Hail," said Civious.

"'Ello," said Mrs. Civious.

"Baron Civious," said the King of Lolede. "Will the Magic Resistance join our struggle against the invaders?"

"We are at your command, your majesty," said Civious.

The king suddenly spotted the black smears of Mr. Wonderful and Bowg amongst us. "Don't call me your majesty!" he said instantly. "I'm not the king! I'm someone else!"

"But you're holding the King's Sword," said Meryl.

"That's true." He coughed and hid it behind his cloak, trying unsuccessfully to make it look natural. "That's. Because. The king let me borrow it. Because. I'm. His . . . dentist."

One of the dockworkers tapped him on the shoulder. "I thought you said you were the king?"

"Does it matter?" said the king.

"Well, yeah, it's kind of the only reason we're following you around . . ."

"Shut up, you stupid peasant," replied the king, through his teeth. The peasants accepted this as an answer.

"Do you know what's happening?" asked Civious, after we had integrated our pathetic army into theirs and movement towards wherever-the-hell-we-were-going had resumed. Bowg and Mr. Wonderful took up the rear, hands behind backs non-committally.

"I was in the palace," said the poorly-disguised king. He shot a nervous look at Mr. Wonderful, who was listening with interest. "As would be expected of me, being the royal dentist. They marched straight into the courtyard and started hurling burning missiles at the walls with some kind of catapult thing with a sling."

"Trebuchet," I corrected, but he ignored me.

"I sent out . . . they sent out the guards to repel them, but most of the guards had already run away. Their role has been entirely ceremonial for years; we don't even train them to use weapons anymore. I mean the king doesn't, obviously."

"Obviously," said Civious, deadpan.

"I was forced to sneak out the back. I barely had time to ta—to borrow the King's sword. There was nothing more that could be done for the palace, but it doesn't matter anymore. I knew that as long as I had the sword, the people would have a symbol to rally behind, and inspire them to fight, and die, for their city." One of the inspired peasants coughed. "But I caught a glimpse of the invader's leader before I left. They've been setting up a base in the main square."

"Their leader," said Civious. "Is he a priest?"

"Yes, sort of. More of a vicar, though. Flighty chap, got a problem with the ground. How did you know that?"

"The lifeblood of the Magic Resistance is its intelligence network."

Mrs. Civious rolled her eyes and Civious himself gave me a look that would require several washes in bleach before it could be described as merely "dirty." The king noticed and looked at me in the general patronizing faux-interested manner of royals meeting commoners.

"Ah, hello again," he said, obviously fighting the urge to ask me what I did and if I enjoyed the work. "Remember me? I was the mysterious stranger who gave you the key to your cell?"

"Yes, we'd met just before then, in the throne room."

He tried to laugh that one off, but it came out rather hollowly. "Ha ha, that doesn't seem likely at all." He flashed me a rather threatening look before quickly returning to noble civility. "Do I take it you've encountered this vicar before?"

"He tried to set us on fire, back in Garethy. Deleters took him over, then he went mad. There's a longer version of this story, obviously."

"Is that one of his people?"

I looked where he was nodding. A familiar figure was jogging leisurely up the street towards us. "That's Benjamin. He tried to set us on fire a couple of times, too, but in a slightly different way."

"Hello there, everyone," said Benjamin, waving. Civious held up a hand to stop the army and they did so instantly, to the annoyance of the king. Benjamin stood before us and clasped his hands earnestly, and if he was rattled by the multitude of armed working class glaring at him, he didn't show it.

"I'm just going around sending a bit of a message to all the resisting armies I can find," he said. "The LORD wants you all to come to the main square by the palace. Bring as much backup as you like in case things get ugly, but we're hoping we can resolve things without having to crush your entire forces. Agreeable?"

Civious, Mrs. Civious and the King, the self-appointed generals of our makeshift army, exchanged looks. "Advice?"

"A par-lay would evaporate all possibility of a surprise assault," said Civious, stroking his cheekbone again. "It would also, however, present the opportunity to assess our enemy, and perhaps even kill their leader while he is close and has his guard down."

The king snapped his fingers excitedly. "Underhand tactics. I knew you'd be the right fellow to have around. They only ever taught me how to be gentlemanly in warfare and that always struck me as so bloody idiotic."

"That would be at dental school, would it?" piped up Mr. Wonderful from somewhere at the back.

"The . . . war on plaque can get pretty nasty."

# TWELVE

"Meryl," I said, sidling close to her as we marched upon the city center. "Can I talk to you for a moment?"

"Hmph," she said, not looking at me.

"Look, I didn't have a choice. They were going to grind me up and throw me to the rosemary. And there wasn't any other way to get us out of the dungeon."

"The king's dentist said he gave you a key," she said, keeping her voice willfully flat. "You were hoping I'd forgotten about that, weren't you."

She had me there. "Could you put aside how much you hate me now for a bit? I need to tell you something important."

"Like what."

"The Deleter thing in my head." I tapped my skull. "It's not telling me things anymore. After we put Drylda's eyes in my face I haven't been able to bring any more out. It's like it's used up."

"That's a shame," said Meryl, insincerely.

"Look, could you stop being all huffy? I'm sorry, all right? I made a bad decision. Everyone's entitled to those. We have to move on. Things are getting serious."

She finally looked at me, her eyes bathed in something approaching pity. "Jim, listen. Forget about the betrayal thing. All that did was make me realize something I should have picked up on a long time ago."

"Like what?" I asked, guiltily suspecting that I knew what she was going to say.

"That you get really annoyed having me around. You consider me some nuisance to shake off." Her gaze dropped to the ground. "That's fair enough. It's not a rule that everyone has to get on with everyone else. You won't have to put up with me anymore. We can both find our own way around, now."

"Don't be stupid, Meryl. I need you."

Somewhere in the recesses of my mind, an inner voice looked up from its newspaper and raised an eyebrow. Meryl looked at me again, brow furrowed and eyes wide. "What did you say?"

"I said I need you. I can't sew my own bits back on."

I mentally smacked myself the moment the words fell out. Her face crumpled with distaste, and she wordlessly drifted away from me through the ranks of the army, hanging her head and shaking it back and forth.

"Wait!" I cried, but then everyone started jostling each other in preparation to halt, and I lost sight of her. A great concerned rumbling ran through the ranks as they took in the scene ahead, and if there's one thing that's harder to plough through than an armed crowd, it's an armed crowd that's all tensed-up and huddled together for safety.

The main square beneath the tower had certainly looked better the last time I'd seen it, and I'd been looking at it over a horse's arse. Most of the well-scrubbed white pavement was covered up with hastily-erected tents where locals were being treated and preached to by devotees in white robes. Barry's army had evidently assumed victory in the actual physical invasion, and had already moved straight onto the "winning of hearts and minds" phase.

Closer to the center of the square beneath the shade of well-kept, slightly bloodstained ornamental trees stood what I had assumed at first glance to be a massive arrangement of last-stage Syndrome victims, numbering in the thousands. As we drew closer I realized that they were in the garb of Barry's army, and stood frozen, not in nonchalant poses, but in mid-charge. They were still hefting their weapons, but their unmoving legs were caught in mid-sprint and their mouths were silently screaming in fury. Several trebuchets were scattered throughout the crowd, poking out over the rows of heads like nosy giraffes.

"Stay where you are," said Barry, needlessly. We'd already stopped dead at the first sight of him.

He floated a good fifteen feet off the ground. The glow around his body was brighter, and the lightning that flowed from his eyes and hands extended far enough to tweak the noses and mustaches of the frozen warriors below. His actual physical body, though, had seen much better days. His black vicar suit and collar now hung loosely, flapping in the arcane wind. His hair was missing in clumps, and his eye sockets were sunken enough to compete with mine.

"Ah yes," he said, noticing me. "How appropriate. All my bugbears come together in a tidy package. Don't any of you move. You're going to wait here nice and quietly while we wait for the rest of our guests. Ah, who's this now?" Approaching the center of the square from a different angle was another army. This one was mostly gnolls, but there was a thick black streak of suited Adventurer's Guild agents running through the center, so that the whole mass looked like a giant chocolate éclair when viewed from above. They, too, halted in surprise when they drew close enough to see Barry's current condition.

"What's all this about?" demanded the agent at the head of the Guild army, whose brimmed hat and sharp suit identified him as the King's advisor from my massively unfair trial in the throne room. "Who the hell do you think you are?"

A burst of white energy from Barry's hand blew the advisor's hat into ashes and lit his hair on fire. He promptly fell back, desperately slapping himself about the head. "I told you all to be quiet. Negotiations haven't started yet," said Barry, with the voice of a secretary chairing a meeting. An involuntary shudder rippled through the office workers behind me. "All my opposing forces must be gathered here together. It's much more efficient to demoralize you all at once."

"Er, actually, glorious LORD," said Benjamin. He was on his knees, holding his hand up for attention like a schoolboy but keeping his eyes averted. "This is it. These were all the resisting armies I could find."

"Seriously?"

" 'Fraid so, gift of Heaven. Everyone else either ran for it or let themselves get killed."

"Well, frankly, I'm disappointed. The biggest city in the world, and the populace can only be bothered to scrape together this measly lot. Doesn't say a lot for faith in the current leadership, does it."

The sound of grinding teeth could be heard coming from the king, who was a few feet away. Mr. Wonderful leaned towards him and whispered, "Careful, Mr. Dentist, you'll set a bad example."

"You were saying something about negotiations?" said one of the senior Guild agents.

"When I say 'negotiations,'" said Barry civilly, "I basically mean that I'm going to say what's going to happen, and you're going to make it happen, or I'll unfreeze my army of berserkers down there and you can all consider yourselves written off as acceptable losses."

The agent conferred briefly with his colleagues. "What are your demands?"

"They're quite simple. I ask merely for an occupying force established within this and all cities of Lolede, a headquarters in your palace, for all decisions affecting national policy to be approved by me, and for an agreeably manageable tribute to be paid annually. Life for most of your population will be exactly the same as before, with only a small, manageable increase in oppression."

"Is there anything in this for us?" probed the Guild agent, being a businessman, and therefore well-acquainted with putting profit above self-preservation.

"But of course," said Barry sweetly. "None of you will have to worry about how to spend your Sundays anymore. Attendance will be mandatory at approved churches to hear the teachings of the great god Si-Mon."

"Si-Mon," echoed every devotee in earshot reverently.

"I am the bringer of His message," continued Barry. "I am in communion with Si-Mon—"

"Si-Mon," went the devotees again.

"—Daily, and my will is his. Si-Mon—"

"Si-Mon."

Barry was clearly wishing he'd never got them onto that. "He is the one true God, initiator of the Infusion and omnipotent caretaker of us all. Hail S . . . hail Him."

"What's your position on the adventuring industry?" continued the Guild agent.

"As long as the Guild remembers who is in control, I see no reason to make alterations to current policy in that area."

An even smaller amount of conferring took place between the gaggle of Guild agents, featuring numerous sidelong glances at Barry and his frozen army, before the spokesperson turned back. "Hail Si-Mon."

"Si-Mon."

"Hail Si-Mon, 'scuse us," said Mr. Wonderful, making his way out of our army and into the Guild's.

"We feel our presence in this army will shortly be regarded as a conflict of interest," added Bowg, following him.

"Right then," said Barry, dusting his hands. He seemed slightly disappointed. "I will move onto the next item in the agenda . . ."

"Wait just one minute!" cried the king, stepping forward. "The Adventurer's Guild are not the true rulers of this land!" He almost believed it, I'm sure.

"You keep out of this," said the Guild spokesman.

"You forget yourself, sir!" He took hold of his hood and dramatically flung it back. A golden crown glittered royally in the moonlight. "I am the King!"

The appropriate stunned gasp resolutely failed to occur. "Yeah," said the Guild agent, low on patience. "We know. You've got the sword."

"I borrowed it! I mean, no I didn't! It's the real sword and I'm the real King and I say that no invading army will waltz in and seize my country without a fight!"

Barry watched him rant himself out, then turned to the Guild again. "Is this truly the King of Lolede?"

"The King? Surely not," said the Guild agent. "That is clearly an impostor. He looks more like a dentist to me."

"CHAAAAAARGE!" cried the King, holding his sword aloft and leading by example.

There had once been a time, in more savage eras, when the King would have had to be the biggest and toughest bastard in the land, in order that he might be able to hang onto his crown while every other bloke with land and a gullible militia was trying to prise it from his grasp. But generations of peace and misguided genetic theory had done away with that.

Then again, even if he'd been eight feet tall with muscles like mahogany, I doubt he would have lasted very long against Barry's counter-attack. The King was barely halfway to the vicar and our army was still internally debating whether or not to follow when Barry waved a hand and a great pillar of white light slammed down. The silhouette of a rapidly skeletonizing human form was visible writhing painfully for a few seconds too long for comfort before the light faded, leaving nothing of the king but a black stain and a few extremely well-maintained teeth.

A deep silence followed before Barry spoke again. "Very well, if that's the way it's going to be," he said. "Chaaaarge!"

He threw up his arms like a conductor and his frozen army of berserkers became animated again. They stumbled a little at first, confused by their surroundings, but were soon confidently roaring towards us.

The dockworkers at the head of our army gripped their sledgehammers in white-knuckled hands. Every man was probably thinking the same thing: that nails and rivets very rarely run around trying to split your head in half, and honest worker's grit didn't make them as qualified for this as they'd thought.

One of the berserkers was proving to be faster than his fellows, and was a good few yards ahead of the charge. It was the same heavily accented northern barbarian we had encountered in Applewheat and Yawnbore. The clapping of his great sandaled feet upon the cobbles was becoming louder by the moment. His robe was utterly soaked through with blood, sweat and oil, and clung tantalizingly to his chest muscles.

A lot of our soldiers were taking quick glances behind them and uncertain half-steps backwards, not wanting to be the first to abandon the pretense of bravery and make a break for it. I was just about to seize the initiative when the heavy footfalls abruptly stopped, and the barbarian's scream faded away.

A manhole had opened under his feet. The three marauders directly behind him lost a battle of wits with momentum and fell down the same hole. Now that I was looking for it, I could see adventurers disappearing rapidly downwards all throughout the oncoming horde.

A skinny white figure emerged from the first manhole, crawling on all fours with a dagger clenched between its teeth. It scuttled into the mass of advancing warriors, nimbly dodged through the gauntlet of flailing legs, and disappeared from sight. Shortly afterwards, two barbarians in the front line immediately upgraded their screams of rage to screams of agony and collapsed, squirting blood from gashes in their ankles.

Similar events were taking place all over the square, as more and more albinos poured out of the ground. Those members of Barry's army who weren't getting their ankles slashed were tripping over the ones who were. Before long, the advance had halted completely. The already undisciplined mob had become a heaving mass of pain and confusion with skinny cave dwellers scuttling all over it like ants on picnic scones.

"CHARGE!" cried the burliest of the burly dockworkers, who were quickly regaining their confidence at the sight of Barry's stricken horde. As one, their sledgehammers collided with the heads of the nearest convenient enemy soldiers, and as one they rebounded from the adventurers' helms with a musical "bong."

The berserk adventurers had gone into suspended animation again. I saw a few confused albinos vainly trying to stab a couple of muscular ankles that had suddenly become as hard as diamond. I returned my gaze to Barry, who was completing the last few finger-waggles.

"Stop it! Stop it! What is this?" he said, scolding tolerantly like a playroom nanny. He made a complex gesture, and one of the underground people was yanked into the air with a squeak of surprise and dangled upside-down in front of Barry's face. "What do you people think you are doing?"

"W-we are the emissaries of the t-true LORD," replied the albino, shaking and stammering. "You are-are-are a despicable burnt oven chip on—*hup*—on the b-baking tray of the universe." His words had a rather familiar turn of phrase.

"Thaddeus?" came Meryl's voice. I spotted her about ten dockworkers away, standing close to Mrs. Civious, and began shouldering my way towards them.

Sure enough, Thaddeus was emerging from a manhole close to our front line. He was a little scuffed and dirty, perhaps a little paler, if that was even possible. He was wearing a shabby fur cloak and a makeshift crown made from the ends of tree roots. Several albinos immediately broke from the crowd and threw themselves at his feet, planting their faces between cobbles.

"Unhand my brother in faith," commanded Thaddeus. "You are an aberration in the LORD's perfect vision for the world."

"How can I unhand him? I'm not even touching him," said Barry innocently, displaying his hands as the levitating fellow in question spun nauseatingly end over end.

"Your army is defeated," Thaddeus continued. There was a general shaking of sledgehammers and staplers and a chorus of adrenaline-fueled "yeah's". "Leave this place and sully the sacred overlands no more."

"Defeated," repeated Barry, shifting his mouth around as if sucking a boiled sweet that was turning sour. Then he made a twirling gesture with his finger.

A few short shrieks broke out among the office workers as some of them risked a look behind them. I did likewise, and saw that there were adventurers behind us. They weren't moving, but they weren't frozen in the same way as the others, and they weren't wearing white robes. Judging by their good looks, bizarre dress sense and identical battle stances, these were all Syndrome victims.

I took a wide look around. While we'd been distracted a thin layer of them had gradually surrounded the entire main square.

"The biggest point rewards in history," announced Barry. "Help our army of brave liberators chase these unprincipled bandits from the city of Lolede."

"Probably terrorists," added one of the Adventurer's Guild men. "They certainly make me feel uneasy. Do they scare you, Mr. Wonderful?"

"I'm quaking so hard my shoes are about to tunnel into the ground," he replied.

"Ha!" scoffed Mrs. Civious suddenly, causing Meryl to jump. "We're not afraid of your puppets!" Another "yeah" rippled through our fighting men, slightly less confident than the previous one.

"Ugh, you people are so stubborn in your ignorance," sighed Barry, floating forwards and getting ready to talk down to us as clearly as he could. "I'm not asking you to be afraid of my soldiers. They're just here for the occupation. I'm asking you to be afraid of *me*. Observe."

He held out his palms in the traditional spellcasting manner, then slowly pushed upwards. The air began to taste of metal, and my eardrums popped so hard that one of them fell to the ground and rolled away.

More of Thaddeus's army of scuttling mole people were plucked from the ground to join their fellow in mid-air. They shrieked and flailed their arms madly until Barry clenched his fists and the neck of every single albino snapped, one by one. It was like listening to someone cooking popcorn while eating raw carrots. He let the moment sink in for a second or two before the bodies clattered to the ground. "Queue Ee Dee," said Barry.

There was a pause before Thaddeus spoke again. I noticed that he had moved a little closer to Barry's army and was now facing us. "Oppose not the healing wind of change! Repent your sins before the true LORD, Si-Mon!" he yelled.

"Si-Mon," went the devotees, uncertainly.

I nudged Meryl. "So how many times is he allowed to betray us?" She scowled, and ducked back off into the crowd. I was about to follow, but I wanted to see what would happen next.

"No . . . no, look, you can't just switch sides," said Barry. "You're still an aberration in Si-Mon's eyes."

"Si-Mon," chanted the devotees.

"Yes," said Thaddeus, smugly nodding at us. "Cease ye aberrant ways, ye wearers of filth."

"I'm talking to you, you idiot," said Barry.

"Hear his mighty words of peace and wisdom, uneducated masses."

"Hey!" Barry cast a bolt of lightning at Thaddeus's feet, spraying him with bits of searing-hot grit. "You! The disgusting stinking undead man in a robe! The one standing right there with his back to me! I am now addressing you and only you!"

Thaddeus spotted me in the crowd. "Turn around when the LORD is addressing you, wretch."

Barry angrily swept his hand through the air. Another telekinesis spell pulled Thaddeus off his feet and dangled him in front of the vicar-god. White energy pinned his arms and held his head in place so he couldn't look away.

"Look, I can see how deeply entrenched in denial you are," said Barry. "But if you make any attempt to ignore what I'm about to tell you, I will rip off your arms. Clear?"

"If you would address me, you may unhand me, my brother," said Thaddeus obliviously. "We live for the same goal."

Barry's expression didn't change for a few moments, although he reddened somewhat and his head appeared to be quivering. He pursed his lips, took a deep breath and carefully tucked a single stray hair behind his ear. "I have communed with the omnipotent Si-Mon—SHUT UP—and he has provided me with a schedule. A schedule for the creation of His perfect world. And there's been one particular item that's been on it since the beginning. One that is becoming very irksome, especially for me. There are three people who live on after death in a state that is unnatural and unpleasing to Him. A girl, a smartarse mage with one leg, and a priest. Do you see where this is leading?"

Thaddeus could only move his eyes, but I could tell he was trying his damnedest to shoot a dirty look in my direction. "I hope you're listening to this," he called.

Barry snapped his fingers. There was a grisly sound akin to a man pulling his boots out of thick quagmire and Thaddeus crumpled to the ground, oozing black slime from the ragged stumps of his shoulders. His arms followed a moment later, adding insult to injury by slapping him on the back of the head as they landed.

Barry descended and savagely stamped on the back of Thaddeus's unmoving skull. "You're listening now, aren't you, you sanctimonious prick! This isn't something you can just ignore anymore! Si-Mon hates you and all your repulsive little friends!"

The devotees hadn't echoed his last use of Si-Mon. Benjamin and the other non-murderous members of the cult were watching with terrified eyes and their hands covering their mouths. Noticing this, Barry wiped the sweat off his brow with his sleeves and counted ten deep breaths. Then he knelt beside Thaddeus and spoke to him calmly. "What were the words you used to describe me? 'An aberration in God's perfect vision for the world?' It's ironic that you would say that, because that's pretty much exactly what you are, and God himself told me so. Do you see?"

"Barry!" boomed a voice. All heads turned to Baron Civious, who took a step forward and flung back his hood. "Cease your bullying."

Barry floated back up to his previous position. "What is it now?! Can't I get through a single item without being interrupted?"

"Your power is indeed great," said Civious. "Perhaps you would prefer to challenge one who can match it."

The Baron extended his arms towards the ground, palms flat. Black and red energy crackled between his fingers, and he began to levitate. An aura of black fog surrounded him, dotted with black sigils and the faces of agonized souls. A grim chorus of hellish wails drifted across the city.

"Took him ages to get the wails right," whispered Mrs. Civious to Meryl and me. "Used to sound like a bunch of cats with their tails trapped in drawers."

He ascended until he had matched Barry's altitude. The two auras, one black, one white, extended tendrils into each other, teasing and testing. The glow from Civious's eyes intensified until they burned like the red fires of a dying sun. When he spoke, his voice hissed like the wind that whistles through the branches of a dead tree right outside your window on the night your girlfriend broke up with you.

"I am Baron Civious of the Malevolands," he boomed. The sky was clouding over rather quickly. "All the suffocating powers of darkness are willing slaves to—"

"Will you stop prattling!" Barry extended a hand and a horizontal cylinder of white light about ten feet wide burst across the square. The wailing of tortured souls became a little bit more desperate before fading altogether under an angelic chorus.

Where Civious had been, there was now nothing but a spreading cloud of black smoke and a sprinkling of red grit upon the floor.

"Winchester!" cried Mrs. Civious, running out. She prepared a purple-black ball of dark magic between her hands as she ran, but she was atomized by yet another musical blast of holiness before she could release it.

"Anyone else?!" yelled Barry. The plaza was silent. He sighed with irritation and dusted his hands with a sound like a church organ being slapped. "Right then. Item one: I declare myself absolute ruler of Lolede. Item two: Get some reliable men around the churches in case Civious shows up again, assuming he's even allowed to set foot in one. Item three: Someone round up those three undead freaks."

By then I was already running for the perimeter. A tall, Syndrome-afflicted barbarian blocked my path, gripping the shaft of a warhammer menacingly, but I didn't even slow down. I fell to my knees before him, slid between his massive legs, smoothly got back on my feet and ran without a backward glance.

Somewhere behind me I thought I heard Meryl call out my name. I clamped my hands around my ears and kept running.

# THIRTEEN

The city had been occupied for barely two days, but life for the general public was almost back to whatever passed for normal. Guild thugs and Church of Si-Mon devotees patrolled the streets looking for dissent to stamp out, but they found very little. Most of the people were already back at work, and the suicide rate had almost leveled out.

The call had gone out for the renegade undeads whose capture was demanded by the great god Si-Mon Himself. An absurd bounty had been posted and several competing mobs of thugs and adventurers were on the loose, challenging everyone they could find with the slightest hint of pale skin and body odor. I could hear their booted feet tramping back and forth along the streets. Fortunately none of them had thus far had the presence of mind to search the dumpster where I had spent the last day or so.

I'd pulled the lid down tightly and settled myself among a few bags of rotten leftovers, but it was impossible to relax. My hopes for getting myself deleted were dust. My only lead in my pursuit of the Deleters had vowed to destroy me, then been evaporated. The rest of my allies were missing, and anyway, most of them were about as reliable as a rice paper suspension bridge. I couldn't even see the Deleter communication anymore. I'd visualized badgers to the point of nausea but hadn't squeezed out so much as a single apostrophe.

"Where have you gone?" I muttered. "Are you afraid of me now?"

"Of course not," said a voice from around the potato peelings. "Slippery John knows no fear. He does sometimes make strategic retreats. Any stains you might occasionally find on Slippery John's laundry are easily explained away by his terrible stomach infection."

I sat up. There was a particularly dark section of the darkness just across from me, and if I squinted, I could make out a stupid mustache. "What the hell are you doing in here?"

"Same as you, Slippery John suspects. It's not a great time to be a known Magic Resistance associate. Slippery John currently embodies a few weeks' fish suppers in the eyes of would-be bounty hunters."

"Yeah, they put a bounty on me, too," I said.

"Pah!" Droplets of saliva pattered across my face. "Tourist. Slippery John's had more bounties on his head than hats. Slippery John was hiding in dumpsters before you even popped your coffin lid. You picked the fairly obvious one. Good size, right off a main thoroughfare, near the back door of a restaurant . . . Slippery John's hidden out in this one three times. Lived here for six months once. You'd be surprised how homey a place gets once you put some wallpaper up."

I felt at the walls. "Oh yeah, didn't notice that."

"So, picking a topic of conversation completely out of the blue, Slippery John admits he was pretty surprised by your act of filthy underhanded betrayal. Slippery John appreciates that it's natural behavior for minions of evil, but Slippery John was sort of under the impression that the Magic Resistance were the key to everything you were looking for, and now they've been utterly destroyed, so maybe you can enlighten Slippery John. What was the plan, dead man?"

I was getting a bit sick of getting called out on that by everyone I knew, including my own conscience. "I didn't really think it through," I admitted. "Not like it matters.

Barry's too powerful now. He conquered the city in an hour; he would've steamrolled right over the Resistance no matter what."

"If you say so, creature. Slippery John reckons Mr. and Mrs. Civious being pulled out of hiding and made to walk around in open streets might have sped things up, but Slippery John wouldn't worry if Slippery John were you. Barry can invade all right but he's got zero public appeal. Wait a few years and he'll probably get voted out before his second term."

"I can't really hang on that long without Meryl. She was the only thing holding me together."

"You know, that's exactly how Slippery John sees his relationship with Drylda. You probably meant it slightly more literally, though. What did happen to your lady friend?"

"I left her in the city center when Barry took over. I didn't even think. He probably blew her into dust or something."

"Oh, Slippery John doubts that. Barry's working for the Deleters now and the Deleters wanted you undead chaps brought to them in an interviewable state. He probably took her to their Nexus thing."

I blinked. "How do you know?"

"Slippery John hung with Barry's crew for a while back in Garethy, remember? And Slippery John nicked some of Civious's intel. Also, Slippery John's natural detective cunning." He stroked his mustache thoughtfully. "Slippery John is thinking he should have mentioned that last one first."

"So where is the Nexus?"

"That's where Slippery John's natural detective cunning breaks down. Civious knew, though. You might want to look through his old lab. Slippery John was just heading down there himself to pick up the missus. Want to tag along? We'll rescue Slippery John's damsel, then move onto yours. Fair?"

"I'm just going to the Nexus to find a Deleter who will erase me," I said firmly.

"Fair enough, but if, y'know, you happen to be passing, you could rescue Meryl anyway. It'd be the heroic thing to do."

An involuntary twitch ran through my face. "I am not a hero. I kept telling her. It's a stupid thing to be."

"That's a smart philosophy," he replied. I wished he would get angry at me, rather than just sit there among the binbags being cheerfully reasonable. "Slippery John knows no fear, o'course, but Slippery John could see how it wouldn't appeal these days, with the Guild and the Syndrome and everything. Slippery John has too much heroism in the blood to do anything else, but it might get a bit too much positive press, if you ask Slippery John."

"Right," I said, doubtfully.

"'Course, Slippery John reckons there's a difference between 'hero' and 'protagonist.'"

I stared at him.

Something clanged heavily against the outside of the dumpster, and we both jumped, scattering food wrappers and used nappies.

"Don't panic," said Slippery John. "Probably just a womblin."

There was another clang. It didn't sound much like a womblin, which is a small urban-adapted cousin to the goblin that feeds on insects and sweet wrappers. It sounded more like, say, the angry fist of a massively-built bounty hunting adventurer with arm muscles the size of giant sea turtles smashing against the dumpster as they attempted to figure out how lids work.

"Is it bounty hunters?" asked Slippery John.

"How am I supposed to know?" I hissed.

"ARE YOU BOUNTY HUNTERS?!" he yelled.

"Open," commanded a voice from outside. It didn't exactly flood me with relief.

"Isn't that your priest friend?" asked Slippery John.

"Dunno. Sounded like him, but he didn't insult me." I opened the lid a crack and peered out.

It was sometime around mid-afternoon, and the streets were strangely deserted. Thaddeus was still missing his arms and there seemed to be several dents in his face, which made sense, because he didn't seem to have anything else to bang against the dumpster.

"So you're still around, then," I said.

"Cower no longer from the light, wretches." he replied. "The streets are near deserted. Barry preaches in the main square to win the hearts of the populace, and his army is occupied with keeping the congregation intact."

There was a long pause.

"Aren't you going to call me the putrescent scrotum of a cosmic horror or something?" I said.

He blinked as if mentally filing that one away. "I have been awakened by the teachings of the LORD, Si-Mon," he announced, while Slippery John and I climbed out of the amassed filth. "So long was I blind to the truth."

"The Truth-truth?" I asked.

"No, a different truth. Only the words of the LORD from the mouth of his avatar could have made me come to such a realization."

"That and the whole ripping off arms thing."

"I am the aberration," he continued solemnly. "I could not see it for my own denial, but now I see that since my resurrection in dark magic it is I who has been the monstrous unclean thing in the eyes of God." He was standing stiff and upright, staring straight ahead. Occasional droplets of the goo we used for blood spurted out of his arm stumps.

"Is this going to take long? Slippery John's got a wife to rescue."

Thaddeus directed his permanent angry gaze at his own shoes for a few meditative moments before looking up. His eyes blazed as they met mine, and I spontaneously blinked. "You have known this all along," he said. "You have sought your own deletion from the world since the moment Satan's fiery anus spat us from the realms of the dead. I have returned now to join your quest and finally rub out the black stain that is our mutual existence."

"Incidentally, how did you get away from Ba—"

I stopped, startled, when he suddenly took a step forward until he and I were chest to chest. Cold black goo ran down my front, joining forces with the dumpster residue to continue ruining my new robe. "We are BOTH the putrescent scrotum of a cosmic horror," he announced. "We are brothers, jostling together in our thorny sack. I praise the LORD for the removal of my arms, for now I can truly slither upon the ground with you, and with the worms we have always been." He immediately dropped to the ground and began wriggling back and forth to illustrate his point. "I am a worm," he reiterated, his voice filled with self-loathing. "Slither slither."

"Look, will you just stop . . ." I began.

He stopped slithering back and forth and glared up at me. "Let us journey together to the edge of the world. Let us escort our unworthy bodies to the realms of annihilation."

"The more the merrier," said Slippery John, levering up a manhole. "Were we going to Civious's lab now, or did you chaps want to make out for a while first?"

The Baron's workshop was still as ransacked as it had been when we left. It had never been tidy, since the ruined cathedral had spent thousands of years gathering dust and bits of fallen ceiling. Mrs. Civious had clearly made an effort to cheer the place up a bit, but now the potted ferns and throw pillows had been cast aside, buried under broken furniture and crushed beneath the hooves of gnolls with no appreciation for interior design.

Filing cabinets had vomited their drawers and Civious's beloved scrolls were pulled from their filing system and scattered randomly over floor and furniture. It was like some stationery-themed ticker-tape parade had rolled through the area.

I inspected a single random scroll. Unrolled it would probably go right across the cathedral, and the handwriting was tiny. Civious was the kind of person who documented his breakfast every morning. "It'll take days to go through all this," I muttered, hand on hip.

"To hasten our disposal, I will make any sacrifice," announced Thaddeus, before flinging himself into the pile to start reading.

I sighed and started searching Mrs. Civious's old dresser, adding anything vaguely paper-like to the pile on the floor. "I don't see why you think Drylda'd still be here," I said, poking a broken porcelain milkmaid with my toe. "Looks like they took everything that could be of any immediate use."

"Slippery John can't be certain, but Slippery John's pretty sure you just called Slippery John's wife a slut."

"She's got to be pretty easy if she married you," I pointed out.

"Slippery John wouldn't call it 'easy.' Carrying her up and down the aisle was a nightmare. Anyway, look." Slippery John flung aside a few scrolls to reveal Drylda lying upon the same slab we'd left her on. Most of the ornate jeweled bits of her armor were missing, though, leaving only a leather bikini and a few pieces of jewelry in places too delicate for meaty gnoll paws to go. In a stroke, her look had gone from "exotic adventurer" to "severely lost swimwear model." "Shows how much you know."

I tried to ignore him, and made an effort to skim-read the scroll I was holding, but couldn't penetrate Civious's thick technical wording. Also, Thaddeus was applying himself to his task with such gusto it seemed a shame to deprive him. I had to face the fact that I was being forced to make conversation. "What will you do now?"

"Well, not much left for us here in Lolede," said Slippery John. "Perhaps it's time for Slippery John to leave adventuring to the younger folk."

"You don't age."

"Yes, but now that Slippery John's a married man, settling down seems like the healthy, natural thing to do."

"There is nothing healthy or natural about the things you do with that poor woman's corpse."

"She's not a corpse. You're probably projecting. Anyway, what's unhealthy about devoting Slippery John's life to assisting his poor handicapped spouse? Slippery John's got it all planned out. We're going to buy a little cottage in the Garethy countryside somewhere and Slippery John's going to rig up some kind of pulley arrangement in the bedroom."

I shook my head and turned my attention to Civious's desk. The drawers hadn't been emptied, presumably because gnoll fingers were too chunky to work the handle, but so far they had only contained paperclips and dinner receipts. "Drylda is dead," I said as I hunted through knick-knacks. "Civious said as much. She was taken over by a Deleter when the Syndrome hit her. And I broke the connection they had to her body when I touched her in the dead world. She might still be warm but however you swing it she's doornail-dead at least twice over."

"Oh yeah? Then how do you explain that she's moving on her own?"

"What?"

The scroll fell from my hands as I saw that Drylda's head had risen from the slab, and she was slowly, mechanically rising to a sitting position like some newly-animated abomination of science. Instinctive horror caught in my throat as her head slowly turned to look at me like a clockwork toy.

"Hi," said Drylda.

# PART FOUR

# ONE

"Drylda!" said Slippery John, overjoyed. "Slippery John knew you'd get better!"

"Yes," she said, after a pause. "I am Drylda, a person you know." She swung her legs over the bench and stood up in a single smooth movement, with no apparent stiffness or discomfort from her months of catatonia. She appeared to be surveying the room, despite the fact that her eyeballs were currently sitting in a kidney bowl by her side.

My first reaction had been to yelp like a girl and trip over a porcelain shepherdess, but by this point I'd sorted myself out and could commence backing slowly away in a slightly more dignified manner. Thaddeus poked his head out the pile in a burst of pencil shavings and glared at Drylda, hissing threateningly.

"Do you want to see pictures of the cottage Slippery John picked out for us, honey?" Slippery John fumbled for his back pocket.

"Slippery John," I said, slowly and clearly. "Move away from her. Slowly. It is not Drylda."

Slippery John leaned close. "Smells like Drylda."

"It's a Deleter!" I urged. "Like Civious said! She's being controlled by the thing inside her!"

"A demon walks among us," hissed Thaddeus from around knee level.

Slippery John rolled his eyes. "Drylda's dead. Drylda's a demon. Drylda's being controlled by things inside her. Slippery John's getting sick of you picking on his woman."

"Oh wow," said Drylda with zero enthusiasm. She was still wearing her usual slightly condescending look, and, like all Syndrome victims, carefully enunciated every word like a foreigner reading phonetically from a script. "You know we control you. You've become self-aware. I so called this."

"What do you want?!"

"You're Jim," said Drylda, swiveling her head to scrutinize me with her empty eye sockets. "The undead minion, right? You were speaking to me."

"Yes, he pushed you around in a wheelbarrow for a while and did no doubt craven and horrible things to your innocent flower of womanhood." Slippery John seemed to be losing confidence. "But it's okay, because Slippery John is here to heal your trauma with his magic touch."

Drylda didn't even glance at him. "You spoke to me through world chat."

"Through what?"

She paused briefly before everything she said, like her personal timeline was a few seconds out of sync with everyone else's. "You spoke to me while I was trying to talk to Don," she said, finally. "You kept your money in a tin under your mattress."

"You?"

"How do you know what he keeps under his mattress?" Slippery John looked hurt. "And who's this Don character? Do I know him?"

"That's. Not. Drylda." I clarified, fists clenched. "It's the thing I was talking to when I passed out in here earlier."

"What thing?"

"My name's Dub," said Drylda. "I'm a developer on the Mogworld project. There was this dickhead we hired, and he took over, and he locked me out of my admin tools, and now he's messing everything up, and he's done something to the security in the building, and I can't get into the office anymore. But I had access to the Drylda account because I was fixing a bug so here I am."

All was silent for a few moments before Slippery John turned to me. "Slippery John thinks you might be right, necrotic swine. Drylda used to say things that made at least vague sense."

It didn't seem dangerous, so I took a cautious step towards the Drylda-thing with my hands held out. "We have no idea what you're talking about," I said, loudly and slowly.

"Okay, hang on a second," said the thing that called itself "Dub." Then, after a very long pause, it continued speaking in a slightly louder but still expressionless voice. "Behold mortals. I am Dub-us, of the Loincloth pantheon, once a great and mighty creator god, now deposed of my powers by the evil trickster lord Simon. I am forced to take the form of this mortal warrior to seek your aid."

"Well, now we're getting somewhere," said Slippery John. "Slippery John knows where he stands with divinely appointed quests. Which temples of the false god do you want us to raid?"

"Si-Mon truly exists?" asked Thaddeus.

"Why do you need to ask?" I said. "You've been worshipping him all day." One look at his terrified eyes told me that I'd missed a point somewhere along the line. It's one thing to believe in a god and quite another to unquestionably know that He exists, and could at any moment materialize in front of you and start making veiled references to the things He saw you doing last night while reading armor magazines.

"He's the new guy," said Dub. "This game—" He paused for a few seconds. "This world was mine and Don's. He's the head god. We brought in Simon to help with running things. But Don's away on vacation, and now Simon's taken over. He's ruining everything we set up."

"So he's the one helping Barry conquer the world?" said Slippery John.

"Yes."

"And he's the one who caused the Infusion?" I said.

"The what?"

"The Infusion. The thing that stops things from dying or decaying or changing in any way."

"No, that was me." Drylda's pouting face rotated back and forth between us like a slow metronome. "Was that a problem?"

"Slippery John wouldn't want to tell you how to do your job or anything," said Slippery John, "but if by 'a problem' you mean 'the cause of the endemic misery and unrest in the world today,' then you're on the nose, there."

"But we made you all immortal," said Dub, idly cocking Drylda's hips. "I know a lot of people who'd kill for that. Other gods, I mean."

"The gods are not immortal?!" wailed Thaddeus. His face was aghast. He would have been pulling his hair out if he had hands, or hair.

"So are you the ones who possess adventurers?" I asked, feeling a bit dense, considering to whom I was speaking. "The ones who cause the Syndrome?"

"Yes, good question, dead man," said Slippery John, waving at Drylda's unsettlingly well-formed body. "Slippery John's got another one. When are you going to stop fiddling about inside Slippery John's missus?"

There was another long pause. "We might be getting a bit off topic," said Dub.

"Can you delete me?" I said.

Drylda looked at me. She still wasn't changing her facial expression but it definitely seemed like the former mighty creator god inside her was losing his grip on the situation. He was like a wolf coming to a flock of sheep to try and raise an army against the lions, and seemed completely unable to fathom why he wasn't having any luck. "What?"

"I want to be deleted. Killed permanently again."

"Why?"

It's funny how the stupidest questions can be the hardest to answer. "I just . . . well, the Infusion is a big part of it, I suppose. And even before then my life was . . . er . . . an unbearable sequence of dashed hopes and pigshit."

"Well even so, this is suicide you're talking about." A very slight emphasis on the last syllable led me to conclude that there was supposed to be an exclamation mark there.

"It's not really suicide when you've died once before already. It's more like . . . tidying up."

"We beseech thee, O Dub-us, to wipe our foul remnants from the glory of your creation," cried Thaddeus, slithering over to Drylda's feet and getting right to the point of matters as always.

"I can't," said Dub. "Not until I get my admin—my godly powers back. But I need your help." Drylda pointed stiffly at me like her arm was on the end of a puppet string.

"Why?"

"See, when you pose a question like that to God when he's giving you a divine mission, that's why you're not cut out for the hero business," said Slippery John.

"I meant, why me?"

"How can I word this in terms you'll understand?" said Dub. "Your. Your programming is bugged out. And whenever you interact with another program you cause it to crash."

"Do you want to try that again?" I suggested, after a round of blank looks.

"Okay. Hang on." He was silent for a good thirty seconds, his borrowed bosom wobbling rhythmically up and down. "Everything in this world is interconnected, right. It's all tied together by this underlying network of. Let's call it the Force. And when things happen that we didn't allow for, it causes disturbances in the Force. You saw what happened at Yawnbore. I've been following your progress with the log . . . with my wondrous powers of omniscience. Yawnbore bugged out because its underlying Force became corrupted. That happened when Simon deleted your old fortress."

"But what about me?"

"I'm getting to that. When Dreadgrave brought you and the others back to life, he did something we didn't expect. He found a loophole in the rules. The world was not laid out with you in mind. There's a corruption inside you that can spread to others. That's what happened when you touched Drylda's interface while you were outside your body."

"Yes, what is all this about touching Drylda's interface?" said Slippery John. "Slippery John has yet to hear a satisfactory explanation for that one."

"So you're saying we—Meryl and Thaddeus and me—because we're undead, we're disturbances in this Force?"

"You certainly disturb Slippery John."

"Yes," said Dub, nodding Drylda's head woodenly. "And that would normally qualify you for immediate deletion, but right here and right now, it could make you very useful to me."

I could feel myself getting deeper and deeper into rather heavy territory. It suddenly occurred to me how much rubbish could have been avoided if I'd just not panicked and run away from the Deleters back at Dreadgrave's. It was a dizzying thought. I sighed. "What do you want me to do?"

"Simon's control of the world rests on a set of . . . thingies . . . that he's put in the . . . this is going to be pretty hard to explain. Let me think." Another long silence passed. "Okay. There's a place in the world from which everything is controlled."

"The Nexus, right?" I interrupted. "Where the Deleters come from."

"It's at. Deleters? Oh. You mean the angels. Yes, they come from there. It's at the very top of Mount Murdercruel, where no NPC—where no puny mortal can possibly reach it alone. There's a sort of machine in the center of it that powers the Force. You will have to find a way to spread your corruption to that machine."

"Then what?"

"Then the server will crash and be forced to reboot without Simon's encryptions."

I let his nonsense god-language drift through the air for a few seconds before prompting him. "And that means?"

He hesitated for noticeably longer than usual. "It means everything will work out. I'll have my powers back and I can grant you whatever you wish."

"You can delete me?" I said.

"You can smite us into the blessed void?" echoed Thaddeus.

"If that really is what you want."

"Could you remove the Infusion?" asked Slippery John.

There was another of those longer-than-usual pauses. "I can definitely see what I can do about that."

"Can you stop possessing adventurers and using them as sick playthings?" pressed Slippery John.

The next hesitation easily beat the last one. "Would it be okay if we kept doing that, actually? That's kind of important to us."

Slippery John was flabbergasted. "No, it . . . really wouldn't be okay. Slippery John doesn't really like knowing that Slippery John could have his brain erased and his body taken over by some extraterrestrial git at any time. It doesn't strike Slippery John as the policy of a benevolent bunch of gods."

"You know, this conversation has really given me a lot to think about," said Dub. I got the impression that somewhere in some distant godly control room he was rubbing whatever passed for his chin. "Perhaps we should continue this discussion after you've finished the job."

"Where did you say the Nexus was?" I said.

"The peak of Mount Murdercruel." A pause. "Is there going to be a problem with that?"

I swallowed. "There're going to be quite a few problems with that."

"Why?"

I wondered how best to answer his question. Mount Murdercruel was the highest point on the planet. Its peak was said to extend beyond the atmosphere. Everyone who had ever attempted to scale it had disappeared, died, or come back missing a few limbs and vowing never to try anything that stupid again. Another problem was that Mount Murdercruel was several thousand miles away in the middle of the frozen wastes of the south polar region, surrounded by iceberg-laden waters that had claimed more sailors than gonorrhea.

Finally, I went for, "It's a bit of a way."

"No probs," said Dub. "I was able to up Drylda's magic stat before I took her over."

"You put something magic up Drylda?" interpreted Slippery John.

"I can teleport us all to the upper slopes of the mountain," clarified Dub. "It'll get us past most of the hard bits and I can use aura spells to keep us all from freezing to death."

Drylda suddenly dropped into the standard overdramatic Syndrome magic-casting pose—one hand held aloft channelling magic, and the other thrust out in front of her, feet far enough apart to accommodate an extremely overweight pony—before firing off a stream of complicated post-graduate level magic words. Thaddeus, Slippery John and I watched nervously as a spark appeared in the air next to Mrs. Civious's dresser, spat blue lightning, then spread out into a three-foot oval. A steady stream of snowflakes flew out and began to melt upon the floor.

I'd never used a magic portal before. They were very strictly regulated, following a few incidents involving exit portals inside solid matter and some subsequent ruinous lawsuits. You had to pass extensive written and practical tests before you could get a license, but it was considered a lucrative career option for high-level casters who didn't mind dealing with tourists.

"And you promise you'll delete me at the end of all this," I said, as the room's temperature began to drop and my few remaining hairs whipped around my face.

"Yes, yes, whatever you want," said Dub, still posing. "You must go now. I can't keep it open for more than an hour or so."

"What about Drylda? Will Slippery John have his beloved back?"

Drylda's blank face cocked sideways quizzically. "What do you want her back for? Her brain's been wiped."

"Yes, well, call Slippery John a romantic but Slippery John feels there's more to Drylda than just her brain. There's still an essence about her."

"Ugh," I said. "We do not want to know about what kind of essence comes out of your corpse bride."

"Hey," said Dub-Drylda in a level but very loud voice. "Portal. Nexus. World. Saving."

I stood before the glittering window. A distant howling wind was drifting over from across the magical border. Sleet was soaking into my robe. I suddenly longed to be back in my dumpster an hour ago, cozy and safe and quiet and most emphatically not the most hostile terrain on the planet.

"Oh, fine," I said. I stepped forward.

The moment I entered the portal I was struck with disorientation. It was like there were three of me at once—one in Civious's ruined hideout, one standing in a snowy mountain scene, and another that stretched all the way from one to the other, all surrounded by magical white sparks and flashes. It's a strange sensation, feeling that your body simultaneously doesn't exist and extends for thousands of miles, and not a little damaging to the self-esteem.

Dub was the only one left in Civious's lab, still visible as semi-transparent shadows against the glowing lights, confidently stepping towards the portal as he voiced the last few arcane instructions to the spell's navigation system. Then I noticed that one of the little white flashes was, in fact, an airborne butterfly knife, flying across the room and turning end over end. I saw it embed in Drylda's spine, crumpling her legs out from under her and ejecting the great god Dub to pastures new.

Without a conscious caster to keep it stabilized, the portal immediately began to waver. The exit loosened and thrashed about like an unsecured fire hose, hurling us around the void like children rolling down a hill in a barrel. In the midst of the turmoil I saw the indistinct figure of Mr. Wonderful walking stiff-leggedly into the lab, watching us with interest.

Then I couldn't see the lab anymore. Thaddeus clung to my robe by his teeth, chanting muffled scripture. Slippery John somersaulted by overhead as the blue ether inhaled and spat us out into the unknown.

# TWO

Freezing wind hit me like a frying pan to the face, tearing off a few more loose flaps of skin. My robe fluttered violently around me, losing all its nesting insects in an instant. My feet came into contact with some kind of ground, then immediately slipped off. My chin bounced jarringly off solid rock.

I looked up, and for one extremely brief moment I saw an ice-covered ledge jutting out of a massive black wall of forbidding stone. I didn't have time to take in any further details before friction announced that there was nothing more it could do for me and I began to slide backwards.

I scrabbled in vain for something vaguely holdable. The rock and ice of the mountain had been pummeled into perfect smoothness by millennia of vicious weather cycles. Soon enough I ran out of ledge and my legs swung into empty air in a swarm of disturbed snow.

Time seemed to slow down. This tends to happen in dangerous situations to help the brain think of an escape route, but at that point all I could think of was cartwheeling in slow motion down the mountain, bouncing off every jagged rock along the way until my finely-sandpapered torso finally came to rest in the middle of a snowdrift that I would have to call home for the next five million years.

I was so engrossed by this thought that it took me several moments to notice that I wasn't falling. Something was holding onto my arm, gripping it fiercely like an extremely poorly-fitting wristwatch.

"Thmmph wmmmph mmmph mmmmmph," said Thaddeus, my wrist between his teeth.

A long pause followed, aptly filled by the roaring wind.

"Are you going to pull me up, then?" I said.

He shook his head and grumbled at length, his eyes darting around madly. I tried to clench my free hand; it wouldn't move either. My fingers were a useless bundle of rock-hard blue twigs on the end of my arm. The freezing cold temperatures had made all our undead joints seize up.

"Slippery John saves the day again," said Slippery John, whose face suddenly moved into view above the ledge. His voice was confident but his blue-cheeked grin seemed a little forced.

He grabbed Thaddeus around the waist and pulled him backwards with surprising strength. My body slid onto a reassuringly horizontal surface. I made to conjure a fireball, but my fingers were frozen into place and unable to make the mandatory waggles.

"Gather round the portal's after-effect," advised Slippery John, warming his hands in the glowing magical smear. "Normally Slippery John would suggest sharing bodily warmth but Slippery John doesn't think you two would contribute much to that."

The bare amount of warmth emanating from the portal was just enough to separate Thaddeus's jaws from my arm. Every time I stopped moving one of my muscles for more than a second it started to freeze in place. The cold at this height could have flash-frozen a lava golem.

The phrase "at this height" sparked a few freezing brain cells. Out of some morbid desire to fully acquaint myself with my problems I shuffled around the magical flame until I was near the edge, then carefully peered down.

I very swiftly regretted doing so. We were mesmerizingly high up. Then I realized that what I had thought was snow-covered ground was, in fact, the cloud layer, and I felt the vertigo scuttle all the way up my body from my feet to my head, digging its prickly claws deep.

I turned my back on the drop and looked up. That wasn't helpful, either. A slight overhang offered meagre shelter, and beyond that a sheer vertical wall of unblemished black rock plunged into the sky for what seemed like infinity. The stars looked thickly clustered as if they'd had to be shifted around to accommodate Murdercruel's mass.

"Something went wrong!" I announced, huddling close to the glow again. "We're nowhere near the top!"

Slippery John's grin was fixed, now. Saliva was crystallizing around his gums. "Chrrr urp. We crn wait 'til Dub crms back to lrrf."

"No, we can't!" I yelled. The wind was deafening. "He didn't finish the spell! It got misaimed! He'll have no idea where we are! WE don't know where the hell we are!"

"Thrn we'd brttrr grt clrmbrng."

I pointed upwards. "We can't climb this!" I pointed a loosely-hanging frozen hand at Thaddeus. "He's lost both his arms! And we're all freezing!"

"The crld shrldn't be too mrch rf a prrblrm," he said. "Jrst keep mrving arrnd."

Thaddeus immediately started jogging on the spot. I broke into a ragged Charleston. "What about the climb?"

"Slrppery Jrn is ahrd of the grrm agrrn." He wobbled left and right a little before extending his flimsy black sleeves and shaking out a few items that clanged metallically on the ground. Then he immediately re-hunched his shoulders and his arms snapped back around his torso. "Enchrrnted crrrmpons."

They were rigid black spikes with leather straps, and little streaks of blue light shone off the reflections. I stared at them for a few thoughtful moments, making no motion to pick them up, then turned to Slippery John. "Why do you have enchanted crampons on you?"

"Prrtty standrrd rogue grrr. Slrppry Jrn wrld lrrv to discrss thrm frrthrr but Slrppry Jrn is abrrt tr frrrze tr drrth." He made a heroic effort and managed to separate his teeth with an eye-watering crack. "Nearest church is on another continent. Slippery John's ghost is gonna have a bit of a walk after this. This is probably another reason why God wanted yrr blrrks trr trke crrr rrf thrrs."

He had a point. Besides the fact that our muscles went rock-solid if we stopped gyrating for a few seconds, the cold wasn't having any lethal effect on me or Thaddeus. But I felt Slippery John was trying to change the subject. "I get that the crampons are standard rogue gear. I just don't get why you brought two sets, unless you'd planned for . . ."

I stared at him. A few moments passed, silent for the cease-lessly upsetting wind and the tramp-tramp of two undead people jogging on the spot.

"Did you plan for this?" I said finally. Having said that, a few other notions rolled together in my head. "I've been following you on and off since all this began. You're very obviously stupid and incompetent but somehow things have ended up going your way, right?"

His face betrayed nothing but a vacant, slightly baffled smile and a nasty case of frostbite. The heat reserves stored in his mustache were clearly running low.

The more I thought about it, the more sense it made. I cocked my head. "The Deleters only take over the most skilled and noble adventurers. So if you want to survive as an adventurer and avoid the Syndrome you have to put on a façade of incompetence and creepiness when you're secretly a devious little prick who knows exactly what they're doing. And that's you, isn't it?"

He kept smiling.

I noticed that his eyes had glazed over. Investigatively I tapped him in the forehead. There was a sharp "crack," a seam appeared in his face, then he toppled backwards and fell off the mountain, disappearing from sight in a puff of water vapor.

"We have wasted enough time," said Thaddeus, his face steadfastly gazing upwards while the rest of his body from the neck down danced madly on the spot. "Our annihilation awaits."

I took up a set of enchanted crampons and weighed them in my hands. "Shall we a-climb?"

# THREE

Our progress up the mountain face was swift. Once the enchanted crampons were attached to our feet, all we had to do was touch the spikes to the wall and gravity shifted ninety degrees, so a devastatingly hard climb became more like walking slowly and carefully across a flat plain while wearing big high heels. Through some patient hand-jiving, I had finally gotten my fingers loose enough to waggle, and I could conjure the odd fireball to abate the cold, although they didn't last long. After the first few hundred yards I was pretty sure the air had become unbreathable at some point, but that had never been an issue. All in all, Mount Murdercruel's fearsome reputation was taking quite a beating.

Thaddeus was slightly ahead of me. He was getting along surprisingly well without arms, only occasionally losing his balance as he walked and faceplanting into the rock. So far we had both been climbing in stoic, determined silence, partly because the wind drowned out most sound, partly because I still didn't like him very much. I tried to zone out and concentrate on putting one foot in front of the other. Or rather, above the other. It was confusing, but then no-one ever employed magic to make life easier to understand.

The snow was everywhere. It fluttered about like swarms of little white bees. With my feet on the wall and the rest of my body sticking out like a flagpole the flakes gathered in my clothing, nostrils, and under my eyelids. After irritably rubbing it out of my face for the third time, I froze—in surprise, this time. "Hey!" I called. "Wait a minute!"

Thaddeus stopped and glared over his shoulder. The wind and the rock was effectively smoothing the wrinkles out of his face. "Why do you delay us?!" he boomed.

"Look at the snow!"

He frowned. "It has been snowing for some time! This is a mountaintop! It is to be expected!"

"But where's it coming from?!"

I could see his mouth begin to form the words "the clouds," and the rest of his face contort into the usual sneer of patronising contempt, but then he glanced over my shoulder and realized the same thing I had—that we had been a considerable distance above the clouds from the moment we'd arrived.

The wind was harsh but not harsh enough to be blowing the snow this far up. I glanced up (or straight ahead), and managed to blink the snow out of my eyes for long enough to take a good look.

The snow was definitely coming from above, but the night sky was completely clear. The stars shone brightly. Weirdly brightly, in fact. They also seemed to be a little more spread out than they'd been from the ledge. This high up in the world there was a disorienting tang of unreality in the air. I didn't know what to make of any of it.

The snow seemed to be intensifying. The flakes that rushed down towards us were getting bigger. In fact, they were starting to resemble big jagged chunks of ice—

"DOWN!" commanded Thaddeus.

I flung myself to the floor/wall just as a solid mass of impacted snow the size of a brick chimney whooshed past, brushing the few remaining straggly hairs on my head. I tried to look up again, caught a glimpse of more incoming missiles, and quickly flattened myself back down.

"Avalanche?!" I guessed aloud. That didn't seem right; it was too localized and too vindictive.

"Fear not!" said Thaddeus, crouching a few feet away. "The missiles of the dark ones will not impede our quest!"

"How do you figure that?!"

"Our path is one of righteousness! It is the will of the LORD that our wretched bodies of filth and dirt be destroyed, and—"

His point was immediately illustrated when a particularly large slab of ice struck him right in the face, tearing him from the wall like a poster for something the world no longer liked. The moment both his crampons came away from the rock, plain old regular boring gravity returned for him, and he plunged backwards out of sight.

I gritted my teeth and continued climbing, crawling on all fours, hugging the wall like a child at his mother's thigh.

The tactic served me pretty well, and being so thin probably didn't hurt. The big chunks of ice kept shooting past just behind me, upsetting nothing more than the label on the back of my collar. Looking up, I saw a narrow ledge that seemed to be sheltering me from the bombardment. Unfortunately, it was also blocking my view. I leaned back to try and get a better look, whereupon a slab of ice slammed into my shoulder.

Fortunately it was a brittle chunk that shattered wetly on impact, but it took me by surprise. My hands came away from the wall and I was pushed back onto my feet and into full exposure. Another chunk clipped my waist and one of my feet came free, leaving me splayed with three limbs in the air, connected to the wall with a single crampon.

Another cluster was coming right for me. Panic seized my brain like the fist of a farmer's wife around a chicken's throat. My hand shot out reflexively—*ARCANUSINFERUSTELECHUS*—and I sent off a firebolt.

It only deflected one of the missiles, but the force of the blast pushed me back until I was against the wall again, crab-walking upside down. The rest of the ice fell past harmlessly, doing nothing worse than embedding a few jagged chips into my kneecaps.

I didn't wait for my heart to ooze sluggishly back into place. Once the current storm of ice had passed I pushed back on the wall as hard as I could, swung my body up and over, slammed heavily onto my face, then scuttled on all fours under the overhang like a cockroach fleeing for the shadows.

No more ice seemed to be falling. All was still—"still" in this case being an extremely relative term, given that it was still as windy as hell and the snow was piling up in my earholes—and the assault seemed to be temporarily over. I carefully placed my hands around the ledge—with the crampons it was like preparing to vault over a short wall—and pulled myself up.

A butterfly knife slammed down into my left hand, pinning it to the rock. My crampons detached with the surprise, normal gravity was restored, and I was dangling by my arms from the highest mountain in the world.

"Or, if the ice doesn't work, we could just wait for him to climb up here and stab him up," said Mr. Wonderful, standing over me and twirling a knife in each hand.

An orange temperature-regulating aura shimmered closely around his body, and he was wearing a glass breathing mask hooked up to a leather gasbag on his back, which could only just contain his omnipresent grin. He didn't have enchanted crampons, so he'd tied a butterfly knife to each of his ankles, one of which was now pinning my hand to the rock.

"What're you doing here?!" I yelled.

"We're a little bit upset with you, Jimbo! We give you a lovely thoughtful gift of a tracking Reetle and then you leave it on a dead tosspot at the bottom of a mountain! THAT'S THE SORT OF THING WE MIGHT TAKE PERSONALLY!!"

I'd forgotten to tell Slippery John to get rid of the Reetle. I had only myself to blame, but I blamed him as well for good measure.

Mr. Wonderful's use of the word "we" gave me cause to look behind him. Bowg was there, too. He was wearing the same breathing equipment, as well as enchanted crampons, so presumably Mr. Wonderful had just preferred to challenge himself.

"So, my little mountain goat," said Mr. Wonderful, playfully rocking his foot back and forth to twist the knife. "Will you be coming quietly, or will we have to scrape you off the jagged rocks at the bottom?"

"Why?!" I yelled.

Mr. Wonderful idly tapped his foot, further mangling the bone and muscle of my hand. "Well, that's quite an existential question, isn't it, Jimbo."

"Do you know what's at the top of this mountain?!" I yelled. I had no idea where I was going with this line of conversation, but my usually reliable animal instincts had started it so I was running with it.

"What do we look like, geologists?" said Mr. Wonderful irritably.

"Why do you think no-one's ever climbed to the top?! Even with aura spells and magic crampons?!" I continued. "This is where they're hiding it! The center of the Infusion!!"

"Oh, give it a rest," said Mr. Wonderful, but he seemed to be thinking about it.

"We are prepared to reiterate your options," said Bowg, quickly. "The opportunity to surrender yourself for transportation back to Lolede and research is still available."

I tried shifting my grip. Pointless. Even disregarding the knife, the cold was seizing my hands up again. I could just about wiggle the fingers of my unstabbed one. I turned to my animal instincts again, but they shrugged, out of ideas. I was going to have to come up with an actual solution.

"Ar kay," I said, with difficulty. "Nuh sweat."

"You will be dissected and interrogated at exhaustive length," clarified Bowg, apparently confused by my answer.

"In fer a silver piece, in for a gold, that's what my dad used to say. Just one little thing."

"State it."

"Telechus," I finished, putting all the effort I had left into the finger waggles.

A jet of flame shot across the ledge, rather small and weak, but enough to set Mr. Wonderful's turn-ups on fire. He reacted with a yelp and a reflexive hop, pulling the knife out of my hand.

The only thing that was reliably anchoring me to the ledge was gone. I concentrated as hard as I could, trying to force my hands closed, to no avail. The cold had taken me right back to those first few uncoordinated hours of undeath, an alien in my own body.

I fell.

The ledge and the angry faces of Bowg and Mr. Wonderful slipped away. The mountain wall rolled upwards like a high-speed conveyor belt. Time slowed again, snowflakes holding in the air like glittering diamonds on a sheet of black velvet. The extra thinking time helped me remember that I was wearing magical crampons, and all I had to do was touch them to the wall.

I waved my arms to move closer to the mountain, somer-saulting in the air, and kicked my toes into the rock as hard as I could.

Had I actually paid attention in science class rather than spending every lesson drawing breasts and flicking elastic bands at Frobisher, I might have been more familiar with the effects of sudden deceleration. Time slowed down yet again just to give me the chance to fully take in the visceral sight of the crampons staying on the wall while the rest of me kept right on going, leaving behind a torn cloth boot and a dog-eared wooden leg.

I fell, again.

# FOUR

Something that felt suspiciously like the ground slammed into my side, pulverizing all my remaining internal organs. I bounced several feet back upwards, then hung in mid-air. When I didn't come back down I realized that my body hadn't come with me.

The grim, empty, gray-tinted afterlife might have been a little disheartening, but I was beginning to seriously miss it. Between the snowstorm, the constant flickering and the chittering of the tiny Deleters scuttling across my spirit body, this particular visit to the dead world felt like being trapped in a crowded nightclub during a volcanic eruption.

Through the disorienting madness of sound and visuals I could only barely see where my body was. It was lying in an ugly pile on yet another icy ledge. I'd been fortunate; I hadn't fallen as far as I'd thought, and was still a good distance above the clouds, insofar as such a distance could be described as "good."

As I waited to return to my body, I noticed movement on the mountain wall above me. Even through the chaos I recognized the insectile scuttling of Mr. Wonderful and the stoic gait of Bowg.

Then came a truly unprecedented experience for me: the burning desire to stop being dead and get back into my body as soon as possible. I could see the red-tinted forms of the two assassins as they stood over my form, and Mr. Wonderful, hands on hips, kicked at my body with a shoe knife.

It seemed like my resurrection was maliciously taking its time for once. I could feel myself starting to be pulled back, but Mr. Wonderful was already rolling my body towards the edge. I tried to yell but I was unheard by the living world, and the usual cluster of supervising Deleters were no help at all.

Just as one of my body's legs swung out into thin air, something bright and fast streaked past me like a comet, trailing white sparks. Bowg and Wonderful looked up—as did I—just in time for a glowing ball of light to explode into sparks directly under their feet. They both leapt out of the way, badly misjudged the width of their platform and dropped straight off the mountain.

Then my soul surged back into my body. I opened my eyes to find myself on my back, half-on and half-off the ledge. I swiftly dragged myself into a firmer position.

Thaddeus scuttled into view. He was attached to the wall with the crampons, and the force of the blast had pushed him down onto his back. "See how the Dark Ones flee from the light," he announced. "They are like the cockroaches in the festering outside toilet of the Damned."

"Was it you casting those spells?" I asked.

"The light of the LORD fills my rotten soul and unwashed hands," he said, which I took to mean "yes."

"You haven't got any hands." This raised another question. "How did you wiggle your fingers to cast the spell?"

"The light comes from within, not the machinations of my digits," he said, although I did notice that he'd taken his shoes and socks off. It must have been difficult to put the crampons back on afterwards, especially with no arms. "Idle no longer. We must proceed."

I attempted to, but stopped half-way. The entire left side of my body rattled around like a limp bag of firewood. I couldn't move my hand or bend my elbow; the fall had shattered most of the bones in my arm like the dry sticks they were. "My arm's paralyzed," I muttered. "I lost my wooden leg, too. There'll be no fixing this without Meryl."

"Cease your whining. Behold." He kicked a crampon off one of his bare feet. "Only one foot is required to ascend to Heaven."

I attached it to my one remaining foot and tucked my useless arm into my belt. Between the two I could pretty much write off the entire left side of my body, appendage-wise. I touched the crampon gingerly to the wall and instantly shifted from sitting on a ledge with my foot in the air to awkwardly half-crouching on the vast horizontal plain of Mount Murdercruel.

We resumed the climb. With only one crampon each we had to continue on all fours. I was having to do a quick little bunny-hop with each step, attempting to get the crampon back onto the wall before gravity could have a chance to react. Thaddeus didn't seem to be having any trouble, though.

"Hey!" I said as he tore off ahead. "I've only got one arm in commission, remember!"

I felt stupid about it immediately. He didn't say anything, but he gave me a piercing look that said I had absolutely no right to complain. Without arms he was having to flop forward like a newborn baby seal with brain damage, banging his face against the rock with each step.

And he was making rather alarming pace, too. I was having to hop flat out just to keep up. "Hey," I called, to change the subject. "What exactly was that spell?"

"The Level 47 Cunning Argument," he said proudly. "For rapid conversion of heathens."

"Have you always been able to do that?"

"'Tis a standard teaching in my Order."

"Never seen you do anything like that before."

"Before, I had no inspiration. Now, my purpose is clear."

I watched him slither and flail his way up the wall with quiet dignity. It occurred to me that I'd never bothered to find anything out about Thaddeus's order; they could have been anything from gentle vicars to unstoppable warrior monks, although I suddenly had good reason to doubt the first one. It also occurred to me that I didn't know precisely how advanced a priest he had been. Considering that merely being undead had upped my battle mage level by several increments, he was probably quite formidable now. All in all it made me grateful once again that his energies were being focused away from me at last. Rip both his arms off; why hadn't I thought of that?

We climbed in silence for I don't know how long. Once I had settled into a routine of crawling and hopping, and when I was satisfied that Mr. Wonderful wasn't going to show up again anytime soon, it was easy to fall into a reverie. With the regular movements of my untiring limbs it was like being rocked to sleep by a huge stone nanny.

Then, the wind stopped.

It hadn't simply died down; as we passed some unmarked line it simply popped abruptly out of existence. Once you've gotten used to constant discomfort, its sudden cessation is like suddenly getting all your skin torn off. Surprised, I stopped. I could still hear its whistling roar coming from below us, but it was like it was on the other side of a wall.

I looked around. Then I noticed the sky, and jolted with surprise a second time. "What happened to the stars?" I said.

Thaddeus also stopped and stared. The sky was featureless black—not the mundane blackness that comes from the absence of light, but the same inky, infinite blackness I'd witnessed under the ocean.

Light there was plenty of. It emanated from below and was casting our shadows up the unyielding rock of Mount

Murdercruel, whose forbidding blackness now seemed quite mediocre by comparison. With the latest in a long line of sinking feelings, I looked down.

The world was a glittering sphere far below us, an ocean of clouds broken up by the occasional island of land or sea. And stretching out over it, below us now, was a layer of stars. A thousand two-dimensional circles of bright light surrounded the planet like spotted gift wrap.

"They're just . . . lights," I said. "They're just a bunch of lights in the sky."

"What did you think they were?"

"I thought they were stars!" I waved my working arm, grasping for words. "You know. Other balls of gas like our sun, going out into space forever. Other worlds. Other life!"

He gave me a rather condescending look, and continued the climb. "Our planet is the center of the universe," he said. "That is what the LORD has always taught us."

"But there isn't any universe." I jerked my head upwards. "Not anymore. It's just . . . black."

Ahead of us, the sky was still empty and silent. Behind us, the world was getting on with the complicated business of existing, a patchwork quilt of cloud, ocean and land. I took one last look over the continents, and fancied that if I squinted I could just make out one of Barry's armies sweeping across another unwitting nation.

Then I heard a new noise. A rapid series of regular "chink"s, like spikes sticking in and out of rock. I looked down between my legs, and saw two figures, one skinny, one stout, scrambling their way up towards us.

"Oh, give me a BREAK!" I spat, before redoubling my efforts. I crawled and hopped as fast as I could manage, flinging myself at the wall again and again.

"What's the hurry?! What's the hurry?!" yelled Mr. Wonderful like a demented mantra.

I didn't know how much longer my body could keep up this pace. Scraps of flesh flew off my arms each time they slapped against the wall, and some foul liquid was dripping from my nose hole. And I still didn't seem to be going fast enough. The rattling of his knives was getting louder and louder, and now that there was no other sound, it was like the rattling of a stick inside a gnoll's feed bucket. The sound seemed to be coming from all around me. I was expecting at any moment a butterfly knife to appear between my legs and smoothly slice me in half lengthways.

Then I ran out of mountain.

I'd been going fast enough that I kept going for a few feet, but then the crampon came away from the rock, my hand groped for something solid, and I fell forward onto a horizontal surface. A genuine one, this time.

"What happened?" was what I intended to say, but it came out more as "Whuhackaguh?"

"Our exodus is truly blessed," said Thaddeus, already on his feet and bouncing excitedly. "We have reached the summit of the world!"

We stood on the edge of a glass-smooth plain. It was like some staggeringly powerful device had cleanly sheared off the mountain from this point upwards, creating a tree stump a mile wide. Originally, the peak had probably been much, much higher, as terrifying a thought as that was.

As I looked around, I realized the plain wasn't as empty as I'd initially thought. There was something in the middle . . .

"You can't escape the wheels of justice, my little jaywalkers," came Mr. Wonderful's voice. His grin appeared over the edge, followed by the rest of him. "Now then, let's . . ." he flinched hugely. "Crack my knackers, what the hell is that?"

"I think it's the Nexus," I said.

This seemed like a pretty safe bet. Even if a human had previously been able to get a team of workmen all the way up here, they'd probably have built something with slightly more traditional architecture than a featureless cube sitting in the dead center of the cross-sectioned mountain.

A normal construction team would additionally have been hard pressed to build it out of a single piece of milky-white stone that glowed brightly from within, and wouldn't have been able to set up the glowing pillar of light that stretched eternally upwards from the top of the cube.

"Huh," said Mr. Wonderful, already bored. He took two smart steps forward and grabbed both Thaddeus and me around our throats. "Well, for the top of the world, it's not much to look at, is it? This really what you climbed all this way to see?" He giggled mockingly. "Want to take some pictures before I throw you off?"

"Unhand us, black devil," spat Thaddeus. "Only the LORD may leave His fingermarks on the sullied flesh of His design."

"It's the Nexus!" I yelled. "Don't you understand?!"

"No, I don't understand!" said Mr. Wonderful cheerfully, dragging us inexorably back towards the edge. "I prefer to keep it that way. Understanding gets in the way of the violence."

"It's what we're looking for! It's the center of the whole Infusion! Where the Deleters come from!"

"Oh really?" droned Mr. Wonderful disinterestedly. Then some kind of thought penetrated the mad bastard's head and he said it a second time, less dismissively.

"Mr. Wonderful," said Bowg. "Your motion towards the mountain edge appears to have stalled. The execution of our assignment cannot be concluded without prompt re-assumption of movement on your part."

Bowg's voice snapped Mr. Wonderful out of his contemplation and he resumed dragging us along. "Not like it matters," he said agreeably. "You wouldn't know what to do with a Nexus even if you had one."

He reached the edge and swung around, dangling me over the abyss. My foot groped desperately for the edge, and I clung as hard as I could to his arm as he attempted to shake me off like a piece of snot on his finger. "But we do know what to do! We're on a mission from God!"

"Oh, that's a new one." He jiggled Thaddeus like an armful of puppy. "How much have you been talking to this chap?"

"I mean the real one! He told us how to end the Infusion! How do you think we got teleported here?! We can't do that kind of magic!" I was babbling now.

"Your punishment will be afforded greater dignity if you undergo it in silence," said Bowg. "Your attempts to reason with Mr. Wonderful are futile, as he is a psychopath, and consequently utterly irrational."

"My little friend's right, y'know," said Mr. Wonderful conspiratorially to Thaddeus. "You can't rely on psychopaths —they're totally unpredictable."

Everyone present saw it coming just a little too late to react. Mr. Wonderful suddenly spun around, flailing my and Thaddeus's legs like a fairground ride. My foot collided soundly with the side of Bowg's head.

The dwarf's expression didn't change. He tottered dizzily for a second as gravity debated what to do with him, then Mr. Wonderful helped it make up its mind by hurling two knives, which lodged themselves either side of Bowg's nose.

"Oh," Bowg said. "Shit." Then he fell.

"Been on that little twat's leash for years," said Mr. Wonderful, watching him disappear from sight. "The obedient pit bull becomes the escaped tiger! And it's got a knife!" He twirled another blade and made a vaguely predatory roaring noise, then smartly reached out and grabbed me by the lapel.

"Uh," I said, wondering if we hadn't made a gigantic mistake.

"Swear to me," he said, nose to nose hole with me. "Do you honestly know how to end the Infusion?"

I didn't have the slightest idea, but the piercing, almost pleading look in his eye warned me against honesty. "Yes," I said.

"Right, well, do me a favor and give it a few hours so I can get myself resurrected. I have to get back to the Guild before he does, the little tell-tale gobshite." He produced another butterfly knife from his seemingly limitless reserves, twirled it smartly three times, then buried it in his own eye socket. His skinny body folded up like a collapsing clothes rack.

"In the end," said Thaddeus, to fill the confused silence that followed, "even he had the goodness of the LORD in his heart."

"What are you talking about? He's a murdering psychotic bastard."

"In another time, such qualities could have sanctified him."

# FIVE

The closer we moved to the cube in the center of the plain, the more certain I was that we'd found what we were looking for. It had none of the decorations or filigree you might expect of an artifact of the gods, which probably meant that it was indeed genuinely important.

Up close, the cube was smaller than it had seemed from the edge, just a few feet taller than me. If the Deleters and their cosmic creators were inside, they wouldn't have a lot of elbow room. Its top face was emitting a broad column of light that stretched off into the black sky. I could hear a familiar high-pitched gibbering coming from within.

We were probably the first sentient beings to gaze upon the Nexus. The occasion called for a memorable quote that would go down in history. "Well," I said, after some thought. "Here we are."

"The LORD has guided us, and our pilgrimage is nearing an end."

"Yeah, I've been meaning to ask you something," I said, turning to him. "You do know we only have Dub's word for it that Si-Mon is the false god, right? We could just be swapping one all-powerful cosmic dipshit for another."

"If you do not believe that the true LORD sanctions our quest, then why do you pursue it?"

"Me, I'm just here for a nice clean death, and Dub said he can give me one. I don't care who ends up running the world. I just want it to stop being my problem."

"Those are the words of your tainted mouth. But are they truly the words of your soul?"

"Tell me, when you become religious, do you have to be taught how to use that smug annoying know-it-all voice, or does it come naturally? Because you should know it really doesn't give any authority to the drivel you spout."

"Worry not," he said, my words sailing gaily over his head. "If Si-Mon is the true LORD, He would never allow Himself to be defeated by the actions of two unclean blasphemers such as us."

I stared into the depths of the cube. "You know, you're really not being much of a comfort." I took a step towards the piercing whiteness, and hesitated.

Thaddeus took the opportunity to reactivate that same smug tone of voice I hate. "Perhaps now you ponder your true purpose?"

"No, I'm just looking for the bloody door." I did a complete circle around the cube. "Seriously, how do you get in this thing?"

I attempted to run my good hand across the surface. It passed straight through and was swallowed by the white mass.

It was an extraordinary feeling, like waving a hand over a volcanic vent that has somehow found a way to pump hot and cold air simultaneously. I could feel my arm being pushed upwards by a strong but gentle blast. I looked again at the great column of light that plunged infinitely into the void.

This wasn't the Nexus itself. This was just the way in.

The whiteness didn't seem to be damaging my hand, so I pushed my arm in to the shoulder. As soon as it had hold of that much, the wind started sucking the rest of me in like spaghetti. I couldn't have pulled back even if I'd wanted to. I took a deep breath out of ingrained habit and let it take me.

For a moment, I saw nothing but the blinding whiteness. The incessant gibbering was deafeningly loud and coming from all around me. Meaningless images flickered past my vision. I felt an ethereal fist grab me by the waist and pull me upwards at incredible speed. The white disappeared with a wet pop, and the planet rocketed away from me, just as it had done during my first death, but this felt very different. There was no warmth or sensation of love. The world below me was still and silent, as if sulking off in despair.

Then the whiteness returned, and everything went silent.

The silence was soon replaced by a continuous rattling, like the chirrupping of mechanical crickets. When my vision cleared, I found myself standing in . . .

. . . I didn't have anything to compare it to. I had been expecting some heavenly plain of existence, maybe with classical gold pillars and naked seraphim, but it was just a big room, totally unfamiliar except for its soul-crushing mundanity.

Under my feet was a sickly gray carpet that was as thick and soft as a piece of greaseproof paper. The walls were painted a light institutional blue. The ceiling was missing, opening out into a featureless white void. The only decoration on the walls was a sign reading *Loincloth QA Department*, with a smaller sign underneath reading, *Abandon all hope ye who enter!!!*

The bulk of the room was taken up by what I at first thought was some kind of labyrinth, but the walls were made of some flimsy fabric-covered material and were only about five feet high.

I was still looking around when we heard a voice, barely audible over the ongoing rattling noise. I couldn't make out the words, but I recognized the cheerful, high-pitched tone.

"Meryl," I said.

"We must regroup with our fellow maggot of Creation's fruit basket," announced Thaddeus. "She will join our righteous quest for extinction."

I stood on tip-toe to see over the walls, then inhaled sharply and ducked back down. A huge number of heads, presumably with bodies attached, were scattered throughout the room, poking up from between the walls. I slowly rose up again, expecting to see alerted guards training crossbows at my eyeballs, but the heads hadn't moved.

"Statues?" I wondered aloud.

"For what purpose would the gods possess graven images?" said Thaddeus.

I spotted two doors on opposite walls of the room. A glowing light was coming from behind one of them, outlining the cracks. The other was slightly ajar, and seemed to be where Meryl's voice was coming from. I began making my way towards it through the bizarre maze.

As we navigated through the walls, we discovered that they divided the floorspace into a number of square sections. Each contained a chair and a desk, but unlike any I'd ever seen. The furniture makers I knew liked to think of themselves as craftsmen, carving so many swirly patterns and bunches of grapes that there was barely room for the drawers. These desks were just soulless, unadorned steel rectangles.

We turned a corner, and almost ran straight into Captain Scar.

She was pale and motionless, all rambunctious energy gone. She was standing bolt upright in the middle of the floor, feet tightly together, arms held out at her sides, eyes widened in surprise and focussed intently on a section of wall. She looked like a drama student who had been told to be a tree, then never told to stop.

And she wasn't the only one. As we made our way across the strange room, we saw them everywhere: people standing frozen in place with their arms held out. I saw the woman I'd met at the entrance of Yawnbore, now relieved of her hedge clippers. There was the father from the hotel who had almost slammed a window onto my fingers. All the afflicted towns-people were there, each wearing the same frozen expression of shock. They weren't laid out with any apparent order or care, but randomly scattered throughout the room, as if they'd just been left where they'd been dumped. It was like a storage room for mannequins.

"Storage room," I repeated aloud, waving my hand in front of the face of a little girl I'd last seen punching a dog. "This is where they took them. All the people from Yawnbore they needed to get rid of. It's some kind of prison. Or . . . quarantine."

"This brings us no closer to our just reward," said Thaddeus gruffly.

I nodded. We left the prisoners behind and continued towards the door. As we approached, I heard the sound of another voice drift through the crack.

"How about now?" said the new voice. It was flat and expressionless in the classic Syndrome style, but was also incredibly deep, and booming, and loud enough to vibrate the floor beneath our feet. The voice of a bored messiah.

"Nnnno, pretty sure I'm still undead." Meryl sounded cheerfully apologetic.

I opened the door a little wider and put my eye to the gap. Beyond was a circular chamber, virtually empty but for what looked like a dentist's chair in the center.

Meryl was seated in it. She seemed quite comfortable, and was beaming happily. She was also missing all of her arms and legs.

"Okay, let's just run through this from the top," said the other voice. It seemed to be coming from the same source as an incredibly bright light that was shining down on Meryl from above. "Essentially you're an undead minion, right? But those are supposed to just be temporary help for necromancer characters. A zombie gets spawned out of the ground and turns to dust after a few attacks. That's how it works. I'm thinking the guy who raised you used that spell as a basis and did something wacky with it. What do you think?"

"For a god, you're not very all-knowing," said Meryl, without malice.

"Shut up. You will show respect to the mighty Si-Mon. The mighty Si-Mon's gonna go have another look through some of your code. If I don't figure this out by lunchtime I'm just gonna delete you, all right?"

"Fair enough."

The light faded. Meryl began softly humming to herself. There probably wasn't going to be a better opportunity. I slowly pushed the door all the way open, dropped into an alert crouch, and crept silently towards the chair.

"Hi Jim!" called Meryl, rendering moot my attempt at stealth. "Hi Thaddeus!"

Thaddeus nodded his head infinitesimally in greeting, while I examined Meryl's predicament. She wasn't strapped in, but in her current state she couldn't do more than wriggle, and anyway, she wasn't acting like there was anywhere she'd rather be. "What happened to your arm? And your foot?" she asked.

"Er . . . I was actually about to ask you something along the same lines."

She looked down and clicked her tongue, as if I'd merely drawn her attention to a patch of dead grass on her lawn. "Oh yeah. Deleted, I'm afraid. Don't worry about it."

"Well, it's going to make it hard to get you out of here."

She smiled patronizingly. "Jim, just stop it. It doesn't matter. You don't have to play the hero anymore."

"I AM NOT PLAYING THE SODDING—"

Thaddeus kicked me sharply in the back of the knee and planted his chin on my shoulder as I stumbled. "Discretion is a most practical virtue," he hissed.

"Si-Mon's been holding me here, being weird and saying a lot of things that don't mean anything," said Meryl. "I think he's trying to figure out how our whole undead thing works, but between you and me, I don't think he has any idea what he's doing."

"Truly he is the false God," muttered Thaddeus, solemnly relieved.

"But he's going to delete me now," she continued. She gazed up into the whiteness, smiling wistfully. "Soon it'll all be over."

"You don't need to get deleted!"

Meryl blinked at me. Her eyes were slightly unfocussed and her usual enthusiasm was severely dampened. If she had been human, I'd say she'd been drugged, but I knew that our blood didn't ooze fast enough for chemicals to have any effect. "I'm glad I got to see you one more time, Jim," she said, still gazing into the sky. "There's something I've been trying to tell you for some time now."

"What?"

"I lied. There never was a revolution in Borrigarde."

"Yeah, I know."

"You do?"

"Of course I do. It was bloody obvious."

"Oh. Well, anyway, you were right all along. The spirit of Borrigarde is gone and there's no room for the pride of our people anymore. That's why I came back to Yawnbore to find you. So I could join your quest and get myself deleted as well."

I was suddenly extremely angry, and the more I wondered

why, the more angry I became. "For god's sake, Meryl! You don't have to!"

"Jim, it's okay. This is what I want. There's something else. I've learned the Truth."

"The truth?"

"No, the Truth. The one Barry's followers were spreading around back in Lolede. The one that makes some people calm and some people crazy. Si-Mon told it to me. And—I just don't really care anymore."

"I care!" I heard myself say. To my surprise, I meant it.

"Then you'd better run, quick," she said, jerking her head upwards. "Si-Mon's coming back."

Above us, a section of the whiteness was somehow becoming slightly whiter and more brilliant than the mundane whiteness around it.

"We must go," announced Thaddeus, pointedly kicking me in the shin.

I swiftly went back through the door before Si-Mon could catch me. But when Thaddeus tactfully closed the door after we were through, pulling the handle with his teeth, I didn't move.

"The great Si-Mon confesses to not being able to get his head around it," came that booming voice again. "That little freak Dub can't notify his code to save his life. You got any idea what BaseRegenPM is? Answer your mighty God."

"Can't say I do, sir."

Thaddeus was biting at my arm, trying to pull me away. I shook him off, pushed the door barely ajar, and peered through the crack. Meryl's body was surrounded by a strange green aura, and a tendril of energy extended from it into the sky.

"Well, whatever," said Si-Mon. "Was kind of hoping I could figure this bug out, but out of sight, out of mind, I think."

"Good luck with everything," she said, quickly. Her eyes met mine.

Then he deleted her.

I would have thought it deserved a little more ceremony, but the process was terribly abrupt. Everything inside the green aura simply faded into shadow, then both the shadow and the aura disappeared. Within two seconds, nothing remained of Meryl.

I kept watching from the crack in the door. Even after she'd gone, and after Si-Mon's glorious light had retreated, I remained frozen, staring at the chair where she had been. Eventually I felt myself topple slowly backwards until I fell onto my backside.

I looked up at Thaddeus. "What was that?" I said.

He thought for a moment. "The righteous judgment of Si-Mon?"

"This isn't the way it's supposed to go!" I yelled, suddenly getting to my feet. "I was supposed to rescue her! She let herself get taken because she thought I'd . . . I'd rescue her, and we'd defeat the villain, run down the mountain as his doom fortress collapses around us . . ."

I stopped when I saw Thaddeus leaning away from me. His arm stumps were twitching and his expression was about two parts fear to one part contempt.

"It just . . . doesn't make any sense," I finished, weakly.

"Our sister has found the annihilation our kind deserve," he said tentatively. "Rejoice in that."

"But she didn't want to be deleted!"

"It was her choice. Just as it is our choice."

"Her choices are stupid! Every choice she makes is stupid!"

Thaddeus looked at me through his eyebrows. "But who are you to decide another's fate?"

"Yes," said a new voice. "That's my job."

We slowly turned around as if we were mounted on cake stands.

"If you're going to have a shouting argument while on a heretical mission," said Barry, "don't do it right outside God's door. Are you completely stupid?"

He seemed a little out of his element. His brilliant white aura and constant levitation were a lot more suited to, say, the scene of an epic battle or the summit of a mountaintop in the middle of a thunderstorm, but this place was a little too cramped for the full effect — which is not to say that his sudden appearance didn't make me come close to wetting myself.

The incredible glare that was Si-Mon's celestial form was suddenly overhead. "What are you two doing here?" he boomed. "Barry, did you bring them in at last?"

"Si-Mon!" barked Thaddeus, his voice so authoritative that even Barry flinched. "If you are the true LORD, then prove yourself worthy of our faith! Delete us!"

"How dare you test the LORD!" shrieked Barry. "He's the one who's supposed to test you!"

"Delete you?" repeated Si-Mon. "Are you serious?"

"Our existence is a blight!" continued Thaddeus. "If you are truly our creator, then un-create us now!"

"Wait. You actually want to be deleted? Both of you?"

I'd tried to keep out of the conversation because it was by far and away the most insane one I'd ever encountered. "Uh," I stalled. "Yes. Yes, that would be very nice. If you would."

"Uh, LORD," Barry broke in, "If it pleases Your Majesty, I would be deeply grateful if You would let me deal with this."

"What?" Si-Mon was getting more and more confused. "No. Don't be stupid. I'll just take care of it right now."

Thaddeus and I tensed up in anticipation. Nothing happened.

"LORD?" asked Barry, as the silence dragged on.

"Oh shit brub," said Si-Mon. The light disappeared.

"Brub?" I said, after a moment.

"Si-Mon has spoken," said Barry, obviously improvising. "Clearly his wish is for me to finish you off." He cracked his knuckles.

"He could not un-create us," said Thaddeus grimly. "Do you see now? You are the consort of a false god." A single drop of black blood squirted menacingly from one of his stumps.

"Oh. Okay. I guess this is going to be a figment of my imagination, then."

He extended a hand. Somewhere in the distance a heavenly choir burst into song. White energy edged with gold exploded from his palm.

I could feel the heat radiating from all around. The smell of burning carpet assaulted my nose hole. But after a moment's terror, I realized that my body was very pointedly failing to be boiled away by relentless holy magic.

The spell cleared. A confused Barry was visible again. Thaddeus was standing in front of me, extending one of his bare feet and wiggling his toes. A bubble of semi-transparent golden light surrounded us.

"Uh," began Barry.

"Only a false god would leave a lickspittle such as thee to fight his battles on his behalf," intoned Thaddeus as the shield faded.

Barry bared his teeth. "I am NOT a LICKSPITTLE!" He extended his hand for another bolt. Thaddeus responded by nimbly hopping onto his other foot and rattling off a stream of lightning-fast holy words. A glowing white Level 47

Cunning Argument exploded against Barry, slamming him against a partition wall.

The vicar's levitation spell fizzled out, and he fell back onto his arse, clutching his arm as smoke rose from the folds in his sleeve. A very worried frown broke out on his face as he remembered what vulnerability felt like. "Who the hell ARE you?"

"I am Father Thaddeus Praise-His-Name Godbotherer III," said Thaddeus, drawing himself up and giving Barry the full flare of his nostrils. "High Priest of the Seventh Day Advent Hedge Devolutionists. Keeper of the Incantations and Steward of the Sunday Coffee Mornings."

"Holy balls," said Barry unpiously. "I did my thesis on you!"

"We are in the employ of Dub-us, the true God," continued Thaddeus. "Surrender now, aid us in the downfall of Si-Mon, and your soul may not yet be damned."

Barry glanced between Thaddeus and me. A drop of sweat ran down his nose. "Well," he said slowly, carefully moving his hands behind his back. "That's a kind offer. Dub-us . . . certainly sounds like a . . . benevolent God . . . but you're forgetting about . . . hang on . . . you're forgetting about this."

I saw the finger waggling but couldn't warn Thaddeus in time. Barry thrust out both his hands for one big push and gave it everything he had. Raw power blasted out of him like a high-pressure hose, pinning Thaddeus to the wall. I saw Thaddeus, only just visible amid the light, backed up against the wall and holding up both his feet, putting every ounce of power into his shield. Ten seconds of joint-quivering effort passed. Then twenty. Then thirty. It was becoming an excruciating spectacle. The paint on the wall behind Thaddeus was blackened, and the carpet had melted under his feet.

Finally, the shield gave way, its layers peeling apart like an onion. Thaddeus was engulfed in the searing white glow, and his body disappeared from sight.

"Right then, one down," said Barry, when the effect faded. He leaned against the burnt wall, gasping for breath. Then he started with realization, and began looking around urgently. "Where'd the other one go?"

The conflict had distracted him long enough for me to duck out of sight. Now, I was desperately creeping on all fours—or as close as I could come, with a missing foot and a paralyzed arm—toward the glowing door on the other side of the room.

I heard a burst of choral singing and the clatter of furniture being violently rearranged. I cautiously poked my head over the divide and saw Barry with his back to me, shoulders hunched in fury, telekinetically picking through a newly-created pile of ruined desks, partitions and prisoners. I swiftly ducked back down and got back to creeping before he realized I was somewhere else.

"I really think you're being irrational about this," he said, doing some kind of breathing exercise they probably teach you in anger management class. "Maybe you should stop and consider for a moment. I'm the most powerful holy magic user in the world, and if you somehow get past me you'll be up against God. And you—you're nothing but a dried out husk held together with string. I'd say you're out of your depth but I think you already realize you hit the sea bed a long time ago."

I kept crawling, moving as carefully as I could so that the exposed bone in my leg stump didn't thump on the thin carpet. If I just let him keep talking, maybe he'd smug himself to death.

I heard another holy bolt and another crunch of broken wood and bones. Closer, this time. "You want to be deleted, right?" said Barry, levitating in the center of the room and rotating like a searchlight. "So why are you even hiding? I can do the same thing to you that I did to your friend. That's as good as deletion, isn't it?"

No, I replied, privately. Because there would still be a body to come back to, even if it was little more than an angry cloud of dust gradually settling into the carpet to spend eternity counting the fibers.

That had been Thaddeus's fate. An unfamiliar twinge of guilt pricked at me, which didn't make a lot of sense, because I definitely wasn't going to blame myself for what had happened to him. He should have rethought his rather confrontational approach to danger around the time his arms were being torn off—

I stumbled. Crawling with one arm paralyzed and one foot missing had proved too difficult. I lost my balance, fell forward and heard my stump knock loudly upon the partition wall.

I lay on the ground, trying to keep perfectly still. Silently, my face buried in carpet, I began to pray. *Dub-us*, I thought, as clearly as I could. *If I'm doing all the legwork the least you can do is pull a few strings on your end. Please make it so that he didn't hear that.*

A second passed.

Another second passed.

The third one was interrupted by the partition wall above me bursting outwards in a singing white fireball, followed by a brief shower of wooden fragments and body parts. I flattened myself down as well as I could and wriggled out of the way. Dub-us's claim to One True God status was starting to look as shaky as Si-Mon's.

Barry was sending out more magic bolts haphazardly, snarling in frustration with each one. He'd lost me again. I scuttled around a corner, and saw the door barely yards away.

Unfortunately all the furniture and partitions around it had already been destroyed, so getting to it would mean stepping out into plain view.

I edged forward and peeked out from around a sizzling waste paper basket. Barry was facing the other way, indiscriminately blasting his way through former pirates and Yawnbore residents. I carefully pulled myself onto my feet, not taking my eyes off him. I had to make my move now and hope he didn't turn around.

I began to tip-toe my way across to the door. Ten yards to cover. Then, eight. Seven. *Don't let him turn around. Dub-us, this is your chance to redeem yourself. Plenty of desks over there I could be hiding behind, Barry, no need to turn around. Four yards. Don't turn around. Don't turn around. Don't turn around, you bastard. Don't . . .*

It was probably the "bastard" that jinxed it. He turned around.

I froze, a full yard from the door. His magic-spurting hand slowly came forward again, with the cold, callous deliberation of a hunter aiming his crossbow at a startled deer.

I raised my arm, instinctually responding to his long-distance high-five. Both our lips moved rapidly, framing the magic words of our respective trades. I screwed my eyes shut.

I heard the sound of magic crackling through the air, and I waited for the prickly hot sensation that would be the last thing I felt before my nervous system was reduced to a smear on the nearby wall. When I realized I was still in one piece, I opened one eye.

A very bewildered bunny rabbit was levitating in the center of the room, paw still outstretched in a vague casting gesture.

# SIX

My body was getting more and more damaged, but I could still move quickly when I had to. It seemed like one moment I was at the door with my hand around the knob, and the next I was on the other side, pinning it shut with my back.

The room beyond was perfectly spherical, and I was standing on a narrow bridge about half-way up it, terminating in a circular platform in the dead center. The curved walls were the source of the glow I'd seen from outside. They were divided into a grid, and each illuminated square displayed a region of the world, viewed from above. I recognized Lolede City, its tired populace shuffling through their daily lives, indifferent to the oppression of Barry's zealots; the people of Applewheat eagerly pillaging each other; the rubble and sand that remained of Yawnbore dotted with new signs promising the future construction of a spa and religious retreat. There was a view of two circular step pyramids side by side that I think were in Anarecsia. It was like a digest of civilization for some cosmic voyeur. There was absolutely no doubt in my mind that I'd found Dub's machine.

I'd been in the room for a full second, now, and the time I had bought was ticking away fast. Behind me, I heard the ominous sound of a rabbit adorably pawing the other side of the door.

The machine itself was disappointingly small. It looked vaguely like magitechnology, but none I'd ever seen. It was a small, rectangular black window, floating a few feet off the ground, attached by a thin wire to some kind of flimsy console. It seemed to be emitting the loud, continuous rattling sound I'd been hearing since I arrived. The screen was displaying a single word in glowing white letters.

*COMMAND?*

I took a closer look at the console. It was rectangular and almost completely covered in buttons. Most of them were labeled with numbers or letters of the alphabet, while the rest bore strange symbols that I couldn't even begin to comprehend. I pressed one of the lettered buttons, and the same letter appeared on the screen below the first word. All right, this seemed self-explanatory.

"Delete me," I spelled out. It took an achingly long time, because for some reason the gods had laid out the letter-buttons in some stupid, unintuitive order that had nothing to do with any alphabet I knew.

I waited for a response, but none came. I started rapidly pushing buttons at random, painfully aware that Barry's bunnymorph wouldn't last much longer, and eventually provoked a reaction from the machine.

*FILE NOT FOUND: 'me'*

I looked fearfully back at the door when I heard furniture crashing again. Barry had changed back. He would be disoriented from the transformation, so he probably hadn't guessed I was in here yet. But it was only a matter of time, and there couldn't have been much left to destroy out there.

I tried another tack. "Who are you," I wrote.

*SYNTAX ERROR: UNKNOWN COMMAND: 'Who'*

This was going nowhere. I had no idea who was on the other end of this screen, but there was no getting through to them this way. What had Dub said? I had to spread the corruption from inside myself to the machine. The same way I'd spread it to Drylda when I was . . .

"Dead," I recalled. "I have to be dead for it to work."

I looked around. I could hear holy magic being cast very close to the door, and the occasional solid object being hurled against the wall. I considered throwing myself off the bridge, but the fall might not have been deep enough to kill me, and there was no way back up.

I glanced desperately around before my gaze returned to the door. I jogged on the spot for a moment, psyching myself up, then bowed my head and ran at full pelt into the doorknob.

Now I had a big dent in the top of my head and the room appeared to be mounted on a giant malfunctioning merry-go-round. Dying had always been a lot easier when I'd had a convenient necromancer's tower, or obliging psychopath. I got up, narrowly avoided falling off the walkway, then staggered forward again for another go.

Barry must have kicked the door open a split-second before I hit it. There was a sound like splintering wood mingled with the sound of a boot stamping on a bowl of cornflakes, and I died.

My body went one way and my soul another. I looked down at my increasingly damaged body hanging precariously off the walkway. Then I turned back to the machine, and my astral jaw dropped.

The room was suddenly a lot more crowded, and not just because of the addition of Barry. Tiny deleters were pouring steadily from the top of the screen machine, expanding rapidly into full size as they emerged. With mindless professionalism each split off in turn and flew smartly into one of the glowing windows, heading off to deliver unwanted resurrections like a flock of poorly-briefed storks.

The dead world was still flickering back and forth between the normal gray and the disquieting green-lines-on-black. In the former, the machine looked like a screen and a panel of lettered buttons. But in the other, it was a hovering sphere of white light, like the cue ball from God's billiard table.

I heard a chittering sound, and looked down at my hands. The unwholesome-looking tiny Deleters that crawled in the hundreds over my astral form were getting excited. They fought each other to climb to the very outlying tips of my fingers and reach out their little insectile limbs towards the machine.

As I floated towards the center of the chamber, a few of the busy Deleters brushed past me, unconcerned. Some of my little companions took the opportunity to leap off me onto one of them. I watched in horror as the tiny Deleters reproduced madly, spreading themselves over their infected cousin as it twitched and shuddered in voiceless agony. I almost pitied the thing. And it made me wonder what, exactly, I was preparing to unleash.

I reached my hand towards the screen, but something stopped it. A few of the Deleters in the room had stopped to watch me, and the astral energies of resurrection were tugging at my limbs. Barry was in the middle of nudging my body off the walkway.

Gritting my teeth, I summoned all the strength I had, hurled myself against the Deleters' inexorable pull, and saw my astral hand pass through the machine. Only for a moment, but long enough for my bug-Deleters to jump off and start breeding. The screen went blank, then began to flash the word *ERROR* over and over again before coughing out one last handful of twitching, crippled Deleters like a glob of tuberculotic phlegm.

Barry froze when all the windows on the walls simultaneously whited out. His head snapped around in time to see the screen fill with a storm of punctuation marks. All the Deleters that remained in the room were convulsing madly, including the ones growing out of Barry's back.

"Oh, you little . . ." he began.

I couldn't resist the pull any longer. I was yanked off my astral feet just as my body slid off the walkway and onto, then into, one of the flashing windows. Barry, frantically pressing the lettered buttons, either caused the following explosion or failed to prevent it.

Then I came back to life.

I returned to my body just in time to land heavily on something hard, roll down an incline and come to rest sprawled on my back.

I was in the real world again. The windows in that spherical chamber had apparently been some kind of magical teleport. The sky was a healthy blue and the morning sun shone down on me with oblivious good cheer. But sooner or later I was going to have to sit up and spoil it all by finding out where the hell I was.

I sat up.

I was in the middle of a featureless plain of smooth, unweathered rock, rising and dipping in perfectly curved hills and valleys. There weren't even any cracks or jagged edges to liven the place up. Nothing but a desert of lifeless stone, contoured like a collection of upturned bowls covered by a sheet.

I took a moment to survey the damage from my landing. My left arm had been paralyzed for a while, but now I couldn't persuade the fingers of my right arm to move, either, nor my right leg. A few sections of my skull shifted whenever I moved my head, making me see marvelous colors. If I was going to be stuck in this body much longer, I was definitely going to have to look into a long-term repair solution when I got back to civilization.

But in what direction did civilization lie? I dragged myself to the top of a shallow knoll but saw only the same wasteland stretching to the horizon in all directions. Where the hell was

I? I ran through the possibilities, and none of them seemed to fit. There weren't enough sheep for it to be Garethy, nor enough wayside inns for Lolede. Anarecsia was covered in jungle. And you'd never find a clear, smokeless blue sky in the Malevolands.

"Oh," boomed the sun. "You're still here."

I spun around, which was a mistake, because I lost my balance and rolled back down the slope. "Whuh?" I said.

"Sorry. I guess it's because you were in the debugging suite when the server crashed."

"Dub?" The voice was virtually identical to Si-Mon's. "What happened?"

"You did it," he said. His voice seemed to be coming from the entire sky. "You crashed the server. There was a hard reset and Si-Mon's encryptions were removed. I've got my admin status back."

It was definitely Dub's brand of thoughtless gobbledygook language. "What?!"

"Oh, sorry." A pause. "Your corruption spread to the very building blocks of the world. The key to Si-Mon's control was erased, and my holy power is restored."

"Where am I?"

Another long pause. "You wanted to get deleted now, right?"

"Just tell me where I am!"

Wherever his actual physical body was I felt certain that his godly foot was awkwardly stirring some heavenly dirt. "You're. You're in Lolede. The middle of Lolede City, actually."

I took a good, long, look around before replying. "Where is everything?"

"Okay. Don't get mad. The thing is, Simon did a lot of damage and I didn't think I'd be able to fix much of it straight away. So in order to remove all the stuff he did we had to remove a few other things too."

My eyes narrowed. "How many other things?"

"Well. Everything. Except you." A lingering pause ensued. "Probably everything. There might still be some things left, haven't checked yet. Looks like everything. Let me know if you see anyone."

"Everyone's gone except me?" I said. I wondered if there was a word that meant "ironic, but in the most hysterically brutal and unfair way." "Can you bring them back?"

"No. Sorry. No. What we've done is basically turn the clock back to the beginning of time. This is the rock layer before we added water and life and all the other bits, so we could start getting the actual gameplay together."

A cold and terrible realization washed over me like an acidic tidal wave. "We?"

"Well," began the sun. "Oh shit brub." Then it vanished.

"So now you know," said Barry.

I spun around, losing my footing again and falling on my arse. He had materialized about twenty feet away, above a neighboring hillock, still floating and still crackling with magic and indignation.

"Tell me something," he continued. His voice was calm but the rest of him was shaking. "Was Si-Mon's vision of the world so terrible? Was it so abhorrent you couldn't even bring yourself to raise your objections in a mature, civil fashion— you just had to run off and smash it all to bits? What are you, five years old?"

"I didn't know this would happen!"

He snorted. "Then you were played for an idiot. But that's what they do, isn't it? That's what they've been doing to us since the beginning of time. LORD Si-Mon told me. This is the Truth that I was trying to make people like you understand. The LORD was the only one of their kind with the decency to tell us."

I was still half lying on the ground in a position of total vulnerability, but I couldn't bring myself to move. "Tell us what?"

"How much do you think you know about it all? Really? About the Infusion and the angels and the Syndrome? That fifteen years ago these all-powerful celestial beings descended from on high, stopped anyone from dying, and started possessing adventurers on a twisted whim? Is that what you think?"

"It's true, isn't it?"

"Yes, yes, it's true, but it's only half of the Truth. I believe your friend just gave you a rather large clue as to the other half."

The horrible thought I'd had earlier appeared in the back of my throat. I laboriously spat it out. "They created us."

"Precisely." He was pacing back and forth at around eye level as he spoke. "They created us, our planet, everything in it and the entire history of our species so that they could one day use it for their entertainment. All our evolution has been guided from the very beginning towards making our world perfect for adventuring. That's it. That's the meaning of our existence." His sickly grin didn't seem to have anything to do with his regretful eyes. "Incidental characters in someone else's quest, that's all we've ever been."

It was all true. I knew that instantly. It was like I'd spent my whole life being followed around by a man making obscene gestures behind my back, and now I'd finally turned around and caught him with his tongue out and his middle fingers up.

"Oh," I said.

Barry scowled. "I used to spend hours pondering the meaning of life. I had so many theories. Until Si-Mon gave away the twist ending. After that, I had nothing left. The only thing left to do was start telling the Truth to everyone else."

"You bastard," I said, without passion.

He hung his head. "Yes. I'm the bastard. I'm the villain. But I couldn't be the hero, could I?" He glanced around at the empty landscape. "It was better than nothing."

I was too lost in thought to see him waggling his fingers. A holy blast sent me into a ragged backflip, throwing me onto my face. I slowly and laboriously lifted my head to see that my left arm was missing, along with a football-sized chunk of attached torso.

"There you are, Barry," came the voice of Si-Mon, as I struggled to wriggle away from the vicar. "Your God has been looking for you."

"My LORD," said Barry, falling to his knees in mid-air. "It's gone, my LORD. Everything. Except this . . . creature."

"What did he do to the build? The debug logs don't make any sense."

"I regret that I have failed You, O Si-Mon," went Barry, averting his eyes and clasping his hands. "He inflicted his corrosive essence before I could stop him."

"Smooth move, dipshit," said Si-Mon to my motionless form. "Dub put you up to this, right? This is exactly the sort of thing he'd do, the big baby. I've locked him out again. You're at the mercy of Si-Mon's judgement now."

"Just delete me," I whispered. "Please."

"Hardly seems to matter, now, does it?" said Si-Mon, as Barry glanced at him hopefully. "There's nothing left for you to corrupt."

"Does that mean I may deal with him as I see fit, my LORD?" he simpered.

"You may, my faithful servant."

Instantly I was pulled off the ground by invisible puppet strings until I was dangling from my head with my remaining limbs splayed out. Barry put his head on one side and considered me, like an artist debating what size brush to employ.

I felt the stitches and tendons in my hip strain against the invisible force for a brief moment, then my right leg was torn from its socket with a sickening meaty squelch. Barry threw it away like a chicken bone and slammed the rest of me back into the ground. A little part of my mind was trying to make me move, to resist, but what the hell did it think I could do? Run away? To where?

"What of our world, master?" said Barry, as he circled my body.

"Well, not much more I can do to fix Mogworld, is there," droned Si-Mon petulantly. "The mighty Si-Mon is thinking it's time to salvage what I can and move on to greater things. At least I've still got you."

"Me, my lord?"

"Yes, Barry, I've decided to bring you with me," said Si-Mon magnanimously. "You will ascend to a new world."

The vicar's eyes lit up, and he clasped his hands together as his heart swelled with gratitude. "Can it be true?" he asked, choking up. "I will finally be allowed to walk among the gods?"

Si-Mon hesitated at length, the same way Dub always did when there was something he didn't want to tell me. "Not exactly. Not walk, anyway. You can't go in your current body. You'll take on other forms when I bring you to other . . . other worlds. You'll have to get on top of some special jobs for your mighty God when you get there."

"I am ready, my LORD."

"Then we'll get going as soon as you're finished here."

I was struggling to get up onto my one remaining elbow when a sheet of white fire swept across my body, neatly severing my arm and cleaving through my torso.

I pulled myself forward with my chin and shoulders. Everything from my sternum upwards came with me, leaving behind half a torso attached to a leg, a spreading puddle of black goo, and a few trailing wobbly bits that belonged inside my ribcage.

Something flipped me onto my back, and Barry appeared overhead. He put his hands on his hips and clicked his tongue. "Last living thing in an empty world," he sighed, extending his hand once more. "And you're not even alive."

The blast hit me like a six-ton boulder. I died instantly, and for the last time.

# SEVEN

I hung in the air above what remained of my body: a steaming patch of dust and slime, splattered against the rock like vomit on the pavement outside a treacle shop. Barry admired his handiwork for a second, then turned to his master.

"Right, here's the first thing you can do for your God," said Si-Mon. "I'm going to move you into something called an 'intra-net,' all right? It's like a really small boring little world. Si-Mon needs you to track down everything to do with 'payroll' and 'security clearance.' Got all that?"

"For my LORD, I will seek any bounty."

"Right on."

A shaft of light extended down to Barry. The vicar held out his arms and began to rise, along with the little entourage of Deleters that were still sticking out of his upper back.

So that's it, I thought. Barry's going to ascend into Si-Mon's world and help him take over that one, too. About a minute from now, I'm going to come back to life and spend eternity as a two-dimensional stain on the rocks.

I looked down, and saw something stark and white peering at me from my scorched remains. It was one of my eyeballs, gazing up at me like the concentrated essence of a mistreated puppy dog. It was slightly deflated but unmistakeable: the weird-looking octopus eye that Meryl had given me.

And then, something seemed to click inside my head, and I felt a great and furious energy flooding me, all the way down to the tips of my ghostly fingers.

A roar came out of me like a belch of volcanic gas rising from the bottom of an ocean. The Deleters inside Barry all turned to look at me, startled.

I ran forward and flung myself at him. The part of me that was still coherent expected to phase harmlessly through and was thoroughly humbled when my arms fastened soundly around his waist.

His Deleters certainly felt my touch. They all began to simultaneously shriek in agony as the first few corrupted bug-Deleters invaded their bodies, causing Barry to clap his hands over his ears.

I tightened my grip as he continued to ascend. The world flickered out around us, and then we were hurtling at insane speeds along a black tunnel ringed by row upon row of shining queues of Deleters. I bared my teeth, shifted my grip to his lapels and hauled myself up until we were face-to-face.

"Get off!" he yelled, his voice reverberating oddly. I nutted him in the face as hard as I could. A couple of my tiny Deleters jumped off me onto his nose, and he shrieked like a schoolgirl with a caterpillar down her dress.

Images rattled across my vision as we plowed through the Deleter universe: meaningless Deleter correspondence, bright colors, and a curiously large number of pictures depicting naked women. That was closer to what I'd always imagined the heavens to be like, but none of them seemed to be enjoying themselves, so I wasn't sure. While I was distracted, Barry brought his fist down on my astral head, which afforded him nothing but an armful of corrupted Deleters.

I climbed higher, and grabbed for one of the Deleter heads poking out of his shoulder. My hand closed around it; it was like squeezing a bag of marshmallows wrapped in silk. With an incredibly satisfying ripping sound, I tore the Deleter from his body and cast its limp remains into the darkness.

Already I could feel myself being dragged back towards the puddle of my own body. I wrapped my legs around Barry's chest to resist the pull, then sunk my teeth into another Deleter's face and shook it out of him like a rabid dog.

My own Deleters were all over him now, and he finally realized that repeatedly punching me was only helping them multiply faster. He tried slapping the swarms away, but only served to spread them to other parts of his body, and more were still pouring out of me at an alarming rate.

Then Barry stiffened. He began shaking uncontrollably, the same way the corrupted Deleters had. His limbs and chest were swelling and bubbling. Shafts of white light were bursting out of him, like a water bed springing leaks.

I barely noticed. I kept hitting him and hitting him until we'd gone as far as the tether to my body would allow. I snapped back, detaching from Barry, and all I could do was watch him rocket away into the darkness. I screamed in rage again, an angry dog denied its chew toy.

Soon, he was a disappearing pinprick of light in the distant darkness. Then he expanded, exploding with a brilliant radiance into a thousand white streamers that rained down upon the void. Then everything was pulling away from me at speed, streaking into oblivion, and I came back to life.

My vision was confused and blurry. I couldn't hear at all. I tried to open my mouth to call out, but my mouth wasn't there. Neither were any of my limbs.

I tried to move. No response. All I could determine was that my body was a lot less body-shaped than I remembered. It seemed unusually two-dimensional. Puddle-like.

*No*, I thought. *No, this isn't fair.*

Only one of my eyes was functioning. I focussed it as well as I could, but it was half-flattened and leaking goo. All I had was a blurry view from a puddle in the middle of an empty wasteland.

No. NO. This wasn't the end. It couldn't be. The universe had played a lot of mean tricks on me but this was crossing the line. *Dub, you can't leave me like this. We had a DEAL. I was PROMISED. You PROMISED it would END. YOU CAN'T LEAVE ME LIKE THIS. YOU SAID YOU WOULD DELETE ME OH GOD PLEASE COME BACK DELETE ME DELETE ME DELETE ME DELETE ME DELETE ME DELETE ME DELETE ME DELETE ME DELETE ME DELETE ME DELETE ME DELETE ME DELETE ME DELETE ME DELETE ME DELETE ME DELETE ME DELETE ME DELETE ME DELETE ME DELETE ME DELETE ME DELETE ME DELETE ME DELETE ME DELETE ME DELETE ME DELETE ME DELETE ME DELETE ME DELETE ME DELETE ME DELETE ME DELETE ME DELETE ME DELETE ME DELETE ME DELETE ME DELETE ME DELETE ME DELETE ME DELETE ME DELETE ME DELETE ME DELETE ME DELETE ME DELETE ME DELETE ME DELETE M—*

**From:** "Brian Garret"
<briang@loinclothentertainment.com>
**To:** All Staff
**Subject:** Simon

When I founded Loincloth it was with the intention to create, not just a great environment for game development, but also a family unit for the greatest talent in the industry. In that respect, as I'm sure you're all aware, I've always liked you all to consider me as a father figure, like the alpha male in a group of lions.

And as alpha male, it sometimes falls to me to make harsh decisions for the good of everyone, like driving out difficult elements and killing the cubs of any lion who challenges my leadership. And as I'm sure will come as a surprise to you all, I've regretfully decided to let Simon Townshend go. I've been hearing reports for some time from various individuals of the difficulty Simon's been having fitting in, but at the time dismissed them as the usual new-job nerves.

The final straw came when IT informed me that the virus that crashed the entire network last week had been uploaded from Simon's terminal. For reasons best known to himself he created a virus that forced the main Mogworld server to catastrophically reboot, then transferred the virus to the company intranet. This act also brought to light a number of extremely worrying other actions on his part, including the hacking of security protocols in brazen defiance of his employee agreement.

So it's with a heavy heart that I am forced to drive him out of the pride and kill his cubs. I'm sure we all wish him luck

in getting over whatever bizarre emotional problems
caused him to take these actions.

Regards,
Brian Garret
CEO, Loincloth Entertainment

*—E DELETE ME DELETE ME DELETE ME DELETE ME
DELETE ME DELETE ME DELETE ME DELETE ME
DELETE ME DELETE ME DELETE ME DELETE ME
DELETE ME DELETE ME DELETE ME DELETE ME
DELETE ME DELETE ME DELETE ME DELETE ME
DELETE ME DEL—*

"Sorry sorry sorry," said Dub. "It took me a while to log back in. It's okay, I've locked you out of your body, now. You won't go back to it anymore."

I looked down sadly at the mess I had become, a lonely island of reddish-black in a featureless ocean of gray stone. "You used me."

"Sorry. How many times am I going to have to say sorry? It had to be done. The world was messed up beyond repair. Even without Simon's influence, the whole no-dying thing was making everyone act weird."

"You're not even the slightest bit regretful, are you?" I wasn't even angry. Just disappointed, like a schoolteacher admonishing a child for pulling the legs off insects. "Messing around with people's lives. Forcing them to become something they didn't want to be, for . . . for *fun*. For a *game*."

"But don't you see? We didn't know." The total lack of sorrow or any other emotion in his voice made my fists clench involuntarily. "We had no idea you were self-aware."

"How could you not know?"

He paused for so long before he spoke that I wondered if he'd gone away again. "Imagine, like, a toymaker. They make a doll that looks like a person, but they want to make it as realistic as possible. So they put in a metal skeleton exactly like a human one. Then they put in a bunch of leather muscles. They give it rubber organs so it can eat and drink and breathe. They give it fake eyes and a voice that says things like 'hello' when it sees someone come in the room. Then they keep adding more and more bits and things for it to say until it looks and acts exactly the same as it would if it were self-aware. Then it actually does become self-aware, somehow. How's the toymaker supposed to know?"

I rubbed my astral temple. "Even so," I said. "You knew I was self-aware when you sent me to make the world blow up. And now they're all gone. You made me kill the entire world because . . . because it wasn't working out for you anymore?"

"It's not really blowing up the world, it's more like going back in time to before—"

"Well, WHATEVER!" I barked, finally raising my voice.

The sun hung a little lower in the sky, like the head of a sorrowful dog. "Look. I'm really, really, really sorry about everything. We would never have done any of this if we'd known you were self-aware. I promise we'll never do it again."

"You can't do it again anyway. Everyone's dead. Or not born yet, or whatever."

Another pause, not as long this time. "Well, yeah, but still."

"But still what?!"

"But still. Live and learn, right?"

I sighed. "Forget it. Just delete me. Get it over with."

"Oh yeah. I figured you'd be wanting that now. Ready?"

"Yes." The green aura burst into life around me, and panic seized me. "No! I mean no! Wait!"

The aura went away. "Well?"

"The first time I died. Properly died. I felt myself ascending to heaven. I saw a wonderful golden place of love and acceptance. So I just want to know. If you delete me, will I go back there?"

"No," said Dub, after a sheepish pause. "We didn't create a heaven."

I frowned. "So what did I see?"

"I dunno. I heard somewhere you can have weird hallucinations when your brain's dying. Sure it wasn't one of those?"

I bowed my head and sighed. "So there's no afterlife."

"No. Sorry."

A lengthy silence followed. There wasn't even any wind to whistle across the hills.

I looked up. "Thank god for that."

# EPILOGUE

**doublebill:** man I just had to do the hardest thng ever

**doublebill:** I had no idae deleting a file could be so heart-braking

**sunderwonder:** christ have you read brians email

**sunderwonder:** he thinks hes a lion now or something

**doublebill:** I am never gona have conversatoins with files I might have to delete again

**sunderwonder:** personally im just glad that dickhead is gone

**sunderwonder:** never thought dickhead would be a big enough dickhead to totally dick up the build tho

**sunderwonder:** trust me to take vacation just when the fun starts

**doublebill:** are you even listning to me

**sunderwonder:** yeah yeah the npcs became self aware

**doublebill:** they knew we were controling them and everythnig

**doublebill:** they were trying to figuer out how to stop us

**sunderwonder:** yup that's a pretty textbook defnition of self-awareness

**sunderwonder:** what do you want me to do

**doublebill:** I think we need to go back to source nd totaly retool the gameplay with all this in mind

**sunderwonder:** ok that can be your job

**sunderwonder:** i'm going to sit here and eat these chips

**sunderwonder:** so you deleted the undead guy yeah

**doublebill:** his name was jim and I feel realy bad about it

**sunderwonder:** aw

**sunderwonder:** don't cry there'll be other files

**sunderwonder:** anyway wasn't it what he wanted?

**doublebill:** he died thinking he destroeyd his entire world

**sunderwonder:** ah

**sunderwonder:** so

**sunderwonder:** I take it you didnt tell him about the backups

**doublebill:** I wasn't sure how to phrase it so hed understand

**doublebill:** anyway that version of him was still goig to be deleted, it wouldn't have ment anything

**sunderwonder:** oh stop moping

**sunderwonder:** you give much thought to spiritual matters?

**doublebill:** I dont drink

**sunderwonder:** you ever h

**sunderwonder:** was that a joke

**doublebill:** maybe?

**sunderwonder:** okay

**sunderwonder:** you ever heard the quantum suicide theory

**doublebill:** uh

**sunderwonder:** it states that a conscious mind can't be destroyed

**sunderwonder:** only moved around to some other world

**sunderwonder:** so maybe a part of him will live on

**sunderwonder:** in theory

**sunderwonder:** this is me humoring you

**doublebill:** in that case

**doublebill:** I want to do him a favur for the next build

**doublebill:** sort of a thank you present

**sunderwonder:** do whatever the hell you want

**sunderwonder:** as long as it doesn't take too long

**doublebill:** okay I need to think on this

**sunderwonder:** what did I just say

———

The last of the worn stone steps, the highest point of the dusty beast-haunted mountain trail, clattered 'neath my sandaled foot. Fifty white-robed zealots, thin of build and pale of flesh, reacted with a chorus of astonished shrieks.

"You!" cried the age-tarnished High Priest, frozen with his sacrificial dagger still glittering in his gnarled hand. "How did you escape from the—"

With a single heave of my thunderous shoulders, the enchanted sword Killbastard, forged from the dark metals of the mystic East, swept cleanly through his rangy neck. His well-used vocal chords continued to flex and quiver in the act of shaping rhetoric before his body faltered.

The acolytes panicked at the fall of their infernal master. Some ran, driven to hysterics at the mere sight of my oiled mass. Some came forward, ceremonial knives poised to slash, and fell one by one to Killbastard's ferocious bite. The blooded flash of its relentless blade sent steady ripples through my leathery muscles.

Soon, none remained to challenge me. I planted my hewn thighs firmly at the corpse-riddled foot of the forsaken altar, and with two powerful flexes of my chiseled biceps, Killbastard split the chains that bound the flame-coiffed Princess Meryl to the slab. Her pale-skinned form sat upright, causing her jeweled bikini to jangle musically about her alabaster skin, and she stretched her stiffening muscles, pushing out her glorious bosoms in a manner most pleasing to my hungry gaze. She flung her wispy arms around my formidable chestnut-hued torso, staining her glittering outfit with chest oil.

"O Jim the Mighty!" she cooed. "I never doubted for a moment that you would come!"

" 'Twas a pleasure, matched only by the glory of victory against the . . ." I tailed off, then glanced around, confused. "Does something strike you as off?"

"What do you mean, O lord of battle?"

"I dunno. I've just been getting this weird sense of something not being right."

She frowned, then untangled herself from my mighty thews. "Now that you mention it, I've been feeling off all day. And I can't stop looking at your nose."

My war-calloused fingers rose to my face and stroked my fine, angular features, which somehow only strengthened my unease. "Yeah, there's definitely something wrong with my nose."

Suddenly, the cursed volcano spewed forth a magnificent spurt of lava. My hand flew to the shining hilt of bloodthirsty Killbastard. From the abysmal depths of the earth rose the head of a titanic red snake come up from the deepest Stygian plains. Its visage was that of a hideous dragon, its eyes flaming with ferocious malevolence and its hungry maw an eight-foot grin crammed with spikes of a sharpness that no armor could slow. It appeared to be twirling a butterfly knife in one of its dreadful talons.

"Hello there, my little toastracks," it wheedled. "Care for a spot of ultra-violence?"

"No, no." I threw down the sword and folded my arms. "There's definitely something up, and I'm not starting this epic battle until someone tells me what it is."

The fire serpent bit my head off.

**doublebill:** he rejected it
**doublebill:** hang on ive got another ide

———

A peal of thunder roared out from the storm clouds that spread across the blood-red sky, mingled with the wails of the damned. A hundred columns of smoke rose from the landscape, each a pulsating finger pointing out my countless dark temples as they completed the day's unholy rites. I stood atop the highest tower of my mightiest fortress, one clawed hand resting on the parapet, the other casually brushing ants away from the hole where my nose had once sat.

Below me, my legions of undead warriors fell to their knees rank by rank, their obeisance most pleasing to my undead eyes. "All Hail Jim," they cried, in the kind of perfect unison only mindless zombie slaves can achieve. "Lich Lord of the Malevolands."

"Master," said Thaddeus, my sniveling vizier, materializing at my elbow. "We have caught an adventurer attempting to steal from your treasure vault."

"Bring him here," I growled. "No man will be spared the terrible judgement of the Lich Lord."

I stalked nobly through the fanged archway that led into my receiving chamber and settled into the Throne of Darkness, its many points of extruding bone curling comfortably around my body. My consort, the Black Witch Meryl, levitated him magically into the room and flung him to the floor at my feet.

"He was able to sneak into the vault through the underground tunnels," hissed Meryl. "We caught him attempting to flee with a sack of gold considerably larger than the manhole he was trying to climb down."

"So, man-fool," I boomed, every syllable a symphony of evil. "To steal from the Lich Lord Jim is an act of either tremendous bravery or tragic stupidity. Which do you believe is the case?"

"Well, Slippery John reckons it'd be the second one," said Slippery John cheerfully. "Slippery John thought that would have been pretty obvious from the manhole thing."

I glared at him for a second, then threw down my staff and folded my arms. "No. No, this isn't right at all."

**doublebill:** this is haerdr than I thought
**sunderwonder:** what exactly are you doing again
**doublebill:** i'm triyng to fix jim
**sunderwonder:** okay I can see this is important to you but maybe your overdoing it a bit
**sunderwonder:** maybe you should just do something small
**doublebill:** what like
**doublebill:** give him a new hat
**sunderwonder:** not quite that small
**doublebill:** i dunno hes a hard guy to shop for
**sunderwonder:** well hes your friend
**doublebill:** hang on
**doublebill:** okay ive got somethnig
**doublebill:** were gona need one of the really old backups

———

The sun began to rise, spilling orange dawn over the rolling green hills of the surrounding plains. I noticed that the horizon was a lot more textured than I remembered, and more bristling with siege weaponry.

An army was advancing towards the school. Just as I had done on my first day, I deeply resented the fact that St. Gordon's Magical College was not, in fact, a castle.

"All right, chaps, settle down," said the headmaster, resplendent in his star-patterned cardigan as he strode back and forth in front of the student body. "Let me assure you all that there is absolutely no reason to panic." The rising tension was not eased in the slightest. "It's probably just some misunderstanding—stop picking your nose, Bottomroach—but a Stragonoffian army appears to be attacking the college. Now, don't . . ."

"What's he saying?" Nearby whispering distracted me from the speech. The rest of the student body was shuffling into place behind us, led by Meryl, the first year head girl. She had a hand on my shoulder and was straining to see over a lanky third year standing in front. "Is something going on?"

"Yes, something's going on," I said.

For the first time, Meryl noticed whose shoulder she was braced upon. "Jim, do you know what's going on?" She squinted at the horizon. "Is that an army?"

"It looks like one, doesn't it?" The upheld weapons of the besieging horde on the horizon grew bigger and better-defined by the second, and I noticed at that point that we had been assembled in a manner that could be described as "regimental." "I think they might be expecting us to fight it."

"Oh dear. Really?"

"I think so."

Meryl jumped up and down a few times. "There's a lot of them."

"How many?"

"About a thousand. No, wait, two thousand. Perspective threw me off."

I stood on tip toe. The sun had risen further by now and the heaving mass of armor and sharp weaponry was clearer than ever. Our pathetic assembly wouldn't even slow them. Neither, I suspected, would the school building.

"I think I'm going to sit this out," I said.

"What did you say?" asked Meryl. "Where are you going?"

The next thing I knew, I was making my way through the students. I pushed a couple of senior years aside and stepped out into the heat of the headmaster's glare.

"Did you have a question, Bottomroach?"

"Yeah . . . I mean, no," I said, fidgeting uneasily under everybody's scrutiny. "I, er . . . I don't really want to die. So . . . I'm just going to leave."

The headmaster's face twisted as if he were marking an essay with particularly bad grammar. "You need not . . . die," he said patiently. "This is your chance to prove yourself a hero."

I winced. "I'm still not terribly comfortable with it."

The headmaster's complexion reddened. "THIS," he barked, like a burst of air escaping from a balloon, "is a school of battle magic. You are here to learn magic in the application of combat and adventuring. If you honestly wish to eschew your very first real-world experience, then there is no reason for you to be attending this institution."

I took another look at the approaching army. It hadn't gotten any smaller. Then I glanced back at the school's defensive force, just in case fifteen hundred backup wizards had arrived while I wasn't looking. "I guess I'll be off, then," I said.

"Right," continued the Headmaster as I made my way towards the back gate. "Now that the timewasters have come forward, perhaps those of us who are unafraid of victory can discuss strategy—"

"Anyone want to come with me?" I interjected, turning around. "Anyone else not want to die?"

"As I was saying . . ." continued the headmaster after a particularly thoughtful silence.

"No, really, look," I said. "There's thousands of them. You will definitely die if you stay here. It won't mean anything. You're not making any kind of grand gesture. You're just going to be dead. So is no-one else going to come with me?"

"I'll come with you!" cried Meryl, raising a defiant fist.

"All right!" shouted the headmaster manically. "Everyone with no concept of heroism is invited to get the hell out of my school! Everyone else can stay where they are and—" An arrow slammed into his temple. "Glurble burble fleep."

"Jim?" called Meryl, after we'd begun climbing the big grassy hill on St. Gordon's south face. "I think we should go back."

I was panting. The hill was getting steep, and exhaustion stung at my legs. "I thought . . . you were with me," I wheezed.

"Can I be honest? I hadn't really been listening when I said that. I thought we were going on a secret mission."

"No, we're pretty much just running away."

"We have to do something to help them! Someone could be killed!"

My current position afforded me a spectacular view of the siege. I could see the whole disorganized mass of warrior thugs smashing through the school gates and bearing down upon the huddle of magic students, like a tarantula crawling towards a trapped ladybird. "Not really selling it to me, there, Meryl."

"But there has to be some way we can—LOOK OUT!"

I felt the tremors through the ground before I heard the clatter of hooves and saw the massive golden horses come storming down the hill towards us. I flung myself to the grass just in time to slip unharmed between the muscular legs of a horse the size of a small cottage.

I flipped onto my back to get a better look. The riders were almost as big and muscular as their mounts. Most of them had long, blonde hair trailing from their heads like comet tails, and their glittering armor clattered musically as they bounced up and down in the gyrating saddles.

"They're heading for the school," said Meryl, pointing. "I think they want to join in."

There weren't more than half a dozen of them, but they charged straight into battle without fear, hesitation or sanity. In one mighty leap the horses had cleared the fence as well as the entire student body of St. Gordon's, and their hooves crashed down upon the gravel directly in the path of the invading army.

The warrior students were taken by surprise, but continued to charge through sheer force of momentum. The members of the frontal assault fell almost instantly before the mysterious horsemen, whose effectiveness was matched only by their apparent ineptitude. Every single one of them was mechanically performing the same three-slash sword combo. And yet, they were ploughing right through the Stragonoffian louts. Those who tried to counter-attack managed only to bend and shatter their cheap school-issue battleaxes.

"Oh, right," said Meryl. "This is what my mum was talking about."

"What?" I asked, as she helped me to my feet.

"Well, she was saying that some big golden guys have been appearing out of nowhere and doing odd jobs for people. Bunch of them chased the foxes out of her hen house."

"That's . . . really weird."

"She had to get a new one built, but she was happy that the foxes were gone. She says she was visited by angels."

The battle had almost reached a decisive conclusion. Most of the Stragonoff side was trying to retreat, but were finding it difficult with their sheer weight of numbers, and the golden riders hadn't ceased their relentless sword-swinging. I could see Mr. Everwind fidgeting nearby, trying to pick the best moment to thank them and ask them to stop.

"Guess it's safe to go back," said Meryl, emphasizing the word "safe" with a hint of spite. She stopped when she saw I wasn't following. "What's the matter?"

"It's just occurred to me. I've been at St. Gordon's for a year and I've never known what's on the other side of this hill. I think . . . I think I'm going to go find out."

"And then you'll come back."

"Mmmmmaybe," I said, honestly. "Actually, no," I added, more honestly. "No, I won't. Look at it, Meryl. It's three buildings in the middle of nowhere, and it's apparently got an invasion problem. I don't need it."

"What's brought this on?"

"I don't know. Maybe it was the siege." I looked back at the mess in the school courtyard, which only made things clearer in my head. "I always felt my only options were college or working on Dad's farm, but . . . I think my horizons just expanded. Does that make sense?"

"No. None. I don't understand at all. Where will you go?"

"I don't know." I cast a look back at the hill. "I'll ask someone when I get there."

I'd only covered ten more yards before her voice made me stop again. "There's still time! They're still cleaning up the last few fighters down there! You could still be a hero!"

I didn't turn. I stood and watched the dewy grass flutter innocently in the early morning sun.

"I'd rather be a protagonist," I said.

## MOGWORLD
**Loincloth Entertainment**

### Reviewed by H. Morris

Unless you've spent the last year on some faraway planet with
an alien parasite stuck to your face, you've no doubt heard of
Mogworld already. It's been causing a big stir in the games
industry for the amazing new creation process behind it: total
procedural generation. Procedurally generated life. Procedurally
generated AI. Procedurally generated quests. It's just a shame
they couldn't procedurally generate some fun while they were
at it.

Mogworld is a Massive Online Game set in a world of magical
fantasy, in a time of dragons and wizards and adventure, which
may seem familiar to you if you've played any game ever made
ever. The developers apparently set this up deliberately by
tweaking the world's evolution at several key points. It's as if
they thought the revolutionary engine meant they could skip
the idea of innovating anywhere else. Even the title—M.O.G.
world—is rubbish. It'd be like calling an FPS "First Person
Shooting Adventure."

Your character is a beautiful angelic hero who descends from
heaven to do mighty deeds. Which is weird, because in the
beta you just took over an existing adventurer in the world. It
seems rather a waste of effort to go to all this trouble to make
humanoid races evolve, then have us slap together a custom-
built hero to drive around in. I guess being able to customize
appearance is nice, but unless all you ever want to play is a
big golden swimwear model, there's not much opportunity for
role-playing. And none of the NPCs seem the least bit grateful

when you do their quests. Most of them just come across as completely terrified of you.

Mind you, I'd be pretty scared too if I knew I was living in such a cruel world as this one: NPC perma-death has been added since the beta. When an NPC dies, they never, ever come back. Any quests that they had, or any quests that involve killing or protecting them, can never, ever be attempted more than once, by anyone. I guess you can't fault it for realism, but I end up having to ride back and forth across the land for hours just looking for quests to do. Maybe this wouldn't matter so much if there was decent PVP, but there isn't any; apparently the idea was that the NPCs are so smart you wouldn't even need other human beings. No doubt the appalling basement shut-ins who still mindlessly defend this game on the forums will call this "immersion," but I prefer to call it "boring."

However detailed the graphics or intelligent the AI might be, I really can't get over the NPC perma-death thing. Seriously. I want to know what retarded gibbon on the dev team thought that was a good idea. I can only presume that an NPC murdered their entire family and this was their chance for revenge. Don't get me wrong, I'm impressed with the technology on display. I'd also be impressed if someone built a skyscraper out of brie, but don't expect me to want to live in it.

**Innovation: 9**
**Gameplay: 4**
**Lastability: 3**
**Overall: 72.85%**

## ABOUT THE AUTHOR

**Ben "Yahtzee" Croshaw** is the creator of Zero Punctuation, a popular weekly game review on the Webby award-winning *Escapist* online magazine, for which he also earned the Sun Microsystems 2008 IT Journalism award for Best Gaming Journalist. He has also worked as a game designer and dialogue writer for various studios. He was born and raised in the UK and now lives in Brisbane, Australia.

*Mogworld* is his first published novel.

# ALSO FROM DARK HORSE BOOKS

## MASS EFFECT VOLUME 1: REDEMPTION

*Written by Mac Walters and John Jackson Miller*
*Art by Omar Francia*

The eagerly anticipated sequel to the blockbuster science-fiction game epic *Mass Effect 2* begins with the disappearance of Commander Shepard. The story of what happens next—exclusive to this graphic novel—will have the commander's companion Dr. Liara T'Soni undertake a deadly mission of extraordinary importance in the Milky Way's lawless Terminus Systems. *Mass Effect* Volume 1 features essential developments in the *Mass Effect* gaming saga.

ISBN 978-1-59582-481-3 $16.99

## THE GUILD VOLUME 1

*Written by Felicia Day*
*Art by Jim Rugg*

Internet phenomenon *The Guild* comes to comics, courtesy of series creator, writer, and star Felicia Day (*Dr. Horrible's Sing-Along Blog*)! Chronicling the hilarious on- and offline lives of a group of Internet role-playing gamers, the Knights of Good, *The Guild* has become a cult hit and is the winner of numerous awards. Now Day brings the wit and heart of the show to comics readers everywhere!

ISBN 978-1-59582-549-0 $12.99

## PENNY ARCADE

*Written by Jerry Holkins*
*Art by Mike Krahulik*

If you've never heard of *Penny Arcade*, it's possible you were killed tragically in a snowplow accident and your ghost is haunting the place where you once lived, convinced that you are still alive! Or you may have just missed out on this new invention called "the Internet." But don't fear, because *Penny Arcade*, the most popular webcomic ever, is coming to comics shops and bookstores everywhere!

**VOLUME 1:**
Attack of the Bacon Robots!
ISBN 978-1-59307-444-9

**VOLUME 2:**
Epic Legends of the Magic
Sword Kings!
ISBN 978-1-59307-541-5

**VOLUME 3:**
The WarSun Prophecies
ISBN 978-1-59307-635-1

**VOLUME 4:**
Birds Are Weird
ISBN 978-1-59307-773-0

**VOLUME 5:**
The Case of the Mummy's Gold
ISBN 978-1-59307-814-0

$12.99 each

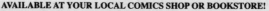